THE BITTERWOOD LEGEND *is a tale known by all dragons: the story of Bant Bitterwood, the most powerful dragon slayer ever to have lived and his vendetta against the all powerful Sun Dragons. Although Bitterwood's death was well documented, there are many that believe he actually escaped death and still lives, killing from the shadows.*

When King Albekizan's son and last hope as a successor is horrifically murdered, the manhunt for Bitterwood begins. The King will stop at nothing to seek out Bitterwood and wreak his revenge, even though his unrelenting need for vengeance could lead to the ultimate downfall of the Dragons and end their reign forever...

JAMES MAXEY

BITTERWOOD

SOLARIS

First published 2007 by Solaris
an imprint of BL Publishing
Games Workshop Ltd
Willow Road
Nottingham
NG7 2WS
UK

www.solarisbooks.com

ISBN-13: 978-1-84416-487-5
ISBN-10: 1-84416-487-X

Copyright © James Maxey 2007

Cover art by Michael Komarck

10 9 8 7 6 5 4 3 2

A CIP catalogue record for this book is available from the
British Library.

Designed & typeset by BL Publishing.

For James Rice, Poet

BOOK ONE

PYRE

Can a man take fire in his bosom,
and his clothes not be burned?

Proverbs 6:27

SEED

1070 D.A. (Dragon Age), The 39th Year of the Reign of Albekizan

F RESHLY PLOWED EARTH and the perfume of women scented the night air. Naked, Bant scurried along the furrows, crouching low as he made his way toward the orchard. All around him women sang out and men grunted with pleasure. Bant strained his eyes in the darkness, fearing that any second some white arm might snake out of the moonless night and pull him close, demanding from him that which was Recanna's.

As he reached the far end of the field, the sounds of passion grew more distant. The black shadows of the peach orchard loomed before him. He paused at the edge of the trees, warmed by the rising heat of the earth, awash in the sweet scent of newly opened blossoms.

"Recanna?" he whispered.

He leaned forward, listening for any faint sound. Behind him, he heard the distant laughter of a woman. He ducked his head and stepped into the orchard, inching forward, his arms held before him. Under the low, thick canopy of the blossoms, even the dim starlight vanished. He saw no sign of his beloved. Had she decided not to come? Worse, had someone else caught her as she traveled through the fields? In theory, on the Night of Sowing, women were free to choose any partner they wished. In practice, no woman could ever refuse any man of the village on this night; to do so would be an insult to the Goddess.

Bant was only fifteen, Recanna fourteen, and this was the first time each had participated in the sowing, the rite of spring practiced in honor of the Goddess Ashera. They had waited a lifetime for this night. If all their whispered plans and shared dreams were to come to nothing now... It was too terrible to contemplate.

"Recanna?" he said again, louder, almost a shout. He held his breath to listen for her reply. His heart sounded like a drum in his ears.

At last, her faint voice answered, "Here."

He crept toward the sound. Bant was all but blind beneath the branches. For a second he thought he saw her slender form in the darkness, a black shape against a gray background. When he drew nearer he saw it was only the trunk of a tree. Then her soft, cool hand closed around his and pulled him to her.

She was naked, of course. From sunset to sunrise on this night, it would be a sin to allow cloth to touch her body. Her soft skin pressed against his.

He felt as if he'd slipped into dream. He wrapped her in his arms, holding her tightly, trembling with joy. He leaned and pressed his lips to her neck, nibbling her, breathing in the rich aroma of her hair. Then he moved his mouth to seek her lips. But she turned her face and his lips fell on her cheek, which was wet, and salty. She shuddered. He realized she was crying.

"What's wrong?" he whispered, rubbing her back.

"This," she said, sounding frightened. "Us. Bant, I love you, but... but we shouldn't be here. I'm afraid."

"There's nothing to be afraid of," Bant said, stroking her hair. "As you say, you love me. I love you. Nothing done in love should cause fear."

She swallowed hard. She was still crying.

"Everything's all right," he said, wiping her tears.

"No," she said. "I know I agreed to this. But, at the ritual, the women who prepared me for the sowing kept talking about the Goddess. They kept telling me of my duty."

"Damn duty," Bant said, grabbing her shoulders and looking her in the eyes. "We've waited so long. I won't share you with the others. I can't."

"But it's the Night of Sowing. The Goddess is good to us. She makes the orchards blossom and the crops sprout. All that she asks in return is this one night of—'

"Hush," Bant said, placing his fingers on her lips. "The old women have really scared you, haven't they? Where's the Recanna I knew just yesterday, the girl so intent on following her own heart?"

"But..." she said.

"There will be other sowings," he said. "There will be time enough for duty."

"But—"

Bant pulled her to him, silencing her with his lips. Despite the warmth of the night, her naked body was cold and she shivered as he embraced her. He ran his hands along her skin, warming her. He didn't break the kiss. She didn't pull away. After a moment her lips grew softer, and she opened her mouth to his. She cautiously placed her gentle fingers against his hips. Her skin, chilled only moments before, grew warm against his. She moaned softly, and pulled him closer. They fell to the earth together, the soil warm and yielding beneath Bant's back.

For the first time Bant understood the deeper meaning of the sowing, the powerful connection between the seasons of the world and the passions of the body. He felt as if he were a part of the earth, a thing of rich loam and hard rock. Recanna's breath against his lips was as sweet and life-giving as the spring breeze. All thoughts of the Goddess were forgotten. Their defiance of the traditions of the village no longer mattered. There was only lingering, sensual tension of the now.

Then, with a gasp, Recanna turned her head and pushed Bant away. She rose to her knees.

"What?" Bant asked, sitting up and raising his hand toward her. "What's wrong?"

"Look," she said, pushing his hand away. "The road."

Far beyond the trees, a single lantern flickered on the distant road, breaking the sacred darkness of the sowing. Who would approach the town on this of all nights? A murmur rose from the nearby fields. They were not the only village folk to have spotted this sacrilege of light.

"It's an omen," Recanna said, her voice once more fearful. "We've angered the Goddess. What have we done?"

"W-we…" Bant's argument trailed into silence. No one would dare light even a candle on the Night of Sowing. The Goddess graced this night with a perfect blanket of darkness. Had he risked too much?

A snap of a twig nearby raised the hairs on his neck. Someone else was in the orchard. By now, his eyes were better adjusted to the gloom. Recanna's pale skin almost glowed. But looking around, all he could see were the silhouettes of the tree trunks. Anyone could be hiding. Then one of the dark shapes broke free from the others and moved closer. Bant jumped as a deep, beefy voice shouted, "Runt!"

Bant knew the voice well. Even in the gloom, the hulking shape of his older brother Jomath was unmistakable. Jomath was two years older than Bant, but a giant by comparison, a foot taller and with thick muscular arms. Bant had always been a target of his brother's bullying. But, if the light on the road presaged something dangerous, it was good that he was here.

"Jomath," Bant said. "I'm relieved it's you. What do you think the light is?"

"Who cares?" Jomath said, striding boldly forward and placing a callused hand around Recanna's frail arm. "Some lost fool, no doubt. Not my concern. What concerns me is to see you and this lovely morsel breaking the commandments. I've been wise to your plotting."

"Ow," said Recanna. "You're hurting me."

"You deserve to be hurt. The commandment is that any woman shall lay with any man on the Night of Sowing. Defiance of this is a great sin. I'm here to save you from your folly."

"Let her go," Bant said, leaping to his feet. "She's in love with me, not you."

"Don't you see the blasphemy in your words?" Jomath said. "On the Night of Sowing, love isn't dictated by our hearts. The Goddess wants all women of the village open to all men. It bonds us, unifies us. Now, it's my sacred duty to bond with Recanna. I've waited a long time for her to come of age."

"Let her go," Bant repeated, clenching his fists. "You don't care anything about the Goddess. You're only doing this to spite me."

"Please, Jomath," said Recanna, twisting in his grasp. "You don't have to be rough. You're right. We've sinned. But at least allow Bant to be the first. We've waited so long."

"Don't speak to me of waiting," Jomath said, his teeth flashing white. "I've wasted far too much time searching these shadows for you. Resist if you like. I find it more pleasurable if you struggle."

"No!" Bant shouted, rushing toward his brother. He punched Jomath in the back with all his strength. His older brother spun around, using his free hand to punch Bant on the jaw.

Bant hit the ground hard, his mouth full of blood. The teeth on the left side of his jaw wiggled with sickening ease as his tongue brushed against them.

When he tried to rise, Jomath kicked him in the belly, forcing his breath out in a painful gush. Jomath kicked him in the guts again and this time Bant vomited, choking on the bile. Unable to breathe and with stars dancing before him, Bant clutched dirt in his fists. He struggled to make his legs obey him. His hate was like a thousand whips lashing him, driving him. Bant had been beaten by Jomath before, but this would be the last time. Bant had no doubt that if he could reach Jomath's windpipe with his fingernails, he would gladly rip it out. Yet his body betrayed him. He remained glued to the ground.

Recanna screamed. Jomath silenced her with a punch then threw her down beside Bant.

"I'll kill you," Bant whispered through bloody lips.

"Empty threats." Jomath lowered himself to his knees before Recanna. Recanna was groaning, barely moving, as Jomath parted her legs. He glanced over at Bant and said, "Watch. You might learn something."

Bant spat at his brother, but the blood-darkened spittle landed on Recanna. Bant closed his eyes tightly until all he saw was a wall of red, a sea of blood. He imagined Jomath drowning in such a sea.

Then, far away, a man shouted and a woman screamed, not in pleasure but in panic. Quickly, the other villagers echoed the scream. Bant opened his eyes to find Jomath standing, ignoring Recanna, and staring off toward the village.

Across the fields, a bonfire rose from the heart of the village.

"This will have to wait," Jomath said, and raced away.

Bant crawled to Recanna's side. Together, they helped each other sit up. Recanna was weeping, her body heaving with great sobs.

"Oh, what have we done?" Recanna moaned. "This has all gone so wrong. Oh, Goddess, I'm so sorry. I'm so sorry."

Bant looked her in the eyes, trying to show courage. "This isn't our fault," Bant said. He prayed it was true. "Come on. Let's see what's going on."

He helped her to her feet. Grabbing her by the wrist, he guided her from the orchard, picking up speed and breaking into a run as they cleared the low branches and reached the freshly plowed field. Alone, Bant could have outpaced Jomath, even with his head start. Jomath had gotten all the brute strength in the family, but Bant's slight, wiry build made him the fastest runner in the village. He slowed his pace, not wanting to leave Recanna behind. And, in truth, he wasn't eager to discover the source of the evil that gripped the village this night. Could Recanna be right? Was this their fault?

At the edge of the village square, Bant stopped, drawing back in fear. Harnessed to a nearby wagon stood a gigantic black dog, as big as an ox. It was the biggest beast Bant had ever seen, save for a brief glimpse of a sun-dragon that had once flown high over the village.

The dog regarded Bant with a casual eye. Its huge pink tongue hung from its mouth as it panted, giving it a friendly, bemused expression. The dog's breath was foul, filling the night with a rotten meat stench. Bant kept his distance from the creature as he led Recanna around the edge of the square to join with the crowd of villagers.

The crowd consisted of the village menfolk, all three score of them. All were still naked from the sowing. The women stood on the nearby hill, clutching their children to them. Everyone's eyes were fixed on the temple of the Goddess. The structure sat in the heart of the village. Its wooden columns were the ivy-covered trunks of ancient trees, and its walls were dense hedges. It held the most sacred artifact of the village: a carving of the Goddess, taller than a man, resting on a pedestal that was once the stump of an enormous oak.

Flames engulfed the temple. The fire roared with a noise like heavy rain. The stone steps leading up to the temple interior were covered with offerings: baskets containing bundles of fresh spring ramps, loaves of brown bread, and a catfish as long as a man's arm. The woven reed baskets curled and warped in the heat of the blaze.

Then, from the smoke and flame rolling from the temple's entrance, a giant stranger emerged, rudely dragging behind him the voluptuously carved mahogany statue of the Goddess. If the smoke stung his eyes or irritated his lungs, the stranger gave no sign. Nor did he cringe from the terrible heat. He kicked away the offerings as he moved forward. He placed the Goddess below him on the stone steps of the temple, moving her heavy wooden body as if it were weightless.

Confused voices ran through the crowd. Had this stranger set fire to the temple? Or was he saving the Goddess from the blaze?

The crowd fell silent as the stranger straightened to his full height, easily ten feet tall, his shoulders broad, unbent by fear or labor. Despite the commandment that no cloth could touch flesh on this night, he wore a black wool coat that hung down to his heavy leather boots. His skin, stained by soot, was as dark as his clothes. The only bright things about him were his eyes, glistening beneath a broad-brimmed hat. His giant right hand held a thick, black book.

In the stunned silence, the stranger opened the book, and read, with a thunderous voice, "THOU SHALT HAVE NO OTHER GODS BEFORE ME. THOU SHALT NOT MAKE UNTO THEE ANY GRAVEN IMAGE, OR ANY LIKENESS OF ANY THING THAT IS IN HEAVEN ABOVE, OR THAT IS IN THE EARTH BENEATH, OR THAT IS IN THE WATER UNDER THE EARTH."

With this proclamation, the stranger opened his long black coat to reveal a woodsman's axe, nearly four feet in length, its finely honed edge catching the firelight. It hung from his belt without touching the ground.

"It may be," the stranger growled, "that you dwell in ignorance, and are unaware of your sin." He lifted the heavy tool with a single hand high over his head. "I have been sent by the Lord to show you the way." The axe flashed down like lightning, splitting the Goddess in twain. The two halves flew apart, clattering on the stone stairs.

From the hillside the women began to wail. Even some of the men were weeping. Recanna clung tightly to Bant, who felt numb. The Goddess was eternal; she had always dwelled at the center of the village. How could this be happening, unless they were in the presence of something—some god— even more powerful than Ashera?

"Now that this nonsense is behind us," the stranger said, "the truth shall set you free."

"Truth?" one man cried, stepping forward. It was Jomath. "You dare speak of truth in the face of such blasphemy?"

"I dare," said the stranger. "Have care. Act not in anger or haste. I am a servant of the Lord. It would be most unwise to oppose me. The Lord has laid waste to nations in His wrath. He will not allow a hair on my head to come to harm."

Jomath's face twisted with rage. His hands were tight fists. But Bant knew his brother well, and could see something in his eyes that others might have missed. Fear. It was on the faces of all the men. Fear of the blasphemy they had witnessed, yes, and fear of the coming wrath of the Goddess, no doubt. But more immediately, Bant saw fear of this giant of a man, this devil standing before the raging flames, his sharp axe gleaming.

Jomath looked back to the men. "Who's with me? Who will join me in avenging this villainy?"

The men looked down in utter silence.

"Cowards," Jomath cursed. He turned to face the stranger. "Let the Goddess give me the strength of the storms, the fury of lightning!"

He bellowed with rage as he rushed the steps. He drove his shoulders into the stranger's stomach with a force that made Bant flinch.

The stranger did not bend. Jomath recoiled from the impact of the blow, stumbling on the steps. The stranger raised his axe. Then, a shout flew from the crowd. A blacksmith's iron hammer flashed through the air. The heavy tool struck the stranger squarely in the face, knocking him backward. Namon, the stout-armed blacksmith, had hurled the weapon and now charged up the steps. Before Namon reached the man, Faltan, the huntsman, rushed from the edge of the burning temple and threw himself against the back of the stranger's knees. The stranger staggered forward, allowing Jomath to grab his belt and pull until all three men and the stranger tumbled. Bant had difficulty discerning whose limbs were whose in the cursing ball of flesh and black cloth that landed in the square.

As one, the men of the village gave a blood-curdling shout and rushed forward, drowning the stranger beneath a human wave.

Bant didn't move to join them. He couldn't, standing there, his arms around Recanna. His heart held an unspeakable desire. He wanted the stranger to live. He wanted the stranger to kill Jomath. Let the temple burn, let the Goddess send her wrath as storms, as floods, as plagues of locusts and flies. Bant feared none of these things. All he wanted was for Jomath to die, to satisfy the hate he'd felt only moments before.

The ox-dog at the edge of the square barked and charged forward, the wagon bouncing behind it like a toy. The beast's teeth sank into the shoulder of one of the men on the ground who screamed as his bones snapped. His scream died as the ox-dog shook its enormous head, sending the man's body hurtling through the air. It landed before Bant and Recanna, splashing them with blood. Bant recognized the man; it was Delan, his uncle, the man who'd been training Bant in the art of archery. Bant realized that it wouldn't be only his brother who died tonight.

So be it, he thought.

Recanna screamed, tugging away from him, trying to run. Bant tightened his grip on her, deaf to her cries. He couldn't bear to part with her, and he didn't dare to turn away from the carnage before him.

The ox-dog tossed men into the sky like rag dolls as the bright-eyed stranger fought to his feet once more, his robes now wet with blood. His axe rose and fell, chopping and hacking. Limbs were severed, skulls split, men died with each blow. The dog tore and savaged the men. Quickly, the few men with limbs still intact slipped and skittered on the bloody cobblestones before fleeing into the night.

The stranger didn't pursue them. He stood in the middle of a mound of bodies, straightening his coat. He pulled the brim of his hat back down over his eyes and wiped his cheek with a gore-encrusted palm. He wasn't even winded.

He kicked the bodies at his feet—two dozen men at least—making a path for him to walk.

With a chill of satisfaction, Bant spotted Jomath, dead among the bloody mound of bodies. It was almost as if his hate had killed Jomath, as if it had been a palpable thing, a force, making his darkest desires real. He knew he should feel remorse or some sense of loss. Instead, he felt something that bordered on joy at seeing his brother's torn and twisted corpse. It frightened him that he was capable of such hate. Nothing could ever wash the blood from him.

So be it.

The blood-soaked stranger walked toward Bant.

"You," the stranger said. "Boy. What's your name?"

Bant looked up into the giant's eyes. They were piercing, unflinching. Bant knew the stranger was studying his terrible soul.

"B-Bant," he said. "Bant Bitterwood."

"You did not fight me," the man said.

"No," whispered Bant.

"Do you fear me, Bant Bitterwood?"

"No," Bant said. In his hatred for Jomath, all other emotion had been lost.

"This marks you as the wisest man in this village of fools," said the stranger.

Of all the words that could have left the stranger's mouth, these were the last ones Bant had expected.

"Tell me, Bant Bitterwood, is this woman you cling to your wife?"

"No," said Bant.

"What is your name, girl?"

She turned her head away as she whispered, "Recanna Halsfeth."

"Are you any man's wife?"

"No," she answered.

"Then the Lord's work in this place shall begin with you. As you stand together tonight, so shall you stand for all eternity. Bant Bitterwood, look upon your wife. Recanna Bitterwood, look upon your husband."

"But—" Recanna began.

The stranger raised his open palm, silencing her. "Do not question the commandments of the Lord."

"T-the Lord?" asked Bant.

"Can you read, Bant Bitterwood?"

"No, sir."

"Then you shall learn. It is important training for all servants of the Lord. He guides us through His sacred words contained within this Holy Bible."

The stranger held forth a black book. Bant took it, surprised by the weight as the stranger released it. He knew it weighed only a few pounds, but somehow, it felt like the heaviest burden he'd ever carried.

Bant asked, "Are you... are you the Lord?"

"No. I am his prophet. My name is Hezekiah. Now go, Bant Bitterwood. Find clothes to cover your nakedness. Your days of living as a pagan savage are no more. Recanna Bitterwood, find clothes of your own then prepare food for your husband. He will need his strength. There is much work for him in the coming days."

Bant looked to Recanna. She was afraid. She tried to pull away but he held tight.

"I know you're frightened," he said to her. "I don't completely understand what has happened tonight, but I have a feeling. I think everything is going to be all right. Please don't be afraid."

"What you feel, Bant Bitterwood," said Hezekiah, "is faith."

Recanna nodded. Something changed in her eyes. Bant realized that she also had faith, faith in him. He stood straighter, feeling somehow more powerful.

He pulled her closer then looked to Hezekiah, who nodded.

"You may kiss your bride," the prophet said.

Recanna surrendered as Bant placed his lips upon hers. The world spun beneath his feet. Gone the musty smell of the fields and the sweet scent of peach blossoms. Here, in this perfect kiss, in the first moment in his life where he felt no fear, no shame, all the world smelled of smoke, and sweat, and blood.

This is how Bant Bitterwood learned that hate could change the world.

This is how Bant Bitterwood found God.

CHAPTER ONE

LIGHTNING

*1099 D.A., The 68th Year of the
Reign of Albekizan*

THE SAD LITTLE fire gave out more smoke than warmth. The hunter crouched before it, turning a chunk of ash-flecked meat on the flat stone he'd placed amidst the coals. The movement of the stone stirred more smoke. The hunter coughed and wiped soot from his eyes. He stretched his bony, knotted fingers above the embers, fighting off the chill. He was a thin man, hair shoulder-length and gray, the deep lines of his leathery face forming a permanent frown. He pulled his heavy cloak more tightly around him.

In the tree above him hung the body of a dragon, blood dripping from its mouth.

The creature was a sky-dragon, the smallest of the winged dragon species. Strip away the ten-foot wings and the long tail, and a sky-dragon was no bigger than a man and half his weight. They were known as sky-dragons both for their prowess in flight and their coloring, the pale, perfect blue of a cloudless day. The hunter had killed many sky-dragons over the years. They weren't particularly dangerous. Despite talons ending in two-inch claws and crocodilian jaws full of saw-like teeth, sky-dragons prided themselves on being *civilized*. The beasts fancied themselves as artists, poets, and scholars; they considered it beneath their dignity to engage in such menial work as hunting.

The hunter had brought the sky-dragon down with a single arrow, expertly placed on the underside of the jaw, the iron tip coming to rest in the center of the dragon's brain. The beast had fallen from the air like a suddenly dead thing, catching in the crook of a tree. The hunter had climbed the tree and retrieved the leather satchel the dragon had slung over its back. He'd tugged at the beast's body but found the corpse jammed too tight to budge. Lowering himself even with the beast's head, he'd stared into its glassy, catlike eyes. Sky-dragon heads always reminded him of goat heads, albeit goats covered in smooth, opalescent scales. With a grunt, he cut out the beast's tongue.

Moments later, a fire had been built and now the tongue sizzled on the flat rock at the center, giving the smoke an oily, fishy tinge. To pass the time as the tongue cooked, the hunter searched the contents of the dragon's satchel. Food, of course. A bottle of wine wrapped in burlap, a loaf of rock hard bread powdered with flour, two apples, some eel jerky. He also discovered a fist-sized crock capped with oily parchment bound with string. He punched through the parchment and recoiled at the stench. The crock was filled with strong-smelling horch: a sort of paste that dragons loved that consisted of sardines, olives, and chilies which were ground together then buried in a ceramic jar and fermented. The hunter tossed the jar as far into the woods as his arm could heave it.

Turning his attention once more to the satchel, the hunter found a map, a rolled-up blanket of padded green silk, and a small jar of ink. He sniffed the cap and judged the ink to be made from vinegar and walnut husks. Several quills crafted from the dragon's own feather-scales were in the bag. No wonder the beasts fancied themselves scholars—they were covered with the tools of writing.

The hunter paused to examine a leather-bound book, the linen paper a pristine white, the opening pages covered with sketches and notes about flowers. The drawings were meticulous. Rendered in dark walnut ink, the flowers had a life and beauty. The blossoms swelled on the page seductively enough to tempt bees.

The hunter ripped out the pages and fed them to the crackling fire. The paper writhed as if alive, curling, crumbling into large black leaves that wafted upward with the smoke, the inky designs still faintly visible until they vanished in the dark sky.

The hunter used his knife to retrieve the roasted tongue and sat back against the tree, oblivious to the blood soaking the trunk. As he chewed his meal, he stared at the ink bottle. It stirred memories. Memories for the hunter were never a good thing.

After he finished the tongue, he wiped his fingers on his grungy cloak. He picked up the book, contemplating the blank pages. Opening the bottle of ink, he dipped the quill and drew a jagged, uneven line upon the page. He tried again, drawing a circle, the line flowing more evenly this time. Across the top of the page he began to write "*A B C D E...*" and it all came back to him.

Dipping the quill once more, he turned the page and wrote in cautious, even letters, "*In the beginning.*" He stopped and drew a line through the words. He turned the page and stared at the fresh parchment, so white. White like an apple blossom. White like a young bride's skin. He lowered the quill to the page.

Dear Recanna,

I have thought of you often. What I would say if I could see you again. What I should have said those many years ago.

Twenty years. Twenty years since last I heard your voice. Twenty years I've been at war, alone.

If only.

Here the hunter stopped. If only. These were weak words, regretful. They had no room in his heart. This was not a night to lose himself in memory and melancholy. Tomorrow was an important day. The most honored ritual of the dragons was scheduled, and he had a special, unscripted role to play.

If only.

The hunter closed the cover on those cursed words and placed the book upon the coals.

Flames licked the edges, dancing before his eyes like ghosts.

THE DRUMMERS BEAT their rhythm as the choir of sky-dragons burst into song, filling the great hall with celestial music. Jandra shivered with excitement as the ceremony began. She was sixteen now, and this was the first time she'd persuaded Vendevorex to allow her to attend the contest. For centuries the sun-dragons had used this ritual as the first step toward the enthronement of a new ruler. She would be the first human to ever witness the ceremony.

More precisely, she reminded herself, she would be the first human to ever witness the ceremony and *survive*. She looked at the two human slaves in their cages across the room. She knew her sympathy should lie with them. Alas, it was difficult to feel any connection to the brutish, wild-eyed men in the cages. Wearing her blue satin gown with an elaborate peacock headdress, Jandra felt more kinship with the dragons that surrounded her.

She sat beside Vendevorex, her mentor. A sky-dragon and the king's personal wizard, Vendevorex was widely hailed as the most clever dragon in the kingdom. As such, the exotic quirks of his personality were given broad tolerance. Jandra was one such quirk. She'd been raised since infancy by Vendevorex, and now trained as his apprentice.

Jandra looked around the great hall, at the eyes of the assembled dragons. They all had a look of disdain as they gazed toward her, from the lowest of the thick-muscled earth-dragons, to the highest of the scholarly sky-dragons who sat around the vast chamber on their elegant silk mats.

Only the immense sun-dragons didn't look upon her with scorn, because they didn't look upon her at all.

The sun-dragons were the nobility of the dragon clans. Twice the size of sky-dragons, they ruled the world with their heads held high in the regal air that came so naturally to them. The sun-dragons sported fiery red scales that faded to orange at the tips. Wispy white feathers lined their snouts, giving the illusion that they breathed smoke.

The drummers and the choir reached a crescendo as King Albekizan and his queen, Tanthia, appeared in the sky, their bright scales in dramatic contrast against the dark storm clouds behind them, tinted a rich red by the sunset. The ceremonial hall was a vast circle hundreds of yards in diameter, half covered with a dome and half open to the sky. Albekizan swooped into the hall, the wind from his wings causing the ceremonial torches that lined the perimeter to flicker. The air took on the scents of patchouli and lavender—the queen's favorite perfumes—as she swooped to rest behind him. The king's dagger-like claws clicked on the marble floor as he crossed the room, drawing closer to Vendevorex and Jandra. He didn't bother to look at them as he took his position on the huge mound of gold cushions that covered the raised dais of his throne. The queen took her place beside him atop a smaller mound of pillows. Two earth-dragons quickly rushed to either side of Tanthia, fanning her with wands of woven palm fronds. When the king and queen had settled into their seats, the drums and choir abruptly stopped.

At the rear of the chamber stood a set of enormous golden doors that led to the bowels of the earth. In the silence the doors slowly swung open, revealing a stooped sky-dragon, Metron, his blue feathers tinting silver with age. Green scarves hung around Metron's neck, denoting his office: the High Biologian, keeper of the ancient secrets. He hobbled forward, supporting himself with a gnarled staff. Despite his stooped, crooked body, Metron commanded respect. Everyone present lowered their eyes in reverence.

Metron trembled as he stood before Albekizan, and Jandra wondered for a moment if the old dragon was about to collapse. The strength in Metron's eyes allayed her fears. The High Biologian turned his back to the king to gaze out upon the sunset. It seemed as if the entire room held its breath. All that could be heard was faint thunder and the torches fretting in the rising wind.

Then, above the wind, came the flapping of gigantic wings. Long shadows raced across the hall as Albekizan's sons spiraled from the sky, spreading their wings to descend with downy grace in the center of the hall. Bodiel, the younger of the two, was the first to land, his outstretched wings nearly blocking from sight his brother, Shandrazel, who touched down behind him.

Bodiel was radiant. The crimson of his open wings blended with the sunset behind him as if all the sky were part of his being. The wind ruffled his feathery scales, making the mane of his long, serpentine neck flicker like flame. Light played on the rings of gold that pierced his wings. He stretched and relaxed the long, powerful talons at the mid-joint of each wing, displaying sharp claws painted with powdered emerald. The crowd nodded with silent approval at the display. Jandra's heart fluttered at Bodiel's beauty.

Shandrazel made no such display, keeping his wings folded. His brooding eyes stayed fixed on the floor. The long, reptilian faces of dragons didn't display the same range of emotions as humans, but Jandra recognized a scowl when she saw one.

Then, the focus once more shifted to Metron as he began the ritual greeting.

"Glorious salutations, oh mighty Albekizan!" Metron spread his wings as he spoke, giving emphasis to his words. "You who own the earth, and all who fly above it, and all who walk upon it. We live in the shadow of your magnificent incandescence! Great is your mercy."

Metron bowed deeply as the assembled dragons lowered their heads to touch the floor. Jandra bowed low, wishing she had a longer neck.

"Greater still is your bounty," Metron continued, spreading his wings once more. "The seed you planted long ago has produced a bountiful crop. Your sons stand before you, mighty and tall. Their wings span the arcs of the heavens. The fire of their will cannot be quenched by rain, or river, or sea. Each is your pride, each is your promise, and one of them, we pray, will be your death!"

The assembly erupted in cheering as Metron lowered his wings. Twice before during Albekizan's reign the dragons of the kingdom had gathered to witness this ritual in which the king's older sons competed to earn the honor of banishment from the kingdom. The hope of the ritual was that a banished son would one day return to overthrow the father, and rule with even greater strength. This was the ritual of succession that had kept Albekizan's family in power since time immemorial, with strong rulers replaced only by stronger ones. In previous contests the banished sons had returned only to be slain by Albekizan.

This year marked the first time Bodiel was eligible to compete. The king's youngest son, Bodiel was universally recognized as the dragon most likely to best his father. He was strong, fast, and charming, a master of politics as well as combat. Shandrazel was larger and, most agreed, smarter, but few believed he could prevail. Bodiel possessed the will to win at all costs. The lust for victory boiling in his blood rivaled Albekizan's and perhaps even surpassed it.

As the sun set, few in the great hall doubted that before dawn Bodiel would defeat his brother, who would be castrated and sent to the libraries to live out the rest of his days in service to Metron. Bodiel would then be granted one day of grace in which to flee the kingdom before all would have the duty to raise their claws against him.

Jandra saw no reason to doubt the consensus of the crowd. She believed that one day Bodiel would return and vanquish his father to seize the kingdom. She hoped he would be a fair and wise ruler.

"Ready the prey!" Metron shouted, tilting his staff toward the open end of the room where a dozen earth-dragons stood guard over the iron cages that held the slave men. The men were lean and tan, their oiled muscles gleaming like brass. Both were rebel slaves famous for their ability to escape; though, as evidenced by their presence, neither had yet perfected the skill of avoiding recapture.

Bodiel would be pursuing Cron, the younger of the two slaves. Shandrazel had the advantage of pursuing Tulk, the older slave. Tulk, though strong and wily, was rumored to be nearsighted. Jandra had reason to wonder if this was true because, from across the room, Tulk was staring at her. Jandra again felt a stirring of guilt. She was in awe of the ritual she was witnessing, swept up in the grandeur. Shouldn't she feel some remorse over the fates of the slaves? She averted her eyes, unable to watch Tulk's face. She stared at the sleeves of her gown, stitched with metallic blue thread to resemble the scales of a sky-dragon.

The thick-muscled earth-dragons grunted as they wheeled the iron cages to small doors in the rugged stone wall. Beyond the doors were mazes, and beyond the mazes lay the vast forest.

"Release the prey," Metron said, lowering his staff to the ground with a crisp *snap*. On cue, the drummers pounded a bass rhythm that filled the night air. The cages rattled open. Tulk tripped as he left his cage. The crowd gasped. Jandra looked up to see Tulk jumping back to his feet. Tulk cast her one last glance then turned from her, vanishing into the dark tunnel. The crowd murmured in hushed tones. A human stumbling from the cage was a bad omen.

"Humans these days are worthless," Albekizan said, addressing the High Biologian. "In my youth the humans had more spirit. They were always finding sharp rocks to wield as weapons, or hiding in tiny caves. I remember how one doubled back and hid within the palace for two days before being captured. Now, the slaves run blindly, leaving a trail of excrement any fool could follow. Why can't we find good prey anymore, Metron?"

"Sire, the laws of nature are strict," the sage dragon answered. "For centuries we have culled the finest men from the villages, only to kill them for their excellence. The breed must inevitably decline."

Vendevorex startled Jandra by interrupting the conversation between the king and the High Biologian.

"Perhaps, sire, a moratorium on the sport of hunting humans might improve things," Vendevorex said. "If you banned the sport for a century, the human stock could recover. They breed at a much faster pace than our kind."

"Bah!" Albekizan snorted, raising his bejeweled right talon dismissively. "You and your softness for humans. They make fine pets and adequate game, but you would let them breed like rabbits. The stench of their villages already sullies my kingdom."

"Their villages fill your larders with food and your coffers with gold," Vendevorex said. "Allow the humans to keep more of the fruits of their labors, and they will improve the conditions in which they live. They dwell in squalor only because of your policies."

"Be silent, wizard," Albekizan growled. "You shouldn't speak to me thus."

"You asked for my opinion, sire."

"Did I?"

"Indeed, sire. Over a decade ago, you commanded me to speak freely in your presence. Your infallible decree still stands to this day, does it not?"

Albekizan ground his teeth and turned away from the wizard. Jandra always feared for her master's

safety during these exchanges. She admired Vendevorex's boldness, but worried one day Albekizan
might be pushed too far.

Metron broke the tense silence by saying, "Sire, it
is time. You may give the word."

Albekizan rose, spreading his wings wide. His
voice boomed through the hall: "Let the hunt
begin!"

Bodiel leapt into the air. The dragons cheered as
he beat his wings against the rising wind and lifted
into the darkening night. But the crowd's cheers
changed to whispered confusion seconds later.
Shandrazel remained standing in the hall.

The king growled. "It may be you failed to hear
me above the thunder. The hunt has begun! Go!"

"Father," Shandrazel said, then paused to take a
breath. After a moment he looked up, facing the
king squarely. He said in a firm but respectful tone,
"You know my feelings. I do not desire your
throne. I will not hunt Tulk. This ceremony is
archaic and cruel. There is no need for blood to be
shed. Simply appoint Bodiel as your successor. Your
word is law."

"And you are breaking that law!" Albekizan
shouted, spittle spraying the floor before him. "I
command you to hunt!"

Jandra drew closer to Vendevorex, who wrapped
a wing around her.

Shandrazel stood unflinching before his father's
anger. With a shrug he said, "I am indeed breaking
your law. Command the guards to arrest me. I
won't resist."

Albekizan leapt from his pillows and raced
toward Shandrazel. He pulled up short of his

rebellious son, their eyes locked. The king's muscles tensed visibly beneath his hide. He stood frozen in rage but Shandrazel did not back down.

All the dragons in the room averted their eyes. No one wanted to witness this shameful confrontation between the king and his son. No dragon would risk the king's wrath by staring. So most heads were turned to watch events outside the hall. The edge of the storm had reached them and rain began to spatter on the marble floor. Illuminated by the still-distant lightning, Bodiel could barely be seen gliding low over the treetops nearly a mile distant, searching the foliage for signs of his prey.

Then, Bodiel folded his wings back and dove into the forest, swift as an arrow racing toward its target. Lightning flashed again, now much closer, momentarily blinding Jandra. The thunder made her jump. Vendevorex hugged her more tightly. When her vision cleared, Bodiel had vanished.

"Oh!" Queen Tanthia cried. "Oh no!"

"What is it, my love?" Albekizan asked. "Is our rebellious son breaking your heart?"

"It's the shadows," Tanthia said, quivering. "The shadows in the room have grown so dark. I feel their chill in my soul."

Albekizan turned his back Shandrazel to face Tanthia. Calmly he said, "There's nothing to fear."

Almost as if his saying it had made it so, the night fell quiet. The thunder faded and the wind shifted, silencing the rain for an instant. At this moment, a mournful, anguished howl rose from the distant forest. Lightning flashed and thunder washed away the voice. The wind twisted, whipping back into the hall with a harsh blast of cold rain, sending the torch flames dancing wildly. Tanthia gasped as one of the torches extinguished, a soul forever lost.

"He's dead!" Tanthia cried. "My son is dead!"

"No," Albekizan said, looking out into the storm. "No human could... could..."

The king fell silent, then turned and rushed past his rebellious son. He leapt into the rain, catching the wind, climbing into the air. Shandrazel paused, gazing after his father, then glanced back at his mother.

"Please find him," Tanthia said. "Find him."

Shandrazel nodded. He walked to the open side of the dome then beat his wings to rise into the night.

Vendevorex took Jandra by the shoulders and whispered, "We should take our leave. The king may need my assistance. It's best that you wait back in our quarters. I will accompany you."

Jandra nodded. Vendevorex sprinkled a pinch of silvery dust in the air. The whispers of the assembled crowd let Jandra know he'd just made them invisible. As they moved quietly from the great hall, Jandra watched over her shoulder as Shandrazel faded into the rain.

SHANDRAZEL HATED FLYING in the rain. He disliked the water in his eyes and loathed the way the wind treacherously shifted and vanished beneath his wings. Yet duty drove him, duty and love. Despite their differences, he loved his father and cherished his spirited younger brother. He hoped that no harm had come to either of them. The only real danger he could imagine was if Bodiel had crashed in a sudden downdraft. But even then, he'd been so low over the trees that the crash couldn't have been fatal. If Bodiel had been diving in pursuit of Cron, what possible harm could the slave have done? Despite his father's keenness for the sport of hunting humans, Shandrazel saw no more challenge in it than he did in his mother's appetite for devouring baskets of white kittens. An unarmed human was a small-toothed, clawless thing. Certainly, Bodiel was safe.

During the confrontation with his father, Shandrazel hadn't watched where his brother flew. He had no idea where to start his search. He blinked through the rain, trying to make sense of the tangled treetops that rushed beneath him. The jagged ends of broken branches caught his eyes. There was a gap in the forest canopy. Shandrazel descended into a small clearing to find his father already there.

A slain dragon hung in the crook of a tree. It was a sky-dragon, not Bodiel. In the dim light, Shandrazel drew closer. The beetles swarming over the dragon's body gave testimony that it had hung here for hours. The body stank; the sky-dragon's bowels had loosened after death. Oddly, just beneath the stench, the air here carried the unmistakable mouthwatering scent of horch.

A single arrow jutted from the dragon's jaw. Shandrazel studied the arrow, which was fletched with a red feather scale from a sun-dragon's wing; black thread wrapped around its split core fastened it to the slender shaft of ash. He then looked closer at the dragon's face. He gasped. He knew this dragon.

"His name was Dacorn," said Shandrazel. "A biologian. He taught me botany during my summer on the Isle of Horses. Who would do such a thing? He was a gentle soul. He had no enemies."

Albekizan paid no attention to Shandrazel's words. He, too, had noticed the arrow. He plucked it from the corpse to examine it. It was a tiny thing in Albekizan's talons, a fragile sliver of wood that Albekizan snapped effortlessly.

Shandrazel raised his long neck and bellowed, "Bodiel!"

"He won't be answering," said Albekizan. His father leapt up, knocking aside branches as he caught the air, rising once more to continue his search in the violent rain. Shandrazel tried to follow but the rain made it difficult to see his father, let alone keep up with him. They flew in ever-widening circles, searching the trees, and soon Shandrazel had lost all trace of his father. He continued his search, hoping that finding the corpse of his former teacher was only a macabre coincidence.

At length, Shandrazel found Albekizan sitting by the riverbank with Bodiel's head clutched against his chest. Bodiel's arrow-riddled, lifeless body lay half in the water—it was possible he'd died further upriver and drifted to rest here. Shandrazel landed, feeling as if his own heart were pierced with an arrow. Never had there been a soul as bold and joyous as Bodiel's. It seemed impossible that he should be dead.

Shandrazel stepped forward, using his wings to shelter his father from the rain. He froze as Albekizan looked at him. Their gazes locked. Albekizan's eyes burned with fury, fury and something more, an emotion he'd not seen in his father's eyes for many years: passion. Albekizan, cradling Bodiel's dead body, was filled with frightening, fiery life.

Shandrazel stumbled backward, his talons slipping in the muddy earth. The air seemed charged, ready to spark.

The king dropped Bodiel into the mud and rose to his full length. In his fore-talon he held a single arrow and he studied the bright red fletching of the arrow as if he were studying his soul. Lightning struck nearby, again and again, shaking the ground. Fire spouted from the tops of the tallest, most ancient trees. Albekizan didn't flinch. Shandrazel couldn't move. As the thunder faded from their ringing ears, Albekizan held the arrow to the sky and shouted a single, bone-chilling word.

"Bitterwood!"

CHAPTER TWO

CIRCLES

B Y THE TIME Gadreel returned to the clearing by the river, the only sound in the night forest was the constant staccato of water dripping from leaves. His master, Zanzeroth—an old sun-dragon who rivaled even the king in size and the finest tracker in the land—still studied the scene. Zanzeroth's golden eyes glowed in the trickles of moonlight seeping through the breaking clouds. Albekizan stood nearby, watching the aged hunter step gingerly over the muddy ground. Albekizan ignored Gadreel. Gadreel hoped the king's snub was due to his fascination with Zanzeroth's methods. The patch of ground they stood on seemed unremarkable to Gadreel, but Zanzeroth had instantly proclaimed it as the site of Bodiel's death, three miles upriver from where his body was discovered. Gadreel suspected, however, that the king ignored him due to his status. It was a simple matter to treat a human as a slave. The notion of a sky-dragon such as himself forced into servitude made some uncomfortable.

"How much longer?" Zanzeroth asked.

"A few minutes, at most," Gadreel answered. As he spoke the distant baying of ox-dogs confirmed his words.

"Good," Zanzeroth said. "The sooner we start, the better. The ground here has told me all it can."

"If you have knowledge," Albekizan said, "give it to me."

"Of course, sire," Zanzeroth said, straightening his stooped form and approaching the king. Next to Albekizan, Zanzeroth's extra years were apparent. The king's hide glistened on his muscular body like paint. Zanzeroth's scales were faded from years under the sun, almost pink along the back. His scales had fallen away at his joints, revealing black hide beneath. His scarred skin sagged over his skeleton, under which his slender, wiry muscles moved like thick ropes. Zanzeroth asked, "Shouldn't we wait for Shandrazel to join us? I'm sure he wants to help find his brother's killer."

"Do not speak that shameful name," Albekizan said, his eyes narrow. "I've placed that traitor under guard for now. His final fate will be left for the morning. We will not discuss this further. For now, Bitterwood is our only goal."

Zanzeroth nodded. He waved his fore-talons toward a patch of mud that seemed to Gadreel no different than any other.

"Here is where the slave, Cron, skidded to a halt as Bodiel dropped from the sky. See the handprint here?" Zanzeroth paused to allow Albekizan time to discern what was being shown to him. Gadreel stared at the chaotic mud and, to his surprise, found he could see the handprint, or at least the heel of a human palm.

Zanzeroth continued: "The human fell and had difficulty regaining his footing." Zanzeroth moved his claw to direct the king's view to a patch of broken ground several yards away. "That is where Bodiel dropped from the sky. Cron's footprints then reappear several feet behind where he stopped—he's jumped away out of fear of Bodiel. There are signs that Bodiel toyed with the human, blocking his moves, prolonging the moment before the kill. And then…" Zanzeroth trailed off, his gaze flickering over the mud, studying it as one might study a book. "And then Bodiel staggered backward. See the marks? Cron fled, passing through the brush… here."

As he said this, Zanzeroth parted a thicket with several bent branches and revealed a man's muddy footprints beyond.

"We could follow Cron with ease but he's not the one who killed Bodiel."

"I know that," Albekizan said. "Bitterwood's to blame. The Ghost Who Kills haunts these woods tonight."

"Perhaps," Zanzeroth said. "But I've yet to see a ghost leave tracks. The murderer of your son was merely a man."

"He's more than a man," Albekizan said. "You'd do well to remember that."

"Yes, sire," said Zanzeroth. He walked to the bush beside Gadreel and touched a torn leaf above his head. "Man or ghost, the assailant struck from behind. Here is where the first arrow passed. That branch, there, is where he wrapped the reigns of his horse. He stood on the large branch in yonder tree to take his first shot."

Zanzeroth stalked back to the center of the clearing, placing his hind-talons in a pair of long, smeared trenches. "Your son stood in this spot. The arrow strikes Bodiel low in the back. In pain, Bodiel spins," Zanzeroth twisted around suddenly, fixing his gaze above Gadreel, "to see another arrow fly forth, burying deep in his shoulder. Bodiel hears Cron running and turns, reflexively fearing the loss of his prize, then catches himself. This is the first instant where he understands his own life is in danger."

Zanzeroth held his wings wide for balance as his talons skittered in the mud, duplicating Bodiel's actions.

"Bodiel leaps but never reaches the bush. His foe is already running through the woods, flanking him, and the third arrow comes from there." The hunter pulled a long spear from the quiver slung on his back and used the shaft to point to a narrow gap in the trees. "The fourth arrow follows swiftly, puncturing Bodiel's lung. Here," Zanzeroth crouched, spreading his wings over the mud, "the prince falls. He's alive but in terrible agony. He screams only for an instant as the fifth arrow lodges in his throat. The prince struggles to rise, unwilling to accept his fate. He crawls toward the water, seeking relief. Still the arrows come. The archer knows Bodiel has mere moments to live but wants him to suffer. The shots that follow aren't meant to hasten death, but to increase agony. The arrows fall upon the tender flesh of the wings and tail. Bodiel at last collapses, his left wing in the river. Slowly, the speeding current drags him from the bank."

Zanzeroth started to rise but slipped in the mud. Gadreel hurried to his side, extending a claw for the hunter to steady himself. Zanzeroth spurned him by digging his hind-talons deeper in the muck and pulling his wings free from the ground with a wet, slurping sound. He shook his wings to clean them, spattering Gadreel with mud that smelled faintly of dung.

"And Bitterwood?" Albekizan said, studying the trees surrounding them. "What became of him?"

"He fled, of course," said Zanzeroth, placing his spear back in its quiver. "On horseback. He's miles away but we'll find him. Even after a hard rain the ox-dogs can follow a horse's scent."

As Zanzeroth spoke, the brush behind him shuddered and then parted as two massive ox-dogs lumbered into the clearing, dragging their earth-dragon handlers behind them. Earth-dragons were solid, squat, no taller than humans but twice as broad, with thick muscular arms instead of wings, and powerful shoulders to support their broad tortoise-like heads. They were strong as mules but their strength did little to slow the powerful dogs. The dogs dragged their handlers to Zanzeroth's side. Their rank breath steamed in the rain-cooled night. Moments later a squad of a dozen earth-dragons, the finest the palace guard had to offer, emerged from the brush.

Zanzeroth took the leashes of the dogs and led them to the spot where the horse had stood. The dogs sniffed and snuffed, rooting through the damp debris of the forest. Suddenly, one froze. The second rushed to the same spot and pushed its nose to the ground. They lifted their barrel-sized heads and bayed with excitement.

"They've found the scent," said Zanzeroth.

The dogs trotted back into the clearing, following the hoofprints through the mud. Zanzeroth unwrapped the leather leashes from his wrist and loosed the dogs. They charged past the king and smashed into the undergrowth, panting with excitement.

The hunt was on. The ox-dogs moved forward in fits and starts, racing when they had the scent, then stopping suddenly to sniff the wet ground where the trail was diluted by washouts. Zanzeroth and Albekizan followed with the soldiers rushing ahead of the king to chop away growth that might slow his progress.

Gadreel was half the size of the sun-dragons, but he still found the dense vegetation suffocating. He wished he could take to the sky to follow from above. As long as Zanzeroth remained earthbound, he must also. Walking through the forest like a common earth-dragon didn't sit well with him.

He looked to the nearest earth-dragon and shuddered. The creature's dull eyes peered out from beneath a sloped, moss-green brow, not even blinking at the gnats that swarmed around its face. Its thick, alligator-ridged tail dragged the mud as it waddled forward. The earth-dragon seemed no more capable of true intelligence or emotion than a human. Yet, as a soldier, the earth-dragon had higher status than Gadreel, a slave. Not for the first time, he silently cursed his father.

Gadreel knew better than to voice his indignation. He'd learned his lesson about showing weakness. Three years past he'd been ill and failed to attend the gathering of his father's clan. Albekizan had issued an order demanding a hundred human slaves from the clan. The clan balked at the idea of parting with the slaves. But wouldn't a dragon slave be worth a hundred humans? His father said he had voted against the idea but had to follow the wishes of the clan.

It had been humiliating, to be placed into servitude at his father's command. To further emphasize his status as mere property, the cunning Zanzeroth, the only dragon who dared best the king on a hunt, had won Gadreel in a bet. Yet in his humiliation, Gadreel could also see hope and opportunity. He found himself almost daily in the presence of Albekizan. One day, he vowed, he would somehow impress the king so greatly that he would be rewarded with freedom.

The ox-dogs paused on the far side of a stream swollen with rain. Gadreel could tell they had lost the scent. Zanzeroth followed the muddy bank, his eyes shining in the darkness as he read the ground.

"Here," Zanzeroth said, at last. The old dragon grabbed an ox-dog by its collar and tugged the beast back across the stream, shoving its head down to mossy stone. Zanzeroth's great strength allowed him to move the giant dog as if it were no more than a puppy. The ox-dog sniffed and growled at the stone. In seconds the dog once more had the scent and bounded off into the forest with its brother quickly following. The dragons chased the dogs and moments later the forest gave way to a cornfield. Gadreel felt relieved to see open sky once more, with bright moonlight illuminating the few faint wisps of cloud. Free from the trees Albekizan beat his wings and took to the air. Zanzeroth followed, and Gadreel accompanied him at a respectful distance.

Moments later Zanzeroth veered and Gadreel could see a riderless horse at the edge of the grassy field. Zanzeroth dove, his rear claws extended. The horse broke into a gallop as the dragon's shadow fell upon it but to no avail. Zanzeroth caught the fleeing horse by the neck, killing it instantly with a vicious twist.

"Damn," the old hunter said as he landed.

"Where is he?" Albekizan said as he touched down nearby. "Where's Bitterwood?"

"We've been tricked, sire." Zanzeroth said. "This is the horse we've been following. I can smell it. But Bitterwood must have dismounted early in the chase. I saw no sign. Perhaps he clung to an overhead branch."

"Damn your incompetent hide," the king shouted. "If we've lost my son's murderer due to your carelessness, I'll have your head!"

Gadreel flinched but his master seemed unperturbed.

"Of course, sire," said Zanzeroth with a slight bow. "The hunt's more interesting if the stakes are high."

By now the earth-dragons had caught up. The handlers grabbed the leashes of the ox-dogs and tugged them away from the steaming carcass of the horse.

Zanzeroth pulled the three spears from his quiver and handed them to Gadreel. "These are only going to get in my way," he said. Gadreel struggled to hold the giant wooden shafts with their gleaming steel heads. Only sun-dragons could ever hope to use such massive weapons effectively.

All stood silently as Zanzeroth crouched down on all fours, his belly touching the wet grass. The aged dragon moved over the ground in a slow, sinuous, reptilian crawl, pausing to study each hoofprint. He sniffed the ground carefully, tilted his head, then crawled forward, paused, and sniffed again. He continued his methodical examination, moving back toward the forest, taking nearly an hour to reach the stream where the trail had been momentarily lost. Gadreel's muscles burned from the effort of lugging Zanzeroth's spears all this time.

Zanzeroth stared at the tracks on each side of the stream with quiet intensity. Gadreel wondered how much sense his master could make of ground that had now been trampled by ox-dogs and a small army of dragons.

Zanzeroth rose, stretching his shoulders until his sinews popped. "The horse was a simple ruse, but effective," he said. "Our quarry dismounted in the water, no doubt keeping to the streambed for some distance. If we run an ox-dog along each side we can discover the point where he leaves the water. We'll have him yet."

"Find him," said the king. "I grow impatient."

Zanzeroth snatched his spears back from Gadreel, placing them once more in his quiver. He took each ox-dog by the leash and led them upstream, wading in the water. He cast his watchful eyes on each branch that hung overhead. After a few hundred yards the ox-dog to his left stopped, sniffed the ground, and let out a low growl. Zanzeroth crouched to study the bank.

"Clever," he said, looking back at the king. "But not clever enough. I have the trail once more."

He loosed the ox-dogs and motioned for all to follow as he raced into the dark woods.

Gadreel's breath came in gasps as he chased his untiring master through the rain-slick forest. The trees were thick here, and the darkness was such that their prey could have been merely a wing's length away and still have been invisible. Ahead, Gadreel could see shafts of moonlight and hoped they were again near the forest's edge. Zanzeroth stopped abruptly and Gadreel nearly collided with him.

The earth-dragons skidded to a halt behind them. One muttered, "The lines." Gadreel looked over his shoulder but couldn't tell which earth-dragon had spoken.

Straining his neck to see around Zanzeroth, Gadreel could see that whoever had spoken had been correct. They had reached one of the bleached, cracked stone lines that stretched endless miles through the kingdom. Some scholars claimed the lines were only ancient roads, built by a long-vanished race of giants. A more common belief was that the barren, flat stone marked a web of evil energy that ran through the earth. In the presence of this cursed ground, the night was unnaturally quiet.

"So, hunter," Albekizan whispered. "You still believe it is only a man we chase? No man alive would dare to walk the ghost lines."

"He will if he's desperate," said Zanzeroth. "Our prey thinks we won't follow because of the curse. But sire, you've known me long enough to know that I've never placed stock in such foolishness. This is merely old rock. We have nothing to fear. The dogs have already run ahead. We'll catch him yet."

"Then we shall give chase from the air," said Albekizan. "The soldiers shall run along the line."

"Sire?" the captain of the earth-dragons said. The light yellow scales on his throat trembled.

"You heard the order," Albekizan said, leaping into the air, his feet never touching the haunted stone.

Zanzeroth followed, and Gadreel, too. The earth-dragons stepped hesitantly onto the crumbling stone line then turned their eyes heavenward and chased their king.

Gadreel was glad to be in the air once more but he had no time to enjoy it. Barely a quarter mile ahead the ox-dogs turned from the line, loping down a steep, vine-covered bank. They turned and entered a small tunnel that ran beneath the broad highway of stone.

As Gadreel landed, one of the dogs yelped. The second dog scurried backward from the tunnel.

Zanzeroth peered into the dark opening. Gadreel strained to see and spotted the first ox-dog, dead, its head crushed by a heavy stone. Zanzeroth took a spear from his quiver, pushed the shaft along the floor, then lifted it to reveal a loop of thin rope.

"A deadfall," he muttered. "The killer has booby trapped his escape route. Cunning, for a human."

"He's Bitterwood," said Albekizan. "The predator. He's no mere human."

Zanzeroth nodded, then took the remaining dog by the leash and led him back over the stone line to the other side of the short tunnel. The dog found the scent once more as the earth-dragons at last caught up. Zanzeroth wrapped the leash tightly around his talon so that the dog couldn't run too far ahead. Gadreel followed, growing ever more nervous. They were walking along the diamond. All the winged dragons were familiar with the place, for it could be seen from the air for miles: four gigantic stone circles surrounded by an even larger diamond of stone. There were several of these constructs throughout the kingdom, in places where the mystery lines crossed in elaborate networks of ramps and bridges. The last remnants, perhaps, of a long-vanished culture. These places were much feared, for four circles was the symbol of death.

To Gadreel's relief, the ox-dog veered away from the edges of the diamond and led them to a large field of broken stone. In the midst of the field sat an ancient, low building formed of vine-covered brick. The sky brightened with the approach of dawn, giving Gadreel some comfort.

As he allowed himself to relax slightly, a whistling noise cut through the air. With a sickening wet *thunk*, an arrow lodged deep between the eyes of the ox-dog. The huge beast sighed then slumped forward, all life gone.

Zanzeroth leapt before the king, spreading his wings wide to shield him. "He's in yonder structure. Take cover, sire!"

"Never!" Albekizan cried. "If Bitterwood is here, no force on earth shall stop me from ordering my soldiers into that building to drag him out, that I may have my vengeance!" He pointed to the captain, then thundered, "Go!"

The captain raised his shield and charged forward, his men following at a tail's length. One by one, they vanished into the dark doorway. Silence followed.

"He's fled deeper," said Zanzeroth. "Or perhaps—"

His words were cut short as a dragon cried out from the darkness, his voice followed by a thunderous rumble. The doorway glowed suddenly with a light to rival the rising sun. A ball of flame rolled forward, led by a blast of searing, turpentine-scented air that threw Gadreel from his feet.

"No!" the king cried. "A suicide trap! How dare he deny me justice!"

"I doubt suicide," Zanzeroth said, flapping his wings in the still-turbulent air. He climbed several dozen feet before shouting, "There!"

Gadreel and Albekizan rose to join him and quickly spotted a cloaked man carrying a longbow, perhaps a hundred yards away, running across the stony field. The light of the burning building gave him a reddish, devilish cast. As Zanzeroth dove toward him, the man dropped his bow and fell to his knees. He struggled to lift a rusty iron disk almost two feet across that was set in the stone. As Zanzeroth stretched his talons toward his prey the disk came free, revealing a gaping hole. Grabbing his bow, the man dropped into the dark circle a half-second before Zanzeroth snatched the air where his head had been.

Zanzeroth looped around to land. Albekizan dropped behind the hole and spun around, his eyes burning red with reflected flame. "So close! So close!"

"He's not free yet," Zanzeroth said, rushing forward, his longest spear in his grip. He jabbed the shaft into the dark hole. Without warning an arrow flashed upward to meet the spear thrust. Zanzeroth jerked backward as the arrow slashed his right cheek and tore open his eye. He stumbled back from the opening in the earth, cursing.

Gadreel gazed at the hole, as black as a starless night, a perfect circle. Albekizan fell to his belly before the dark ring, thrusting his fore-claws into it, grasping blindly, his need to capture Bodiel's killer blotting out all caution. The hole was much too small for a sun-dragon to enter.

Gadreel swallowed hard and stepped forward. If ever there was a moment where he might prove himself worthy of greater esteem than a slave, this was that moment.

"I'll go," he said.

"Hurry," Albekizan said, rising. Gadreel lowered himself tailfirst into the darkness. He entered a tunnel barely eight feet in diameter and found it half-filled with rushing water. He heard echoes from up ahead and inched forward in pursuit, holding his wings as high as he could to keep them from becoming waterlogged. His eyes adjusted to the dim light that filtered in from the opening behind him. He saw no sign of the human.

The light behind him faded as he crept forward but was replaced by a dim glow far ahead. When he reached the new light, he found another metal disk still in place above him, perforated by four holes. The glow of dawn seeped through and he felt exposed. He reached up to try to lift the rusted disk, but couldn't budge it.

Taking a deep, calming breath, he moved further into the gloom. As darkness engulfed him once more, he felt something swirl around his legs, entangling them. He tried to kick himself free but lost his balance in the rushing water. He fell, dragged beneath the chill current, tossed and scraped against the rough walls. He flailed, unable to tell which way was up. He swallowed foul, brackish water and felt his heart freeze within him. The flame of his life began to flicker.

Then, through the murk, he saw four tiny circles. He'd been washed back to the last disk. He dug his claws into the walls and thrust his head toward the light. He gulped in dank, moldy air, the sweetest air he'd ever tasted. He found his footing and reached down to grasp the heavy weight that still entangled his legs. He pulled it free, lifting it into the light. It was Bitterwood's cloak.

Bitterwood.

The insanity of his pursuit struck home. Bodiel had been no match for the demon. Zanzeroth, the most skilled hunter in all the land, had been bested. What chance had he, a mere slave? He studied the darkness before him. The roar of water masked all other noise. Perhaps Bitterwood was near. But Gadreel knew in his heart that the only reason he was still alive was that Bitterwood was long gone. Gadreel abandoned his chase and inched his way back toward the entrance.

He reached the open hole and stretched to grab the edge. The king's enormous talon reached down, grabbed him by the scruff of the neck, and lifted him clear.

"Did you find him?" Albekizan said, setting Gadreel before him.

"I-I…" Gadreel said, staring deep into the king's hopeful eyes. Gadreel felt he should lie, should tell the king he'd fought the killer. But he only sighed and shook his head. Gadreel lifted the cloak. "I found this, sire."

Albekizan took the cloak and stared at it, his eyes filled with emotions that Gadreel could not fathom.

"I saw no other sign of him," Gadreel said. "The water was quite powerful. The current pulled me under. No doubt, the man we chased has drowned."

"No," said the king, softly. "Not this monster. This dragon-slayer, he'll not die a careless death. You did your best. Be grateful to have escaped with your life."

Gadreel nodded. The king didn't seem angry about his failure. Somehow that didn't comfort him.

"Go tend your master's wound," Albekizan said.

Zanzeroth was squatting on the ground, pressing a bloodied bundle of leaves to his injured eye. No one alive knew more about the medicinal properties of forest plants; the entire world was his pharmacy. "'Tis not a mortal wound, sire," said Zanzeroth, his voice a curious mixture of confidence and agony. "We'll head back to the castle for more earth-dragons and fresh dogs. The hunt will continue. In daylight our prey no longer has the advantage of shadows."

"No," Albekizan said. "I admire your spirit, old friend, but we need not chase this demon into further traps. There's a solution to this problem, an obvious one. We've paid a horrible price this night. I vow this—the debt of Bitterwood will be repaid in blood."

Gadreel stared at the open circle at his feet. Outside the tunnel, free of the rushing water, he felt shame that he'd abandoned the chase. His failure lodged in his gut like an icy stone. He'd been brave enough to enter the hole; why hadn't he been brave enough to stay? Proving his worth to the king no longer seemed important. The next time he faced Bitterwood, he must prove his worth to himself.

CHAPTER THREE

STONE

A T MID-MORNING, after giving his orders to Bander, the earth-dragon in charge of the palace guards, Albekizan went to the roof of the palace to bask in sunlight. The night had left him with a chill despite the warmth of the day. It was late summer, nearing the time of harvest. The sky was flawless blue. From his high perch Albekizan surveyed the patchwork of land splayed out in all directions. The deep green forests, the golden fields, and the broad silver ribbon of the river: Albekizan ruled every inch of this land as undisputed master. His kingdom stretched from the impassible mountains two hundred miles west to the endless ocean a hundred miles to the east, north to the Ghostlands and far, far to the south, to the endless, trackless marshes that had swallowed many an army.

It was said that Albekizan owned the earth and was master of all who flew above it and all who crawled upon it. In over a half century of rule, he had bent the world to his will and had assured that there was no destiny other than his destiny. He woke each day secure in the knowledge that if he desired a thing, nothing and no one could deny him.

Until this morning.

Beloved Bodiel was dead. He wanted to trade his wealth and power, his own life, even, to undo this horrible truth. But there was no one with whom he could demand such a trade.

Albekizan rushed to the edge of the roof, a great platform of stone, and leapt into the sky. His wings caught the wind; he soared upward, his face toward the mocking sun. In his youth he'd often tested his boundaries, climbing ever higher in pursuit of the yellow orb that remained beyond his reach. He pushed himself again, beating his mighty wings until they ached, scaling the sky like a ladder, upward, upward, until the chill in his blood was replaced by fire, by the burning in his chest, by the heat of the breath that rushed from his throat in gasps as he pushed to his limits, then beyond.

The sun grew no closer than it had in his youth. There were some things above even a king.

Exhausted, Albekizan tilted earthward and abandoned his futile chase.

From high above, his palace looked like a rocky mountain. A vast mound of stone heaped upon stone, the palace had been under construction for a thousand years, started by ancestors so long distant that their names were now legend. Asrafel, the Firebringer. Wanzanzen, the Lawgiver. Belpantheron, the Just.

Over the centuries, stone quarried from the western mountains had been floated downriver to this rich plain and used to build the home of kings. The structure was in many ways more fortress than palace, with cliff-like walls designed to hold back enemy armies. From the sky the palace was a maze of courtyards and towers, winding alleys and great halls half open to the sky, as befits a race born to rule the air. Despite being built of gray granite, the palace was awash in bright colors with terrace gardens alive with riotous flowers. The fiery flag of the sun-dragons—goldthread suns set against scarlet silk backgrounds—flew by the thousands, on poles rising from every corner of the complex. Inside the palace the colors vanished. Over the centuries, as stone piled upon stone, the oldest rooms of the palace had become ever more enclosed. Immense caverns became hidden deep within the rock, connected by narrow, twisting passages. The vibrant, explosive life of the external palace hid a cold, stony heart.

Albekizan landed on the highest rooftop with the lightness of a leaf. Indeed, as he touched down, the wind of his passage sent a dried leaf skittering across the polished stone before him. Albekizan took the presence of the dry, dead thing as a sign. Autumn lay close. Cold days were coming to the kingdom.

He paused, steadying himself against a wall as he caught his breath. He looked over the fields and spotted a small army of earth-dragons at work piling wood in a nearby field. Albekizan's heart skipped as he realized they were at work on his son's funeral pyre.

"Bodiel," he sighed.

Then, taking a slow, deep breath, he steeled himself. Once certain that his eyes would betray no emotion unbefitting a king, Albekizan marched down the wide steps into the dark depths of his home.

Albekizan descended ever further into the bowels of the palace, drawn to the very heart, the nest chamber. This was the most deeply enclosed structure of the palace, set upon the very bedrock of the place. The cool, dank air of the chamber stirred primitive memories. This was his birthplace. More, it was where he had first gazed upon Bodiel, damp from birth. He'd licked away the thick, salty fluid that had covered his son's still-closed eyes. The taste once again lingered on his tongue. The birth memory quickly faded, pushed away by the sour thought of Bodiel's adult body clutched against his own, damp with rain and blood.

When he entered the nest chamber he found he was not alone. Tanthia waited there, beside the vast fire-pit which lay cold and black. He almost didn't see her in the darkness. The lanterns that lit the immense room had all been shuttered so that only a sliver of light from those in the outer hall penetrated the shadows.

Albekizan stood silently, contemplating his queen as she turned her head toward him. He felt he should say something, that it was his role to give her strength.

The only thing he knew to say was, "Bodiel will be avenged."

Tanthia's wet eyes glistened in the gloom as she fixed her gaze upon him.

"I am convening a council of war," Albekizan continued. "This crime shall not go unpunished. There is no corner of the earth where the guilty may hide."

Tanthia inhaled slowly. Then, softly, she said, "This is all you have to say in comfort?"

"What more need be said?" he asked. "Last night's events demand vengeance."

"Talk of vengeance is not the same as talk of grief," she said, her voice trembling. "I hear no pain in your voice. Where are your tears? Come with me, my king. Come with me to the Burning Ground. By now, Bodiel lies in state. Stand by my side as I go see him."

"No," said Albekizan. His eyes were fixed on the ancient rock beneath his claws, polished smooth by the passage of his uncountable ancestors. Could Tanthia not feel the gravity of this place? Here, at the heart of all history, was no place for weakness. "Not yet. At nightfall, perhaps, I will go. But I've already seen my son dead. I've held his cold body. Do not lecture me about the proper way to grieve."

"You sound angry with me," Tanthia said.

"You hear what you want to hear," said Albekizan, turning away. "I'm sorry to have disturbed you. I will go now."

"Please," said Tanthia. "Stay with me. Share the burden of this grief."

"Grief cannot be my priority," Albekizan said, not looking back. "I have summoned Kanst. I must ready the armies. The longer we hesitate, the longer Bitterwood has to work his evil on this world. I hope you understand this."

Tanthia replied only with sobs. Albekizan sighed, stepping through the chamber door. In the hall he sensed a presence and could hear scraping against the stone around the nearby corner. Albekizan breathed deeply, catching a familiar scent in his nostrils. He knew who shadowed him.

"Bander!" he cried, summoning the captain of the palace guard.

In the time it took Albekizan to blink the earthdragon dashed around the corner and snapped to attention.

"Sire," Bander said, "I didn't want to intrude but—"

"Are they ready?" Albekizan asked.

"Kanst has arrived, sire," said Bander. "He waits in the war room with Metron and Zanzeroth." As he spoke, his voice wavered. The hard, beak-like face of earth-dragons gave little hint of emotion, but Albekizan could recognize a touch of fear in Bander's eyes. "As for Vendevorex, sire, the guards continue their search."

Albekizan nodded. He wasn't angered by this failure of Bander's guards. Vendevorex possessed the power of invisibility. He would be found only if he wished to be found. "Continue the search. The wizard is vital to my plans. What of my second order?"

Bander looked relieved. "The guards are gathering the humans even now, sire."

"Good. I want their stench removed from this castle—"

"Please?"

Tanthia's voice interrupted them. Albekizan turned to see his mate standing in the chamber door, the feathery scales around her eyes darkened by tears.

"I beg you," she said, her voice raspy and weak. "Come with me to the Burning Ground."

Albekizan narrowed his eyes with displeasure. "I consider this matter settled. No amount of tears will revive Bodiel. Go and wait at the Burning Ground until the ceremony if you must. I will see to the business of saving my kingdom."

Upon hearing his words Tanthia collapsed, all strength gone.

"You're so cold," she sobbed. "So cold. The stones in the walls are warmer than your heart."

Albekizan turned from his mate and stormed away, grinding his teeth in anger. But when he reached the end of the hall he stopped and turned to study his fallen queen, her crimson wings stretched across the ancient bedrock, her body heaving with sobs. Albekizan walked back and crouched beside his queen. Touching her shoulders, he helped her to rise. He brushed his talons across the delicate scales of her cheeks.

"Tanthia, my love, it pains me to see you grieve. Nonetheless, mourning is a female's burden, and her luxury. My duty is to avenge my son. I must go and consult with my advisors as to the swiftest path to achieve justice. Later, when the moon has risen and the day's work is done, I will join you at the Burning Ground and watch as Metron lights the pyre. Then I will hold you and assist with the burden of grief. Go now. Wait with our fallen son, until the night comes."

Tanthia stood, her legs still trembling, but her head held high. "Yes, my king," she whispered, and returned once more to the nest chamber.

Albekizan turned away and saw that Bander now conferred with another guard in panicked, hushed voices.

"What is it?" Albekizan demanded.

Bander snapped back to attention. "Sire, my guards have searched every room of the castle. Vendevorex cannot be found."

"No doubt the wizard plots some dramatic entrance," Albekizan said. "He thinks it beneath his dignity to simply walk into a room. Call off the search. I'll wait no longer. Come."

VENDEVOREX, IN FACT, did not consider it beneath his dignity to simply walk into a room. Dignity played no part in his comings and goings; strategy was the key to his movements. He'd served Albekizan for close to fifteen years and he'd decided long ago that life would be more comfortable for him if he maintained his own agenda. Thus, while the night had found Albekizan and Zanzeroth in frenzied pursuit of Bitterwood, Vendevorex had chosen a different course. He'd been present in the forest at Bodiel's murder scene, watching invisibly from a tree as Zanzeroth pointed out Cron's and Bitterwood's trails. As the hunting party left in pursuit of Bitterwood, Vendevorex followed Cron's path. It wasn't that he was unconcerned with the capture of Bitterwood. He was simply confident that the deed was within Zanzeroth's grasp. The old tracker could follow a single snowflake through a blizzard. And when they caught up with Bitterwood—or to the person pretending to be him—it seemed likely that that the small army accompanying the king would prevail. How dangerous could one man be, after all?

Cron's trail led for several hundred meandering yards through the thickets of the forest. Vendevorex didn't possess Zanzeroth's skills as a tracker, but he didn't need them. The king had been right. These slaves left a trail anyone could follow.

At last he found the young slave hiding behind a fallen log with a shelter of branches pulled over him. It wasn't a horrible hiding place, except that Cron's teeth were chattering loud enough that he sounded like some sort of nocturnal woodpecker.

From ten feet away, Vendevorex said, "I am your friend, Cron."

Cron gasped, then clenched his jaw, silencing his chattering teeth.

"You have nothing to fear," Vendevorex said. "Rise, I wish to help you."

"W-who are you?" Cron whispered.

"Tonight, I am your last, best hope," Vendevorex said. "You're safe for the moment. But when the king finds his prey tonight, I have no doubt he'll come looking for you. It's best that you be long gone."

Cron rose into a crouch, looking around the dark forest with fear in his eyes. Vendevorex chose to remain invisible. But he placed a burlap sack near the log and backed away.

"The sack before you... do you see it?"

Cron looked around, trying to find the source of the voice. At last he looked to the ground and spotted the sack.

"I have brought you clothes and food," said Vendevorex. "You will also find a knife within the pack."

Cron crawled over the log toward the burlap. He reached out carefully and poked it. Then he pulled it toward him and fumbled at the cord that closed it with trembling fingers. At last he tore it open. He found a heavy cloak within which he draped over his body. In doing so, a loaf of bread fell from the bag, landing on the muddy ground. Cron snatched it up and began to hungrily devour it.

Between cramming in mouthfuls of bread, Cron said, "You sound close. Why don't I see you?"

"I wish to remain an anonymous benefactor for now," said Vendevorex.

"You're invisible," said Cron. "That kind of narrows down who you might be. Venderex, right? The wizard?"

Vendevorex remained silent.

"You have that human pet, right? The girl? She was there tonight. She's beautiful."

"You have me confused with someone else, friend," Vendevorex said.

"Right," said Cron, wiping his mouth and digging through the bag's contents in search of more food. His eyes lit up as he pulled out a hard-boiled egg. "What I want to know is what a person has to do to get to be a dragon's pet. It seems like a pretty soft life."

"I don't believe the girl you speak of is a pet," Vendevorex said.

"She was dressed like a dragon, all those feathers," said Cron. "What I'm wondering is, is there, you know, sex involved? Do dragons find humans attractive? I know some girls get hot over dragons. I have a sister who—"

Vendevorex bristled at the speculation, but there was no time to correct this fool's uninformed opinions. He interrupted Cron, saying, "You must return to the river with all haste. Can you find the place where you witnessed Bodiel drop from the sky?"

"Yes," said Cron, spitting out a fleck of eggshell. "I thought I was a goner. Why didn't he chase me?"

"You... didn't witness what happened, then?"

"I turned and ran the second I saw him," Cron said. "What happened? And why are you helping me?"

"What happened isn't important," said Vendevorex. "Just know that I am someone who has no patience for needless death. Your lot in life has been a cruel one, Cron. There is little I can do to change it. Return to the river. The area is abandoned. The king's party is miles away by now. When you arrive, you will find a small boat and, if my luck holds, you may also find Tulk waiting for you. Take the boat and go as far downriver as you can before morning. If you reach the town of Hopewell, seek the advice of a man known as Stench. He'll give you shelter for a day or two. This is all I can do for you."

"I know old Stench," Cron said. "Thought he'd be dead by now."

Vendevorex didn't answer. He'd done what his conscience demanded and he could risk no more. He crept away silently. He had little time left to find Tulk.

IT WAS EARLY morning when Vendevorex returned to the palace. He was exhausted, having flown a score of miles that night, following Tulk and Cron from above as they paddled downriver in their canoe, making sure they avoided immediate capture. When at dawn they had put the canoe to shore as he'd advised and disappeared under the canopy of the forest, he felt he had done all he could.

Returning to his chambers, Vendevorex went to Jandra's room. He sighed when he found she wasn't there. In truth, it wasn't a surprise that she'd defied his orders to stay put. He knew where to find her.

Invisibly, he flew outside the palace walls to a row of wooden shacks that lined the base of the palace. These were the quarters of the human servants who labored within the palace: the cooks and chambermaids, the workmen and washerwomen who dwelled meekly among the dragons. Vendevorex landed on the muddy pathway that wound among the shacks, wrinkling his nose. The shantytown smelled of rotting garbage and excrement. Within the palace an elaborate and ancient system of aqueducts and pipes carried fresh water to all corners of the edifice, and flushed away waste. Here, open, stinking ditches served the same purpose. Filthy children in rags played in the muck, laughing, seemingly unaware of their squalor.

Perhaps the king was right to regard humans as a lower race than dragons, thought Vendevorex. He shook his head to chase away the thought. The humans didn't live like this by choice. If a man were ever to try to live with the wealth and comfort of a dragon, Albekizan's tax collectors would simply come and take it away. Humans lived in squalor because this was all Albekizan would allow.

As he walked unseen past the hovels, he heard at last the familiar sound of Jandra's voice. He turned a corner to find her talking with Ruth and Mary, two of the palace kitchen maids. Ruth and Mary, by his estimate, were in their mid-twenties, but their hard lives made them seem middle-aged. Fifteen years ago, when Jandra had first come into his life, he'd turned to Ruth and Mary's mother for advice in raising a human child. Their mother had passed away some years ago from disease, but Ruth and Mary maintained a friendship with Jandra to this day. Jandra would frequently steal away to gossip with them.

And this morning... such gossip.

"Is it true that Bodiel is dead?" Ruth whispered.

"I hear that Cron killed him," Mary said. "He had a bow and arrow hidden in the woods."

"All I know is what I saw," said Jandra. "In the midst of the storm, Bodiel vanished. Albekizan and Shandrazel chased after him. Then Vendevorex rushed me back to my chambers before I could see anything else. He told me to wait for him then disappeared. I tried to get some sleep but couldn't. I kept hearing shouts all throughout the palace."

"They were making quite a ruckus," said Ruth.

"Some soldiers came by looking for Vendevorex about an hour ago," Jandra continued. "I hid from them and overheard that the king wanted Vendevorex to come to the war room. I figured that if Vendevorex is going to be tied up, I had a chance to come see you two."

"If Cron did kill Bodiel, it will be horrible for his family," said Mary. "The king will have them all killed."

"But it won't be their fault," said Jandra.

"Do you think that matters to Albekizan? I've heard that in villages where they can't pay the tax, he takes the babies and devours them as their parents watch."

"That's nonsense. The king isn't... isn't cruel or unjust," said Jandra, not sounding at all like she believed it.

"What would you know?" said Ruth, bitterness in her voice. "You live sheltered by the wizard. You don't know what the world is really like."

"Don't be mean," said Mary. "It isn't Jandra's fault that she's the wizard's pet."

"I'm not his pet," Jandra said. "I'm his apprentice."

"Either way, he whistles and you come," said Ruth.

"If I obeyed him always, I wouldn't be here," said Jandra. "I don't do everything the old goat says."

Vendevorex decided he'd heard enough. With a thought he allowed his aura of invisibility to fall away, revealing himself behind Jandra.

Ruth turned pale. Mary turned a bright shade of pink.

"What?" said Jandra.

The two women didn't speak.

"What?" Jandra asked. "Is... is he...?"

"*Baaaa*," bleated Vendevorex.

Jandra whirled around. "Ven!"

"You will return to our chambers at once," said Vendevorex. "I have a most important homework assignment for you. You are not to leave until you finish it."

Jandra swallowed hard and nodded.

"Don't be mean to her, please," said Mary, quietly. "She only came for a little visit."

Vendevorex didn't acknowledge her. He grabbed Jandra by the wrist and dragged her away.

"This is a dangerous morning to be defying me, Jandra," he grumbled. "I can confirm one rumor: Bodiel is dead."

"Then Cron...?"

"Not Cron. Bitterwood."

"B-but Bitterwood is only a myth, you said. A boogeyman dragons use to frighten their young."

"Perhaps there is a man behind the myth after all," said Vendevorex. "With any luck, Zanzeroth has Bitterwood's corpse displayed in the war room right now, and that will be the end of this affair."

As they reached the edge of the shantytown, Vendevorex released his grasp on Jandra's arm. She rubbed the area he'd held.

"Go back to our chambers. Go to the third bookshelf, the biology texts, you know the ones?"

"I think so. Yes."

"There is a book concerning the alchemical properties of sea mollusks. Don't leave the chambers until you memorize it."

"What? Why?"

"There will be a test," Vendevorex said.

"But—"

"Go!" said Vendevorex. "Time is of the essence."

"Aren't you coming with me?"

"No," said Vendevorex. "I'm wanted in the war room. I'll need a few moments to prepare a dramatic entrance."

CHAPTER FOUR

fLIGHT

THE WAR ROOM was the size of a cathedral, the towering roof supported by a forest of white columns. High arched windows opened onto broad balconies that overlooked the kingdom. A rainbow of tapestries covered the walls, embroidered with scenes from Albekizan's unparalleled reign. On one tapestry stood a youthful Albekizan, posing in triumph on the corpse of his father. Nearby was Albekizan in ceremonial gold armor, leading his armies to victory against the cannibal dragons of the once notorious Dismal Isles. It had been the first in a string of triumphs against the smaller kingdoms that had once ringed the land. While the tapestries caught the eye with their bright colors, the most arresting feature of the room was the gleaming marble floor, inlaid with colored stone, precious metals and gems into an elaborate map of the world. Zanzeroth, Metron, and Kanst waited for the king within the vast space.

Zanzeroth was in a foul mood. He crouched in the middle of the world map, his belly covering the spot on which the palace rested. He studied the map with his remaining eye, finding in its jagged contours something of the king's soul. For the map, he knew, was a lie. It showed the world as a narrow sliver of land a thousand miles in length, a few hundred miles wide at its thickest part, surrounded by trackless ocean. It showed, to be blunt, all the world that Albekizan had conquered, and not all the world that was. Over the decades Albekizan had supported the myth that there were no lands other than a few stray islands beyond the borders of his kingdom. But Zanzeroth was old enough to remember that, in his youth, he'd learned differently. He'd traveled far in his younger years. There was a kingdom north of the Ghostlands, a vast land of ice populated by dragon and man. And beyond the western mountains Zanzeroth had explored a huge continent: a land of immense rivers and trackless deserts, endless forests and impassable mountains. A third species of winged dragons made their homes in those wild lands, dragons so large they regarded sun-dragons as dwarves, just as the true world dwarfed the small sliver of earth dominated by Albekizan.

If Albekizan didn't rule a place he deemed it did not exist. For many years Zanzeroth had thought this a harmless quirk of the king's ego. Now he wondered if the king's blindness to reality would lead them all to doom.

Far across the room near a broad balcony, Kanst, a sun-dragon and general of the king's armies, spoke with Metron. Zanzeroth listened to their conversation with distant interest. He tilted his head to catch their words. This tiny movement created a change in the map to which his eye was drawn. One of his spiky neck scales, pink and ragged, had fallen out. He could barely move without losing them these days. He sighed, contemplating the dull scale against the polished floor. He could see something of his eventual fate in this single scale. He wouldn't so much die as simply flake away to dust. The conversation between the general and the High Biologian caught his attention once more as they lowered their voices to whispers... the surest way to get his attention.

"Bodiel was the kingdom's greatest hope," Kanst said, his voice hushed—or as hushed as a beast like Kanst could muster. Kanst was an enormous bull of a dragon, heavy and squat. He wore steel armor polished to a mirrored finish that was unblemished by any actual blow from a weapon. Albekizan liked Kanst, which again to Zanzeroth spoke ill of the king. Kanst was all bluster and polish. The king had a bad habit of surrounding himself with advisors who were more show than substance. Kanst and Vendevorex were the two best examples.

Kanst continued his murmurs with the High Biologian. "Shandrazel hasn't the thirst for blood that's necessary for victory. What now? Will the king abandon Tanthia for a younger bride in hopes of another son? Or will he willingly turn the kingdom over to someone more capable of running it?"

"Someone like yourself?" Metron said.

"I'm not implying—"

"Then speak not of the matter," said Metron.

"It's only that time is the enemy," Kanst said. "Even if the king were to father another son, will he remain strong enough twenty years hence to hold the kingdom together?"

Metron dismissed the notion with a wave of his fore-claw. "You're young, Kanst, and think age is a barrier. But in twenty years Albekizan will be younger than I am now, and I am more than able to perform my duties. Indeed, the king will be younger than Zanzeroth twenty years hence, and he's as sharp and strong as any dragon in the kingdom."

Zanzeroth felt Metron's words like sharp blades stabbing at him. The hunter interrupted, saying, "Age matters, Kanst. Let no one tell you it doesn't. I'm almost a century old and I feel it. They'll tell you experience matters, but they lie. Once I would have had the speed to dodge the arrow. I'd trade all my experience for the strength of my youth."

"Don't be so hard on yourself," Kanst said with perhaps a hint of condescension. "You survived when Bodiel did not. If it is truly Bitterwood we face you should consider yourself fortunate."

"There is no 'if,' Kanst!" Albekizan thundered as the tall iron doors to the war room opened. The king strode into the room followed by Bander, the captain of the guard. A dozen members of the guard followed, their armor and weapons clanking as they marched into the room and took their ceremonial positions along the wall. "We deal with fact: Bitterwood lives!"

"Of course, sire," said Kanst. "I never doubted Bitterwood's existence. I've always felt there was substance behind the shadows."

"As Zanzeroth here learned only too well, yes?" Albekizan said with a glance toward the tracker.

Zanzeroth held his tongue. He was tempted to point out that he'd claimed all along they pursued a man, that it was the king who regarded their prey as some supernatural ghost, but he knew this was an argument he would not win.

"Sire, I have done the research you requested," Metron said. "I conferred with my fellow biologians and have the answers you seek."

"And?"

"The minor rebellion of the southern provinces two decades ago is the source of the Bitterwood legend. Bitterwood was a leader of the rebellion. He preached a vile philosophy of genocide against all dragons. Even when the rebellion was crushed his radical rantings earned a small, faithful band of followers. The band eluded your troops for many years, but in the end they were chased into the City of Skeletons, where they were slain."

"You are telling me that it's a dead man we faced tonight?" said Albekizan.

"No, though one popular version of this legend holds that Bitterwood's vengeful ghost still haunts the kingdom. A rival telling holds that Bitterwood eluded death and continues to fight to this day, alone, no longer placing his faith in other humans who have failed him."

"So you have nothing but legend to give me?"

Metron shrugged. "Sire, the truth is somewhat mundane, I suspect. All evidence leads me to conclude that Bitterwood died twenty years ago. Only his legend lives on. Now other humans occasionally summon the nerve to slay a dragon—usually in the most dishonorable ways, striking from ambush—and when your troops investigate, Bitterwood is blamed by the humans to keep us chasing after a myth."

"The man who killed my son was no myth," said Albekizan. "Bitterwood fletches his arrows with the feather-scales of dragons. We pulled thirteen pieces of evidence of his existence from Bodiel's body."

"Yes, sire," Metron said. "However, we should consider that the feather-scales of dragons are hardly a rare commodity. We shed old ones as new ones come in."

Zanzeroth felt Metron's words stabbing at him. At his age, he was losing his old scales without the assurance that new ones would replace them. He stared at the large, black patches of naked hide that covered his once-crimson fore-talons.

"Our servants and field hands no doubt discover fallen feather-scales all the time," Metron continued. "What if a human, familiar with the legend, is using it to his advantage to create fear among us? I've checked the records and found hundreds of dragon deaths over the past twenty years attributed to Bitterwood. It's likely that other men have blamed Bitterwood for murders they themselves performed."

"No," Albekizan said. "I am certain that one being, be he man or ghost, is responsible. I've seen him with my own eyes."

Now it was the king's words that stabbed at Zanzeroth as he realized that he would never see anything with his eyes again.

"Still, I am not blind to the possibility that other humans assist Bitterwood," Albekizan said. "That's why I've called you here. We are going to devise a way to remove the stench of humans from

my kingdom forever. I've tolerated their kind far
too long. They breed like rats. Their dung-encrust-
ed villages spread disease. They create nuisance by
leeching off dragons as beggars and thieves. Now
their greatest crime of all: they give shelter to Bitterwood. We must eliminate every last safe harbor
for the villain. We can only be certain of victory
over Bitterwood when all the humans are dead."

For a moment no one spoke. Zanzeroth wasn't
quite sure what Albekizan meant. Did he want to
kill all the humans in the nearby villages?

Metron broke the silence by clearing his throat,
then asked, "All humans, sire?"

"Every last one."

"From what area?" he asked.

"From the world," answered Albekizan.

Again, there was a long silence as Kanst looked to
Metron, who looked to Zanzeroth, who studied a
patch of air near the king with rapt fascination.

"Respectfully, sire," said a voice from the empty
air Zanzeroth watched, "you've gone quite mad."

Albekizan whirled around, searching for the
source of the rebellious voice, looking straight past
the point where Zanzeroth's ears fixed the sound.

"Show yourself at once, wizard!" Albekizan commanded.

In a spot a yard from the suspicious voice, the air
began to spark and swirl. The sparks fell away like
a veil to reveal a sky-dragon, his wings pierced with
diamond studs, sparkling like stars against his blue
scales. Light gleamed from his silver skullcap. His
eyes were narrowed into a scowl of disapproval.
Vendevorex, Master of the Invisible, had made his
grand arrival.

"Very well, sire," Vendevorex said. "You see me. Now hear me. Humans and dragons have existed side by side for all of history. Mankind poses no threat to dragons; indeed, humanity makes our lives more pleasant. If you kill the humans, who will tend to your crops? Who will do the basest of labors? The humans as a race didn't kill your son. Bitterwood alone is responsible. Turn your resources to finding him. Don't distract yourself with a costly war against all mankind."

"The humans number in the millions," Albekizan said. "Bitterwood could hide among them for years. But if all die, he dies."

"Then consider this," Vendevorex said. "Your course of action could lead to rebellion among dragons you now count as allies and friends. The earth-dragons won't be eager to tend the fields. Many sun and sky-dragons keep humans as pets. Do you expect them to sit idly while you slaughter their companions?"

"I anticipate resistance," Albekizan said. "But my war against the humans will take place on many fronts. Metron's battleground will be the minds of dragons."

"Sire?" said Metron.

"In your role as protector of all knowledge, do you not teach that millions of years of evolution have produced the dragon as the highest form of life? We are by rights the masters of the earth. The human religions claim that they were created separate from other species. If they are not part of nature, why should we tolerate them? Your task, Metron, will be to educate all dragons to this fact. Persuade them to the logic of our cause."

"Of course, sire," Metron said, though Zanzeroth could hear traces of doubt.

"Ah, Metron, I expected more spine from you," Vendevorex said. Then, addressing Albekizan once more, he said: "Even if all dragons stood with you, which they won't, the humans themselves will rise against you. They may not be our physical equals, but they are capable of great cunning, and they outnumber dragons ten to one. You rule them now because they expend their aggression in petty tribal squabbles. They bicker and war over not just the meager resources you allow them, but also kill each other in the name of competing mythologies. More humans die each year at the hands of fellow humans than are killed by dragons."

Albekizan stood silent. It seemed to Zanzeroth that he was actually considering the wizard's argument.

Vendevorex expanded on his case. "Humans have the skill and the passion to fight; we are fortunate that they turn their energies against each other rather than on us. If you wage war against them, they will certainly unite. We will face an army of Bitterwoods. How many dragon lives are you willing to throw away in pursuit of your madness?"

The king didn't react angrily to this insult, as Zanzeroth expected he would. Instead, Albekizan said in a patient tone, "That is why I summoned you, wizard. I've tolerated your insolence all these years because I recognize you as the most clever of all dragons. Your task will be to devise the most efficient method of eliminating the humans. You are adept at curing disease. Could you not create a disease as well, one that slays only humans?"

"No," said Vendevorex.

"Then perhaps some poison would serve our purpose, something which could be introduced into their wells."

Vendevorex closed his eyes, shook his head, and took a deep breath… a breath that, to Zanzeroth's ears came from well behind the place where the wizard stood. Was his lone eye playing tricks?

"I don't mean I'm incapable of doing as you ask," the wizard explained as if speaking to a child. "I won't do it because I find the idea abhorrent." The wizard looked around the room. "Kanst, I'm not surprised by your silence. You've never displayed the smallest hint of backbone. But Metron, you must know better. And Zanzeroth—you, of all dragons save myself—you have always spoken truth with the king. Will you not stand for the truth now?"

Zanzeroth nodded. "You're correct, wizard. Sire, let me be blunt. I don't believe Bitterwood to be beyond our grasp. You called off the hunt too early. His trail may yet be warm. This genocide you dream of is unnecessary. That said, you've won every battle you've ever fought. I have no doubt you can achieve this goal if you desire it. You have my loyalty. If it is to be war against the humans, sire, I stand beside you."

"Cowards, the lot of you," said Vendevorex. "I want no part of this."

"I anticipated your answer," said Albekizan. "Your close companionship with the human girl— Jandie is her name? Jandra? I believe this clouds your judgment. If you will not help voluntarily, consider this: this morning, I ordered all humans within the castle be gathered together and slaughtered." As the king spoke he glanced toward Bander, who nodded toward the guards. They drew their swords and crept toward the wizard. Albekizan continued, "I have spared your pet, for now. Assist me and she will live, the last human who will ever be allowed a natural death. Defy me and she dies. A simple choice."

Vendevorex calmly studied the approaching guards then looked the king squarely in the eyes. "If she's been so much as scratched you will regret it!"

"Don't threaten me, wizard," the king growled. "Bander! Place this fool in chains. A few days in the dungeon will change his mind."

"Y-y-yes, sire," Bander said. His arms trembled as he lowered his spear toward Vendevorex. "P-place your talons above your head!"

"Gladly," the wizard replied, spreading his wings wide. The ruby in his silver skullcap glowed brightly. With a crackle Bander's spear crumbled to ash. The black particles swirled from the shocked dragon's talons, flying in a dark stream toward the wizard to encircle him in a shadowy vortex.

"Kill him!" shouted Albekizan.

The guards rushed forward. A weighted net was thrown over the black vortex, the wind of its passage causing the miniature tornado to collapse into an expanding cloud. One by one the earth-dragons lunged, tackling the cloud of ash. The sound of steel striking steel, then ripping muscle and cracking bone reverberated through the hall.

Zanzeroth drew his hunting knife, a yard-long blade that would have been a sword in anyone else's grasp. He flung it with a grunt, missing the black vortex by a wide gap, the blade whizzing beneath the beak of one of the guards to fly out the open doorway before burying itself in the mortar of the stone wall beyond.

By now, the ash lost its momentum and drifted to the stone floor. It was difficult to make out from the tangle of bloodied limbs and gore exactly what had happened. When the earth-dragons who could stand had finally risen, all that remained on the marble floor was the tattered remains of one of the guards, chopped beyond recognition. Of the wizard, not even a single scale could be found.

"He's gone?" said Bander.

"Surround the palace at once," Kanst ordered. "Summon the aerial guard. The wizard must not escape."

"If he survives, I fear he could prove quite a powerful figurehead for a human resistance," said Metron.

Albekizan shot the High Biologian an evil glance. Then he turned his focus on Zanzeroth. "Find him," he snapped. "Do something more useful than almost killing a guard with an ill-thrown blade."

Zanzeroth nodded. "Yes, sire." He wandered into the hall and yanked his knife free from the gap between the stones. As he suspected, there was a thin, wet red line along the edge. He held the blade to his nose and sniffed. The wizard's scent was unmistakable; no other blood would smell of lightning. Perhaps a foot more to the right and this would have been over. Zanzeroth felt confident he could find the escaped wizard in short order, but on a deeper level he felt a certain satisfaction in letting the wizard go, for now. The king had created this mess by placing his trust in such a fool for so long. Let Albekizan deal with the consequences.

"The wizard won't have long to cherish his freedom," Albekizan snarled. "Bander, see to it that the human girl is killed. We'll not need that traitor's help. Once you've seen to her death, go at once to the dungeon. Bring me Blasphet."

"B-B-Blasphet!" Bander said, his turtle-like beak hanging agape.

Blasphet? thought Zanzeroth, realizing for the first time that the depth of Albekizan's hatred of Bitterwood might be greater than his own.

"Blasphet?" said Metron. "Sire, surely—"

"Silence," growled Albekizan. "I've given my order. Despite his deeds I've kept Blasphet alive for a day such as this. No dragon that ever lived has more of a genius for killing. Bring him to me. Bring me the Murder God."

ON THE WESTERN side of Albekizan's palace, a winding maze of chambers led to a star-shaped room that was home to Vendevorex, Master of the Invisible. The room itself was a nearly impenetrable labyrinth of piled books. Lining the walls were dusty shelves filled with handblown bottles of all sizes and shapes, their murky contents gleaming in the light of the small window slits that lined the chamber. Jandra sat at a desk in the middle of the labyrinth, a massive tome cracked open before her, the pages bearing colorful detailed drawings of clams and snails. For a Master of Invisibility, sometimes her mentor could be incredibly transparent. This assignment was obviously meant to keep her out of his way while he investigated Bodiel's murder.

The knock on the chamber door came as a relief to Jandra. While normally a devoted student, she welcomed the excuse to take a break from reading about snails. She brushed her long brown hair back from her eyes and went to the door. Vendevorex never had visitors but sometimes while he was away servants would sneak up to talk to Jandra in hopes of acquiring some minor potion or charm. She knew enough of Vendevorex's art to help most supplicants. The salve she mixed really could heal burns, and while the love potions she provided were only colored water, they gave people confidence and courage, which often brought them the love they sought.

Unfortunately, when she opened the door she didn't find a serving girl or a stable hand. Four earth-dragon guards awaited her, one carrying iron manacles.

"Come," said the dragon with the manacles.

"Where?" she asked. "Why?"

"Don't question me," the guard snapped, reaching out to grab her arm, his claws digging into her skin.

"Ow! All right! I'm coming!" she said. She contemplated turning invisible but couldn't see how it would help while he held her. Once he released her she would have more options.

The guard locked the manacles around her wrists. The cold steel clamped her as tightly as the earth-dragon's scaly grip. They dragged her by her chains into the hall. In the distance she heard a woman scream.

"What's going on?" she asked.

"Silence!" The guard slapped Jandra's face.

Jandra's head spun. The earth-dragon guards were no taller than her, but they possessed incredible strength. Earth-dragons were slow and a bit dimwitted, but still dangerous. It was safest to cooperate. She bit her lip and walked on, now pushed by the pointed end of a spear. Another cry echoed through the hall, a man this time. The guards weren't merely after her, apparently, but after all the humans in the castle. Was this tied to Bodiel's disappearance? If so, she could expect only the worst from Albekizan.

Where was Vendevorex? Why was he allowing this to happen?

To her surprise the guards led her not to the dungeons, but to another tower. They unlocked the manacles and shoved her into a large, comfortably furnished room, though once the heavy door shut behind her it was as secure as any dungeon cell. She moved toward the room's single window when she heard the shouts outside. Through iron bars she looked onto a courtyard where perhaps twenty humans stood, lined before an earth-dragon wielding an axe. To her horror, a woman was being pushed down to her knees. An earth-dragon guard roughly slammed the victim's head against the chopping block. It was Ruth!

"Stop!" Jandra cried out. Mary, next in line, looked up to the tower.

"Don't look!" Mary shouted through tears.

"No!" Jandra screamed as the axe rose.

She turned away in helpless anger as the executioner performed his task. The wet *thunk* sent a chill up her spine. Mary was screaming.

Jandra slammed her fist into the stone wall and sank to the floor, sobbing. How could even Albekizan order such a thing? What did Ruth and Mary have to do with Bodiel's death?

Mary kept screaming for what seemed like an eternity. And then she stopped.

Jandra buried her face in her knees and bit her lips. This couldn't be happening.

There was a gust of wind from the open window, followed by a scraping sound as claws clenched stone.

"Jandra," grunted a disembodied voice. "Stand away from the window."

Jandra raised her head. "Ven! Where are you?"

"Uhn. I'm clinging to the wall outside. Not much to hold onto." The iron bars shifted, rust flaking, as unseen talons grasped them. "It seems I may have made a strategic error in sending you back to our quarters."

"What's going on, Ven?" Jandra said, jumping back up to the window, wiping away her tears. "Those people in the courtyard, they—"

"They are being executed, yes," said Vendevorex. "Don't think about it. You are in terrible danger; my first priority is your rescue. Stand back."

"Why is this happening?" Jandra said, grabbing the iron bars, so cold and immobile. She sought Vendevorex's claw but couldn't find it. Apparently, he was no longer holding the bars.

"There's no time to answer your questions now," said Vendevorex. "I must steady myself to disintegrate the mortar holding in the stones around the window. The stones will collapse inward. Stand back. Hurry!"

Jandra let go of the window. She wiped her cheeks again as she stepped toward the middle of the room. "Do it."

Dust trickled from beneath the window. With a *crack*, several large stones broke free and crashed to the floor. The iron bars landed on top with a loud *clang*.

"What's going on in there?" a guard shouted through the door.

"I-I tripped," Jandra shouted back. She grabbed a pitcher of water that had been left in the chamber and thrust her hand into it. Concentrating, she worked the water into steam, filling the room with fog.

"Hurry," Vendevorex said, climbing through the hole in the wall and turning visible. "I'll fly you out of here."

Jandra dashed to his side. She paused when she spotted the long, open wound on his cheek.

"You're bleeding," she said.

"It's not important. I'll heal it when there's time. For now, we must fly."

"But you haven't been able to carry me for years," Jandra said as she heard the guard's keys rattling at the lock. "Oh, we should have thought this through!"

"I have," he said. "Flying with your weight isn't so much a problem as taking off. But with a forty-foot drop I'll build sufficient speed to carry you. Hurry!"

Jandra went to her teacher's breast and hugged him by the neck as she had done when he carried her in the harness years ago. She clasped her heels around his waist just below his wing-folds. The fog swirled as the door opened.

Vendevorex leapt. Jandra closed her eyes as they plummeted, the wind whistling past her ears. Then her stomach twisted as their downward momentum changed abruptly to forward motion. Vendevorex grunted with each beat of his wings. She opened her eyes and saw the stone wall of the courtyard mere yards away. But in the instant it took for her eyes to snap shut once more Vendevorex veered upward, clearing the wall by inches. Needle-sharp pains pricked along the back of her scalp as the rough stone snatched away strands of her flowing hair.

She opened her eyes again. They were flying above the forest. In the distance she could see the gleaming silver ribbon of the river. They soared far higher than the tallest spires of the palace now, and it seemed as if she could see forever. It was odd to be overcome with nostalgia while fleeing for her life, especially given the horrors she only just witnessed, but the sight of the world from on high brought back her earliest childhood memories, soaring high above the world, the wind rushing past, clinging to Vendevorex for warmth and safety.

"We've got a problem," Vendevorex said, his voice barely audible above the wind. "We're being pursued."

Jandra looked back. A score of sky-dragons were rising from the roof of the castle. It was the elite aerial guard—the swiftest, most agile fliers in Albekizan's army. Her heart sank.

"Oh no," she said. "You'll never escape carrying me! You... you should save yourself."

"Don't even think of letting go," Vendevorex said. "Our only chance is invisibility. You'll need to create the illusion. I'm too taxed at the moment to concentrate."

"I-I'll do it," Jandra said. "I've been practicing."

"Take care. You'll find that the wind makes the illusion difficult."

Impossible is more like it, Jandra thought. Vendevorex was good enough to turn invisible in the wind and even in rain. He could walk and fly invisibly while Jandra could only maintain the effect if she stood still. She could not reveal her doubts to Ven now, however.

Jandra clasped her mentor's neck more tightly with her left arm while her right arm reached into the pouch of silvery dust she kept on her belt. The wind snatched most of the dust from her grasp the second she pulled her hand free, carrying it beyond the range of her control. She knitted her brow in concentration, envisioning each individual particle of dust in her palm, feeling it come to life. She released it, and with effort kept enough of the dust close to her to make the light deflection possible. The tiara on her brow grew warm as she extended the control field, bending the flight of the dust to her will, swirling the motes into a sphere large enough to encompass Vendevorex's wingspan. Suddenly the sunlight dimmed as the particles began to follow the reflective pattern Vendevorex had taught her.

"Well done," Vendevorex said, his voice weak. "Maintain control. And please, ever so slightly, relax your arm."

"Sorry," Jandra said, realizing she was choking him. As she thought of this the sunlight brightened once more. She gritted her teeth and snapped the dust back into the pattern.

"I can't believe I'm getting this to work," she said. "I've screwed it up every time I've ever tried it."

"You've put in the practice," Vendevorex said. "All you've lacked, perhaps, was the motivation."

The pursuing dragons drew closer now, but their heads swayed from side to side, searching. Ven actually slowed his pace, dropping low, skimming over the tree branches. The guards pressed forward, passing above them, traveling in the direction Vendevorex had held the whole time they'd been visible. A lone straggler remained behind them.

"We're losing them," she whispered as Vendevorex banked toward the river.

"I can't go much further," Vendevorex said, the strain evident in his voice. "Once we clear the river I'll need to land. From there we'll continue on foot."

"Where are we going?" Jandra asked.

"I don't know," Vendevorex answered, sounding hesitant, even lost.

The wind around Jandra grew suddenly colder. She'd never heard these words from her mentor before, or even this tone. Vendevorex always knew what to do, always had everything plotted and planned and under control.

Her mind drifted for a moment as she considered the implications. Then, suddenly, she snapped back to attention. The lone member of the aerial guard who'd still been behind them was diving straight toward them, a blue streak, still a hundred yards away, but closing fast. When she'd allowed her mind to wander the invisibility had been disturbed by the rushing wind.

The guard held an eight-foot long spear in his hind talons. He zoomed toward them quicker than she could think, closing the distance by a dozen yards a second. She tried to will the invisibility back until, with a sudden jerk, the dragon whipped his rear claws forward and released the spear.

"Ven!" she shouted.

Vendevorex snaked his neck around just in time. The spear passed through the air where his head would have been if he hadn't looked back.

Alas, they were too close to the treetops. Jandra felt leaves and twigs snatching along her clothes until her shoulder collided on the tip of a pine. The tree was limber; it bent against her momentum, bruising her shoulder rather than breaking it. But it was enough to wreck her grip. Suddenly, she was falling. She closed her eyes as she flew toward the thick limbs of a second pine. The branches ripped at her as she skidded along the thick needles, then suddenly she was back out in open air, her limbs flailing. She opened her eyes in time to see the surface of the river rushing up to meet her. She tried to draw a breath of air but was too late. She smashed into the river, sucking water into her lungs.

Disoriented, she kicked and clawed, trying to make sense of what was up and what was down. To her relief, she suddenly broke back through the surface. She coughed out the water then drew in great gasps of sweet air. The river wasn't deep here near the water's edge. Her feet found traction on the rocky bottom. When she stood the water was barely above her waist.

She staggered toward the shore, rubbing her eyes, half-blind from the water streaming from her hair. She stumbled when she reached the bank as her waterlogged gown tangled around her feet and she slipped on the slick rocks.

She crawled further onto the rocky bank, still coughing and spitting out water. Suddenly, the top of her head collided with something hard. She looked ahead and found herself staring at scaly blue legs with knees that bent backward and sinewy talons sporting two-inch, pitch-black claws. A long blue tail twitched behind the legs, catlike.

"Ven?" she asked, then looked up. It wasn't Ven. The aerial guard who'd thrown the spear loomed over her, a long knife clutched in his fore-talon.

Jandra flinched as the guard reached for her.

Then, from the tree line, a voice: "Stop!"

It was Vendevorex. He stepped from the trees, looking more frightened than she'd ever seen him. He seemed smaller somehow, diminished in his fear.

"Please don't hurt her," he begged. "We surrender. We won't resist."

The guard turned from Jandra to face the wizard. "Don't move," he growled.

"No sir," Vendevorex said. "Just please, don't hurt us."

"It's not me you'll have to worry about," the guard said, stepping toward Vendevorex.

Then suddenly, the guard vanished. The small, frightened image of Vendevorex shimmered then broke apart. From the thin air before her came a muffled cry of pain and the sickening smell of burning flesh.

Jandra searched the sky. The rest of the aerial guard was nowhere to be seen. She clambered further up the shore and rose to her feet, shivering, chilled by the water and the close call of the fall.

Vendevorex allowed his circle of invisibility to break apart. He stood ten feet away with the body of the aerial guard at his feet. The guard clawed helplessly at his jaws, emitting small, muffled grunts through his flared nostrils. The skin around his mouth was melted together. Large talon-shaped holes had been burned into his wings; he would never fly again.

"When your brothers find you and cut your mouth open, I want you to give them a message for me," Vendevorex growled. His eyes glowed as if lit by an internal sun. "My decision to run should not be interpreted as a sign that I am weak or defenseless. Anyone who attempts pursuit will face a fate much worse than yours. If I didn't want you to tell your brothers this, I would have killed you already. You live only because you retain this slight usefulness to me."

The guard rolled on to his back on the rocky bank, still clawing at his immobile mouth. His eyes were waterfalls of tears. Jandra turned away, feeling sick.

"Let's go," Vendevorex said, moving to her side. "Upriver, toward Richmond. You'll find it easier to maintain the invisibility while we walk."

She nodded, noting the coolness in his voice, the utter lack of remorse for the way he'd just maimed the guard for life. She didn't look back as she raised a field of invisibility around them. They headed west along the riverbank, watching the skies for further signs of pursuit.

CHAPTER FIVE

WOUNDS

ZANZEROTH TOOK ADVANTAGE of the chaos in the war room to slip away. Albekizan was shouting orders to Kanst, who was shouting orders to Bander, who shouted orders to the soldiers. Zanzeroth had known the king since he was a mere fledgling. He could remember the sharp, eager young dragon who'd accompanied him on hunts, long ago. Albekizan had been a most cunning stalker of prey in his prime. It pained Zanzeroth to see how age had changed the king into a creature that now confused shouting for action.

As he found the next drop of the wizard's blood around the corner, Zanzeroth felt the despair that had gripped him earlier lighten a bit. Even with half his sight, he could still follow wounded prey. Of course the wizard was no challenge, not at the moment. Zanzeroth need not follow a trail to find him. The wizard's next move may as well have been marked on a map. He would head straight for Jandra.

But Zanzeroth had bigger prey in mind, and a bigger challenge. What had happened to Bitterwood? Earlier he'd been held back by Albekizan, slowed by the all-but-useless Gadreel, and even the ox-dogs had led him on a wild goose chase. Zanzeroth had allowed himself, over the years, to become part of the king's court, to be a member of a crowd. It had been too long since he hunted alone.

Of course, by now, Bitterwood's trail would be cold. But was it only coincidence that Cron had led Bodiel straight into Bitterwood's trap? Could Metron be right about the deeds of Bitterwood being the responsibility of more than one man? There was no time like the present to find out.

METRON WATCHED FROM the balcony as the aerial guard flew in ever-widening circles in search of Vendevorex. It would be for naught, he knew. Ever since Vendevorex appeared in the court all those years ago, dazzling Albekizan with his mystic powers, Metron had known this day would come. Vendevorex had never shown the least deference to Albekizan. Metron had known all along that Vendevorex, despite his apparent power, was nothing but a fraud. After all, who better to spot a fellow fraud than he?

Still he wished that Vendevorex had cooperated. Having read the most ancient of the texts in his duties as High Biologian, he understood deeply the irony of the king's plans. Fraud or no, the wizard didn't lack compassion or wisdom, and could perhaps have changed what was to come. A kindhearted fraud had to be preferable to an honestly wicked dragon such as Blasphet.

"Have they found him yet?" Albekizan asked from inside the war room.

"Sire," Metron said. "I fear the wizard has escaped."

The king's claws scraped on the marble floor. Metron looked back to see the king's massive head jutting through the doorway to peer out over the forest. With his neck extended, Albekizan's face was level with Metron's. Metron was used to looking up to Albekizan's presence. To have their eyes on the same level was mildly unnerving. Albekizan had the head of the world's most effective predator; his powerful jaws were large enough to swallow a man whole with its sharp, knifelike teeth. Though he knew he was not in danger, a chill still ran down Metron's spine as he contemplated the imposing natural weaponry of the sun-dragon. No wonder these beasts ruled the world.

Albekizan studied the horizon with another biological advantage of the sun-dragons: forward-facing eyes with vision sharp enough to put an owl to shame. After a moment of scanning the surrounding skies, the king said, "The wizard will keep running. Invisibility, when you consider it, is the ultimate refuge of a coward. He'll run back to the Ghostlands, or wherever he came from. He's no threat."

"Yes, sire," said Metron.

"It's lucky I kept Blasphet alive all these years," Albekizan said. "He'll take to the task more willingly than Vendevorex, I wager."

"Sire, have you considered the dangers of releasing Blasphet? He was jailed not for poisoning humans but for poisoning dragons. Tanthia will not be pleased to learn that her brother's murderer walks free once more."

The king tilted his head to look upon Metron, as if giving consideration to his words. He looked as if he were about to speak, then stopped.

Metron, sensing doubt, started to press his argument. "Tanthia has always been—"

"I will explain the matter to her," Albekizan said, cutting him off. "She will want Bitterwood dead, will she not? She's blinded by grief at the moment... but I know, on the morrow, my queen will thirst for justice. It's in her royal blood. Blasphet's dangerous, yes. But so is fire. Properly handled, both can be powerful tools."

"He's here," Kanst said from inside the war room.

Metron left the sunwashed balcony and followed Albekizan into the shadowy room. His sight was blocked by Albekizan's broad, crimson back. Metron moved to the side for a better view of the room. In the center of the world map stood a withered sun-dragon, the scales of his wings so long hidden from light they had lost all color, becoming transparent, revealing the black hide beneath. Blasphet's eyes, red as sunset, burned as he looked upon the king. He shook his manacled limbs, causing the heavy iron chains to clatter. The earth-dragons who guarded him jumped at the noise.

Their skittishness was justified. Blasphet had killed thousands of dragons; the true numbers were uncertain as his preferred weapon was poison.

Many of his victims died in their sleep or with the symptoms of a wasting fever. The number was further complicated by the fact that, in his prime, Blasphet had founded a cult in which a loyal band of humans worshipped him as a god and carried out assassinations in his name. It had taken years to track down and kill the cult members after Blasphet had been imprisoned.

"Albekizan," said Blasphet, the Murder God. His voice was raspy, as if he hadn't spoken in years. He bowed slightly then gave a spooky, moldy chuckle. "I suspect I know why I'm here. The news has reached even the dark hole you keep me in. If you plan to accuse me of a role in Bodiel's death, I can only express my deepest regrets that you've blamed the wrong dragon."

Albekizan reared up, his shoulders held back. He puffed out his chest, making himself as physically imposing as possible. He said, in his firmest tone, "Blasphet, if I thought you had harmed my son, only your head would be brought before me now. Your body would be digesting in the bowels of my ox-dogs."

Blasphet seemed unimpressed by the king's bravado. "Tanthia would no doubt be pleased with that turn of events. Is she still unhappy you kept me alive after I killed Terranax?"

"You were not brought here to discuss Tanthia or her brother."

Blasphet shrugged, a movement that made his faded scales rustle like dry leaves. "What, pray tell, am I here to discuss? This seems an odd time for idle chatter. Don't you have a funeral to attend?"

"It's said that since you have resided in the dungeons, no rat has been seen there. In addition, many guards have been lost to a strange wasting sickness. You are responsible, no doubt."

"Of course," Blasphet said, his eyes twinkling. "There is a mold that grows on the stones of my cell that possesses the most intriguing properties. I use whatever test subjects are near in my experiments."

"You find no difference between the life of a rat and the life of a dragon?"

"Mere anatomy. Life is life, no matter how it's packaged. Every living thing burns with the same flame. It all may be extinguished with equal satisfaction."

The king nodded his head, as if Blasphet had just said exactly what he wanted to hear.

"If it's life you care to extinguish, and it matters not which form of life, we have much to discuss. I've brought you here to offer you freedom, should you accept my challenge."

"Challenge?"

The king drew close to Blasphet, much closer than Metron thought wise, chains or no. Metron grew more alarmed for the safety of the king when he drew his face mere inches from Blasphet and said in a low, even voice, "Look at what you've done with your poisons. You've ended the lives of a few random dragons, some humans, a rat or two. Does it satisfy you? Or do you long for a greater task? Imagine not the death of an individual. Imagine the death of an entire species. Are even you capable of such a thing? Could even you slay every last human in my kingdom?"

Blasphet raised a manacled talon to scratch his chin. His lips drew back to reveal his yellow-gray teeth. "Every last one? There are millions. The resources required would be enormous."

"All I have would be at your disposal," Albekizan said, his voice quieter, almost a seductive whisper. "My treasure, my armies are yours to command. For all purposes in the matter of the elimination of the humans, you will possess all the powers of a king."

"What do I care for the powers of a king?" Blasphet asked. "I was a god, once. Yet even for a god, the task is a daunting challenge." Blasphet's eyes ran along the map of the world as if sizing up its scale. "The humans would flee before a direct onslaught. The survivors would take up arms against us if we failed to kill all in one sweep. I've worked intimately with humans in the past. They can be most tenacious. The war could last for centuries."

"I know this," said Albekizan. "Which is why I'm consulting with you rather than Kanst."

Kanst's eyes narrowed at the slight.

"The key would be subtlety." Blasphet's voice fell to the same conspiratorial tone as the king's. "Somehow draw them into a trap, kill them before they ever suspect danger…"

"Ah," said Albekizan. "I see it in your eyes. This task interests you. Should you refuse me now, this will taunt you, torment you as you rot away in that cell."

"Is this offer honest?" Blasphet asked. "You never were one for clever schemes, but I can't believe you would trust me. What was that I was yelling at my trial? 'I'll kill you? I'll kill you all?' You remember that, don't you?"

"I don't trust you, but I do understand you. If you desired, you could kill me right now. You've no doubt hidden several poisons on your body. Something you could spit, perhaps? Or some paste beneath a claw that could kill with the merest scratch?"

"Of course," said Blasphet. "It may be that I've poisoned you already and it's only a matter of time before you begin to bleed from every bodily orifice. That would be most satisfying. You, weeping tears of blood."

"You haven't poisoned me," the king said with a confidence Metron didn't feel was justified. "You'll be no threat to me or my court because you dare not risk this opportunity. You are free to murder on a grand scale without fear of punishment, indeed, with the guarantee of praise and respect. You were worshipped as a god, once. Now, you have the opportunity to enter history as the architect of the greatest single feat of the dragons. Your freedom to act will be your shackles."

"Perhaps," Blasphet said. "This does hold... promise. You know me better than I thought, it seems. Well played. I accept."

"I knew you would," Albekizan said, stepping back. "When we were growing up there was no dare you would not accept. Your will was thought to be even greater than my own. That's why it surprised everyone when I bested you in the hunt."

"Indeed, brother," Blasphet replied. "Indeed."

ZANZEROTH TOUCHED DOWN on a stony island in the middle of the mud-brown river. It had been too long since he'd spent time here; almost a century ago this spare, stony wasteland had been his only home. He'd not been born to the comfort of a king's court. Or perhaps he had... he'd never known his true parents. He'd been left to fend for himself in the wild as a fledgling, and had survived on his own for a decade, living from the land, the only meat in his belly coming from prey he'd killed with his own claws. When he was ten he'd been captured by Albekizan's father, Gloreziel, for the crime of poaching in the king's forest. But rather than killing the young, feral dragon, the king had taken him under his wing and set himself to the task of civilizing the snarling brute Zanzeroth had been at the time.

The civilizing had taken, but not completely. Zanzeroth still felt most at home making his bed beneath an open sky. While he'd adapted to the nobles' fashion of hunting and fighting with weapons, he still, while hunting alone, enjoyed the sensation of digging his bare claws into squealing, wriggling prey. And if there were any better pleasure in this world than laying on a warm rock with a full belly and licking drying blood from his talons, he had yet to experience it.

Having grown up in the king's court and knowing Albekizan since before he could even speak, Zanzeroth could claim to be the king's oldest friend, though friend wasn't the right word, perhaps. In Albekizan's world, all other sentient beings were subjects, enemies, or prey. "Highly regarded lackey" was no doubt the most accurate label for Zanzeroth.

Zanzeroth found the familiar gap in a pile of mossy stone, lowered himself and thrust his head within. Any sane observer would have judged it impossible for the old dragon to squeeze his bulk into such a tiny hole, but Zanzeroth was practiced at the maneuver, knowing when to exhale, and knowing when to push and twist and kick. In seconds he was through the gap and into the hidden, dank cave that was his true home.

In his youth the cave had felt enormous, a world of its own. Now Zanzeroth recognized that it was smaller than the smallest room in the palace, too small to stand straight in, barely thirty feet from front to back, and half again as wide. The place still had the familiar smell of decay. During the spring melt off, the island often flooded; he remembered waking to rising water many times.

Around the room were ledges that always remained inches above the high-water mark. These ledges contained Zanzeroth's treasures. He cast around the ledges, each item provoking memories. Here were the antlers of the largest buck he'd ever killed. The tusks of an enormous boar he'd killed on a hunt with Gloreziel had been gilded by the king and presented as a trophy. He found his old whip, thirty feet of braided leather. He remembered the summer he'd spent mastering it. In his prime, he could knock flies from the air.

But what he'd come here for was hidden behind a trio of human skulls. These had been leaders of the southern rebellion twenty years ago. Their tattooed, tanned hides now decorated the king's own trophy room. Behind their skulls were the trophies of real value: their swords. Still gleaming and razor sharp despite decades in a damp hole, the swords had been made from a mysterious metal

that never rusted. He'd kept the blades hidden
from the king but did risk showing them once to
Vendevorex. The wizard had declared that the
blades weren't magic, but were, in fact, remnants
of a lost technology, crafted from something called
"stainless steel," a type of metal that hadn't been
made for a thousand years. Despite the wizard's
explanation, Zanzeroth always felt there was
something supernatural about the swords. A thousand year-old blade shouldn't have a mirrored
finish. Zanzeroth studied himself in the narrow
sliver of silver, his one good eye golden in the dim
light seeping through the gaps in the rock above.
He examined his torn cheek, his scaly hide stitched
together by Gadreel with a horsehair thread. The
wound was swollen and black with dried blood. It
was going to be an interesting scar.

His whole body was a mass of interesting scars.
Why did this wound haunt him so? He'd had close
calls before. Indeed, one of the three ancient blades
had once cut a foot-long gash in his chest that provided him with the rare opportunity to gaze upon
his exposed ribs. Why did this fresh wound so
remind him of his mortality? He was old, true, but
still healthy, still in command of his wits. But for
how much longer?

He bundled up the three blades in an old bear
hide and tossed them from the cave. On a whim he
decided to take the whip as well.

He slithered back out into the open air. Now, to
find Cron. This wasn't a particular challenge since
he'd found Cron's trail earlier at Bodiel's murder
scene. Following it was as easy as following a hallway. Broken branches, torn leaves, footprints in the

mud: all led to a thicket a quarter mile away from where Bodiel had fallen. Zanzeroth found the impression of Cron's body in the forest debris behind a fallen log. The slave had apparently hidden there for some time before rising again. More interesting than the impression of Cron's body, however, were the many breadcrumbs and the discarded apple core. Cron did have an accomplice after all. Bitterwood? Zanzeroth searched for a second set of human footprints and instead found the hind-talon marks of a sky-dragon. He bent low to catch the scent, an all-too-familiar one. Vendevorex. He should have known the wizard had been involved in this. The wizard's fondness for humans was well known.

And yet… Why would Vendevorex have plotted against Bodiel? Helping Cron survive may have fit within the wizard's quirks, but working to harm Bodiel seemed too *active*. There was more to this story than footprints alone were going to tell. Perhaps Cron himself would be more talkative.

"WAIT HERE," SAID Vendevorex, peering through the branches toward the town beyond.

Jandra stepped forward for a closer look. She was glad they were hidden by the trees and not relying on her maintaining the invisibility shield. It left her free to use the same technique she'd used in the tower to turn the water into mist to gently dry out her clothes and hair, which were still damp from her plunge into the river.

They were hidden within a small grove of trees on the outskirts of Richmond, a human town several miles upriver from Albekizan's palace. Richmond was a thriving place, built beside rapids in the river. A canal running through the town connected the broad, deep river below the town with the swifter, yet still-navigable river that wound up into the mountains. A gateway between the ocean and the mountains, Richmond bustled with activity as the wealth of the kingdom flowed through it. Vendevorex and Jandra watched the nearby river docks. A few dozen people could be seen going about their business.

"Where are you going?" Jandra asked.

"I think our best course at this point will be to take a boat," Vendevorex said. "We can save our strength rather than exhausting ourselves on foot."

"When you say take a boat, do you mean steal a boat?" Jandra asked.

Vendevorex turned his long, narrow face to her. His face was back to normal. He'd taken ten minutes to concentrate on the cut to his cheek, and now there was little sign of the wound, only a thin, pale line of blue scales that were fresher than the others.

"Yes," he said flatly. "I mean steal."

"But—"

Vendevorex raised his talon to his mouth in a gesture of silence.

Jandra clenched her jaw at the dismissive signal. She understood, of course, the danger they were in. But it always bothered her the way that dragons treated human property as their own. "People need—"

"These people are all dead," Vendevorex said. "You saw the slaughter in the courtyard. It's only a matter of time before the king's troops descend on this place. Albekizan means to kill every last human in his kingdom. These people have much greater things to worry about than a missing boat."

Jandra could hardly breathe. She had thought that the king was slaughtering only the palace workers in retribution for Bodiel's death.

"Did... did you say..." she could barely think the thought, let alone speak it.

"Every last human," said Vendevorex.

"We have to stop him!" Jandra said. "We have to go back!"

"We would return to our deaths," Vendevorex said. "We escaped due to the haste with which I acted. We had the element of surprise. I turn invisible, not invulnerable. You of all people know how many of my magics are based on illusions. In a direct, violent confrontation with Albekizan, I could possibly best him, but then what? If I kill him, we'll wind up with anarchy, or worse, under the rule of a buffoon such as Kanst. I see no immediate good options."

"B-but, you're his advisor. You can reason with the king, can't you?"

"Albekizan's notion of reason was to lock you in a cell to blackmail me into assisting him. I defied him, Jandra, for your sake. I won't throw away our lives by returning to the palace."

"Then, what? We sit idly by while all of humanity is slaughtered?"

Vendevorex shook his head slowly. "I... I need time to think. Let me secure a boat. There may be allies we can contact. Albekizan's decision to wipe out the human race will meet with opposition from other sun-dragons, I'm sure of this."

"We should at least warn the people of Richmond," Jandra said. "Give them time to flee."

"We'll do nothing of the sort," said Vendevorex. "We must be careful to leave no clues of having passed this way. I'm certain Albekizan's troops are searching for us. Worse still, he may put Zanzeroth on our trail. We can't be careless."

"I can't believe you," Jandra said. She was thinking about the cries from the courtyard. She remembered the wet sound the axe made as it fell. Perhaps Vendevorex was content to allow these people to die, but she would have no part of it.

Without another word, she ran. Vendevorex reached to grab her but she slipped past his grasp and dashed from the trees, heading for the docks.

"Run!" she shouted. "Run! Albekizan wants to kill you!"

Instead of running, the men working on the docks merely looked up, bewildered. As she drew closer and her shouts grew more urgent, more people emerged from boats and buildings to see what the commotion was.

She reached a gray-bearded man who stood coiling rope at one of the nearest boats.

"Calm down, girl," the man said. His eyes twinkled with bemusement against his leathery, tanned face. "What's wrong?"

"You're all in terrible danger," she said. "You need to run. Albekizan plans to kill everyone."

The old man chuckled. "Is that right?"

More men approached.

"What's wrong?" a young man shouted as he strolled up.

"This girl says the king wants to kill us!" the old man said, sounding amused.

"He's doing a good job of it," another man shouted. "Takes half my wages in taxes, he does. That wicked old beast is starving my family."

"Let the king try something," another man shouted, brandishing a large, dangerous-looking hook. "He shows his scaly hide around here, I'll give him what for."

Jandra was out of breath. She bent forward, resting her hands on her knees, and said, "Please. This isn't a joke. He's killing people right now in the palace."

A tall man appeared on the deck of a large boat twenty yards away.

"Oi!" he shouted to the assembled men. "Get back to work. We're behind schedule already."

The gray-bearded man shouted back, "Girl here says Albekizan's killing people. I reckon this means we can take the rest of the day off."

The crowd of men laughed.

Then, as one, the men turned pale and sucked in their breath, their eyes fixed behind Jandra.

Jandra turned.

Albekizan dropped from the sky, only a few steps away. As his shadow fell over her she suddenly felt very, very small.

Albekizan landed, his weight on his hind claws, his enormous wings spread for balance, the tip of his tail swaying like a cat's with prey in sight. His red scales glistened as if wet from blood. His eyes smoldered with hatred.

"You mock me?" he roared. "I'll kill the lot of you!"

Suddenly, the dock shuddered and banged with the panicked dance of a hundred feet. The men behind Jandra fled, some leaping into the river, others racing for the narrow alleys of Richmond. Inside of thirty seconds she faced Albekizan alone.

She swallowed.

Albekizan lowered his serpentine neck, bringing his face close to hers. His head was bigger than a horse's, the long jaws capable of opening wide enough to close around her torso with a single chomp. His white teeth glistened with saliva. The white wisps of feathers around the king's nostrils swayed with each breath. Yet... she didn't *feel* the breath, though his face was now inches from her own. And the perfumes the sun-dragons soaked themselves in... There was no smell.

"Ven?" she asked.

"That would be a lucky break for you, yes?" Albekizan said in her mentor's voice.

"I can't believe you'd frighten me like this," she said.

"More importantly, I frightened the townsfolk." The image of Albekizan fell away in a shower of sparks revealing her master at the center. "You've got your wish. They are warned."

"Yes," she said. "Yes, I suppose they are. Let's steal a boat and get out of here."

"An excellent suggestion," said Vendevorex. "I wish I'd thought of it myself."

CHAPTER SIX

SPARKS

TULK AND CRON had hardly spoken to one another on their daylong flight along the riverbank. Tulk felt there should be a bond between them; they had been, literally, in the same boat earlier, drifting downriver until the dawn made travel by water too risky.

Yet Cron barely looked back as he raced through the woods. He showed no willingness to slow his pace or assist Tulk, who lacked his companion's youth and stamina. It was all Tulk could do to keep up.

At last, Cron paused at the forest's edge, allowing Tulk to catch up. Tulk looked out at a large, reddish blob in the distance. He had no idea what he was looking at.

"Where are we?" Tulk asked between gasps for breath.

"That ship down there," said Cron. "It's Stench's place."

Tulk was confused. His eyesight wasn't great but he certainly wasn't overlooking the river. They were facing dry land. "What ship?"

"You really are blind, aren't you, old man?" Cron said.

"I see you well enough to knock in your teeth, boy," said Tulk.

"That big rusting thing down there… It's a ship. It's ancient. It's on land now but centuries ago they say the river flowed through here."

"Is it Stench's place?" Tulk asked. He'd heard of the tavern many times, but having spent most of his life in captivity, had never had the pleasure of drinking an ale there. "I've heard that it was made of iron. I never believed the stories."

"It's true," said Cron. "A priest of Kamon told me it was once a ship that could sail the oceans, built by humans before they angered the gods and fell from grace."

Tulk felt as if he'd been slapped.

Cron, apparently sensing the offense, said, "What?"

"You spoke the blasphemous name."

"Oh," said Cron. "You're one of them."

"You're a Kamonite?" Tulk spat after saying the name to remove its evil from his tongue.

"I'm not saying," said Cron. "I take it you are a follower of Ragnar that you find such offense in his name?"

"Kamon is an abomination," said Tulk, spitting again. "His lies have corrupted thousands over the years. He turns people from the true path and preaches that dragons are divine things, the offspring race of angels and men. He wants us to be inferior and subservient to dragons."

"True. And the followers of Ragnar believe that we're to fight the dragons at every turn," said Cron. "We see how well that philosophy is working out. Men *are* inferior and subservient to dragons. The world will be a better place for everyone once we swallow that."

"You mock Ragnar's teachings?" said Tulk. "Speak truthfully. You know Kamon's—" Tulk abruptly stopped speaking in order to spit, "—heretical philosophies, but of course, so do I. I will not condemn you for mere knowledge. But to practice his teachings is beyond all decency. Are you, or are you not, a follower of that foul prophet?"

Cron sighed. "I don't think it's any of your business. Besides, we have other things on our minds than a discussion of philosophy."

"I am duty bound to slay followers of Kamon," said Tulk, stopping to spit once more. He clenched his fists. He had to know the truth. Traveling further in the company of a Kamonite could risk his very soul. "We travel no further until you answer my question. Ragnar himself would slit my throat if he knew I'd traveled this far in the company of one of the fallen. Do you follow Kamon's teachings?" He spat once more.

"If you keep spitting," Cron said, "you're going to turn to dust."

"I'd sooner be dust than the companion of a heretic."

"I don't see any guards around Stench's place," said Cron, turning away from Tulk. "I'm making a run for it."

The young man sprinted off. Tulk followed, afraid of being stranded. They dashed across the open ground that led to the red, boxy blob. As Tulk got within a hundred feet of it, he could see that Cron had spoken the truth. Stench's place *was* shaped like a ship, a hundred feet long, lying on its side. Could such an enormous structure have ever floated on the water? If it had been seaworthy once, it was no longer. Age had rendered most of the ship into a mound of rust. Holes gaped in what had once been solid plates of iron. The rear of the ship had collapsed under its own weight at some point. What had once been a hatch in the deck now served as a door, reachable via rickety wooden stairs.

"Stench!" Cron cried out as he vanished into the dark reaches of the hold.

"I'll be damned," echoed a reply from the darkness. "Cron! Is it really you?"

Tulk carefully made his way up the stairs and poked his head into the dark doorway. The first thing he noticed was, unsurprisingly, the stench. Swamp water saturated with the bloated corpses of skunks was the only odor he could compare it to. No wonder dragons steered clear of this place. He'd heard their sensitivity to smell was more developed than that of humans.

What had once been a hold of the giant ship had been converted into a bar. The room was long and thin; a wooden ladder led down to the floor, which at one time, Tulk assumed, had been a wall. A half dozen patrons sat around, too drunk to move, slumped against the wall on low couches. A wooden plank at the end of the room served as the bar itself. Behind the bar was a metal barrel full of some sort of flaming liquid. The smoke rising from the blue-green fire carried the horrible odor that permeated the place. A bald, withered man stood next to it, smiling a toothless grin.

"I see you brought a friend," the old man said. "Tulk, I'm guessing. I heard you both escaped."

"Word travels fast," Cron said. "Is there a price on our heads yet?"

"Could be," said the man who Tulk guessed to be Stench.

Tulk climbed down the ladder. He said to Cron, "If there is a price on our heads, you shouldn't be reminding people of it."

"We're all friends here," said Stench. "No one will turn you in. Besides, I've been told to treat you well by someone I'd rather not mess with."

"Venderex, right?" Cron asked. "The wizard. He saved us. Why's he doing this?"

"Can't say," said Stench.

"I've heard he has a human companion," said Tulk. "I thought I saw a girl at the ceremony. I kept trying to make her out. I can't be sure, though."

Cron chuckled. "I noticed you gawking. Next time you're in the presence of Ragnar, ask him to fix your eyes. That girl stood out at the ceremony. There were more eyes on her than on us, I wager."

"You saw her?" Tulk asked. "It's true? The wizard has a human for a pet?"

"Raised her like a daughter, I hear," said Stench.

"That's horrible," said Tulk. "I'd rather be a slave than a pet."

"Lucky you wound up in the right line of work, then," said Stench.

"I don't think it would be so bad to be a pet," said Cron. "And, if humans and dragons are related as Kamon teaches—"

"Again you speak his name!" Tulk said, his voice echoing against the metal walls.

"Take care," said Cron. "This is a bad place to be sympathetic to Ragnar. Right, Stench?"

"Look," said Stench. "You're both in a bad place, period. Cron, you know I'm a loyal Kamonite like you. Every man in here is. But none of us have the luxury of squabbling about religion right now. If the king has his armies looking for you, I've got to get you both far down the river as soon as possible. You can spend the night here in my hidden room. Tomorrow, I'll smuggle you downriver in a fishing boat. But when you reach the sea, you're on your own. Tulk, if you do follow Ragnar, put aside your hatred of Kamonites long enough to get to the ocean. And Cron, can you not provoke him? It's like you're trying to pick a fight."

"Sorry," said Cron. "I'm not in the best of moods. I've spent all day expecting to be murdered at any second. Knowing that it might be a fellow human that does the deed is a bit much to swallow."

Tulk couldn't believe this cruel twist of fate. Alone in a den of Kamonites. To be faithful to the teachings would mean certain death. How many could he kill before he died, especially since he had no weapon? He gazed at the fire barrel. Perhaps he could somehow… then he dropped the thought. He didn't want to get any closer to that smoke than he already was.

"What in the name of all that's holy are you burning?" Tulk asked, nearly gagging as he thought about the odor.

"My own special blend of herbs and skunk glands dissolved in a hundred proof alcohol. You like it?" said Stench. "There's pockets of stagnant water all through this place. Without the smoke we'd be sucked dry by mosquitoes. And as a bonus, it keeps dragons away. People get used to the smell. Dragons never do."

"No," said a loud, deep voice from the other side of the wall. "No, I don't think I could ever get used to this smell."

Tulk looked toward the iron wall in the direction of the voice. Then the whole room shook as something slammed against the metal. The noise was deafening. A shower of rust flakes fell, coating Tulk's skin. Suddenly the room trembled again, as a red, scaly fist larger than Tulk's head punched through the metal. The fist withdrew to be replaced by dagger-like claws that gripped the edges of the aged metal. The room shuddered as the claws peeled the metal back, popping the rivets free. The wall flew away, tossed over the shoulder of an enormous sun-dragon sporting a bandage covering his right eye.

"Gentlemen," said the dragon, "I've had a very bad day. I'm planning to take it out on you."

ZANZEROTH LOOKED AT the frightened humans cowering before him. He could barely see them. Even if he'd had both eyes, the smoke stung so badly it was all he could do not to clench them shut. He tossed the bundled swords into the exposed room.

"Weapons, gentlemen," said Zanzeroth. "The finest swords this world has ever seen. One of those blades had a taste of me about twenty years ago. I'm giving you the chance to finish its meal."

The humans didn't move. They merely stood, slack-jawed and trembling. Zanzeroth sighed, reached out to unroll the bundle and revealed the swords. Then he took the bear skin that the swords were wrapped in and stepped back from the room to get away from the smoke and to give the men room to maneuver. There were nine people; six of them looked too inebriated to stand. But fate must have had a hand in this, given that he only brought three swords.

Zanzeroth ripped a strip from the bear's hide and brought it to his face, blindfolding himself.

"I assure you, I cannot see you," said Zanzeroth. "And thanks to that horrible smoke, I can't smell you. You will never have a better chance to slay me."

"We don't want to fight," one of the men said.

"Then I'll kill you without you putting up a struggle. Or you can kill me first. I'll be fighting unarmed. Tooth and claw versus steel. I honestly think you have a chance."

"Why are you doing this?" another asked.

"To find out if you have a chance," Zanzeroth said with a slight nod. "To find out if I'm still the dragon I think I am. I'll silently count to three. Then I will kill you if you choose not to fight."

Zanzeroth fell silent and spread his wings. Sightless and without the benefit of smell, he could rely only on his hearing and the sensitivity of his wings to small changes in air pressure. In theory, he should know if one of the men rushed him.

And in practice, the sound of their footfalls on the iron floor fixed their positions in his mind. He heard the scrape of metal against metal as the men grabbed the weapons. Then, one said, "Kamon teaches obedience to dragons. If one asks us to kill him, who are we to deny that wish?"

Suddenly, two feet rapidly advanced. A grunt. A rush of wind ruffled the feather-scales of his wings. One of the men—the youngest, Cron, judging by the stride—had leapt from the ledge on which they stood and became level with Zanzeroth's chest. With his sword extended the arc of his dive would drive the shining steel blade deep into Zanzeroth's gut.

It was a bold and powerful attack, if the blade had stood any chance of reaching its target. With a flap of his wings Zanzeroth launched himself a yard into the air and kicked out with his powerful hind claws. His kick hit home. His talons sank into his opponent's torso, snapping bone, puncturing lung. He kicked again to send the corpse flying and readied himself for the next attack.

Only, as he listened, he heard another blow, of steel striking bone, followed by a gurgle. With a *clang* a body fell to the iron floor. Then, a movement in the air... another of his foes had leapt... but not at him. The unseen man leapt to the side. He heard the man hit the ground and collapse. And the third man... The third man was responsible for the wet gurgling noise from directly in front of him.

With a sigh, Zanzeroth removed his blindfold.

The oldest of the three men lay before him with a sword in his back. Off to the side the slave Tulk was struggling to his feet. Zanzeroth took a moment to look at Cron's body, slumped on top of the rusting metal. Zanzeroth felt pleased at the amount of damage he'd done to his opponent. He'd given death every chance to take him and survived, even blind and unarmed. It hadn't been age that had cost him an eye... it had been carelessness. He could never regain his youth but he could sharpen his wits. Zanzeroth felt certain that when he met the man who'd taken his eye, even if he was the legendary Bitterwood, their next fight would end very differently. And were he to stumble over a certain invisible wizard... well, an invisible foe and a visible one are one and the same when your eyes are closed.

Tulk was now limping off and making quite good speed considering that his ankle was broken. Without bothering to look at the slave, Zanzeroth freed the loop of braided leather from his hip and whipped it to the side, snaring Tulk by his damaged ankle. Tulk shrieked like a wounded rabbit as Zanzeroth pulled him from his feet and dangled him before his eyes.

"Why did you kill your friend?" he asked.

"He was no friend!" Tulk shouted. "He was a filthy Kamonite!" Tulk spat, the spittle landing on Zanzeroth's leg. "His kind shall not be suffered to live!"

"I see," said Zanzeroth. "Since you're in a talkative mood, I want you to tell me what you know about Bitterwood."

"Bitterwood?" Tulk asked, plainly bewildered. "Why do you want to hear ghost stories?"

From the tone Zanzeroth could tell this wasn't a bluff. Tulk knew nothing of Bitterwood's involvement. "If it wasn't Bitterwood, who killed Bodiel?"

"I don't know!" said Tulk. "You have to believe me! Neither Cron nor I knew Bodiel was dead until we were told so."

"By whom?" Zanzeroth asked, giving the dangling human's leg a jerk.

"I didn't see him!" said Tulk, his voice cracking with pain. "Cron and Stench said it was the king's wizard. But I never saw him. I only heard a voice in the night."

"You are proving to be something of a disappointment," said Zanzeroth. "Shouting out the answers is robbing me of a good excuse to torture you."

"There's no need for that," said Tulk, sounding resigned. "You've caught me. I'm a slave. Just take me back."

"So you can escape again? I don't think so. And as a slave, may I point out that you disobeyed a direct order to fight me? And killed a man who might have? I don't think I need to wait for Albekizan's orders to know your fate."

Zanzeroth lifted the human higher. He carried him to the smoking barrel.

"Please," said Tulk. "I've told you everything I know!"

"I believe you," said Zanzeroth. Then he lowered the struggling man headfirst through the flames into the smoky liquid. Tulk splashed and struggled, sending the foul-smelling goop everywhere for a moment or two. Zanzeroth grimaced, knowing this wasn't something he would enjoy licking from his talons.

Tulk's struggles grew increasingly feeble. He fell still, then kicked once more. Then once again.

Finally, Zanzeroth dropped him into the barrel. He stepped back, gathering his prized swords. Some of the horrible fluid had splashed onto one of the blades. If this didn't corrode the finish, nothing would. Zanzeroth glanced back at the half dozen drunken men who still held their positions, staring at him in terror.

"Gentlemen," said Zanzeroth. He tilted his head toward the bar. "Drinks are on me."

Then with a leap and a flap, he took to the sky.

As NIGHT FELL, the dragons assembled at the edge of the Burning Ground. This ceremonial field was a circle many hundreds of yards across, the ground now permanently blackened with the soot of many generations of funeral pyres. Earth-dragon guards stood around the edges, their bodies painted in solemn ceremonial hues of gray. They stood as still as statues as the royalty of the kingdom strode past.

At the center of the dark circle was a tower of pine logs and, on a platform at the peak, Bodiel rested, surrounded by flowers. The air was rich with the scent of pine.

This was the first time Albekizan had seen either of his sons since the previous night. He glanced toward the piled logs that bore Bodiel's corpse. For a brief instant, he thought he saw his beloved son breathe once more. It was only a trick of the light as the warm evening breeze sent a ripple across Bodiel's feather-scales.

Shandrazel stood defiantly before Albekizan. The king studied his surviving son. He should have felt pride. Shandrazel had grown into a marvelous specimen. The prince was equal to Albekizan in size; his scales had the richness and luster of rubies, his face bore the sharp, clean lines of his noble heritage. It was only when the king looked into his eyes that he felt his heart sag. Bodiel's eyes had always been proud. Bodiel's eyes were windows through which his strength and fire could be seen. Bodiel's eyes were eyes that watched the world, constantly searching for threat and opportunity. Bodiel had possessed the eyes of a warrior born.

Shandrazel had none of these qualities. He had the eyes of a dragon who looked primarily within himself. There had always been an introspective, contemplative side to Shandrazel that Albekizan recognized as weakness. Shandrazel was a dragon who valued thought over action.

"You disappoint me, Shandrazel," Albekizan said. "It breaks my heart to reward your cowardly performance in the contest. Only countless generations of tradition lead me to say what I will say next. By default, I decree that you have won the contest with Bodiel. As your reward, you are to be banished. Should we ever lay eyes upon one another again, it must be in mortal combat."

"If I refuse?" said Shandrazel.

"You will not refuse," Albekizan growled.

Metron, who stood beside the king, said, "It is the way, Shandrazel. It is written in the Book of Theranzathax that the victor of the contest must flee from his father. Return only when you feel strong enough to defeat him. In this way the kingdom will be assured a mightier king."

"I didn't win the contest. I didn't even chase the human."

"When one of the contestants is slain, the other wins. It is written," said Metron.

"I know what's written. I don't choose to obey the words of someone who died ten centuries ago. There's no logic behind them. Father, you boast of having conquered the entirety of the world. Where, precisely, am I to flee?"

"Shandrazel," Albekizan said, "if you do not flee now, I will slay you where you stand."

Shandrazel looked into Albekizan's eyes. Albekizan steeled himself, letting no hint of regret show in his features. In Shandrazel's eyes, he could see confusion. Shame welled up in Albekizan's soul. How could his royal bloodline have produced such a weak, unpromising candidate for the throne?

"But—" said Shandrazel.

"Go!" Albekizan cried, lunging forward. If Shandrazel didn't leave, Albekizan felt sure that he would sink his teeth into his son's throat, even though it would break all law and tradition.

Shandrazel stepped back, cast one last glance toward his sobbing mother, then turned and opened his wings to the night sky. In minutes he was only a small dark shadow against the stars. Shooting stars began to slip from the heavens like tears.

Albekizan walked back to Tanthia's side.

"Light the pyre," Metron said.

The choir of sky-dragons rose in pitch as the heat of the torch touched the kindling. The fire ate hungrily, rising quickly up the stacked wood to lick at the flowers wreathing Bodiel. The smoke soon took on the acrid aroma of burning scales.

Metron opened the ancient leather-bound tome he held. He spoke the words written in the Book of Theranzathax without ever glancing down at the text.

"Asrafel crawled onto a bed of dry branches, and poured oil on his fevered brow, and called for his children.

"And he spoke, 'In the winter, we breathe steam, for within we are flame. The fever that burns me is the flame of my own life, and no longer shall my skin stand between the world and myself. As long as this flame burns, I am alive, and as smoke I shall mingle among you. You shall breathe me and I will become part of you, and as I touch your eyes you shall cry, not in sorrow, but in joy, for I am with you still.'

"As he spoke the oil upon his brow smoldered, and the flame within him burst free, to blaze in the night. His children took up branches from the flame, and forever nourished these torches, using the light of Asrafel to carve the world from darkness."

Metron closed the book and approached the bonfire that now howled with life. He placed an unlit torch into the fire and when he pulled it forth it burned with the presence of Bodiel. Metron turned to stand before Tanthia.

"Take this flame and never let it die. May the love of your son blaze hot and bright."

Tanthia moved her mouth as if speaking, but her words couldn't be heard over the roar of the bonfire. She accepted the torch, holding it tightly in her grasp.

All the while, Albekizan looked on, watching the sparks rise from the bonfire to mix among the stars. As each tiny red point vanished in the darkness, he experienced the loss of his son once more. He stared again at the bonfire, feeling himself at one with the raging flame. The inferno sizzled and cracked and roared, and the noise was music to Albekizan's soul. In the religion of flame, heaven comes when all the world is ash.

CHAPTER SEVEN

SCHEMES

S HANDRAZEL ROSE INTO the starry night, not believing the turn his life had taken. Behind him the chorus sang as the pyre was lit; it broke his heart that he wasn't even allowed to mourn his brother.

The most difficult thing to swallow was how plainly he'd been warned that this moment would come. Since he'd been a fledging, he'd been taught the ceremony of secession. He'd witnessed the drama unfold over the years as one by one his older brothers vanished, banished from the kingdom, or disappearing in shame into the libraries of the biologians. Why had he never accepted that this would be his fate? Why had he been so certain that he, alone, among countless generations of royalty, could break the chains of superstition and introduce a new age of reason?

By now he was far beyond the river. He was a swift, powerful flyer; miles could pass during a moment lost to thought. It did him no good to fly blind. He needed to pick a destination. There must be some place in the kingdom where he could find shelter.

He looked to his left, searching the heavens for the pole star, But for some reason the stars were blotted out. He startled as he realized that he was in the company of another sun-dragon, dark and hidden in the night.

It was Zanzeroth. He raced toward Shandrazel on an intentional collision course. Shandrazel banked hard, pulling up to avoid the old stalker. His speed and strength gave him the edge; Zanzeroth passed beneath him with a yard to spare. Without warning, something snaked through the air with a *snap*, entangling his leg. Searing pain flashed up his spine as his body whipped to a halt. Then suddenly, he was falling, dragged by Zanzeroth's dead weight as the old dragon folded his wings. Shandrazel stretched to grab as much air as he could to slow their descent. Still they plummeted.

Then, yards above the treetops, Zanzeroth opened his wings once more, catching his own weight. Shandrazel tried to recover from the sudden change in balance, skimming along the treetops, but it was too late. The branches snatched and dragged at him, yanking him into the canopy. He crashed unceremoniously onto the leafy floor of the forest.

Shandrazel lay there, stunned, all breath knocked from his body, until sharp claws wrapped themselves in the fringe of scales along his skull and jerked his head back. A cold sliver of steel pressed against his throat.

"You're working with the wizard, aren't you?" hissed Zanzeroth. "You're up to your eyeballs in this. You could have won the contest fairly. Instead you conspired to have your brother killed."

"That's insane," Shandrazel spat.

"Is it? Who profits more from your brother's death?"

"I wanted no profit! I publicly defied my father and pleaded to have Bodiel appointed king!"

"A clever cover," said Zanzeroth. "I confess, I was fooled until I had time to eliminate the false leads. Then I was left with the obvious."

Shandrazel had heard enough. He jerked his head backward, slamming into the old dragon's snout. He raised his fore-claw to catch the wrist that held the blade to his throat and twisted, forcing the weapon away. Zanzeroth was a skilled, experienced fighter, but Shandrazel had youth, speed, and strength to spare. He yanked the stalker free from his back, slamming him to the ground. A tall, narrow pine toppled as Zanzeroth's hips cracked against it. Shandrazel sprang to his feet, bracing for a new attack.

"You senile old idiot," Shandrazel said, his voice crackling with anger. "Your stunt could have killed us both. All over some baseless theory!"

Zanzeroth's wings lay limp as blankets on the forest floor. The twitch of his tail revealed him to be conscious, however. The old dragon took a ragged breath, then chuckled.

"If I'd wanted to kill you, the whip would have gone around your neck rather than your leg," Zanzeroth said.

"And if I wanted to kill you," said Shandrazel, "I'd snap your old neck in two before you ever saw me move."

"I believe you could," said Zanzeroth. "You never lacked ability as a warrior. Only bloodlust. You fight only with your brains, never with your heart."

"You didn't chase me down to critique my fighting techniques," said Shandrazel.

"Didn't I? I honestly believed you planned Bodiel's murder. But if you had, would I still be alive? You'd have killed me to silence me. I'm disappointed, not for the first time tonight. I guess you might be innocent after all."

"You should know I'm no murderer," said Shandrazel.

"But I had hope," said Zanzeroth with a sigh. "Hope that you were a schemer, a deceiver, a cheat, and a killer. Hope that you had what it takes after all."

"What it takes?"

"To come back," Zanzeroth said. His joints popped as he rolled to his belly, raising himself on all fours, stretching his long neck to limber it. "I hoped you'd do your duty and kill Albekizan."

"You're his oldest friend," said Shandrazel. "How can you wish such a thing?"

"What is the future you envision? A world where your father grows increasingly old and feeble until death claims him in his sleep? This is not an honorable way to die. In his decline, the kingdom would crumble. A loving son would sever his jugular while he still enjoys life."

"A world where old dragons may die in their sleep doesn't frighten me," said Shandrazel.

Keeping his eyes fixed on Shandrazel, Zanzeroth rose. Shandrazel tensed his muscles as Zanzeroth reached for a pouch slung low on his hip. The hunter's old, dry hide sounded like rustling paper as he moved. He untied the clasp of the leather bag and produced two round, red things the size of melons. He tossed them toward Shandrazel's feet.

They were severed human heads, their bloodless white faces in sharp contrast with their gore-soaked hair and the brown-crusted stumps of their necks.

"Cron," said Zanzeroth, "and Tulk."

Shandrazel supposed it to be true. The faces were too distorted by death to be recognizable.

"Did you think you would spare them last night by not hunting?" Zanzeroth asked.

Shandrazel shrugged. "I hadn't given their ultimate fates a great deal of thought. But yes, part of me hoped they'd be forgotten in the confusion."

Zanzeroth cast his gaze down at the severed heads. He stood taller as if drinking in the sight of them gave him strength. "Do you enjoy looking upon dead men, Shandrazel?"

"Of course not," said Shandrazel. "What kind of question is that?"

"Perhaps not so much a question as a warning. Your father plans to kill all the humans. He will build monuments from their bones. Pyramids of human skulls will rise from the fields. The species will be driven into extinction."

"I don't believe you," said Shandrazel.

"The beauty of truth is that belief plays no part in whether it happens or not."

"Why would father do this?" said Shandrazel.

"Is it important?" asked Zanzeroth. "From where I stand, the only thing that's really important is that no one can stop him. Nothing will save the humans... except, perhaps, a new king."

"You've come here to tempt me, then," said Shandrazel.

"Take my words as you wish," said Zanzeroth, turning away and limping into the shadows. "I will take my leave."

SAFELY BEYOND SHANDRAZEL'S sight, Zanzeroth slumped against a tree. His head throbbed from the blow Shandrazel had dealt; his whole body was bruised and numb. He could barely feel his left leg. There was no doubt about it. If Shandrazel grew a spine, he would be a formidable match for his father. Perhaps the prince's misguided sense of affection toward humans might save them yet.

Not that Zanzeroth gave a damn about the human race, as a lot. But somewhere among them was the man who stole his eye. With the king's policy of killing off the whole species, Bitterwood, or the man pretending to be him, might be lost. If the king were to poison the wells of the humans, and his assailant were to die anonymously, just one bloated corpse among millions, Zanzeroth would never find satisfaction. Thus, it was in his best interests to complicate the king's plans. And if Shandrazel was to be the tool, so be it.

SHANDRAZEL FLEW THROUGH the night and day, past the point of exhaustion. Tradition held that he had twenty-four hours to escape the kingdom. At nightfall, all subjects of the king were duty bound to kill him. His older brothers were all reported to have flown toward the Ghostlands, the cursed, dead cities that littered the northern wastes. There were rumors of powerful magics within the Ghostlands; Shandrazel had himself been tempted by the promise of exploring the unknown. And yet the day found him heading south, deeper into the lands held by Albekizan rather than to the possible safety of the north. He was determined to reach the one place in the kingdom where he knew he would find kindred spirits: the College of Spires.

Evening was evident in the blood-touched tint of the clouds. His target was finally in sight. From the seemingly endless canopy of emerald trees that blanketed this rolling land, the hundred gleaming copper spires of the college emerged. This was a city built long ago by biologists as a place for the finest minds of the kingdom to gather and study the great mysteries of life. And more so than his father's castle, this was the place Shandrazel truly thought of as home. He'd been educated here, spending years studying the collections of tomes and scrolls and leather-bound journals housed in the libraries. More importantly, he'd been challenged here; the Biologian Chapelion, Master of the University, had taken him under his wing (though, not literally, given that Shandrazel was twice his size) and mentored him. Through endless hours of arguments, he'd taught Shandrazel the art of discerning truth from fiction. Some called Chapelion the ultimate cynic, a skeptic who believed in nothing. But Shandrazel knew, in fact, that Chapelion was the ultimate romantic—so deeply in love with truth he would never be seduced by convenient or comfortable falsehoods.

Shandrazel could credit Chapelion for his own stance against the ancient mythologies that shackled the races of dragons. If there was one place on earth that was certain to provide sanctuary, it was here.

The dense forest canopy gave way to green rolling hills dotted with tall oaks. Sky-dragons on the gravel paths below pointed toward the sky. Some rose to join him, shouting out his name. Soon, he traveled with a score of young sky-dragons. From the nearby spires, bells chimed a welcome.

Shandrazel spotted a good landing site. He angled his wings to slow himself, drifting gently down toward a white fountain that sat in the center of the college. A trio of marble sun-dragons craned their necks toward the sky from the center of the fountain, water bubbling from their open mouths and spilling into a pool below, green with water lilies. Shandrazel came to rest on the edge of the fountain, his talons grasping the familiar stone. The scent here was well remembered; the lively, humid air of the fountain square brought back recollections of debates stretching through long, warm nights. For the first time in two days, he felt safe. The sky-dragons that shadowed him landed as well, joining a growing crowd. In the moment it took Shandrazel to regain his breath after such a prolonged flight, he was surrounded by a sea of blue faces, all eyes fixed upon him. His name was spoken a hundred times in tones ranging from curious and excited to worried as the crowd speculated on the reason for his presence. From the cacophony of voices speaking his name, his ears found a welcome voice.

"Shandrazel!" It was Chapelion. The Master Biologian emerged from the crowd, draped in the green silk scarves that denoted his rank among the scholars. "You've come back!"

"An interesting assertion," said Shandrazel, falling back into the ongoing joke he shared with his former mentor. "I admit there's anecdotal evidence to support your claim, but do you have any substantive proof?"

In response, Chapelion punched him in the thigh.

"Ow," said Shandrazel.

"Ow, indeed," said Chapelion. "Why have you come here? Where is your mind? How can you be so thoughtless?"

"Thoughtless?"

"It's nearly nightfall," Chapelion said, looking up at the red sky. "In moments, I and everyone in this crowd will be bound by law to slay you. This is a dangerous gamble you are taking, Shandrazel."

"You, sir, are the dragon who taught me that an unjust law may be disobeyed in good conscience. This is no gamble. I've come here to seek sanctuary and your advice."

"You'll receive neither," said Chapelion.

"Please," said Shandrazel. "If you'll listen to me, I—"

"No!" snapped Chapelion, his scaly brow furrowing until his eyes were mere slits. "Your presence here dooms us all! We are scholars, not warriors. If Albekizan's armies come here, there are no walls to protect us, no gates to defend."

"He need not learn I'm here," said Shandrazel. "Is there a dragon among this crowd who would betray me? I know I can count on your loyalty. We citizens of the college are bound with a camaraderie that may endure any test."

"You fool!" said Chapelion. "Did I teach you nothing in your years here? You dare speak of camaraderie when your reckless action could mean the death of every student before you. You speak of loyalty yet apparently give no care that Albekizan may torch these hallowed spires and render to ash the accumulated wisdom of three hundred generations. Leave this place!"

"But, sir…" Shandrazel's voice trailed off as Chapelion turned from him. From the tower the evening bell tolled, marking the arrival of sunset.

"Kill him," barked Chapelion as the crowd parted to allow him passage.

The crowd closed once more in his wake. In mass, the sky-dragons crept toward Shandrazel, their eyes showing fear.

"Stay back!" Shandrazel shouted, lowering his head and opening his jaws wide to brandish his perfect, knifelike teeth. "I don't want to hurt anyone!"

Then from behind, a stone smacked into his shoulder. Shandrazel spun, his talons extended. He was completely encircled. The sky-dragons were pulling the larger stones from the gravel walkways. A second stone flew toward him, glancing his wing. He retreated back into the shallow waters of the fountain. More rocks rained down. He was fortunate that the pathways held few stones larger than pebbles. But though the stone missiles caused little physical pain, each blow hammered into Shandrazel's mind the awful truth. He was alone. There was no shelter here.

A splash in the fountain behind him signaled the rush of one of the bolder students. Shandrazel whipped his tail in an arc, catching his unseen attacker in the neck. There was a louder splash as the dragon fell. Shandrazel growled then charged to the edge of the fountain, snapping his jaws inches from the nearest student. The crowd roiled as dragons stumbled into one another, trying to avoid Shandrazel. He raked his wings across the crowd front, knocking students from their feet and causing shouts of panic to fill the air.

A circle expanded around him. Outnumbered a hundred to one, a sun-dragon was still a terrible force. In their wide, frightened eyes, Shandrazel could see every dragon before him wondering if they would be the one snapped in twain by his powerful jaws. Their fear stirred his soul to anger. Was this how a fellow scholar was to be treated?

Then, like a flood, shame washed away the anger. What was he doing? Was he prepared to fight and kill every last one of these students? If he wasn't, he knew his father would. Chapelion was right, as always. Shandrazel had betrayed these students by coming here.

"Anyone who tries to follow me is dead," he growled, then spread his wings and rushed back toward the fountain. He leapt to the rim of the fountain and flapped with all his might, taking to the air, the downbeat of his wings knocking the smaller sky-dragons from their feet. He skimmed over the crowd, rising slowly, climbing with effort among the spires. His wings felt like lead; he'd flown two hundred miles to come here.

Two hundred miles, to reach the start of a journey to which he saw no end.

FOG COVERED THE moonlit valley as Jandra watched from the window of the log cabin. Vendevorex was asleep; the cooler clime of the mountains in which they'd taken refuge these last two weeks seemed to stir an unspeakable weariness in her mentor. In the hours when Vendevorex wasn't sleeping, he would take mysterious trips down into the valley to conduct business which he wouldn't discuss with her.

Jandra's world had shrunk to the four wooden walls of the rustic cabin and a circle of a hundred yards around it that she'd been gleaning for firewood. She was bored. She'd gladly devour a book on the anatomy of mollusks if she'd had one handy; she'd even read the acknowledgements and the footnotes.

She went back to where Vendevorex lay in the corner. He was curled onto a pad of wool blankets with a patchwork quilt draped over him. His chest heaved slightly as he slumbered.

A small fire still glowed in the fireplace but cast little warmth. An iron pot hung on a hook over the fire; it held the leftovers of a stew of squirrels and some potatoes Vendevorex had smuggled from a farmer's cellar. They'd been eating the same stew for three days now. Jandra couldn't help but think back to the feast held at the palace the night before the contest. She imagined the tables piled high with roasts and freshly harvested vegetables and crusty breads frosted with white flour. She could still taste the grilled trout she'd consumed that night; for dessert she'd had fresh strawberries in syrup.

She sighed, trying not to think of it. Looking out over the moonlit fog she suddenly felt cold. To fight the chill, Jandra lay down beside Vendevorex, resting her head on his shoulder and pulling the large quilt over her as well. The quilt was musty. It had been in the cabin when they found it; there was no way to tell how old it was. The wool pads beneath her were rough and scratchy.

Resting next to Vendevorex triggered dim fragments of memory. When she'd been a mere baby he'd cradled her. His musky, reptilian scent made her feel that all was right with the world. She had no memories of her parents before Vendevorex. He'd told her they died in a fire and she alone had survived. She'd asked if she might still have surviving relatives, some distant cousin perhaps, but Vendevorex claimed that his research into the matter was fruitless. Her dead family had been migrants that had come to work Albekizan's harvest. No one knew where they'd come from. Jandra had no idea what her birth name might be.

And most of the time, that didn't matter. Now that they were on the run, homeless and hunted, she wondered about the truth. Did she have remnants of a family out in the far reaches of Albekizan's kingdom? Was there someone in the world she might yet turn to for help in this awful time?

Vendevorex was lucky, sleeping as he pleased. Jandra hadn't slept soundly since they'd left the castle. Hours passed in the darkness as she alternated between dwelling on her worries and drifting through her memories.

Sometimes, in the weightless, dark void of pre-slumber, she could still smell the smoke of that long-ago fire that had taken her family, and still see the blue talons reaching down into her crib to rescue her.

Then, just as sleep was taking her, Vendevorex stirred, waking her. She could tell from his breathing that he was fully awake. However he set his internal clock, an alarm had been triggered. She sat up and asked, "Is something wrong?"

"No," he said, rising and freeing himself from the quilt. He stretched, his broad wings touching the far walls of the cabin. The diamonds that studded his wings glimmered red in the firelight. "I'll be back in a few hours," he said.

"Where are you going?"

"Gathering," he said.

"At this hour? What? Are you going to steal more potatoes?"

"Perhaps. Or I may go and see about acquiring better quarters. I should say no more," Vendevorex said, shaking his head. "I don't want to raise false hope."

"Ven, I need hope, false or not," Jandra said. "Another day here in this cabin and I'll go crazy. We can't just wait here while Albekizan is killing the entire human race."

"Then I can give you genuine hope," said Vendevorex. "The slaughter has yet to begin, according to my sources. Albekizan killed the workers of the palace and then stopped. No broad order to kill humans was issued to the kingdom at large. Perhaps his rage has abated. More likely, I fear, he's merely taking the time to plot a bolder strategy. If my meeting tonight is fruitful, we may soon be in a better position to gather news."

"Meeting?" Jandra asked. "Who are you seeing? I want to come."

"That would be unwise," said Vendevorex. "Again, I've said too much."

"Ven, you wouldn't have said it unless you really wanted to tell me. It's out in the open now. What's going on?"

Vendevorex moved to the window of the cabin and looked out over the valley. He studied the scene for a moment, lost in thought.

"Very well," he said. "As you know, Tanthia had a brother who was killed by Albekizan's brother, Blasphet. His name was Terranax, his wife was Chakthalla. She dwells in a castle about fifty miles from here. She manages these lands for Albekizan; socially, she is well connected. More importantly, she has an affection toward humans."

"She treats them like show dogs, you mean," said Jandra. "I know her by reputation. She buys and sells humans based on their breeding."

"Precisely," said Vendevorex, sounding pleased that Jandra understood this point. "As you see, she has an economic interest in thwarting Albekizan. More, if what I've learned of is true and Blasphet is involved in this dirty work, then she has an emotional stake in stopping the scheme as well. She's our best hope."

"Fine," said Jandra. She had little use for the sundragons who bred and displayed their pet humans; perhaps that was because she was only a mutt in their eyes. As a foundling, she had no noble lineage to boast of. But mutt or no, she was willing to swallow her pride if it meant getting access to an actual bed and to something to eat besides squirrel stew.

"I've long maintained a network of trusted contacts," Vendevorex continued. There is a sky-dragon within Chakthalla's court named Simonex who I've corresponded with through this network. I'm meeting him tonight, to work out the details of an alliance with Chakthalla."

"I'm coming with you," said Jandra.

"You'll stay invisible," said Vendevorex.

"Of course," she said. She was surprised he wasn't arguing against the idea.

"You won't make a sound. In fact, breathe as little as you possibly can. We cannot risk spooking Simonex. He is fully aware that speaking with me could land his head on the chopping block should the king learn of it."

"You won't know I'm there," said Jandra.

"Let's go," said Vendevorex, heading for the door.

Invisibly, the two of them headed down the winding, root-covered path that led to the river. The damp night air smelled of mushrooms and moss. The ground was slick; slimy rocks lay hidden beneath rotting leaves. Vendevorex held her hand to guide her over the most treacherous ground. She felt guilty that her presence was slowing him. He could simply have flown down the mountain if she hadn't insisted on coming along.

At length they reached a large rock by a stream that fed into the river. Vendevorex paused in the open area. Then, he faded into the fog, only to reappear several yards away in the center of the rock. In actuality, he still hung back near the edge of the stone, his claw still clutching Jandra's hand.

"Started to think you weren't coming," said a ragged voice from the fog. Jandra strained her eyes to see a figure emerging from the wispy cotton of the air. Vendevorex flinched.

"You're not Simonex," he said.

"Simonex?" said the sky-dragon who approached them, still half-veiled by fog. "Oh, you mean this fool?"

The sky-dragon now stood mere feet from Vendevorex's doppelganger. He lifted a severed head high, revealing the tortured visage of a sky-dragon, eyes open and dull, the tongue hanging limp from its slack jaw. In her horror Jandra noticed a second detail—the sky-dragon who stood before Vendevorex's double had only tatters for wings. The membranes that stretched between the extended fingers that formed his wing struts had been slashed, a punishment reserved for sky-dragons convicted of property crimes such as the murder of humans. This irreversible injury crippled the sky-dragons, severing them from their namesake element. It also marked them permanently as outcasts; she'd heard rumors that these tatterwings would retreat to the wilds and band together into thuggish gangs.

As she recalled this a second sky-dragon appeared beside the first, then a third. From the edges of the stone two more appeared. She held her breath as she heard a rattle in the bushes next to her. A tatterwing carrying a long, crude spear crept no more than five feet to her right, crouching as if to spring.

With a final one stepping out from the other side of the stream, she counted seven tatterwings, all armed. Poor Simonex never stood a chance.

The lead tatterwing dropped Simonex's head and rested his fore-talon on the hilt of the sword he had slung to his side. "Before your friend died he told us you work for the king," the tatterwing said, sounding smug. "Said there'd be quite the ransom for you. In the meantime, those fancy jewels in your wings will make a good down-payment."

"You'd not live to spend your ransom," Vendevorex said calmly. "There is no corner of the earth you will not be hunted if you attempt to harm me."

"We'll take that risk," the leader said, drawing his blade. The steel edge was jagged, more saw than sword. Suddenly, three large rope nets swirled from the fog, flying over the area. Two nets fell over the spot where Vendevorex's doppelganger stood. They fell harmlessly to the ground, causing the illusion to flicker and shimmer. The leader drew back, eyes wide as if he'd realized that he was standing before a ghost.

Alas, the third net was badly thrown. Jandra leapt away as it headed for them. The tatterwing to her right rolled out of the path of the spreading hemp.

Unfortunately Vendevorex didn't react as quickly. The net hit the edge of the circle of invisibility, then wrapped around her mentor. Vendevorex gave a mumbled curse as his concentration broke, leaving him visible.

"By the bones!" the tatterwing across the stream exclaimed when Vendevorex's double vanished. "What's happening?"

"It's the king's wizard!" the lead tatterwing shouted. He sounded panicked and was swiveling his head, searching the shadows. Suddenly, his eyes focused on the wizard's netted form. He pointed his jagged blade toward Vendevorex as he cried, "He's too dangerous to hold hostage! Kill him!"

The nearest tatterwing rushed forward, his spear held level with Vendevorex's heart. Invisibly, Jandra dove into his path, tripping him. This ruined her invisibility; she gambled that there would be a moment of surprise in which she might dart back to safety and vanish once more. Unfortunately, the tatterwing fell on her. She fought to get out from under him. She rolled to her back to find a second tatterwing rushing at her with a spear.

Before the dragon reached her, a loud sizzling sound, like bacon in a skillet, drowned out even the water in the stream. The net that covered Vendevorex flared in a searing flash, disintegrating and freeing him. All the tatterwings reflexively raised their talons to shield their eyes.

Vendevorex pointed his left wing toward the dragon with the spear that had been charging Jandra. The dragon yelped in shock as his spear crumbled to ash and took a large chunk of the flesh of his talons with it.

"You murder my associates?" Vendevorex said, his voice trembling with rage. "You threaten me and my companion, attacking us with ropes and pointed sticks? Fools!"

Vendevorex drew his shoulders back, seeming to double in size. "I am Vendevorex! I control the building blocks of matter itself! Know that your actions have brought my judgment upon you!"

White balls of flame engulfed the tips of both wings. Vendevorex lunged out and touched the flame to the snout of the dragon near Jandra, who stood staring at his damaged talons. Shrieks echoed from the hills as Vendevorex pushed the dragon's suddenly limp body away. The tatterwing fell to the stone, his face boiling to pink mist, revealing his skull.

Jandra kicked free of the dragon who had fallen on her as Vendevorex leaned and plunged the flame into the dragon's spine. This one didn't even have time to scream before he died.

Jandra struggled to her feet. She rose to find herself face to face with Vendevorex who said in a firm tone, "None can escape."

Jandra understood. A single survivor could reveal their location to the king. And who knew if Simonex had told them about Chakthalla? As Vendevorex turned to face the leader of the tatterwings, Jandra grabbed the fallen spear of the dragon she'd tripped. She set her sights on the tatterwing on the far side of the stream who'd turned to run. Luck was with her; he tripped on a root, hitting the ground hard.

Jandra had never killed before. She'd never even carried a spear. But there are moments in life when one discovers the most primitive actions are built into the very muscles. She jumped the stream, the spear tucked tightly against her body, both hands gripping with all her might. With her full weight she drove the shaft into the back of the tripped tatterwing, feeling the slips and snaps as the stone tip worked its way through hide and muscle and gristle to the ground beneath.

The tatterwing thrashed and gasped, its talons scraping the earth, still struggling to rise. The air suddenly smelled of urine. Jandra released the shaft and staggered back, unable to believe what she'd done. She turned to find Vendevorex surrounded by a mound of charred corpses. His foes all died so quickly and quietly. The smoke from his victims wafted across the stream; she braced herself for a horrible scent. Instead, the aroma reminded her of roast venison.

The weak, wet calls for mercy from her victim lingered for several long moments until Vendevorex caught his breath, crossed the stream, and silenced him.

Jandra sat down by the stream, her eyes closed, her cheeks wet with tears. She grew sick to her stomach; her hands felt slick with blood, though in truth, there wasn't a spot on her.

Vendevorex placed a fore-talon on her shoulder.

"It had to be done," he said.

"I know," she sobbed, wiping her cheeks. "I know."

"I apologize. I failed to train you for a moment such as this," said Vendevorex. "I've sheltered you from the darker side of our arts. I've show you illusion and minor transmutations. As you've seen, there are more... aggressive skills to be learned. In the morning we'll begin your lessons."

Then he left her and began to dig through the satchel of the fallen leader. She went to the stream and splashed water on her face. It helped; she no longer felt quite so close to losing her dinner. Her body trembled as the adrenaline worked through her. She looked at her hands. Had they really killed someone? Though it happened only a moment before—the corpse of her victim was in the edge of her sight, the spear thrusting up like a young, straight tree—it all felt so distant. Like a memory from years ago, a different life.

She wiped the tears from her cheeks. She could kill if she needed to. The knowledge gave her a grim strength. It was good to know, in a way. She'd wanted hope earlier in the evening; now, in the least expected fashion, she'd found it.

Vendevorex rose with a folded sheet of paper in his claw. He opened the paper, agitating the molecules of the air above it to create a soft light by which to read. He nodded his head slowly as he studied the words.

"It's from Chakthalla," he said. "These tatter-wings had no idea the treasure they carried. Albekizan would give half his kingdom to know the contents of this letter."

ALBEKIZAN STIRRED FROM his sleep, sensing an alien presence in the room. He opened his eyes to the dim light of the chamber. Among the shadows something rustled like dry leaves. He raised his head for a better view. A shadow moved toward the large table on the far side of the room.

Then, a scratch, and a spark. A match had been struck. An oil lamp flickered to life revealing the dark-scaled hide of Blasphet.

"I couldn't sleep," Blasphet said, placing a roll of parchment on the table. "I confess, I feel rather giddy. I've been contemplating the task you gave me. Quite a thorny problem. I now have a solution."

"Blasphet," Albekizan said, standing, stretching, fighting off the stiffness of interrupted sleep. "It's late. Why did the guards let you in?"

"They wouldn't. I killed them," Blasphet said with a shrug. "It was depressingly simple. No challenge at all in killing such a dim-witted lot. Try to replace them with something a little brighter next time."

"I assigned all my best guards to cover you," Albekizan said.

"Oh dear," Blasphet said. "I have more bad news for you then. But that can wait. This can't. Come. Look. Isn't this the most marvelous thing you've ever seen?"

Albekizan glanced at the parchment. Blasphet raised the lamp to cast a better light. A nearly impenetrable maze of parallel and perpendicular lines covered the surface of the parchment. Albekizan looked closer. Slowly the lines began to make sense. They were roads, buildings, walls, aqueducts, and sewers. It was the map of a grand city.

"What is this?"

"This is the ultimate destination of mankind," said Blasphet. "Their final home. Do you like it?"

Albekizan rubbed his eyes. His brother was insane; this was a given. Albekizan normally wasn't surprised or disturbed by Blasphet's odd tangents and flights of fancy. But this?

"I asked you to plot the destruction of all mankind and you design a housing project. This is unexpected, even from you."

"Yes, well," said Blasphet. "If the humans expected this it could never work. But I took inspiration in your words. I thought that was a very insightful thing that you said, telling me that freedom would be my shackles."

"Hmm," said Albekizan. "I suppose I did say that."

"This is the Free City," said Blasphet. "It's the city of humanity's dreams. What they will never know, until it's too late, is that it is the city of our dreams as well." Blasphet ran a claw dreamily along the lines of a major street.

"If you say so," said Albekizan.

"You can't see it, can you?" Blasphet said. "Let me explain the beauty of this plan."

Albekizan said, "Go on."

And, come the dawn, Albekizan considered the inky paper stretched out before him to be the loveliest thing under all the sky.

BOOK TWO

CROWS

For man also knoweth not his time:
as the fishes that are taken in an evil net,
and as the birds that are caught in the snare;
so are the sons of men snared in an evil time,
when it falleth suddenly upon them.

Ecclesiastes 9:12

PROLOGUE PART TWO

SPEAR

*1078 D.A., The 47th Year of the
Reign of Albekizan*

RECANNA PLACED BANT'S breakfast before him: a large, flat golden biscuit covering half the plate beside a scramble of eggs, the yellow flecked with diced green onion. A black-rimmed sliver of orange cheese leaned on the edge of the plate. As Recanna poured him a mug of white, frothy buttermilk, Bant looked around the table to the bright eyes of his two beautiful little girls. They lowered their eyes respectfully as Bant said, "Let us pray."

"We give thanks, oh Lord, for the bounty before us," Bant said. "We give thanks for the new day."

He continued the prayer for some time before concluding, as he always did, with the things he was most personally thankful for: his newborn son, his beautiful daughters and, most of all, for Recanna.

His son Adam gurgled and mewed throughout the prayer as if offering his own thanks.

When Bant finished his meal he kissed Recanna's cheek and then stepped from his cabin into the soft dawn light. He faced a busy day. He needed to complete his chores and prepare for tomorrow's sermon. He smiled. Knowing how every moment of his day would be spent gave him a warm feeling. He felt very much at home in the world. He found joy in his labors, whether tending to the orchards or aiding his fellow villagers.

The morning light danced through the peach orchard, causing the dew-covered leaves to sparkle with a million tiny jewels. Truly, he dwelled in the new Eden.

He couldn't know, yet, that today the serpents would arrive.

By MIDDAY, THE southern sun pressed down on Bant like a giant hand, making the slightest movements laborious. If the rains had been steadier last spring, he might have avoided working in the heat of the day. All the cooler hours of the morning and evening were spent tending the fields. The village couldn't afford to lose a single plant. This left the middle part of the day to such drudgework as reshingling a roof. Bant hadn't planned to spend this long on the task; it was only a few wooden shingles that needed replacing after wind damage from the previous week's thunderstorm. Bant lay his hammer down and wiped the sweat from his eyes. He would welcome a thunderstorm if it came along now, wind damage or no. He glanced toward the distant stream, longing for a dip within its cool waters. A cloud of dust caught his eye; someone was approaching from the northern road.

Bant squinted, shielding his eyes. Three huge lizards—gray in color save for the rust-red scales along their throats and bellies—lumbered along the dirt road. At first glance they appeared low to the ground, but when Bant compared them to the trees they passed he realized the lizards stood taller than horses, and only their great length made them appear squat.

As the great lizards grew nearer, Bant could make out the riders who looked like men astride the high-backed leather saddles. But they weren't men; they were earth-dragons. Their scaly skin was the color of moss. Their heads sat broad and low upon their shoulders, their dark eyes set wide apart. A teal fringe of spiky scales jutted from their necks.

Bant climbed down the ladder, moving to meet the dragons as they rode into the town square. He could only vaguely recall the last time the dragons had visited, well over a decade ago. The dragons had then demanded a tenth of that year's harvest and the older townsmen agreed to provide it, citing an ancient agreement. The town lay in the land of dragons and the Dragon King had the right to take as much as a quarter of the harvest. The elders said dragons were abundant in the north but ventured south to collect taxes only rarely, seldom appearing more than once in a score of years.

Bant wished some of the elders had survived to advise him now. If the dragons wanted a quarter of the harvest this year, it would be difficult. Christdale suffered from a shortage of men. Only male children his age and younger had survived Hezekiah's initial teachings unmaimed. Now only a dozen able-bodied men could tend the crops, and they had to provide for a community of nearly a hundred. The Lord in his mercy always provided enough but there was seldom much surplus.

The three dragons rode into the center of the village. They dismounted and spoke to one another in a strange, hissing speech. Two carried long spears tipped with metal. The third dragon, the apparent leader, had a scabbard hanging from his belt from which the bejeweled hilt of a sword jutted. From the windows of their houses the villagers watched but none approached, leaving Bant alone with the visitors.

The sword-dragon finished conferring with his associates. He faced Bant and said, "I am Mekalov. You are this town's leader?"

Bant found Mekalov's speech difficult to follow. The creature's hard, beak-like mouth didn't move as it spoke; the noise seemed to emanate from deep within his throat. It didn't help that the dragon's breath distracted him. Perhaps the heat played tricks with his eyes, but foul, fishy garlic fumes spilled from Mekalov's mouth in visible waves.

"Well?" Mekalov demanded. "Answer me!"

"We are led by no one but the Lord," Bant said.

"Bring this lord to me," Mekalov said.

"He is already here," Bant said.

"If you are the lord, then gather your subjects. There is work to be done."

Bant smiled politely. He knew that Mekalov didn't understand him. He wondered what Hezekiah would have to say about attempting to tell a dragon about God. Would it be a waste of time?

Then, setting aside the theological musings, Bant asked what slowly dawned on him as the important question: "What work?"

"A week from now Albekizan's tax collectors will arrive. By then you will gather in this square half of this year's harvest along with half of all livestock in the village."

"Half?" Bant said. "But... but the agreement is for no more than a quarter."

"Perhaps, in this backwater, you have not heard the good news," said Mekalov. "Albekizan commemorates the miraculous birth of a new son, Bodiel. This is a celebration tax in his honor."

"But—"

"Need I remind you that the very ground you stand upon belongs to Albekizan? Anything that grows here belongs to him, and him alone. You live merely as a parasite, feasting upon food that is not your own. We are not taking half *your* harvest. Instead, Albekizan is allowing you to keep half of *his* harvest. Be grateful for his generosity."

"The Good Book tells me give unto Caesar that which is Caesar's," Bant said, "but I won't starve my friends and family. When the collectors arrive we will give them what we can spare."

"We're not here to bargain, human. We merely inform you of what will be. You will comply or you will die."

Bant searched his mind for the proper scripture for guidance. He wanted to follow the will of the Lord, but what was it in this matter? That he yield to authority, obey the dragons, and have faith that all would be well? Or that he oppose the dragons and stand against injustice?

Bant knew that the Lord was on his side no matter what. He drew his shoulders back and said, "We do not fear death. We will not submit to evil."

"What a curious attitude," Mekalov said. The earth-dragon drew his sword from his scabbard, the blade singing like the fading peals of a bell. Before Bant could react the blade tip was thrust beneath his chin, stopping just short of his throat.

Mekalov narrowed his eyes. "How about now? Now do you fear death?"

Bant swallowed hard. He whispered, "Yea', though I walk in the valley of the shadow of death I will fear no evil."

"Humans have never been known for brains," Mekalov said. "But you're something else, boy. Too stupid to be scared, eh? Think there's something to be gained by this little display? Continue with this foolishness and this village will burn. Its people will be enslaved, if they are lucky. You can prevent that only if the next words from your lips are, 'We will obey. We live to serve Albekizan.' Go on. Say it."

Bant's mouth seemed suddenly too dry to allow speech. Was this mere vanity that caused him to resist? Pride that goeth before the fall? As his mind whirred another voice shouted, "TOUCH NOT MINE ANOINTED, AND DO MY PROPHETS NO HARM!"

Bant stopped staring down the length of the sword, shifting his gaze toward the church. Hezekiah emerged from the dark, windowless interior. He stood on the steps like a tall pillar. His black robes wrapped about him like shadows.

"Hmmph," said Mekalov to his fellow dragons. "Another idiot. Let him serve as an example to the lord, here. Kill him!"

A spear-wielding dragon charged toward the church. Hezekiah stood, unflinching. With a grunt the dragon guided his weapon to its target, planting the spearhead in the center of the prophet's belly, driving it deeply into him until the point lifted Hezekiah's robes from his back. Hezekiah remained standing, looking stern.

"HE WHO LIVES BY THE SWORD," Hezekiah said, without a trace of weakness in his voice, "SHALL DIE BY THE SWORD!"

Hezekiah placed his hands upon the shaft that pierced him and began to push it deeper until it reached the midpoint. Then he reached behind him and grabbed the spear and pulled it free. He held the spear before him, examining its gleaming point. Not a drop of blood stained its surface. The dragon before him staggered backward, his beak dropping open in shock.

"AN EYE FOR AN EYE!" Hezekiah shouted as he hurled the spear at his attacker. The spear struck the dragon with a *crack* like thunder. The dragon's body toppled backward, as his head, eyes wide with surprise, fell to the ground between his twitching legs.

Bant shifted his gaze back to the sword at his throat. It hovered unsupported in the air a brief second before falling to his feet. Mekalov tripped twice in his haste to reach his scaly steed but at last reached the saddle and dug his claws into the beast's sides. He pulled the lizard's reigns to turn it back in the direction they had come and set off in pursuit of the other spear-dragon whose steed already thundered down the road in a trail of dust. The third lizard steed—its reptilian brain oblivious to its master's death—stood contentedly by the village well munching on clover.

"Hezekiah!" Bant shouted, running to the preacher's side. "Are you all right?"

"Of course," the prophet said, smoothing his robes.

"But-but-but how?"

"The Lord provides."

Bant nodded as the land around him began to blur.

"Why do you weep, Bant Bitterwood?"

"I... I didn't know what to do," he sobbed. "They could have killed Recanna, Adam, everyone. I didn't know what to do. I didn't know what to say."

"Did you do as the Lord guided?"

Bant wondered. Had the Lord guided him? Or had his pride? Hezekiah might be able to endure such a serious wound through faith alone, but Bant knew his faith did not equal the preacher's. For when he had stood in the valley of the shadow of death, when the sword had been at his throat, he *had* feared evil. He dared not reveal this to Hezekiah.

"Yes," he said, wiping away his tears. "I did as the Lord guided."

"Good. For the Lord provides guidance for me as well. Before the winter comes I must leave this place. The seed of the Lord has brought forth a plentiful harvest in this town. Now we are needed elsewhere to sow other fields."

"We?" Bant sniffled.

"Yes," Hezekiah said. "You are ready for the next phase of your training. You will travel for a time as a missionary, Bant Bitterwood."

"But," said Bant, "Recanna... the harvest..."

"Recanna will stay to care for your children. The harvest will be complete before we are ready to leave. For all else, we will trust to the Lord. Return to your labors, Bant Bitterwood."

"Yes," Bant said, as Hezekiah walked back up the church steps and disappeared into the shadows beyond the open door.

But Bant didn't return to his labors, not for a long time. Instead he looked at the dead dragon before him. The head gazed up at his, the eyes still wide with surprise. Flies already gathered to drink the red pool that grew around the dragon's corpse.

He couldn't help but think of the last time he'd seen this ground drenched in blood, that night long ago when he'd first kissed Recanna. The sight of blood had satisfied him. Blood had been a promise, then. Blood could carry justice, and blood could give hope. Blood had washed the land of its old ways and brought about a new world. Now the blood carried a different promise.

As the red liquid crept toward his worn leather boots, Bant took a step back. The sun shone strongly yet a chill ran up his spine. Something awful was coming. He couldn't define it, he didn't know when it would come, or how, but it was there, in the future, revealed by the dark rivulets before him. He shuddered as the cracked, dusty earth drank the cursed blood.

CHAPTER EIGHT

ZEEKY

1100 D.A., The 69th Year of the Reign of Albek-izan

"TOUCH NOTHING," ZANZEROTH said. Though angered by his master's assumption that he would disturb the scene, Gadreel held his tongue. He had grown used to Zanzeroth's mood by now. For months Bitterwood had eluded them, though not by much. Zanzeroth's instincts led him again and again to Bitterwood's trail, but always the trail was lost when it returned to the river. They had followed their prey nearly two hundred miles now, and Gadreel doubted they would ever catch him.

Perhaps this time would be different. Even Gadreel could see the leaves were relatively fresh, no more than a week old. The hunter tugged at the pile of wilting branches. He lifted them one by one, holding each to his eye, searching for any clues it might hold before tossing it aside. He repeated the task until at last the hidden boat was uncovered completely.

"Step carefully," Zanzeroth said. "We need to flip this over gently."

Gadreel grabbed the end of the flat-bottomed boat and helped Zanzeroth to lift it, taking care not to disturb the ground around or beneath it. They set the boat aside. As they moved it the odor of charred wood caught his nostrils. Gadreel saw that their care had been merited for beneath lay the remains of a campfire.

Zanzeroth knelt next to the ash-filled ring of rocks. He lowered his scarred snout close to the ground and sniffed. The master hunter then examined the site pebble by pebble, and by following Zanzeroth's eye, Gadreel began to see the nearly invisible scuffs and scratches that made Zanzeroth frown in contemplation. Zanzeroth continued to crawl over the arcane runes, piecing together syllable by syllable the story they told.

"It's not Bitterwood," he said, rising at last, stretching his limbs. His joints popped as he limbered them, unleashing a flurry of pale scales. "A human's been here, but the boot prints are too small."

"Then we're wasting our time," Gadreel said.

"What does time matter to a slave?" Zanzeroth said.

Gadreel wanted to answer Zanzeroth's insult with the strongly worded speech he had recited in his mind again and again. But he didn't. Zanzeroth had treated him abusively ever since he had climbed from the tunnel carrying Bitterwood's cloak. Words wouldn't turn aside the hunter's anger. Only Bitterwood's death would bring peace to the hunter, and so to Gadreel.

"I merely meant," Gadreel said, keeping his voice low, "that it is a shame that this lead has been unrewarding."

"Unrewarding? I think not," Zanzeroth said. "Following this trail will prove most satisfying."

"Why?"

"How is it that even with two eyes you are so blind?" The hunter used a fore-claw to circle a small footprint in the dirt.

"I see the footprint, master," Gadreel said, looking closer. "From the size I assume it is the footprint of a child or a woman."

"But don't you see this as well?" Zanzeroth's claws pointed to the faint outline of a feather beneath the sandy dirt. He pulled the feather free of its grave and held it to the light, revealing it as the pale blue wing-scale of a sky-dragon.

"A sky-dragon and a human female traveling together," Zanzeroth said. "Surely this tells you whose trail we've found."

"Why?" asked Gadreel. "Many dragons have human companions. It's not uncommon to find human and dragon footprints on the same site."

"Even though you weren't present, surely you must have heard rumors. Albekizan wanted the matter kept secret, but how can you not have heard about Vendevorex?"

"He's the king's wizard," Gadreel said. "It's common knowledge that he's taken ill. He's been too sick to leave his bed for months."

Zanzeroth's one good eye rolled up in its socket. "I wondered what kind of fool would be taken in by that lie."

"Lie?"

"Vendevorex turned traitor the day after Bodiel's death. He disobeyed the king's orders and fled with his pet human in tow. Now Albekizan wants him dead. He's not as big a prize as Bitterwood, but he's worth following. Besides, I have a theory that Bitterwood and the wizard may be connected somehow."

"But," said Gadreel, "if Albekizan wants Vendevorex dead, why the lie? Why not just announce a price on the wizard's head?"

"Because soon Albekizan will start his master plan against the humans and the wizard's loyalty to humans is legendary. It's best to have everyone think Vendevorex is ill rather than free and hidden somewhere in the kingdom."

"Albekizan fears the humans might turn to Vendevorex for assistance?" asked Gadreel.

"It's possible," said Zanzeroth. "Even if the wizard never turns up again he's still likely to be a hero to humans. One thing I've learned is that humans would rather spread a rumor than breed. You've seen what they've done with Bitterwood. They think he's everywhere at once, ready to leap from the woods to save them at any moment, even though none of them have ever seen him. They think he's a ghost or a god. If they would build such a legend around a mere man, imagine what they would do with a dragon wizard. But that's not the real reason Albekizan wants to keep the wizard's treason quiet."

"Then, why?"

Zanzeroth shook his head as if disgusted to once again be explaining the obvious. "Albekizan has built his empire at the expense of many a former friend. More than a few sun-dragons would shelter Vendevorex, given the chance, and use him as a weapon in an open rebellion. In fact... we can't be far from Chakthalla's castle."

"Three miles," Gadreel answered. He'd spotted the graceful towers and colorful windows of Chakthalla's palace during his reconnaissance flight of the area. Chakthalla was the widow of Tanthia's brother, Terranax. She managed this mountainous corner of Albekizan's kingdom.

"She lost her mate to Blasphet," Zanzeroth said, "I wonder if she's learned that the Murder God is now among the king's closest advisors?"

"Perhaps we should pay her a visit?" Gadreel said.

"Aye," said Zanzeroth. "But first we should pay a visit to Kanst. His troops are camping near the village of Winding Rock in preparation for the round-up of humans after the harvest to take them to Blasphet's city, I imagine Kanst might enjoy a visit with Chakthalla as well."

ZANZEROTH LED GADREEL to the east toward Kanst's camp. Evening was coming on. The sun behind them cast their long shadows onto the earth. Below, a small band of humans trudged along a dirt path by the edge of a field. They looked up, their eyes wide and frightened, as the dragons' shadows fell over them. Zanzeroth always loved the effect of the light at this time of day. The black outline of his shadow possessed a grand, ominous life of its own.

Half a mile away from Kanst's camp, the shrieks of an injured earth-dragon reached Zanzeroth's ears. Gadreel's flight slowed when he, too, noticed the sound.

"By the bones," Gadreel said, sounding worried. "What's that noise?"

"I warned Kanst that the slop he feeds the troops would eventually kill someone," Zanzeroth said.

As they raced ever closer to the camp, the source of the agonized cry became obvious. An earth-dragon was running through the camp, enveloped in bright white flames. The charred outlines of his body revealed his headlong rush straight through the walls of tents. A trail of crisp, smoldering footprints led straight as an arrow back toward Kanst's personal tent.

As Zanzeroth landed a few yards from the action, the earth-dragon at last fell as the tendons of his legs turned to ash. The ground around him began to boil. All the dragons in the camp fled the horrible flames, save one. A youthful sky-dragon, bearing the wing-ribbons that marked him a member of the aerial guard, rushed toward the fallen earth-dragon and tossed a thick woolen blanket over him to smother the fire. He jumped back when the plan failed; the blanket erupted into a bright blaze.

The air took on the stench of burning sheep.

"Bring water," the sky-dragon shouted, though no other soldier remained to hear him.

"Too late for that," Zanzeroth said, walking toward the fallen dragon. He stepped around the wisps of smoke that wafted toward him. "Take care not to breathe the fumes," he said. "A large enough dose will kill you."

"What could possibly burn like that?" Gadreel asked, staring as the dragon's body sank into the bubbling ground.

"It's called the Vengeance of the Ancestors," said Zanzeroth, "and it confirms Vendevorex is near!"

As he spoke, the giant armored form of General Kanst appeared over the tent tops. He moved toward them in slow, clanking steps. Despite the clatter of his movements, he'd apparently heard Zanzeroth's comments for he said, "It confirms nothing of the sort."

"Only the wizard can create this flame," Zanzeroth said. "I've seen it before. So have you, though I assume your memory isn't what it once was. Have care. This magic flame burns everything."

"Everything but iron," Kanst said, unclasping his massive breastplate. He dropped the heavy oval of steel over the burning pit, capping the flames. He dropped to all fours and began to slap out the fiery footprints with his iron gauntlets. "It's one reason I've spent the last decade and a half lumbering around in this armor."

The young member of the aerial guard found an iron shield lying on the ground and began beating out the flames elsewhere.

Kanst rose and said to Zanzeroth, "I see I have at least one soldier worth his gruel." Then, to the sky-dragon, "You, son. What's your name?"

"Pertalon, sir," the dragon answered without stopping his work.

"Pertalon, I like your face. I'm giving you a promotion."

"Sir," Pertalon said, standing straight. By now the flames were all extinguished.

"Come with me. You too, hunter. You'll be interested in this."

Kanst led them back along the charred footprints. They arrived at the largest tent in the camp, a palace built from gray canvas that covered almost an acre, Kanst's personal home away from home. The wall they approached was neatly marked with the charred outline of an earth-dragon.

Leading them inside, Kanst said, "It was roughly fifteen years ago that the wizard first demonstrated the effects of the Vengeance of the Ancestors. On quiet nights I can still hear the screams of the family inside that cabin. I wasn't a general back then, only a soldier."

"We all knew you were destined for greatness," Zanzeroth said. "You were a cousin of the king, after all."

"No matter my heritage, I knew power when I saw it," Kanst said. "The Vengeance of the Ancestors was naked, unquenchable power. The wizard controlled it. And ever since that night, so have I."

Kanst took them to a row of a dozen cauldrons: huge, black, cast-iron affairs used to cook stews for armies. "That dead fool must have thought I was hiding supper in these things," Kanst said. He lifted the iron lid a crack. White light as bright as the midday sun filled the room.

"I snuck back to the cabin later that night and found a few tendrils of the flame still flickering among the ruins. I placed them in an iron pot and carefully fed them. The wizard had said that below a critical mass the flame dies out. For fifteen years I've maintained that critical mass, feeding the fire with whatever fuel I had at hand. It really does burn anything—hard, dense fuels do especially well—stones, bricks and, from time to time, the remains of a particularly thick-skulled and disloyal soldier."

"Albekizan knows of this?" Zanzeroth asked.

"Of course. It's why he elevated me to general. But I'm certain that the wizard never knew. Aside from the king, the only dragons to know about the flames are the rare and trusted few I've selected to help me maintain the stock."

He glanced toward Pertalon. "You rushed into danger while everyone else fled. You followed my lead to squelch the flame without waiting for my orders or asking a single question. Now your job will be to help keep this fire alive."

"Sir," said Pertalon. "It will be an honor."

IT WAS A dark, cloudy night in Winding Rock. The windows of the score or so wooden houses that composed the village proper glowed with candlelight. A lone figure slipped along the streets; a small blonde-haired girl, clutching a bundle of blankets tightly against her chest. She dashed behind the largest house on the street, pausing to press her ear against the back door.

"Okay, Poocher," Zeeky whispered as she carefully slipped her knife through the crack in the back door, lifting the latch. "You need to be really quiet."

She looked down at the piglet snuggled warmly in the wool blanket. Poocher looked back, his dark eyes full of understanding.

Zeeky slowly cracked the door open. The kitchen should be empty; she had watched the last of the help leave just after dark. Only Barnstack himself was still inside, but everyone knew the mayor was half-deaf. Even though the light still burned in the front room, Zeeky couldn't wait any longer for him to turn in. The night grew colder by the minute and her stomach was a hard knot. She didn't mind so much that she hadn't eaten since yesterday, but poor little Poocher had to be starving.

Barnstack's kitchen was the size of her father's house. The warm space smelled of stewed beef, onions, and sauerkraut. Pots and pans hung from the ceiling, gleaming in the faint light that seeped around the door leading to the front room. Zeeky tiptoed inside, easing the door shut behind her.

Cradling Poocher, she crept toward the pantry. The silence was suddenly disturbed by a series of bangs. She looked around, terrified that she had knocked something over. But the noise came from the other room. Someone was knocking at the front door with a force that sounded like hammer blows. She held her breath as she listened to the silence that followed. Then the sound erupted again followed by the creaking of floorboards as the mayor limped to the door.

"You shouldn't knock so hard," Barnstack hissed loudly, though he probably thought he was whispering. "Do you want the whole town to know?"

"I'd been knocking for five minutes. Answer your door more promptly in the future," replied a deep, smooth voice.

"I came as soon as... oh, never mind. Come in before someone sees you."

"We are alone?"

"What?" Barnstack shouted.

"Are we alone?" the strange voice said forcefully.

"Yes, yes. I sent the help home hours ago."

Zeeky tried to peek through the gap between the doorframe and the door to the front room, but she couldn't see with whom Barnstack spoke. No matter how hard she tried, she couldn't match the deep voice with any of the village men.

Barnstack said, "Heavens, the night's turned cold. Would you like some tea?"

"It would be rude to refuse," the stranger answered.

Zeeky gasped as Barnstack came into view, shuffling toward the kitchen. She hurried for the pantry. When she opened the pantry door she saw a row of cured hams hanging from the ceiling. She closed the door before Poocher could notice and looked around for another hiding place. As light poured into the kitchen from the opening door, she crawled beneath a large table and climbed into the seat of one of the chairs, curling into a tight ball. With her left hand she scratched Poocher beneath his chin to make sure he'd keep calm.

From her vantage point, she watched the elderly man walk slowly toward the stove. She looked at the doorway to the front room. Her eyes grew wide. The visitor's legs were green, scaly, and thickly muscled. A broad, pointed tail hung behind the legs, reaching to within inches of the floor. The tail swayed as the stranger followed Barnstack into the kitchen.

Barnstack stirred the coals in the fireplace as he hung the teapot on the metal hook within. He tossed a slender wedge of wood onto the coals. The smoke reached Zeeky's nose; she prayed Poocher wouldn't sneeze.

"There," Barnstack said as the flame took life. "It will only take a few minutes."

"Your hospitality is appreciated," the visitor said. "I hope this means you are receptive to our offer."

"What?"

"Our offer," he repeated, louder this time. "I hope you intend to accept it?"

"It's generous," Barnstack said.

"Yes."

"Too good to be true, almost."

"It may seem that way at first. But think about it. All of Albekizan's wealth flows from the labor provided by your village and countless other villages like it. Is it any wonder he would choose to repay you?"

"Everything good comes with a price," Barnstack said.

"Consider your past labor as advance payment."

"But if everyone accepts this offer, who will plant the crops next year? Who will harvest them? If everyone goes to this Pre-City…"

"Free City."

"What?"

"Free City." The visitor said the words in a warm tone, as if he were talking about some place wonderful. "It"s called Free City, not Pre-City."

"Oh," Barnstack said, sounding confused. "I thought it was called Pre-City because they were still building it. They only started it a few weeks ago, yes?"

"True. It's a testament to the king's leadership that he's devoted enough money and labor to the Free City that it is already open to humans. Free City awaits those lucky few who will live the rest of their lives in peace and plenty."

"Lucky few? You said it was for everyone."

"Everyone in this village, yes. Of course, it couldn't be for everyone everywhere; as you say, who would do the work? No, Free City is a reward to those villages that have served Albekizan faithfully and completely over the years of his reign. Your village is among the chosen. We are especially pleased by the teachings of your spiritual leader, Kamon. His vision of harmony between man and dragon is most enlightened."

The hair rose on the back of Zeeky's neck as Barnstack pulled the chair across from her from under the table. Poocher started to wiggle but Zeeky held him tighter and rubbed his belly, calming him. Barnstack sagged into the chair.

"Forgive me for sitting. My knees ache when the weather turns cooler. You insist we meet so late. Yes. Yes, that was my other question, Dekatheron. The secrecy. You want me to move all the people of my village from their homes into this Free City. You say it's for their good. Yet you insist that we meet in secrecy."

"The very fact that you ask that question answers it," Dekatheron said. "Humans distrust dragons. I want to persuade you before we approach the others. Many of them will no doubt speak against us. I must know that you will stand with me and won't be swayed by their objections."

Barnstack sighed loudly. "I'm an old man. I have good land and a comfortable home. Leaving for a city so far away, a place I've never—"

"Barnstack, may I remind you, you have no land," Dekatheron interrupted. "You humans may divvy up its usage however you please, but the land belongs to Albekizan. This house, this kitchen, the chair you sit it, belong to him. You are his guest. If your host offers you the use of more spacious quarters, it is impolite to refuse, just as it would be impolite of me to refuse your tea."

"But—"

"Albekizan has allowed you to farm his land for generations. The years of his rule have been marked by peace and prosperity. Now he offers further largesse."

Barnstack paused a moment, contemplating the dragon's words. "I suppose it's as you say. I promise to talk to my people. Perhaps the young will want to go. But I want to stay."

"I understand," Dekatheron said, walking to the table. "Perhaps this will change your mind."

A sudden metallic clatter rained upon the table. A gold coin rolled from the table's edge and bounced against Dekatheron's clawed foot. He leaned down, reaching for the coin, his beaked, tortoise-like profile suddenly visible to Zeeky. He then tilted his head toward the fire as the kettle whistled. He rose, taking the coin with him.

"There must be a hundred coins here," Barnstack said.

"More than enough to start a new life anywhere, even at your age," Dekatheron said as he moved to the fireplace, his claws clicking against the wooden tiles. "In Free City your housing, food, and clothing will be provided at no cost. The gold can be used for luxuries befitting a man of your authority."

Poocher's snout twitched as Dekatheron carried the aromatic kettle to the table. Zeeky sniffed deeply; the steam smelled of apples, lemons, and cinnamon.

"Very well," Barnstack said. "When we finish with the harvest, I will ready the town to move."

"Then it is settled?"

"Yes," Barnstack said with a grunt as he rose from his chair. "Come, let us return to the front room. The chairs there are easier on my back. You'll still have some tea, won't you?"

"Of course, friend."

Barnstack left the room carrying the kettle and a pair of cups. Dekatheron followed. Zeeky let out her breath in relief. Dekatheron suddenly turned toward the table. Zeeky held her breath again as Dekatheron walked toward her. He reached the table, and with his clawed hand he scooped the coins back into the leather pouch. He then turned and walked into the front room, closing the door behind him.

Zeeky crawled from beneath the table and stood on shaky legs. She saw a basket of fruit sitting on the counter near the cutting board. She grabbed it and silently slipped out into the night.

"Poocher," she said. "We sure picked a good time to run away. Free City or not, I don't trust nobody green."

Poocher snorted and shook his head in agreement.

DEKATHERON PULLED HIS cloak close about him as he hurried along the dark streets of the town. He checked his pocket again for the agreement Barnstack had signed, wondering at the ways of kings. Only Albekizan would want a soldier who couldn't read to obtain the mark of a man who couldn't write on a document that would never be honored.

Barnstack had been right about one thing; the night had turned cold. He turned from the road, going deep into the woods, his eyes searching the darkness for a good spot to rest. He wished he wasn't so far from the rest of Kanst's army. He would have to sleep on the ground tonight. He'd rather spend the night in a warm tent heated by a proper fire. He could almost smell the smoke.

He stopped to sniff the air. He *did* smell smoke. Was it from the village? The wind was from the wrong direction.

He followed the scent, moving cautiously through the darkness. His attempt at stealth, however, was foiled by his surroundings. The leaves crunched beneath his heavy feet with each step.

He came into a small clearing and found a circle of stone, within which smoldered the dim remnants of a fire.

He knelt down and grabbed a stick, stirring the coals. Feeble golden flames flickered to life.

Dekatheron looked around. He could see no sign of whoever had built the fire. He listened, but the night made no sound now that he'd stopped moving.

No sense in letting the fire go to waste. He tossed in the stick he used to stir the fire, then gathered some pine needles and tossed them on as well. As they flared up he searched the area for more sticks and branches. In a moment, the fire was burning properly again. He held his claws toward the blaze, warming them.

Now that the fire had taken the chill from his stiff claws, it was time to take care of the rest of his body. He dug into the pocket of his cloak and found a small ceramic flask that was stopped with a cork. He popped the cork to unleash the powerful, musk-sharp stench of goom, a powerful alcohol distilled from wild swamp cabbage and seasoned with cayenne. He tilted his head back and gulped down the eye-watering brew. The vapors gave his whole head a hot, buzzy feel.

Then, there was a whistling sound, and his right arm went numb. The flask tumbled from his suddenly useless claws, toppling to his chest. The goom spilled all over his torso. The burning sensation wasn't unpleasant. He looked down, his eyes struggling to understand what he saw in the dim flicker of the fire. He found a stick jutting from his arm: a long, straight stick, decorated at the top with feathers.

Dekatheron sniffed. Beneath the goom and the rising smoke, he detected a hint of fresh blood. He noticed the flask resting against his thigh. He reached for it, wondering if there was any goom left.

Another whistle.

Now there was a stick in his chest. He touched it with his left claw, stroking the red feathers, wondering if this was some sort of goom fantasy that made him imagine that he had sticks growing from him. Where the stick met his chest, air leaked with a bubbling hiss. It reminded him of the noise of Barnstack's kettle.

He realized he was suddenly very tired. He fell onto his back. Spots danced before his eyes. It would be good to sleep. High in a nearby tree, the silhouette of a cloaked man crept among the branches.

CHAPTER NINE

PET

MURALS COVERED THE high ceilings of the grand dining hall. The scene displayed the history of the world, according to dragons, as huge reptiles from a vanished age crawled from the swamps, took flight, and carved the world from untamed forests. In the shadows of the trees tiny humans looked on in awe of the ancestral dragons.

No one had ever seen an ancestral dragon, of course. They'd lived long ago. But their bones were abundant in the rocks of the earth. Their black, polished skeletons decorated the halls of biologians, with the choicest relics finding their homes in the castles of sun-dragons. A skull as long as Jandra was tall hung on the wall of the dining hall.

Beneath this stone skull, at the head of the dinner table heaped high with roasts and breads and fruits, sat the sun-dragon Chakthalla. Jandra thought that Chakthalla could pass as Tanthia's double; the same poise and dignity possessed by the queen was reflected in Chakthalla's noble features. Each scale of her face seemed crafted from rubies, then placed in precise symmetry by a master jeweler. Her scales glimmered as they reflected the candlelight of the chandeliers. Chakthalla was the product of fine breeding, a dragon whom, long before her birth, had been sculpted by her bloodlines to possess a regal bearing.

Jandra wondered whether, perhaps, one reason why Chakthalla and Tanthia looked so similar to each other in her mind was because of the simple fact that she rarely was in the presence of female dragons other than the queen herself. Dragon society was heavily patriarchal. Unlike most birds or reptiles, dragons gave birth to live infants, and mortality during birth was high. It wasn't unusual to encounter male dragons over a century old. Encountering a female over thirty was a rarity. This imbalance in the longevity of sexes allowed males to control nearly all the wealth of the kingdom. Only the occasional widowed female dragon might hold a position of authority as Chakthalla did.

Seated next to Chakthalla was a human male, perhaps five years older than Jandra. The man reflected a similar attention to breeding. He was handsome to a fault, with long blond hair and chiseled features. His bronzed skin glowed; his broad smile revealed teeth white as fine porcelain. He was dressed in silk, his clothing cut to show off his slim, well-muscled physique. Jandra hadn't been properly introduced to him yet—she'd only heard

Chakthalla refer to him as "Pet."

"Pet," Chakthalla said. "Show Vendevorex your little trick. The one with the apple."

"Yes, Mother," Pet answered, smiling as he stood in his seat and stepped onto the table.

Pet somersaulted gracefully across the dishes, darting his hand out as he passed over the fruit dish. He landed on his feet, now holding an apple and a napkin in one hand and a silver knife in the other. He threw the knife and apple straight into the air and in rapid motion tied the napkin around his face. He knotted the impromptu blindfold in time to snatch the falling knife and apple.

The items didn't remain in his grasp for even a second. The apple left his hand, then the knife, and soon both floated in a constant arc above his head, his hands merely tapping them as they reached the bottom of the circle.

Jandra watched the performance, impressed by Pet's skill, yet vaguely disturbed by the scene. She had been relieved to learn that Chakthalla would allow her to eat at the dinner table with Vendevorex. Some dragons allowed humans at dinner tables only on platters. Chakthalla's liberal attitude toward human companions had obviously been shaped by her love of Pet. That bothered Jandra as she watched Pet perform like a tamed bear. She wondered how many hours of practice he'd put into the act solely to please Chakthalla.

Pet sliced the apple in half midair and then sent the pieces up in the air to be quartered. With a flick of his wrists, two of the quarters went flying, one landing in the center of Chakthalla's plate, the other landing slightly to the side of Vendevorex's. Pet caught the third quarter in his mouth as he pulled his blindfold free with a flourish and bowed. Jandra lost track of where the final quarter of the apple landed.

"Very good, Pet," said Chakthalla.

Pet bit a chunk from his apple, swallowed, then said, "Oh, but Mother, I have been remiss. It seems not everyone was served."

Pet back-flipped from the table landing next to Jandra. He stood with such grace that Jandra suddenly felt clumsy merely sitting still. Now that he stood close to her she noted the breathtaking jade color of his eyes.

"It wouldn't do to have this lovely lady go without her share," Pet said, taking Jandra's hand. His long slender fingers were softer than her own; his nails were trimmed in perfect arcs. Pet turned her palm upward, revealing the last quarter of the apple in the center of it. He closed her fingers around it, then leaned and kissed the back of her hand with his warm pink lips.

"How sweet," Chakthalla said. "I think Pet likes your little Jandy."

"Jandra," Vendevorex corrected.

Pet returned to his seat next to Lady Chakthalla. The regal dragon reached out her bejeweled talon to stroke his long blond hair. He rolled his eyes with pleasure. Jandra felt slightly ill.

She was bothered that Pet called Chakthalla "Mother." Though she never addressed him as such, she sometimes thought of Vendevorex as a father. He had raised her for as long as she could remember. Since her true parents had died when she was only an infant, Vendevorex was the closest thing to a parent she would ever have.

But what place did she occupy in Vendevorex's heart? Vendevorex never discussed emotion. He treated her kindly and was often smotheringly protective, but it wasn't quite the same as affection. Did he think of her as his daughter? His apprentice? Or merely his pet?

Vendevorex asked, "Have you received any word, my lady, from your friends?"

"Not as yet. Be patient. These are delicate matters we inquire about."

"Of course," Vendevorex said.

"I'm sure things will turn in our favor," Chakthalla said. "Albekizan has made many enemies over the years. It what you say is true and Albekizan does plan to kill all humans, we shall not want for allies. Thinning out the village rabble is one thing, but there are many others who feel as strongly about their darlings as I do about Pet. You, of course, understand the bond between a dragon and her best friend."

"I understand," Vendevorex said.

"My messengers will mention your name in their queries," Chakthalla said, a tone of pride in her voice. "Vendevorex is a name that carries a great deal of weight."

"And a great deal of liability. I am sure, my lady, that you use extreme caution as you speak my name. If Albekizan learns I am here, it will endanger your life and destroy our plans."

"I assure you, I know who to trust," Chakthalla said.

As Jandra looked away from Chakthalla, she saw that Pet had his gaze fixed squarely upon her. She looked down at her plate and stirred the spiced potatoes with her fork. She had little experience dealing with human males, but she had a strong suspicion of what Pet's stare meant. Many dragons who kept humans as pets bred them. Pet certainly looked like a thoroughbred. Jandra felt relieved that she didn't have a pedigree. No sense in giving Chakthalla ideas, especially since she wasn't sure what Vendevorex would say to such a proposal.

AFTER DINNER, VENDEVOREX walked the halls of Chakthalla's palace, lost in thought. Jandra followed close behind but he was barely aware of her. He was thinking of the solid stone walls of Albekizan's abode. The king's home was built for defense with high, solid walls, slits for windows, and guard towers in all directions. Chakthalla's home was a much more open space. The elegant ceilings were roofed with wooden arches which would fall beneath the first catapult assault. Huge, decorative windows filled with tinted glass panes lined the upper halves of the rooms. When war came, the glass would fall like deadly rain. Chakthalla's home was built for beauty, not for battle.

"How much longer will we have to stay here, Ven?" Jandra asked.

Vendevorex's brow furrowed at the question. He faced her and said, "For weeks, you've only expressed impatience at the slow crawl of the negotiations that brought us here. Don't tell me you are in a hurry to leave."

"I'm not," she said. "But it's been almost two months since Albekizan decided to wipe out the human race. I want to tackle our problems head on, take action."

"Action and problems will seek us out. It's foolish to invite them before their time."

"You've been training me to fight," Jandra said. She tightened her jaw and threw back her shoulders, looking as fierce as her five-foot tall, slender frame could manage. "I'm tired of sitting around waiting on all this letter-writing and spy games."

"The history of the world is shaped as much by the exchange of letters as it is by the waging of war," Vendevorex said.

"But there will be war, won't there? Someone has to stand up to Albekizan."

Vendevorex paused, contemplating her words. He found it difficult to believe Jandra was so hungry for war. He suspected she might have another motivation for wanting to know how long they would stay here.

"You seemed ill at ease tonight at dinner," Vendevorex said.

Jandra shrugged. "Something about this place disturbs me."

Vendevorex nodded. "I was thinking the same thing. But I need a safe place to gather my thoughts. We can count on Chakthalla's loyalty. She despises Albekizan."

"I don't trust her," said Jandra. "It sounds like she's bragging to her friends that she's sheltering you."

"We can only have faith that her words will reach the right ears."

"I think you trust her too far," Jandra said.

Vendevorex analyzed the edge in Jandra's voice. Annoyance? Jealousy? He wished he were better at understanding her moods. He knew that humans experienced a stage of intellectual growth in the years following puberty which was characterized by unpredictable emotional swings. He tried not to think about it. There were more important worries.

"Well?" Jandra asked.

"What? Do I trust her too far? Obviously, I don't believe so. That could prove suicidal. There are many, many secrets I keep from her—and from everyone."

"Even me?"

"Even you," Vendevorex said. He thought again of the ultimate secret he kept from her, then chased it quickly from his mind. She would never learn the truth of her origins. "But I see no reason to keep you in the dark," he said. "My decision to come here was one made in weakness. I doubt that our paths will intermingle with Chakthalla's for long."

"What do you mean?"

"Now that I've spent time in Chakthalla's company, I see that turning to her was a futile hope. Chakthalla is planning a rebellion the way she would plan a holiday picnic. It's something she'll invite a few close friends to for an afternoon's diversion. None who stand with her have the wits to know what they are up against, or the strength of will to make their rebellion work."

"But you stand with them," Jandra said. "You have the wits and the will."

"No," Vendevorex said, shaking his head. "The situation has spun beyond my control. For too many years have I watched Albekizan in his ruthless quest for power. Indeed, I've helped him gain power. I've killed for our king, Jandra. I've used my abilities to harm some of the very dragons who would now have the greatest chance of success against Albekizan."

"You couldn't know this day would come," Jandra said. "You did what you thought was best at the time. You told me it was good for the dragons to be united under a strong king."

"So I believed. It was certainly to my advantage."

"How so?"

Vendevorex contemplated his answer. There were still many, many things he didn't wish to reveal.

"No one in this kingdom knows of my past. I arrived seventeen years ago, a stranger to all. I used my status as an outsider to cultivate an air of mystery. I eventually made my way into Albekizan's court. I was given respect, power, wealth: all things that had eluded me in my former homeland. As Albekizan's power increased, so did mine. I always spoke freely with him, told him whenever I felt he grew too ruthless or cruel. This appeased my conscience. But I never made any move to stop him, nor did I ever refuse a share of the bounty of his conquests."

Jandra looked confused. "Your former homeland... where was it?" she asked. "How could it lie outside of Albekizan's kingdom?"

"Ah, to be as innocent as you are now." Vendevorex placed his fore-talon on Jandra's shoulder. "Let's just say the world was once a much larger place."

"What do you mean?"

"Albekizan controls only a small sliver of this world, isolated geographically by mountains to the west and an ocean to the east. But beyond the mountains there are other lands. I was born in one of these faraway kingdoms. I was the youngest of seven brothers. I had little chance of ever inheriting land or power, and less chance of taking it forcefully. So I left, seeking my fortunes in the frontier beyond. It was the beginning of a journey that is now rather difficult to explain."

"I can't believe it," Jandra said. "A whole world beyond the mountains? Why didn't you ever tell me?"

"It never seemed important. I have good reasons for not discussing my homeland. But now, it seems, I have even better reasons to return to it."

"Return to it?"

Vendevorex nodded. "Until tonight, I hadn't made up my mind as to the best course of action. I clung to the hope that it would be possible to fight Albekizan. Now, my consultations with Chakthalla show this to be folly. Our best hope lies on the other side of the mountains."

"The best hope to stop Albekizan? You think we can find allies there? Your family, maybe?"

Vendevorex shook his head. "We must think of ourselves now. If we stay here we will throw our lives away for a lost cause."

"But if we run, who will fight for the humans?" Jandra asked, her voice rising.

Vendevorex recognized her emotions stirring again. He tried to calm her with reason. "The humans must fight for themselves. United, they may succeed. A war of attrition favors them due to their superior numbers. In the end, humans may simply outbreed their way to victory."

Jandra grew pale. Vendevorex tried to interpret

her eyes. Was she reassured by his words? No, there were tears forming. He'd disappointed her instead of reassuring her. He sighed. Why did she have to make things so difficult?

"Don't you care about the countless millions who will die?" she asked softly.

"Jandra, you're too young to understand," he said firmly, hoping to end this discussion. "I'm not heartless. I've given up all my power and prestige. I won't assist Albekizan in genocide. But I also won't risk my life in such a lopsided cause."

"You aren't willing to die for humans."

"It's not—"

"You aren't willing to die for me?"

"Don't put words in my mouth. I've raised you for many years now. You mean a great deal to me."

"I mean a great deal… that's all?" Jandra said, her voice trembling. "It is true then. I'm nothing more than a pet to you."

Vendevorex hadn't expected this response. "What?"

"I'm not blind or deaf. Chakthalla acts as if I'm your pet and you say nothing to make her think differently."

He shrugged. "It's simple courtesy not to hurt the feelings of our hostess."

"But you think nothing of hurting my feelings, do you?" Jandra said through clenched teeth.

"I admit," Vendevorex said, on the verge of exasperation, "that I often have trouble comprehending the logic of your feelings."

Jandra sucked in her breath, looking for all the world like she was getting ready to shout. Then she turned and walked away, fists clenched. He hoped she would walk off her anger. Vendevorex felt a good deal of relief that this confrontation was behind them. When conditions were more favorable he would make things up to her.

ZEEKY COULD SEE the castle against the sunset. She'd been this close to the castle only once, last year when her father had taken food to the next village. He had told her the castle belonged to a dragon and that Zeeky should never go near the place. Zeeky had wanted so badly to visit.

The castle was lovely. On foggy mornings its graceful spires seemed to float in the sky. She often saw dragons in flight, their shadows falling over her as they passed above. Some of her friends were frightened by the shadows. She was always thrilled. She wanted more than anything in the world to touch the skin of a dragon; she imagined it to be soft and smooth, like snakeskin. She once dreamed that she was a dragon perched on the castle wall, looking over the valley.

Now she was finally going inside the castle walls. It was the only place she could think of to hide Poocher where her father would never follow. She wasn't sure what dragons ate—horses, maybe—but she knew without a doubt what her father ate, and from the moment she'd laid eyes on Poocher she'd known she couldn't let it happen.

It was well into night when she reached the small village that lay just outside the castle walls. The full moon dominated the sky, pierced by the dark silhouette of the castle's tallest tower. Zeeky's excitement at being so near the castle was somewhat muted by her exhaustion. Poocher snored softly in her arms and she felt as if she could simply lie down on the ground where she stood and drift away.

But that would be stupid. The villagers would find her and return her to her father, and then what would happen to Poocher? No, she would have to find shelter. Fortunately, she could make out the dim shapes of farm buildings across some nearby fields. She slipped through a wooden fence and made her way toward a barn. A dog barked angrily, the sound growing rapidly nearer. The large hound materialized from the darkness.

"Shhh," whispered Zeeky, pressing a finger to her lips. "You'll wake everybody up."

The dog stopped barking and approached her, sniffing. Zeeky scratched the old hound behind its ears.

"That's a good boy," she said. She had always gotten along better with animals than people. Animals listened to her. People spoke to her

The dog walked with her to the barn. She noticed a chunk of bloody fur in the dirt in front of the door.

"Poor thing," she whispered, guessing that the dog had caught up with a rabbit earlier. The dog picked up its meal and wandered off toward the farmhouse.

She slipped into the barn, pausing to let her eyes adjust. The moonlight outside was like daylight compared to the gloom of the barn. She stepped forward carefully, holding a hand before her, until at last she touched the ladder that led to the loft. She climbed slowly. Poocher was awake now and if he began to squirm she didn't want to drop him from the ladder.

As her head reached the top of the loft an arm thrust down from the darkness, grabbing her by the collar. She screamed but was instantly muffled by the large, rough hand that clamped over her mouth. She clasped Poocher with both arms as her assailant lifted her the rest of the way into the loft.

"Stop squirming," said a deep, gravely voice. "I'm going to let go of your mouth so you can answer a few questions. I'm not going to hurt you, so don't scream, understand?"

Zeeky nodded. The man's hand left her mouth. He still held her by the collar from behind so that she couldn't turn to face him.

"Did you have a good dinner tonight?" he asked. "I smelled fried chicken up at the house. Can you get me some?"

Zeeky didn't know how to answer.

"C'mon. Talk. You got nothing to be afraid of."

"I... didn't have dinner tonight."

"Oh?" the man said, sounding curious. "Why not? You being punished or something?"

"I can't tell."

"What did you do?"

"I didn't do nothing. I didn't eat dinner here 'cause I don't live here."

"Then what are you doing in this barn?"

"What are *you* doing in here?" Zeeky replied.

"Trying to get some sleep without some nosy kid butting in."

"I'm not nosy. I didn't know you were up here. I'm just looking for a place to spend the night."

"You a runaway?"

"No. I'm... I'm an orphan."

"Huh," the man said. "Well, me too. So I guess you got as much right to pass the night here as I do."

The man let go of her collar and Zeeky spun around. She found a skinny old man with gray, thinning hair and tattered clothing. Spread on the straw beside him was a large gray cloak which held a longbow, a quiver of arrows, and a long knife in a leather sheath. The old man smiled, showing two teeth missing from the bottom.

"I see you brought a pig, kid. Good thinking. Kind of a runt, though. But split between just the two of us—"

Zeeky squinched her eyes and said in the sternest voice she could muster, "Poocher's not for eating. He's my friend."

"Oh." The man shrugged. "Whatever. Not much meat on him anyway. Guess we're stuck with potatoes," her loftmate said, holding out a large spud. "Want one?"

"Thank you," Zeeky said, taking the potato. "What's your name? Mine's Zeeky."

"Zeeky? Never met anyone named Zeeky."

"Well, now you have."

"You got some sass in you kid. I like that."

"What's your name?"

"If you knew that, I'd have to kill you," the man said.

"Why? Are you a bad guy?"

"Could be," he answered. "I stole these potatoes."

"I stole fruit last night. Stealing food isn't always bad."

"The way I was raised, it is."

Zeeky shrugged. "Then we both must be bad guys."

"Ah," he said, nodding. "We're brother outlaws then."

"But I'm a girl."

"Okay, brother and sister outlaws."

"You gonna tell me your name?"

The old man started to say something, then stopped. He smirked, then asked, "Can you keep a secret?"

"Sure."

"Okay. Then keep this one real good," the stranger said, leaning close to her. His breath smelled of rotting teeth as he whispered, "I'm *Bitterwood*."

"No," Zeeky said.

"No?" The old man leaned back away from her. "I thought sure I was."

Zeeky rolled her eyes. She hated when adults treated her like she didn't know anything. "Bitterwood's this hero, okay? He lives in a big castle and he rides around on this big white horse and he has a shiny sword and a fancy hat with feathers in it. He fights dragons who are mean to nice people."

"Oh," the man said. He scratched his head, looking confused. "So... I'm not Bitterwood?"

"No, silly."

"Huh," he said. "Then I'm at a bit of a disadvantage. I must have forgot my name. Why don't you just call me... Hey You."

"Hey You?"

"Hey, for short. Mr. You if you're feeling formal."

"Okay, You."

"That's Mr. You to you," he said.

"You're silly," Zeeky said. "I like you."

Mr. You's lips bent slightly upward into an expression not quite a smile. "Thank you," he said. "Not many people like me."

"Maybe if you didn't scare little girls in barns, people would think you were nicer," she said.

"Could be," he said. "I don't normally try to scare anyone. It just happens."

"Maybe you need somebody to hang out with you and give you advice on not scaring people."

"Like a little girl?" Hey You said. Then, his partial smile faded. He nodded as he said, softly, "You might be onto something. People did like me more when I had a little girl. I had two of them, actually, a long time ago."

"Did something happen to them?"

He looked down into the straw and mumbled, "Yes." Then he took a deep breath and said, "Enough chit chat. If you want, you can stretch out on my cloak and I'll sleep on one of them straw bales. We gotta get up before dawn if we want to avoid being caught."

"Okay." Zeeky didn't need much convincing. She stretched out on his cloak, which was soft and smelled of smoke, and within less than a minute was drifting to sleep, dreaming of dragon castles, barely hearing the dog frantically barking in the distance.

JANDRA STEPPED FROM her sandals so that she would be able to climb more easily. The window had been built to allow a sun-dragon to stand comfortably at it and look out. She could just barely reach the bottom edge of the window if she jumped. She was used to navigating furniture and rooms scaled for beings twice her height. One advantage of the lifestyle was that it had made her a good jumper and a great climber. She pulled herself into the window, the highest in the castle, and looked out over the surrounding farmland. The moonlight bleached the night of all color, but still she could see the rectangular patchwork of farms, the wide river beyond and, far in the distance, the long ridge of mountains that bordered the rich valley.

The houses below looked idyllic. She wondered what it would have been like to have been raised in a normal house rather than a castle tower. She knew that Ruth or Mary would have thought she was crazy. They would have given anything for a taste of her life of privilege and comfort. But tonight she would rather be in one of those small farmhouses than here in the abode of dragons.

Sitting in the window, the cool night air playing against her hair, she remembered her last flight with Vendevorex. It seemed so natural to soar above the earth. It wasn't fair that humans were forever earthbound. If she could fly on her own she would never touch ground.

"A lovely night, fair Jandra. Made all the lovelier by your presence."

Jandra looked back. Pet was behind her, standing on the stairs that entered the tower chamber. He still wore his dinner finery: black pants and boots, a green silk shirt that matched his eyes with a necklace of gold and emeralds. She missed her old wardrobe, all the elaborate headdresses and gowns, now forever lost, she supposed. Having fled with only the clothes on her back, Vendevorex had used his abilities to create a simple cotton blouse and skirt for her. They were nicely crafted and fit her well, but compared to Pet, she may as well have been dressed in burlap rags.

"You look sad," Pet said. "Is something bothering you?"

"It's nothing," she said. She noted the ease with which he'd read the emotions on her face. Why couldn't Vendevorex be as tuned to her feelings as this stranger? "I just felt like looking at the moon."

"So I'm not intruding?" Pet asked.

"This is your home," she said, turning her face away. "I suppose you can go wherever you want."

"You look as if you wish to be alone," Pet said. "I wouldn't want to be where I'm not wanted. If you want me to go away, I will."

"Thank you," Jandra said.

"But before I go," Pet said, "I want you to know I understand."

"Understand what?"

"Your sorrow. Your loneliness," he said in his soothing, lyrical voice. "Sometimes, when we feel the greatest need to be alone, it's the moment we should most welcome the company of others."

Jandra supposed he meant the words to come across as wise. But they struck her instead as unsolicited advice. She got enough of that from Vendevorex. "You presume much, Pet."

"Do I? I caught a glimpse of the turmoil in your soul. It's in your eyes. You're all alone. I know your master doesn't understand. He can't."

Jandra frowned. "Vendevorex isn't my master.

He's my… teacher."

"But he's not human. He'll never be sensitive to your needs."

Jandra shifted in the window, turning her full back to him. "I thought you said you would leave."

"You haven't actually asked me to leave. I believe I know why."

"Oh?"

"You look out into the moonlight and it haunts you. You're a human living among dragons. You will never be recognized as an equal to the dragons, but neither will you ever be at home among mankind."

Jandra didn't want to let him know how right he was. She remained silent, staring into the night. Her gaze fixed on the farthest fields, her eyes drawn to movement, a large mass creeping along the river. A herd of cattle, perhaps. Did cattle come out at night? She turned away from the view to study Pet once more. His eyes continued to look right through her. Was she really so transparent?

She didn't want to discuss her feelings with him, so she changed the subject. "Is Pet your real name?"

"No. My true name is Petar Gondwell. But Chakthalla prefers to call me Pet."

"Why do you let her?"

"Why not? It makes her happy."

"But don't you want your own identity? Don't you want what makes you happy?"

"Making Chakthalla happy makes me happy."

Jandra felt a little ill hearing this, thinking of how she enjoyed pleasing Vendevorex when she did well with her lessons.

"You don't like my being Chakthalla's pet," he said in a matter-of-fact tone. "It makes you question your servitude to Vendevorex."

He is perceptive, thought Jandra.

"You dislike the idea that people are owned by dragons," Pet ventured. "You want your freedom."

"I have my freedom," Jandra said. "Vendevorex doesn't own me. He's just... my mentor. My parents died when their house burned down. He's raised me but he doesn't own me."

"Ah. If you are free then you can leave his service at any time."

"I suppose. But..."

"But?"

"I don't know where I would go."

"Ah." Pet nodded. "That is a problem, isn't it? He has you bound by ignorance of the world. This shackles you far more effectively than iron."

Jandra thought about Vendevorex's revelation of lands beyond the kingdom. Had he kept her in the dark to limit her possibilities? Who knew what lay beyond the mountains? Perhaps there were places where humans ruled dragons. That would certainly explain his reluctance to discuss them.

"I won't say that Vendevorex has me in shackles," she said. "But it bothers me the way he's always keeping quiet about his plans. He just announces our next move and expects me to follow. He never consults me."

"It's the way of dragons," said Pet. "They can never consider humans as equals. Asking a human for advice is as absurd to them as us asking a dog what the weather will be like."

Jandra nodded. "I must admit, you surprise me. You seemed so subservient to Chakthalla. I just assumed you let her do all your thinking for you."

"She thinks she does all my thinking for me. In truth, I am the sole master of my fate, fair Jandra. Humans are dealt a very bad hand. In the villages, men struggle to survive. Some become comfortable but none may become wealthy. The only humans to gain a semblance of power are the prophets that seem to grow like mushrooms after floods and plagues. But what do prophets do with their power? Wage war against the non-believers in the next village who are following their own prophet. In the end, there is little profit in prophecy."

"No," she said. "I suppose not."

"But to live among dragons is a far different fate," Pet said. "As a favorite of a dragon I am showered with jewels. I sleep on sheets of silk; I drink from cups of gold. All Chakthalla asks in exchange are a few tricks and a sympathetic ear."

"It sounds attractive when you put it that way," Jandra said. "But still, to be a pet... have you no pride?"

"I take pride in a job well done," Pet said with a slight bow. "I am an actor, a singer, an acrobat, a poet: a master of diverse arts and talents. I think of Chakthalla as my patron rather than my keeper."

"But Chakthalla owns you," Jandra said. "You don't have freedom."

He shrugged. "A vastly overrated commodity in my opinion. Do I want the freedom to be poor? Do I want the freedom to tear my food from the hard earth, to struggle daily to endure? No. This way is better. As Petar I could pursue nothing but daily toil. As Pet I can pursue the finer things in life. Beautiful women such as yourself, for instance, are found only in the courts of dragons."

"Please," Jandra said, rolling her eyes. "I'm not beautiful."

"Oh dear. He doesn't tell you, does he?"

"Doesn't tell me what?"

"Vendevorex never tells you how lovely you are."

Jandra lowered her head. "No. He doesn't."

"Dragons know nothing of human hearts. The loveliest woman never sees her own beauty with her eyes until she sees it with her heart."

Jandra sat quietly, contemplating his words. Beautiful? Pet was beautiful. Bodiel had been beautiful. She was just plain. Wasn't she? She felt slightly dizzy at the possibility.

"I think," she said, "I should go back to my chambers."

"Why?" Pet asked.

"I'm tired," she said, though she wasn't. She was nervous for reasons she didn't quite understand, but she couldn't tell him that. "It's been a long day."

"Vendevorex will expect you to sleep in his quarters?" Pet asked.

"I suppose," she said. "I normally do."

"Do you always do what he wants you to do?"

"I don't sleep there because he wants me to. I sleep there because we're on the run. Where else am I to sleep?"

"My chambers. I have the most wonderful bed. The moment your body touches it, I guarantee you will be in ecstasy."

"Oh," she said. "I, um…"

"There are many areas in which a person may be shackled by a lack of knowledge," Pet said slyly. "I have a key. I can teach you many things. Open doors to worlds you haven't even dreamed of."

Pet's gaze met hers and held it for a long moment. She found his stare most unsettling.

"I should... should go now," she said. Yet her body didn't seem to agree. It remained frozen on the window ledge, her lips parted, her eyes fixed on his deep emerald eyes. With effort, she turned away, looking back over the fields. The moving mass she had seen in the distance was much closer now, practically at the castle walls. It no longer looked like a herd of cattle. What was going on? Then she noticed a score of lights in the sky, moving more erratically than stars. She focused upon them and could see the dark shapes of sky-dragons above. They swooped closer and she saw that the lights came from small iron pots dangling from chains.

"Oh no," she said.

She spun around and jumped from the window. She landed, to her surprise, in Pet's arms. He lowered her to her feet, his face only inches from her own. Then, without warning, he lowered his lips to hers. She'd never been kissed before. She stood there, stunned, all but paralyzed with the shock of it. He smelled wonderful. Pet wrapped his arms around her. She noticed how well her body fit against his. Could this really be happening?

A voice in the back of her head kept yelling that she had more important things to attend to at the moment, and at last she listened to this voice. She summoned the strength to push Pet away.

"There isn't time for this! I've got to get to Vendevorex!" she said.

"That's your fear speaking, fair one," he said, his voice a gentle coo. "It's not the voice of your heart."

"No! You don't understand!"

Pet grabbed her by the arms and kissed her again. She struggled but his strength was far greater that hers. This time it wasn't even mildly pleasant. She beat at his back with her clenched fists.

At last he broke the kiss, pushing her away, but not letting go of her arms, "I apologize. Your beauty has caused me to lose all caution. I've pushed you too far, too fast. You're scared. You're young, confused by the stirrings in your body, confused by the burning in your soul."

"It's not my soul I'm worried about!" she snapped, but her words were drowned by the beating of wings. Light bright as day flashed through the window. A burning cauldron crashed against the far wall then clattered as it bounced around the room, throwing flames in all directions.

CHAPTER TEN

WAR

THE FLAMES SPREAD across the far wall as the iron pot rolled to rest. A river of flames spilled down the steps, cutting off their exit. The stone stairs hissed and popped as the flames ate at them.

"Don't breathe the smoke!" Jandra shouted, grabbing Pet's arm and pulling away from the flames. "It's poisonous!"

"It's burning the rocks in the walls!" Pet yelped.

"It's called the Vengeance of the Ancestors," Jandra said, letting go of Pet. She studied her surroundings. "It burns rock, wood, even water. Everything but iron." The only way out was the window. She leapt up to grab the ledge then scrambled quickly up the rough stone. Once perched in the window she leaned down and extended a hand to Pet.

"How do you know about this?" Pet asked, taking her hand.

"Vendevorex invented it," Jandra said as she helped Pet climb onto the ledge next to her. "At least the wind is blowing in our favor. We'll be safe from the smoke in here. You know this castle better than me. Isn't there another window below us? Maybe twenty feet?"

"Y-yes," he said, not taking his eyes from the flames.

Jandra studied the flames as well, trying to guess how much time they had. The Vengeance burned thoroughly but it burned slowly when dense materials like stone were its fuel. Even though it had splashed over half of the room, it would take a long time to spread to this wall. Unfortunately, the Vengeance had ignited the wooden roof beams that now burned with conventional flames. The breeze from the open window that kept the worst of the smoke away also fueled the fire that devoured the beams. The thick wooden shafts supported the tall, thin metal spires that topped the towers. It wouldn't take long before it all collapsed on top of them.

Outside the window Jandra could see other fires burning across the castle. The dark shapes of sky-dragons swooped and glided among the rising smoke. She looked down. To her relief, no flames were directly below them.

"Take off your shirt, Pet," she said.

The panicked look vanished from Pet's face. He raised an eyebrow as he asked, "If we're going to die, you want to die in a passionate embrace?" He gave a confident grin as he began unlacing his shirt. His fingers flew with well-practiced speed.

"You really have a one track mind, don't you?" Jandra said. "Silk is very strong. It will make a good rope."

"My shirt isn't long enough to reach the lower window," Pet said, sounding a bit disappointed.

"It will be," Jandra said, taking the shirt from him the instant he pulled it over his head.

She dipped her fingers into the small pouch of silver dust she carried on her belt. She carefully closed her right hand around the sleeve of his shirt then closed her eyes, so as not to be distracted by the flame. With her left hand she pulled the small tuft of silk she had left showing and began to pull it from her hand. Instead of the shirtsleeve, a silk cord as thick as her little finger emerged from her grasp. Pulling more rapidly, she soon ran the entire shirt through her right hand, leaving her with thirty feet of coiled silken rope.

"Good trick," said Pet, nodding appreciatively.

"It's not a trick," Jandra said. "What you did with the apple... that was a trick. This is something much more complex. I've been studying with Vendevorex all my life. He's teaching me how to reconfigure the basic building blocks of matter." Jandra stood up on the wide windowsill. She reached up, tying the rope around the roof beam that extended outside the tower. She dropped the rope. The end dangled just below the lower window.

"Okay," she said, "Let's—"

She was cut short by a horrendous creaking. She looked into the room and saw that the Vengeance had climbed the far wall and cut into the copper plates that formed the roof. She yelled, "Don't breathe!"

But it was too late. A large copper plate twisted free and fell into the room amidst the Vengeance of the Ancestors, sending large billows of smoke toward them. Jandra tried to inhale one last breath of clean air in the instant before it reached them. Instead, her lungs filled with the awful smell of phosphorous and sulfur. Her lungs felt full of needles as she began to cough uncontrollably. Dark spots danced before her eyes as her strength failed. She was vaguely aware of her feet slipping from the ledge as she tumbled backward into the night air.

"WHAT'S HAPPENING?" ZEEKY mumbled as Poocher's squeals awakened her.

"Sorry to disturb you," Hey You said as he lifted her in his arms and set her onto the straw. "I need my cloak. There's work to be done."

"What's that noise?" Zeeky asked, hearing guttural shouts in the distance, and the faint clangs of metal against metal.

"War. The dragons fight the dragons."

"Why?" she asked, sitting up.

"That's of no concern to me. Whatever cause dragons are prepared to die for tonight, I feel obligated to help them along. The family in the farmhouse should be awake by now. I'm going to leave you with them."

"No!" Zeeky protested. "They'll take me back!"

"Back where?"

"Oh. Ah," Zeeky muttered, hugging her knees as she looked at the floor. "To the orphanage?"

"You can always run away again," Hey You said as he fastened the sheathed knife to his boot. "Running away's easy."

"Why can't I go with you?"

"I'm going someplace little girls shouldn't go."

"Where?"

"To hell, eventually," Hey You said. While he tied his cloak around his neck he stared at her straight in the eyes and asked, "You coming voluntarily?"

"What's 'voluntarily' mean?"

"Fine," he said, scooping her up under one arm and lifting his bow with the other.

Zeeky screamed as Hey You jumped from the loft. But the ground was closer than she guessed and when they hit, Hey You curled into a ball around Zeeky and rolled forward once, then sprang to his feet. It happened so fast Zeeky didn't even get dizzy. She could hear Poocher squealing frantically above them.

"Wait!" she yelled. "I'll go! I'll go! But I have to take Poocher!"

"Forget the pig," Hey You said as he carried her from the dark barn into the starlit night.

"No! He's my friend!"

Hey You stopped and muttered several words Zeeky had never heard before. He put her down and darted back into the barn. He leapt to the ladder leading to the loft, bounding up the rungs quicker than she could blink. Poocher squealed more emphatically as Hey You again leapt from the loft, this time curling into a ball around Poocher as he landed, then rolled to his feet. Now that she wasn't part of the jump, Zeeky thought it looked fun.

Hey You grabbed her by the hand and ran across the yard. Lights glowed from inside the farmhouse. Zeeky could see flames at the dragon's castle, with the tallest spire engulfed completely in a pillar of fire, blazing like the world's largest candle.

Hey You pounded on the farmer's door. "Open up!" he shouted. "It's a fellow human who summons you."

The door opened quickly and Hey You dragged Zeeky into the house, into the presence of a frightened-looking family. The farmer and his wife looked young, much younger than Zeeky's own parents. Zeeky was relieved to see that they had a girl, a little smaller than Zeeky. Her own family was all boys except for her mother.

"I need you to watch after my daughter for a short time," Hey You said. "We're travelers, far from home, and I know no one who can watch her."

"But…" the farmer said.

"Where are you going?" the wife asked.

"To battle," Hey You said.

"To attack the castle, or to defend it?" the farmer asked.

"To attack the dragons," Hey You answered. "Will you watch her or not? Time is short."

"Of course," the wife said.

"But…" the farmer said.

"Of course," the wife said more firmly.

The farmer shrugged and said, "Of course."

"Good. She comes with a pig," Hey You said, handing Poocher to the farmer. "Don't eat it."

"Um," said the farmer.

Zeeky tugged Hey You's pant leg. He looked down into her eyes. She said, "Promise you'll come back?"

Perhaps it was only a trick of the dim light, but it seemed to her that Hey You's face turned ghostly pale. He stared at her for a long moment before whispering, "I promise."

Then, he turned to the farmer and his wife and said, more firmly, "Thank you both for your kindness."

Before another word could be spoken he stepped backward through the door and vanished into the night.

JANDRA WOKE UP. The ground lay far beneath her, swirling, spinning, swimming in colors. A heavy weight pressed against her stomach and she remembered she was falling. She closed her eyes, bracing for impact.

But the wind wasn't rushing against her face. The seconds it should take her to reach the ground were dragging by. She opened her eyes again, blinking to clear her vision. The rope swayed above her, or rather, beneath her, since her head was pointed earthward. The lower window crept ever closer. Looking down and then up, she found herself face to face with Pet's butt. His feet were pressed against the wall for balance. She was slung over his shoulder. He grunted with each inch as he lowered them, hand-over-hand, down the rope.

"You awake?" Pet asked, his voice strained.

"How'd you know?" she said, coughing as the remnants of smoke in her lungs raked her throat.

"You aren't limp anymore."

"You caught me when I fell out the window?" she asked. She could vaguely recall his strong hand wrapping around her wrist at the last second.

"I'm a sucker for a damsel in distress," he said.

Pet's feet reached the top edge of the lower window.

"Almost there," Jandra said.

Pet stepped down, feeling for his next foothold, but his foot slipped into the open window. They lurched sideways, slamming into the wall. Pet cursed as he struggled to maintain his grip on the thin, slick rope.

Suddenly, they lurched down even further, another three feet, placing them well past the top edge of the window. Jandra watched as comets of flaming oak and copper rained past them, exploding on the distant ground below.

"The beam's shifting!" Pet yelled. "It's going to break!" His toes touched the lower edge of the window but his body angled out into space. Jandra knew he couldn't pull himself into the window with her weight on him. She tried to rise, reaching her hand up behind her to grab the rope.

"Don't struggle!" Pet said. "I'm losing my grip!"

Jandra's hand found the rope and she pulled herself up, taking her weight from his shoulder. Pet lost his toehold on the ledge and they swayed away from the window, the rope twisting. As it swung back in Jandra let go, her momentum taking her onto the ledge. She waved her arms for balance then quickly turned. Pet had swung back out. As he swung once more toward the window, Jandra grabbed him by his belt.

"Let go!" she said, pulling backward as he started to sway away.

Pet released the rope and they both tumbled from the ledge, falling backward into the tower. They landed on a soft cotton cushion, big enough for a sun-dragon to curl up on comfortably. Shadows and light danced around the chamber as flaming debris fell past the window.

Jandra lay trapped beneath Pet's muscular body, looking into his face which was framed by a mane of golden hair. His bare chest pressed firmly against her breasts. His lips were inches from her own. She stared into Pet's deep, emerald eyes, seeing the powerful emotion that stirred within them.

"What the hell is going on?" Pet shouted, his voice cracking with fear.

"The castle is under attack," she said.

"Yes! I know! We were almost killed!"

"Calm down. Panic won't help."

"I don't see how it's hurting anything!"

"You're hurting me," she said. Her breath was still painful and his weight on her wasn't helping. "Get off."

"Oh," he said, looking as if he just now realized he was on top of her. "Right. Sure." He rolled off, sitting up, looking dazed. "This just isn't how I planned to spend the evening at all," he whined.

She sat up, bracing her back against the wall.

"As soon as I catch my breath, we'll go," she said.

"Where?" Pet said, shaking his head. "It looked like the whole castle was on fire. Why is this happening?"

"Albekizan must know we're here," Jandra said, taking a deep breath and then coughing again. "We need to find Vendevorex. Fight by his side to defend this castle."

"Fight?" Pet said, twisting a long strand of his golden mane around his fingers. "I don't know anything about fighting!"

"Would you calm down?"

At that moment the rope hanging outside the window slackened and the flaming roof beam roared past the window. Glowing embers showered the room. Thin white twigs of smoke rose from several spots on the cushion.

"We're going to die!" Pet screamed.

"If we stay here, probably," Jandra said, struggling back to her feet. "Come on." Jandra grabbed Pet's hand, helping him rise. She pulled him toward the hallway. "Vendevorex will know what to do."

Halfway down the hallway she heard a crash behind them. The crash kept rumbling for an absurdly long time. Smoke and dust rolled through the corridor as the hot wind at her back pushed her to move faster. She suspected the whole tower had finally collapsed, but she didn't dare look back. She pushed ahead, ignoring the needles in her chest, dragging Pet along.

The further they went, the more her breath returned. Soon, she broke into a run with Pet still in tow. Racing through the halls of the castle, Jandra heard the sounds of battle all around. She hadn't been in Chakthalla's palace long enough to get a feel for what kind of army she commanded. She'd seen perhaps a hundred earth-dragon guards but nothing like the force outside the castle walls. And Chakthalla's earth-dragons had seemed to exist primarily as dolls to be costumed in elaborate uniforms. She'd seen very few of the rough, ill-tempered brutes that populated Albekizan's ground forces.

Still, Albekizan's army was *outside* the walls. This battle wasn't over yet. Vendevorex could even the odds, she was certain. The Vengeance of the

Ancestors the attackers used must have come from a supply Vendevorex had created. He could extinguish it with a wave of his hand. Better, he could turn it against the attackers.

They ran through the long, tall passageways to Vendevorex's room. Luckily, this section of the castle was silent; the battle was being waged far from this area. But when Jandra pushed open the door to his chambers her heart sank. Empty. Vendevorex was nowhere to be seen. *Of course,* she thought, *he would already be at Chakthalla's side.*

"Jandra!" Vendevorex said, his voice coming from thin air.

"A ghost!" Pet cried, jumping at the sound.

"Calm down," Jandra said. "He's only invisible."

"Calm down! Of course!" Pet began to chew his immaculately trimmed nails. "I see invisible dragons every day!"

"My apologies," Vendevorex said, shimmering into view as the air around him erupted in sparks. "I didn't mean to frighten you, Pet."

"Don't worry about him," Jandra said. "We've got a bigger problem. The attackers are using the Vengeance! You've got to put it out."

"That would be unwise," Vendevorex said.

"What?" She couldn't believe she'd heard him right.

"The castle is woefully under-defended," Vendevorex said with a calm, observational tone that one might expect if he were discussing the weather. "It will fall to Albekizan's forces no matter what we do. Better he gain possession of ruins than another base from which to command his armies."

"I can't believe this," Jandra said. "You're conceding defeat before we've even started fighting?"

Vendevorex sighed. He placed his claw on her shoulder and looked her in the eyes and explained, as if to a child, "We aren't going to fight. We're going to run. I fled the castle of Albekizan because I cared for your safety. It would be foolish now to endanger your life fighting a battle we cannot win."

Jandra pushed his claw away. She poked his scaly chest with her finger as she said, "This isn't like running from Albekizan. He wanted to kill you! Chakthalla wants to help you!"

"You must see that her desires are not supported by her resources," Vendevorex said.

Jandra felt like slapping him.

"For what it's worth, sir," Pet interrupted, "I have a box of jewels in my room that could be of great assistance in a relocation. If you'll take me with you, please."

"What?" Jandra said, cutting him a withering look. "You're going to run, too? This is your home!"

Pet nodded. He looked sheepish as he said, "Please don't think ill of me. I'm a good person... I really am. But your master is making a lot of sense."

"If you were a good person, you'd stay and fight!"

"Think about this," Pet said. "If Chakthalla wins this battle, what then? The king will send a bigger army. We won't stand a chance. Your master is right. Please listen to him."

"Stop calling him my *master*," Jandra snapped. "My relationship with Ven is nothing like what's between you and Chakthalla. Tell him, Ven."

"I don't possess enough information to assess the state of Pet and Chakthalla's relationship," Vendevorex said. "In all candor, this isn't the best time to discuss this."

"So you truly don't care for Chakthalla?" Jandra asked Pet. "When you look at her all lovey-eyed and call her Mother, that's only an act?"

Pet shrugged. "I'm a good actor. I know who butters my bread. Unfortunately, Chakthalla's not going to have any butter left once this place burns down."

"Well argued," Vendevorex said. "It sounds cold but it's simple truth. Chakthalla is doomed. We doom ourselves by remaining."

"You're both cowards!" Jandra shouted. "You're looking out for your own skins and not thinking twice about the ones who will die. They're dying because of you, Ven! They're dying from the weapon that you created. The king wouldn't be attacking if it weren't for you stirring up the possibility of rebellion."

"Jandra," Vendevorex said, lowering his voice. "We will not discuss this now. Gather your belongings."

"What about me?" Pet asked.

"Retrieve your jewels," Vendevorex said. "You may accompany us from the premises under the shield of invisibility."

"Fine," Jandra said. "You've got a new pet, Ven. You won't be needing me. I've got more important things to do."

Jandra turned and raced toward Chakthalla's chambers, blinking away the tears that blurred her vision. Vendevorex shouted her name, calling her back, but she had no reason to listen to another word he said.

JANDRA FOUND CHAKTHALLA in the throne room, a cathedral-like hall that jutted perpendicularly from the main castle. The stained-glass windows along the tops of the side walls danced with the lights of the flames outside, casting colorful shadows around the room, painting the white marble floors with scenes of ruby dragons floating in amethyst skies above emerald fields.

Chakthalla's throne was a giant, gilded pedestal, draped with blood-red satin. Chakthalla slumped on her throne, her head lowered to the floor, her eyes fixed on the doorway in which Jandra stood. Her expression was blank as if she were numb with shock. Her ruby wings draped to each side, spreading onto the floor like carpet. Her fore-claws clutched her breast as if she were feeling her breaking heart. The flickering light gave the illusion that her feathery scales ruffled in a breeze. At her side was a huge spear, twenty feet long, the sort only sun-dragons such as herself could wield.

"My lady," Jandra said, hurrying forward. "I've come to help defend your castle."

Chakthalla followed Jandra with her eyes as she advanced but she did not speak.

"Chakthalla? If you'll tell me what to do to help, I'll do it. My skills aren't as great as Vendevorex's, but I can turn invisible, and transmute simple materials, and—" Jandra stopped short as she reached the throne.

Chakthalla continued to stare at her but now Jandra could see the dark blood seeping down her chin.

Jandra's eyes moved to the dragon's bejeweled talons. She could see the fine red scales glistening with moisture. Wet red spots dripped to the marble floor.

Chakthalla dropped her claws to her sides. The enormous gash in her breast was revealed. Her eyes closed as her body convulsed, sliding clumsily from the pedestal and sprawling at Jandra's feet.

A long metal blade protruded from Chakthalla's back, gleaming in the firelight. Suddenly, a claw so deeply green it looked black rose from behind the pedestal. Long nails dug into the satin. Then the assassin leapt to the top of the throne, crouching upon it. It was an earth-dragon, one of the Black Silences, a unit in the dragon army bred for espionage and assassination. Some mutation had rendered this subspecies of the earth-dragons a deeper hue than their brethren, and had gifted them with unnatural speed. The dragon's scales were so dark they sucked in the light around him. His eyes burned like dim coals as they studied Jandra. Then his gaze shifted toward the blade in Chakthalla's back.

"Why not try for the sword?" the assassin hissed. "You might make it."

Jandra turned to run, reaching for the dust in her pouch so that she could become invisible. She tossed the dust into the air but too late. The dragon tackled her squarely in the back and she fell forward. The assassin was no taller than her but he was solid. His weight crushed all breath from her as he pressed her to the cold, hard floor.

Still pinning her down with his mass, the dragon wrapped his left claw into her hair and pulled her head backward. Her mouth opened in a silent, breathless cry of pain. The sharp nails of his right claw flashed before her eyes.

"Chakthalla was too important to play with," the assassin whispered, his beak next to her ear. "Now that my work is done, I think I deserve a moment to revel in your screams."

He drew his claw along her cheek, his nails dragging along her skin with just the proper force to not cut her. Jandra felt the sharp claws caressing her cheek, her chin, and her throat. The slightest extra pressure would open her veins.

Fortunately, there were still traces of silver dust on her fingers. The combat training Vendevorex had subjected her to would prove useful after all. She grabbed the dragon's wrist and concentrated. With the same talent she'd used to turn Pet's shirt into a rope, she began to reshape her assailant's hide and bones. His wrist melted beneath her fingertips... too slowly. He shrieked in pain. Then, with a slashing motion, he yanked his injured claw up and out.

For half a second Jandra felt nothing. She tried to breathe and wound up swallowing blood. She coughed, spitting a fine spray of crimson on the marble before her. It was only then that she understood her throat had been slit.

fLESH

"YOU'LL DIE FOR that," the Black Silence snarled. Jandra heard a blade being drawn from its sheath. It sounded very far away, far beyond the heartbeat that pounded in her own ears. She pressed her hand to her throat. Air bubbled from the gash beneath her bloody fingers as she coughed.

Jandra tried to concentrate. There was still a chance to use the dust lingering on her fingers to reshape the flesh of her own throat, to knit the wound. But her mind was locked up, frozen.

The weight on her spine shifted as the Black Silence pulled her head back further. The blood gushed between her fingers more freely. She peered up to see the tip of a dagger high overhead. When it fell it would plunge into her throat. She closed her eyes, anticipating the blow.

Three seconds later, the dagger failed to fall. A rain of fine particles fell against her face. Suddenly the claw that pulled her hair went slack. Her face hit the marble with a tooth-jarring *thump*. She opened her eyes as a hilt bounced on the marble floor before her, its blade only a shard of crumbling rust. Fine red flakes continued to drift to the floor. The weight on her back vanished as the Black Silence let loose a pained gasp.

The assassin gurgled, then squealed. The smell of burning flesh tainted the air.

Hands fell upon her shoulders—a man's hands— rolling her over until her head lay in his lap. She looked up into Pet's concerned face.

"It's going to be okay," he said, pressing his fingers to her throat, pinching the torn flesh closed. "Ven says to keep calm and he'll help you."

She gasped for breath. She sucked blood into her lungs... but air as well. How bad was her wound? Where was Ven? The room was spinning slowly. She cast her gaze about the room but couldn't find him. Her assailant's screams came from a patch of air before her. His voice faded in a series of brief, weak sobs. No one could be seen in the hall except for Pet and herself. Then she spotted the smoke hanging in the air, the bottom edge of the cloud cut into an almost perfect arc. The assassin's voice rattled into silence.

The upper half of the earth-dragon's body appeared suddenly as it slumped to the floor, the charred flesh of the face flaking away in the outline of a three-fingered hand, revealing the skull beneath. Without warning the dragon's legs appeared, and Vendevorex also, standing at the slain assassin's feet. Smoke rose from the foretalons of the now visible mage, and his eyes were narrowed in a look of grim determination.

He crouched beside Pet and said, "Move."

Pet moved his hands away from Jandra's throat. Vendevorex's claws touched her, exploring the wound. She arched her back in agony as his nails probed beneath her skin.

"Don't struggle," he said. "I'm going to knit your trachea closed. The wound didn't reach the jugular. In five minutes this will only be a bad memory."

Jandra nodded. For once she appreciated Vendevorex's cool, emotionless approach. He was looking at her wound as mere matter to be rearranged. If he was frightened or worried by the task, it didn't show in his impassive expression.

He worked in silence for several long moments. The distant sound of battle grew louder but Vendevorex's eyes never strayed from the task. Pet continued to cradle Jandra's head in his lap and didn't let go of her hand. Her eyes met his. She saw all the emotion that was missing from Ven's face… the worry, yes, but also the hope.

Jandra realized, suddenly, that her breathing was easier. There was no blood in her mouth anymore. She swallowed and found no pain.

"Perhaps now you can see the logic of my position," Vendevorex said, wiping the remaining blood away from her throat. It felt as if his fingers were stroking smooth, unbroken skin. "Chakthalla is dead. Staying here provides the possibility of defeat without the slimmest hope of victory. Will you come with me now?"

"Okay," she whispered. Her throat tingled, the way an arm that has been laid on too long will tingle when the pressure is released.

"Good," said Vendevorex.

"Great," said Pet, breaking into a smile. "Let's get going. I just have one small thing I need to do."

Pet helped Jandra to her feet before going to Chakthalla's body and kneeling before it. Pet lowered his head as he took her limp claws. Jandra was moved by his sorrow until she saw him pull the golden rings from Chakthalla's talons and then rudely let her limbs drop back to the floor.

He stuffed the rings into his pocket as he stood. "I'm ready," he said without a trace of remorse in his voice.

Jandra turned to Vendevorex. "This is the wrong place and the wrong time to say this," she said.

"Then don't say it," said Vendevorex.

"I have to," she said. "I don't know what you feel for me. I don't know if you think of me as your daughter, your apprentice, your slave, or your pet. It doesn't matter. I love you, Ven. You're like a father to me."

"How touching," a deep voice said from the doorway.

Jandra turned to see a huge spear flashing through the air as fast and straight as a ray of light. It dug into Vendevorex's side, sending him to his knees. Vendevorex gave a pained cry as he grabbed the spear with both hands, struggling with its weight.

In the doorway stood Zanzeroth the hunter and his slave Gadreel, both of whom Jandra recognized from Albekizan's court.

"Gadreel, take care of the humans," Zanzeroth said, drawing a long blade from a leather sheath strapped to his waist. "The wizard's mine."

VENDEVOREX SUMMONED A shield of invisibility to swirl around him—not that it mattered while the spear jutted from his side. The long shaft lay beyond the edge of his shield, betraying his position. The pain made it impossible to concentrate but he couldn't give up now. He'd just saved Jandra's life. If he didn't pull his wits together, that would all be a waste. She'd die just as surely as he would.

He squeezed the shaft with his claws, twisting it slightly, purposefully increasing the pain, to focus the agony from a cloud that fogged his mind into a tight beam that pierced his center. His mind clear, he set to work, reaching into the very forces that bound the wood together, loosening them. The spear shaft glowed brightly, then vanished with a sizzle in a spray of bubbling light.

Vendevorex rolled forward as Zanzeroth landed where he'd been when the shaft hit. Zanzeroth held a long, curved knife in one claw and a whip in the other. Vendevorex could tell by the way the hunter held his head that his circle of invisibility was working perfectly. Zanzeroth couldn't see him.

But a pool of blood marked the spot where Vendevorex had been, and a line of red drops marked the path where he'd fled. Zanzeroth whirled his whip in a half-circle behind his head then flicked it. The leather raced around Vendevorex's neck before he even knew what had happened. With a savage yank Zanzeroth jerked

Vendevorex forward, out of his field of invisibility. Vendevorex fell to the marble before Zanzeroth's feet. Zanzeroth loomed above him, nearly twice his size, and Vendevorex could only flail helplessly as the hunter placed his clawed foot onto the back of his neck, pinning him.

"This need not be painful, wizard," Zanzeroth said. "Albekizan wants your head. You can keep everything else."

JANDRA SCURRIED BACKWARD. She grabbed the assassin's sword from Chakthalla's back with a wet *slurp* as Gadreel flew toward her. Gadreel was a sky dragon like Vendevorex, slightly taller than a man with a wingspan twice his height. She was out matched physically, but if she could hold out for even a minute to get out of his line of sight and turn invisible, she stood a chance.

She ducked and Gadreel's claws raced by, inches above her. She heard him flap his wings up to land before he hit the back wall of the chamber. She threw a handful of dust into the air, turning invisible just as he spun around to attack again. Now she could strike him by surprise. With luck she'd kill him before he ever knew what hit him. The sword was heavier than she had guessed, however, and her hands were drenched with slick sweat and her own blood, making it hard to hold. Her breath came in loud, ragged gasps that she feared would betray her position. Her throat was okay now, but it felt as if half her ribs were broken from the assassin's tackle.

Gadreel drew his own sword and inched forward, slicing the air before him savagely. Jandra crept to the side to strike at his back as he passed.

To the surprise of both of them, Pet let loose with a bloodcurdling cry and charged Gadreel while carrying Chakthalla's oversized spear. Jandra was impressed; not many humans could wield such a huge weapon. Alas, Pet didn't wield it well. His charge was slow and clumsy. Gadreel turned away from Jandra to face the attack.

VENDEVOREX GROWLED, HIS rage rising with the humiliation of being under his former ally's talon. He raised his fore-talon to grasp Zanzeroth's ankle. Flames burst from around his claws.

Zanzeroth cursed and jumped backward, freeing Vendevorex. The old dragon beat at the flaming scales on his ankle, extinguishing them.

"You dare?" Vendevorex snarled, rising to full height and ignoring the pain that pierced him. "I am the Master of the Invisible! I control matter itself!" He spread his wings and crafted the simple illusion that made him double in size. "Have you forgotten who you are dealing with?" he shouted. "I am Vendevorex!"

"I am unimpressed," said Zanzeroth. With a flick and a flash, his long silver knife sliced through the air.

Vendevorex choked as the knife sank squarely into his shoulder, paralyzing his right wing. He pulled the knife free with his left claw and staggered backward. Before he could blink Zanzeroth stood before him, raking his claws savagely across Vendevorex's eyes. The old dragon then twirled, slamming Vendevorex's belly with his heavy tail. Vendevorex began to fall, all strength gone, when Zanzeroth spun back around and grabbed him by the throat. The old sun-dragon lifted Vendevorex as if he were weightless, holding him in the air as steady as a gallows.

"You scare the king," Zanzeroth said, taking the knife Vendevorex still held in his feeble grasp. "But I've studied you for years. You're one-tenth magic and nine-tenths bluff. You need time to think to do your tricks. Right now I'm guessing all you'll be thinking about is this!"

Zanzeroth sank his knife to the hilt into Vendevorex's belly.

"And this!" he shouted, pulling the knife free and driving it home again.

"And this!" The knife once more plunged into Vendevorex's gut.

"And this!"

"And this!"

The hunter's voice seemed to fade, washed away by the roar within Vendevorex's ears. Zanzeroth's leering face vanished behind a growing dark veil Vendevorex could no longer feel his body. Only some slender thread of intellect remained, coolly observing the scene. He felt as if he were outside himself, watching the sad, limp doll dangling in the giant dragon's grasp. He stared with grim fascination as blood and feces and urine showered onto the marble around Zanzeroth's feet. Then, as the world around him went black, leaving him alone in a vast, formless void, he set to work.

PET CRIED OUT savagely as he charged with the heavy spear of his former mistress. Gadreel pivoted at the last second, dodging the tip, then knocked the shaft aside. Pet tripped forward as the spear flew from his hands. His momentum took him straight toward Gadreel who raised his sword to strike.

"No!" Jandra shouted, leaping onto Gadreel's back and thrusting her own sword with all her strength. The blade tore into the dragon's wing near the junction with his back. Gadreel cried out in pain, bringing his sword down against Pet, but poorly aimed. The flat of the blade whacked the side of Pet's head, making the steel blade tremble. It pealed like a bell. Pet's eyes rolled toward the ceiling as he fell to the floor.

Jandra braced her feet and pushed forward, pressing her weight against her sword. The blade struck something hard within the dragon, then lurched sideways, tearing from the skin of his back. Jandra fell against Gadreel and as she slammed into him, the sword twisted from her wet hands.

The dragon turned, grabbing Jandra by the arm, digging his claws deep into her muscles. He flung her around, releasing her. She slammed against the heavy throne pedestal, then fell atop Chakthalla's body. She looked up at the spinning world. She could see Zanzeroth tearing viciously at Vendevorex's belly. Pet lay helpless on his back, knocked senseless. Gadreel advanced toward her, his sword held ready to strike. Yet he moved cautiously and his eyes watched her warily.

There was no one to help her. Her head throbbed, keeping her from concentrating enough to turn invisible. She wondered briefly where Chakthalla's guards were. Surely some still lived; there could be a last-second rescue.

Almost as if wishing it made it happen, four earth-dragons rushed through the doors of the throne room, spears lowered for attack. These dragons weren't bedecked in the fine uniforms that Chakthalla forced upon her guards. They must have been awakened by the noise of the battle, and rushed into combat in their half-naked, savage state. Hope stirred within Jandra as she saw the bloodlust in their eyes.

"Sir?" one of them asked.

"Everything's under control here," Zanzeroth answered, releasing his grasp on the wizard's throat. Vendevorex sagged lifelessly to the floor.

Jandra's heart sank. The dragons were soldiers of the king.

With Vendevorex dead, she didn't know what she had left to live for. She watched as Zanzeroth lifted one of Vendevorex's wings, limp as cloth, and used it to wipe his gore-soaked knife clean.

Jandra couldn't find the will to raise her arms to defend herself as Gadreel stalked carefully forward. She looked up into his golden eyes and found no hint of mercy there. Beyond Gadreel she saw one of the stained-glass windows that ran along the room's upper half. The pane she gazed upon portrayed a scene of a dragon battling a small group of humans. All around the great beast the humans' torn bodies lay scattered. A lone survivor knelt before the dragon, his arms raised, begging to live. The look in the stained-glass dragon's eyes and the gape of its long, open jaws over the man's head showed there would be no mercy.

A shadow flickered behind the glass, darkening the scene. It looked almost like the form of a man. Just as Gadreel prepared to strike, the window shattered.

Gadreel looked over his shoulder. Zanzeroth glanced up at the noise. Shards of colorful glass fell to the ground like a broken rainbow. The dark form of a cloaked man stood in the window, outlined by the flames of the castle wall beyond.

"You!" Zanzeroth shouted.

The figure pushed aside his cloak and raised his bow as the soldiers drew back their spears. An arrow whistled through the air in a red streak. The closest earth-dragon fell, an arrow jutting from the orb of his right eye. Before his body hit the floor a second arrow flew home to the heart of the next dragon. With a speed Jandra's eyes could barely follow, the human nocked a fourth arrow as his third arrow sliced into another soldier's throat. The final earth-dragon spun, preparing to run, when the arrow pierced its kidney.

The human then turned his attention toward Zanzeroth who flapped his wings, trying to get airborne. The hall—huge by human standards—was too small for the sun-dragon to build up sufficient speed. Arrows sank into his shoulders, his back, and his wings as he cried in pain and frustration. Then, in a wound that made Jandra shudder, an arrow sank into Zanzeroth's nostril, the tip of the arrowhead suddenly visible in the roof of the dragon's gaping mouth.

Zanzeroth roared with pain. "Thith cannot happen!" the sun-dragon shouted with an almost comical lisp as he crashed to the floor. "I am the hunter! You are the prey!"

"You can track me through hell," the man answered, taking aim for Zanzeroth's heart.

Unfortunately, the hall was more than large enough for a dragon of Gadreel's size to take wing.

The dragon slave turned from Jandra and leapt into the air. Despite his injured back Gadreel strained to beat his wings, climbing toward the window.

"Not this time!" Gadreel cried.

The human turned toward the voice. With fluid grace he sank two arrows into Gadreel's chest. If the dragon felt any pain Jandra couldn't tell. Gadreel continued to climb higher in the air before folding his wings to his side to dive forward, letting his momentum carry him into his foe. Jandra saw the human drop his bow and reach for the knife strapped to his boot. Gadreel struck the man in the center of his thighs and both toppled through the window into the courtyard beyond. A handful of blue feathers drifted in the window as a few arrows that had knocked free from the man's quiver clattered to the throne room floor. In seconds, this was the only evidence of their passing.

No longer able to see the combatants, Jandra sat up, holding her head to fight her dizziness. Pet was on his hands and knees. As he groped around, trying to steady himself, his hands fell upon one of the stranger's arrows. He lifted it, studying the red feathers of the fletching, looking bewildered, half-awake. Zanzeroth was on his feet now, moving toward the broad oak doors of the far end of the room, limping away as quickly as he could manage.

Vendevorex lay as still as a corpse. Jandra rushed to his side, praying her eyes deceived her. Blood pooled around the wizard in a circle the size of his wingspan. Her feet slipped in the warm fluid as she sank to her knees. She lifted Vendevorex's head into her lap. Where Zanzeroth's claws had torn his cheek into a series of ragged flaps, she could see the teeth at the back of his jaw exposed. She cradled his head as if it were an infant. Vendevorex was the only family she had ever known, the only life she had ever had. She knew, in her heart, that other humans had meant nothing to Vendevorex. He'd defied the king only for her. She was as responsible for his death as Zanzeroth. She felt sick; chills racked her body. She worried she was about to vomit. She let loose a long, low wail of anguish as tears burst from her eyes, running down her cheeks like acid.

"D-don't... c-cry," Vendevorex whispered.

Jandra couldn't believe her ears. She wiped her tears, trying to clear her vision. Vendevorex had opened his eyes, ever so slightly.

"I might... m-make... it," he said, his voice quavering. Blood bubbled at the corner of his mouth. "T-this is no more difficult... than healing your wound." His eyes closed as he whispered, "It's o-only a question of s-scale."

"He's still alive?" a man asked.

It wasn't Pet's voice.

Jandra looked over her shoulder to see the man who had attacked the dragons standing once again in the window. His arms and chest were soaked with blood, but from the way he stood, she could tell it wasn't his own.

The man crouched down in the window. Still holding onto the ledge, he shifted foward and dropped to a hanging position. He dangled for a second, then let go, falling the rest of the distance and rolling backward as he hit the floor. His momentum carried him back to his feet. He cast a disdainful glance at Pet as he began to walk across the room.

Jandra quickly but carefully moved Vendevorex's head from her lap, placing it gently on the floor. She stood to face the man who strode toward her.

"You can't have him," she growled, clenching her jaw. She dipped her fingers into the dust pouch. "I'll kill you if you try."

The man stopped, a deeply etched frown showing on his weathered face. His eyes studied her own. Then he smirked, ever so slightly, as if amused by Jandra's threats.

"You know who I am," he said.

"Yes," Jandra answered, raising her fists, using the dust to create the illusion of flames around them. "You're the Death of All Dragons. The Ghost Who Kills. You're Bitterwood."

CHAPTER TWELVE

BAIT

Z ANZEROTH LIMPED INTO the courtyard, seeking refuge in a niche in the high stone wall. He paused, glaring into the shadows behind him, watching for the slightest movement that would indicate pursuit. He snapped the arrow that pierced his shoulder, leaving the head still buried inside. He then grabbed the arrow that jutted from his nose and thrust it deeper until the entire arrowhead was in his mouth. He snapped the shaft then worked the arrowhead free with his tongue, spitting it out. That had certainly been unpleasant.

Reaching around, he grasped an arrow in his back. It had hit bone and wasn't buried deep. Zanzeroth freed it with a grunt. He studied the arrow, fletched in red feather-scales. Bodiel's, perhaps? Would his own feathers one day guide the flight that brought another dragon low?

"No," he growled softly.

The flames flickering behind his enemy had painted the picture of a devil, but Bitterwood was only a man. He used a man's weapons and would have a man's weaknesses. All that was needed was to attack the man's heart.

His path to victory now clear, Zanzeroth gathered his will to climb a long row of steps leading up the castle walls. He kicked aside the body of a fallen guard. From the finery, he could tell this was one of Chakthalla's defenders. From atop the wall he surveyed the fighting below. The castle's forces still fought here and there, though the battle was plainly lost. Zanzeroth spotted Kanst in a nearby field, shouting orders to his troops. Zanzeroth leapt into the night sky, the cool air rushing across his body, soothing the pain that cut through him with each downward thrust of his wings.

He landed less than gracefully, his legs buckling on impact. He slid forward across the muddy ground, grinding dirt into his open wounds. The world swirled into a bright shower of red stars. Zanzeroth willed them away. He couldn't pass out until he told Kanst what he'd learned.

Earth-dragons rushed to his side, helping Zanzeroth to rise. Kanst ran forward, shouting for the battle medics to follow.

"By the bones," Kanst said. "What happened to you? Was it Vendevorex who wounded you so?"

"You insult me," Zanzeroth said, pausing to spit blood. "The wizard is dead. I gutted him easily."

"Then who...?"

Zanzeroth lifted the crimson shaft of the arrow before Kanst's eyes. "Look at the feathers. Tell me."

Kanst froze as he saw the arrow. "B-Bitterwood?" he whispered.

"He's within the castle," said Zanzeroth. "He took me by surprise. You can see by the wounds in my back he fought less than honorably."

"All the soldiers will be sent against him," Kanst said. "He won't escape."

"He can, if brute force is your strategy." Zanzeroth spat again. It was hard to talk with blood filling his mouth with every movement of his tongue. "Bitterwood moves more swiftly than any human I've ever seen. He's also unbound by any of our notions of honor or pride. He strikes from the shadows. Cowardly, yes, but effective. Chakthalla's castle is a maze of flame and smoke. Send your soldiers in there and he'll slay them at his pleasure."

Kanst nodded, looking consternated. "I trust your judgment. Still, I see no option but to give the order. Albekizan will have my head if I don't."

"Albekizan can rot," Zanzeroth said. "Bitterwood is my quarry. He's made a tremendous error in showing himself tonight."

Kanst eyed Zanzeroth's wounds then shook his head. "I won't allow you to go back inside. You're in no condition to hunt."

"A hunter who knows only the art of stalking prey will starve," Zanzeroth said. "There are times when a snare is the proper tool. Do as I tell you and we'll capture the so-called ghost by sunrise."

JANDRA WATCHED BITTERWOOD's dark eyes, looking for the slightest hint of mercy. She found none.

"Witch or no, you can't stop this," Bitterwood said, staring at the flames around her fingers. He raised his bow and placed an arrow against the string.

Jandra started to protest that she wasn't a witch, but decided it might be to her advantage to let him think that she was. Jandra placed herself in the path of the arrow to shield Vendevorex. She said, "You'll have to kill me before you can kill him. With my dying breath, I'll place a curse on you so powerful your great-grandchildren will mourn the day you crossed me."

"Thou shall not suffer a witch to live. Exodus 22:18," Bitterwood said.

Jandra had no idea what he was talking about.

Bitterwood stared at her, his face betraying no emotion. Jandra expected his fingers to let the arrow fly at any second. But the seconds dragged by, each longer than hours, and at last he lowered the bow.

"Witch or not, I've never shot a woman. A human woman, that is," he said. "Still, I'd kill you to kill the dragon you shelter, if it wasn't a waste of an arrow."

Bitterwood gave Vendevorex a dismissive glance. "Look at him. With those wounds he'll never see the dawn. If he does... you can't stand in my way all the time."

"Why would you kill him?" Jandra said, letting the illusion around her fingers fade away. "What great wrong has he done to you?"

"He's a dragon," Bitterwood said, shrugging. "He breathes. Crime enough, I think."

"He's more than a dragon! He has a name—Vendevorex. He has a long life behind him, filled with joys and sorrows. He deserves to live as much as you."

Bitterwood said nothing.

Jandra continued, "I thought I had lost him forever only moments ago. It nearly killed me. Now I have hope he will live. It's like getting my own life back. Vendevorex is my family and my friend. You say you won't raise your hand against me, but if you kill him, you murder me. I love him more than anything else in the world."

"You… *love* him?" Bitterwood asked, sounding utterly disgusted.

"Yes. Like a father. I never knew my real family. He's raised me for as long as I can remember. I probably wouldn't be alive today if he hadn't taken me in."

Bitterwood frowned. Jandra searched for the faintest hint of understanding in his eyes.

"You must know how it feels," she said, "to care for someone. Someone whose life you would fight for. Someone you would beg for. So please. *Please*, if you have the faintest trace of kindness within you, spare him. Spare me."

Bitterwood grimaced, then turned away. He raised the back of his hand to her and said, "This conversation is pointless. You delude yourself into thinking he'll survive. He's got more blood on the floor than he does in his veins. But if he does pull through, what the hell. I'll leave him alone. Maybe one day he'll be the last dragon on earth."

A silence followed his words. From the outer chamber Jandra heard the curses and clashes of battle. Chakthalla's few remaining guards must have rallied there. But they couldn't hold out for long. Even if Pet helped her move Vendevorex, where could they run? The only doors from the room led toward the battle or out to Chakthalla's private garden, a walled area with no exit save for flying.

The sounds of metal striking metal, of dragons crying their final cries, grew ever closer. Pet sat where Gadreel had dropped him, still looking dazed. Bitterwood busied himself cutting arrows free from the bodies of the earth-dragons he had slain. Jandra could see his quiver held only a few remaining shafts.

"Been a busy night," Bitterwood said as he yanked an arrow free and studied the tip for damage. "Looks like I'll run out of arrows before I run out of dragons."

Then, from the distance, a new sound could be heard over the clash of swords. The faint wail of a trumpet was echoed by another, less distant horn, and another followed this.

"What's that?" Pet asked.

"Curious," said Bitterwood. "That's the signal for retreat. The king's army is breaking off the attack." Indeed, the noise in the outer chamber nearly ceased as the invaders fell back. The handful of guards left alive chased after them.

"But... they were winning!" Jandra said.

"Maybe they don't know that," Bitterwood said. "I killed dozens of the king's soldiers. It's a mess out there. Smoke everywhere. If that big sun-dragon I shot up made it outside before he died, he might have panicked the forces."

Jandra wondered how long it would be before the assault resumed. Would she have time to help Vendevorex? She needed help and she had few choices in allies.

"Bitterwood," she said. "All you want to do is kill dragons."

"Yes."

"Well, all the dragons outside want to kill Vende-vorex. I think we should make a deal."

"I'm listening," Bitterwood said.

ZEEKY STIRRED AS a hand vigorously shook her arm. Sleep was slow to release its hold on her. The sheets were warm and soft, and it had been too many days since she had slept in her bed. Then she remembered this wasn't her bed.

She opened her eyes. Merria, the little girl, was shaking her. The worn, wearied look in her eyes made Zeeky think she hadn't slept at all. How late was it? The room was still dark.

"They're here," Merria whispered.

"Who?"

"Dragons."

Zeeky sat upright. Poocher rested at the foot of the bed, waking with a snort as she moved. From beyond the bedroom door she could hear Hodan, Merria's father. She had difficulty making out all of his words through the wooden door but he was plainly arguing.

His words were met with the rough tones of the voice of a dragon, shouting, "Silence. You'll come now."

Hodan raised his voice again. There was a loud *clap* and his voice fell silent. Clatters and bangs, like furniture overturning, echoed throughout the room. Alanda, Merria's mother, screamed.

"C'mon," Zeeky said, grabbing Merria by her arm. "We have to run."

"No!" Merria said, struggling to get loose. "I want my mommy!"

Footsteps pounded toward the door. Zeeky let go of Merria, who jumped from the bed and ran toward the door. Zeeky swept Poocher into her arms and searched the darkened window next to her bed for the latch to the shutters.

She pushed the window open as lamplight spilled into the room from the opening door. Her legs were tangled up in the sheets so she leaned from the window and dropped Poocher the few feet to the ground. She then toppled forward, letting herself fall, kicking her legs free of the sheets. Just as the tangled cloth released her, the sharp-nailed claws of an earth-dragon closed around her ankle. Poocher squealed loudly as Zeeky was lifted away from him, back into the farmhouse.

"Run, Poocher!" she yelled as her attacker dragged her across the bed, then through the bedroom into the common room. The table was toppled to its side and not a single chair remained upright. She kicked her free leg wildly, striking her attacker's arms.

The dragon who carried her showed no pain, and when he spoke he merely sounded amused. "This one shows a little more spirit."

"Good," a voice from outside the door of the farmhouse answered. "Bait's better if it's wiggling."

CHAPTER THIRTEEN

ARROWS

"No," Bitterwood answered, barely giving her proposal a second's thought.

"But we can help you with your fight if you help us," Jandra said.

"I've already agreed to spare his life. You can't seriously expect me to help save it."

"Fine," Jandra said, seething with frustration. "Then go. We'll do this on our own."

She noticed from the corner of her eye that Pet had finally cleared his head enough to stand and walk toward them. "You'll help me, won't you, Pet?" she said.

"Um, Mr. Bitterwood?" Pet asked, ignoring Jandra.

"What?"

"Can I go with you? At least until we can get away from the castle and to a decent-sized town somewhere?"

"No," Bitterwood said.

"Please? I can pay you with gold and jewels and…"

Bitterwood raised his hand to silence Pet. "Look at you. You're no villager. Everything about you screams that you're a dragon's companion. If you enjoy their company, seek help from them."

"But—"

"Enough," said Bitterwood. "There is work to be done. The dragons within the castle are weakened and disoriented. I give you fair warning—when the dragons outside the walls strike again, they will find all the defenders dead."

"You're condemning us to death!" Pet cried.

Bitterwood turned and walked into the outer chamber. As he disappeared into the shadows, he said, "You feasted at the table of dragons; you slept on soft beds beneath their roof. It's fitting that you rot among their corpses."

"You bastard!" Pet yelled into the dark hallway. "I hope the dragons kill you! I hope they rip your arms from your sockets!"

"Shut up," Jandra said.

"Did you hear his tone? That sanctimonious bastard thinks he's too important to help us. If I see him again I'll knock his teeth out."

"I said shut up!" Jandra gave Pet her nastiest glare. "I've had all I can take of you. A minute ago you were willing to abandon Ven and me to save your skin. You're a coward, Pet. Talking big just makes you look smaller."

"Don't talk to me that way!" Pet said.

"What are you going to do?" Jandra planted her hands on her hips. "Knock my teeth out?"

Pet threw up his hands. "You're the most infuriating woman I've ever met! Women normally fall all over themselves to see me smile at them. You're talking to me like I'm common trash."

"Oh, I think you're very uncommon trash. Now why don't you just run along and find one of those women who like you so much? I need to figure out how to save Vendevorex."

Pet started to say something and then stopped. After a pause he said, "It's so quiet outside. Even the roar of the flames has lessened."

"The Vengeance doesn't burn forever. If the air is still, its own smoke eventually smothers it."

"I'm sorry," Pet said.

"That it doesn't burn forever?"

Pet shook his head. "I'm sorry I yelled at you. I lost my head. You're right. This situation hasn't brought out the best in me. But I'm calm now. I want to stay and help you."

Jandra rolled her eyes. "You're just too scared to try to make it out of the castle alone."

"I'm not a coward."

"Then go." Jandra pointed toward the door.

"No." Pet crossed his arms. "A minute ago you said you needed my help to save Vendevorex. Just tell me what to do."

"Fine," Jandra said. No matter how much she loathed him at the moment, Pet was the only other person in the room. She had to take whatever help she could get. "We need to find a place to hide him."

"How can we move him without injuring him further?"

"I don't know," Jandra said, looking at Vendevorex. He seemed to be sleeping restfully. His wounds had scabbed over and he no longer lost blood, but Jandra feared that moving him might injure him. "I've seen him heal himself before. That wound was much smaller, a cut on his cheek. He closed that cut within minutes, but this...? I don't know how he's doing this. Our only hope is that it will take hours for him to heal and not days."

"I'm not sure I see what the problem is," Pet said. "You can turn us invisible, right?"

"If they bring ox-dogs, invisibility won't help much," she answered, kneeling next to Vendevorex. She placed her fingers lightly on his brow. He was hot as a hearth. "But just sitting here talking won't help anything either. Is there an armory in the castle?"

"Of course," Pet said.

"Then we should go while the battle has paused," she said as she stood up and wiped her hands on her dress. "The right weapons might make all the difference."

"We've still got that sword," Pet said. "And I bet the hallways are full of stuff."

"Swords aren't going to help. Neither of us is a match fighting a dragon hand-to-hand. But Bitterwood does well with a bow. If we were armed the same, firing from a position of invisibility, we'd stand a chance."

"I don't know," Pet said. "Have you ever fired a bow? They aren't as easy as they look. I practiced with them for a while, trying a trick where I could shoot an apple from the head of a volunteer."

"Oh," Jandra said, perking up. "So you know how to use one?"

Pet lowered his head, shaking it slowly. "I never had a second volunteer."

"Dragons are bigger targets than apples."

"True enough," Pet nodded. "I don't have a better idea. Let's do it. The armory isn't far. If we move invisibly, we can cut straight across the castle walls. We can make it there and back in five minutes."

PET HELD JANDRA'S hand, guiding her across the main wall. She told him they couldn't be seen but he wasn't so sure. *He* could still see them. But he could see himself earlier as well, when Vendevorex had cloaked them with invisibility, and that time they had passed crowds of dragons without reaction.

This trip, however, they met no dragons who could have reacted to their presence. Their path was strewn with dead bodies, both of the attackers and defenders of the castle. Most had died engaged in combat with one another, but here and there arrows stuck from the bodies. Pet noted that most of the dragons Bitterwood had killed were shot from behind. For a supposed hero, Bitterwood wasn't interested in taking chances. He was looking out for his own skin. Yet when Pet displayed the same concern for his own safety, he was labeled a coward.

The night had grown exceptionally dark. The moon had crawled from the sky hours ago. Soon it would be dawn. From outside the walls he could hear the distant shouts of dragons and the crying of children, human children. He peered over the wall as they moved but all he could make out of the surrounding village was dim shadows. Had the invaders turned their attack against the village? He hoped not. He knew quite a few of the village women; indeed, there were many fair-haired children of the village he suspected were his own. He hoped they would be all right. If he had Bitterwood's skill in combat, he'd be out there now, saving the villagers. But he was no fighter. He was an acrobat, an artist, and actor. If there were some way to save the villagers by putting on a costume and performing in a drama, he'd be the right man for the job.

They descended from the wall through the tower, moving toward the armory. They paused as they approached the door. From inside came torchlight and the scuffles of something moving around.

"Go ahead," Jandra whispered. "They can't see us. Let's see who it is."

He crept carefully forward, peeking into the door. He breathed a sigh of relief when he saw it was a human moving inside.

But as he exhaled the man reacted, spinning around toward the noise. It was Bitterwood and he fired an arrow toward the doorway before Pet could even blink. The arrow whizzed over his shoulder, barely missing his ear.

"Hey!" Pet shouted.

"Wait! It's only us!" Jandra shouted, and the air before Pet sparked and swirled.

Bitterwood's eyes grew wide. "Are you trying to get yourself killed?" he said. "You take a foolish gamble creeping up on me."

"Don't you bother to look where you're shooting?" Pet said.

"I don't always have that luxury," Bitterwood said. "I've saved my life many times over by firing blindly." Bitterwood shook his head, then leaned against the wall for support. "You should be grateful it's been such a long night. Were I not so tired... Where I ten years younger... I wouldn't have missed."

"It doesn't look like you miss often," Jandra said. "It looks like you've killed all the dragons... on *our* side. Now that you've killed our defenders, would it be asking too much to kill some of the dragons attacking the castle?"

"There won't be time," Bitterwood said. "It will be morning soon. I strike at night."

"Easier to hide when it's dark, isn't it, 'hero?'" Pet said.

"Yes," Bitterwood said. "Precisely." He then returned to the work he'd been doing when they'd interrupted. The armory was a shambles, ransacked by the invaders, but some weapons remained. Bitterwood was gathering what arrows he could find from the clutter. Pet wondered if he should mention the arrows that had fallen from Bitterwood's own quiver that still lay beneath the window in Chakthalla's throne room.

"The legends say you only use arrows you make yourself," Jandra said.

"Some legends also say I can fly," Bitterwood said. "Fletching my arrows with dragon scales gives my attacks a greater psychological impact. Still, an arrow guided by a goose feather can do the job just as well."

"Leave some arrows for us," Pet said, finding a longbow leaning against the wall. "Lucky they didn't take this. This is a good bow."

"Not that lucky. Dragons are mediocre with bows, at best," Bitterwood said. "The red and blue ones prefer to fight when flying, using a long spear held with their hind claws. The green ones sometimes use bows but they can't hit the broadside of a barn. They are only effective in mass assaults, not in attacking an individual target. I don't think an earth-dragon can focus on distant objects as well as we can." He handed Pet a handful of arrows. "If you have the guts to fight a dragon, a bow's a good choice. Pick your target and don't panic, and you can kill them before they ever get close."

"I have the guts, old man," Pet said.

"I doubt it," Bitterwood said. "But I guess you'll find out."

Bitterwood placed the rest of the arrows he'd gathered into his quiver and walked past Pet and Jandra with no further word.

"Bastard," Pet snarled as the archer vanished around the corner.

"I noticed he escaped with his teeth," Jandra said.

Pet shrugged. "He's an old guy a foot shorter than me. It wouldn't be fair to fight him."

"Not fair to you, maybe."

"Would you stop taunting me? I'm not a—"

"We'd better get back," Jandra said, cutting him off. "It can't be long before morning."

Almost as if it had heard her words, a cock began to crow in the distance.

After Jandra again made them invisible, Pet led her back up the tower to cross the wall leading to the throne room. The sky had brightened in the east since they had passed by minutes before. In the fields below he could see the enemy army, gathered together in a huge circle, and within the circle stood the villagers.

"What are they doing?" he asked, stopping to study the scene.

"I don't know," Jandra said. "But it doesn't look as if they're getting ready to attack. Maybe Vendevorex will have time to heal."

In the middle of the circle, Pet could see three flat-bedded wagons, drawn together to make a large platform. A huge sun-dragon stood on the platform with metal armor gleaming on his chest.

"Damn," said Jandra. "That's Kanst. He answers directly to Albekizan."

"What's he up to? Why has he gathered the villagers?"

"Who knows?" Jandra said. "Let's get back."

"Not yet," Pet said. "I want to find out what's going on. I know many of these people." Although from this distance, he couldn't recognize anyone.

"There's not time for this," Jandra said, tugging his arm. "Vendevorex has been alone too long already."

Pet held his ground. "This is something important. I can feel it."

"Maybe Kanst is just going to lay down the law for the locals. Tell them they have new bosses now."

Pet was annoyed by Jandra's dismissive tone. "What will it take to make you take me seriously for once? I want to watch this. We need to know what the enemy is up to if we want to get out of here alive, right?"

Jandra grimaced. "Okay. Fine. Stay here. I'm going back."

"I won't be invisible if you leave."

"Nobody's left alive to bother you." Jandra waved her hands toward the corpse of a fallen guard. "Stay low on the wall. They can't see you from down there. Don't be such a crybaby."

"Arg!" Pet cried in frustration. Then, worried that he'd been loud enough to be heard below, he hunched lower to the wall and whispered, "Will you stop that? What is it going to take to make you stop thinking I'm a coward? I attacked a dragon with a spear three times too big for me to use properly. I've stuck by your side to help you save your master when I could have just ran. What does it take to impress you? Do I have to go down there and fight them all by myself?"

"Aw. Have I hurt your feelings?" Jandra asked.

"Yes!" Pet hissed. "I don't think I deserve this constant ridicule."

"You're right," she said. "I'll try to space it out more."

Pet threw his hands in the air. "Fine!" he said. "I'll stay here alone. Get back to your master."

"I told you not to call him my master," said Jandra. "I'm his apprentice, not his slave."

"There are some chains you don't even know you're wearing."

Before Jandra could respond, a booming voice from below shouted out a name.

"Bitterwood!"

The word echoed through the stone walls. Pet could make out a large, armored sun-dragon standing on a platform, using a wooden cone to amplify his voice.

"Zanzeroth must have survived," said Jandra. "How else would Kanst know—"

Kanst's shouts drowned her out. "We know you are defending the castle, Bitterwood! These villagers are special to you, I think. Maybe you have family among them. You've tried to save them by picking us off one by one. A good strategy, if you had the time."

Kanst motioned with his claw and an earth-dragon dragged a young boy onto the platform, his arms and legs bound, his screams nearly drowning out the words that followed.

"Time is up, Bitterwood."

The green dragon held the boy up by his blond hair, his toes just off the platform. Kanst drew his sword, slowly, ceremoniously, from the scabbard. The deliberateness of the action only added to the shock of what followed. Savagely, the sword flashed through the air in a silver arc. The body toppled sideways. The earth-dragon held the boy's head toward the castle walls.

The villagers erupted in noise, men cursing, women weeping, children crying. The dragons that surrounded them rushed in, shouting for them to be silent, enforcing their orders with blows from the blunt ends of their spears.

After order was beaten into the crowd, Kanst continued: "That boy can be the last to die today, Bitterwood. You can save the rest by coming forward now. We give you a quarter hour to show yourself. Then they die, minute by minute, one by one. The children first, as they may be your own blood. Then the women, as one of them may be your mate. Then the men, brothers, perhaps, or fathers. Should they, by chance, all be strangers, so be it. Perhaps you'll have the stomach for the slaughter being carried out in your honor."

Kanst looked toward the castle walls and waited as the body of the boy was carried away and a little girl was selected from the crowd.

BITTERWOOD DIDN'T LOOK back. He couldn't. He heard the words but he wouldn't feel them, couldn't feel them unless he looked. The fight would continue on another battlefield. No matter what the cost.

His path carried him toward a barn where he hoped to find a good horse. All the dragons would be in the fields by the castle. Their stunt only assisted him in his escape by focusing their forces to control the crowd.

As Bitterwood reached the door, he heard a snuffling noise. Looking to his side he saw a piglet, free from the other animals, looking at him with big black eyes.

Bitterwood knew this pig.

"Damn," he sighed.

He remembered his promise to Zeeky. He remembered the promises he'd broken in the past. If he abandoned her, it would haunt him, but he was already haunted. What was one more ghost?

He sat down on a bale of hay, his body leaden. He'd never felt so tired in all his life.

"I'm sorry," he whispered to the ghosts.

"HE HAS TO!" Jandra said as she raced for the throne room.

"He won't," Pet answered as he chased her.

Jandra rushed through the doors, expecting to find the scene just as she left it. But something was missing. Vendevorex was gone.

"Vendevorex!" she yelled.

"I-I am here," he answered weakly. The air glittered, revealing him. He lay near where he'd fallen but was now propped against the wall. Many of his wounds had closed but fresh blood seeped from the larger wounds that remained. "Do you have... any water? I tried... to condense some from the air. Didn't have... the s-strength."

"Pet! Where can I find water?"

"There's a fountain in the garden," he said. "Follow me."

He led her through the side door that led to the walled garden. The water sparkled in the morning light making Jandra aware of her own thirst. She could drink directly from the fountain but what of Vendevorex?

"What can we put water in?" she asked.

"Hold on. I'll find something," Pet said, going back into the throne room. Jandra knelt by the fountain and drank deeply. The water was cold and clean as freshly melted snow. The garden was filled with pink flowers, opening their buds to the rising sun, filling the air with perfume. Yellow-breasted songbirds flitted among the branches of the low trees and greeted the day with music. The beauty made her feel ill. The garden was too lovely, too peaceful in light of the horrors she'd seen.

"Here," Pet said, returning. He carried the pack she had seen him with earlier. He pulled a golden goblet from it and handed it to her. "I guess I won't be needing this after all," he said.

"Thank you," she said as she took the goblet.

Delicate engravings of butterflies covered the golden cup. It was the loveliest thing she had ever seen and it broke her. The goblet fell from her hands as tears began to stream from her cheeks. She began to tremble, her body weak with sorrow.

Pet sat beside her. He took one of her hands and squeezed it. "It's okay," he said, stroking her hair with his free hand. "It's okay."

"No," she said, shaking her head. "They're going to die. Kanst doesn't bluff. It's all my fault."

"No," Pet said. "It's not your fault."

"The dragons wouldn't be here if Vendevorex weren't here. He's only here because of me. Maybe things would have been better if the guards had just killed me the morning after Bodiel died. I've been holding on to such foolish hopes. I thought... I thought everything would be all right. I thought we could win."

"You can," Pet said. "Vendevorex will be okay. You'll both live through this."

"But it's too late for the villagers," Jandra said. "They're dying because of me."

"Hush," Pet said. "Don't torture yourself. This isn't your fault. It's Bitterwood's. He's the one who killed Bodiel. He got the dragons all worked up. If he has a heart in him, he'll turn himself in and end this."

Jandra sniffed, wiping her cheeks. "A minute ago you were the one saying he wouldn't surrender. I don't think he gives a damn about saving people. He only wants to kill dragons. He won't give himself up. We can't do a damn thing to stop Kanst. I think we've proven tonight that we're both pathetic at fighting."

"Shhh." Pet hugged her tightly for a long moment. Then he broke the embrace. "Bitterwood is going to surrender. You have my vow."

"Oh, what good is your vow?"

Pet turned Jandra's face toward him and brushed her hair away from her face. "You can't worry about that right now," he said. "Vendevorex needs you, honey. He's thirsty, and hurting, and probably more scared than you are. Be strong for him, okay?"

Jandra swallowed. "Okay."

Pet helped her to rise. He picked up the goblet from the green carpet of grass and filled it with water.

"Take this to him," he said, then he sat by the fountain and lowered his face to take his own drink.

Jandra entered the throne room, breathing deeply. She would be strong, for now, at least, while Vendevorex needed her. She knelt and held the cup to the wounded wizard's lips and helped him to drink.

"More," he whispered as he swallowed the last drops.

Jandra returned to garden, both for water and to find Pet, to thank him for his words. She also felt a need to apologize for her earlier insults. Perhaps she'd expected too much of him. But Pet wasn't sitting by the fountain anymore.

"Pet?" she asked.

Only the colorful birds answered, singing joyfully as they danced among the hedges.

ZANZEROTH WATCHED AS Kanst gave the order. The earth-dragon lifted the little girl roughly by the hair. She screamed in pain and fear as Kanst slowly slid his sword from his scabbard.

"Stop this!" a man yelled, his voice coming from outside the circled humans. "I'm here."

Zanzeroth smiled with satisfaction. The guards on the far side of the circle stood aside and the crowd parted. Zanzeroth struggled to rise, ignoring the pain of his injuries. He couldn't wait to see the look of defeat in his enemy's eyes.

The general motioned for the soldier to lower the girl. The cloaked figure walked forward haltingly, his shoulders sagging, his bow dangling from his weak grip, as if surrender sapped all his strength.

As the figure reached the platform, two earth-dragons rushed to him, knocking the bow from his hands, each grabbing an arm. They ripped his cloak away, exposing an old man, his skin weathered and tan, his hair thin and gray.

"A valiant attempt," Kanst said. "Alas, I'm not so easily fooled. You are not the one we seek."

The old man looked up as Kanst's words sunk in. Anger flashed in his eyes. "Are you mad?" he asked. "I'm Bitterwood. I've done as you asked. Let these people go."

"Zanzeroth," Kanst said. "Twice you've stood in the presence of the Ghost who Kills. Tell me, is this the man we seek?"

Zanzeroth looked at the aged figure before him. His clothes were caked with blood—Gadreel's? Though he'd never been close enough to meet Bitterwood's gaze, this man's eyes looked as he'd imagined: hard, hateful, as dark and cold as a grave. But the old man was short, and while his arms revealed hard, wiry muscles, they were far too thin. The demon who stood in the window the night before had strength and stature. Still, if the

Bitterwood who killed Bodiel were the same as the Bitterwood of legend, he would be old by now. Could this unimpressive specimen truly be the fabled dragon-slayer? It seemed impossible. If only the arrow hadn't pierced his nose; the scent would reveal the truth. As it was, he couldn't smell a damn thing.

Zanzeroth weighed his answer carefully. If he named this old fool as Bitterwood, and dragons continued to die, no doubt Albekizan would have his head. His eye fell on the quiver slung over the old man's shoulders. It was filled with arrows fletched with goose feathers. This told him all he needed to know.

"This is an imposter. Put him with the others," Zanzeroth said. "Continue the executions."

"No!" the old man shouted. "I am Bitterwood! I killed three score of you during the night! I am—"

An earth-dragon struck the gray-haired man hard in the stomach, silencing him. While the two dragons continued to hold him, another dragon began to bind his arms with rope.

"I like your spirit, old man," Kanst said. "Your willingness to sacrifice yourself for others is admirable. I'm going to reward you by changing the order of the executions. You're next."

"But," the old man gasped painfully, "no one else will come forth. I'm the man you seek! I am Bitterwood!"

"No he's not!" a man shouted.

The crowd turned. On a nearby hill, astride a white stallion, another man could be seen. He was tall, broad-shouldered, his face fair, his hair long and golden. He was dressed in black silk and a velvet cape, and he held in his hand a well-crafted longbow. Over his shoulder a quiver hung, holding only three arrows, the feathers gleaming red in the morning sunlight.

The man shook the horse's reins and rode toward the platform. The crowd of humans murmured, excited.

"Release them," the stranger said in a firm, commanding voice. "The war is over. I'm the one you want. I'm Bitterwood."

CHAPTER FOURTEEN

MASKS

SCREAMING WITH RAGE, Zanzeroth lumbered toward the man on the white stallion as fast as his wounded frame would carry him. The horse bucked, panicking. The man somersaulted to the ground with acrobatic grace then turned his steely gaze toward Zanzeroth's charge.

"Stop him!" Kanst bellowed.

Pertalon, a sky-dragon half Zanzeroth's size, dashed into the hunter's path. Both tumbled into the assembled humans, sending them scrambling in fear. The soldiers plunged into the crowd, beating people down with their spear ends, preventing them from fleeing. A mob of earth-dragons rushed toward the man in the velvet cape, surrounding him in a wide circle. Most kept a respectful distance from the fabled dragon-slayer, but two of the braver—or perhaps dumber—members of the guard ran forward and grabbed his arms.

Pertalon and Zanzeroth rolled on the broken ground, each seeking to best the other. Zanzeroth had the advantage of size but his wounds sapped his strength. Pertalon proved to be a skilled brawler. In seconds, the smaller dragon had pinned his much larger opponent.

"Damn you!" Zanzeroth howled. "Why do you deny me my justice?"

"Justice is for Albekizan to dispense," Kanst said. "Tell me, are you the one willing to face the king? To say we had Bitterwood captive, then killed him instead of giving Albekizan that pleasure?"

"I demand my revenge!" Zanzeroth said.

"I deny it," Kanst said.

Kanst turned back to his captive, the blond-tressed hero of the humans who stood stoically in the grasp of the two earth-dragons. Borlon, the captain, stood nearby, a two-handed sword gripped tightly in his chunky green fists, his eyes wide in an alert expression that was set somewhere equally between fight and flight. Kanst said, "Chain this man, then take him to my tent. Keep him constantly under guard. Under no circumstances allow Zanzeroth to come near. Use whatever force is necessary."

"Yes, sir," Borlon answered. Then, he cast his gaze toward the assembled crowd. "What about the villagers we've gathered? Should we let them go?"

"Why bother?" Kanst shrugged. "In less than a month we were supposed to escort them to the Free City. We will take them now, as we return to the palace with Bitterwood."

Kanst turned to Zanzeroth. His armor clanked and clattered as he lowered himself to all fours to address the pinned hunter. "Old friend, I know you are a dragon with more than his allotment of guts and guile. I'm tempted to put you in chains to ensure Bitterwood survives. Still, in the years I've known you, I've come to respect you as a dragon of unparalleled integrity. If you give me your word, as one sun-dragon to another, that you will not seek revenge against Bitterwood until he is presented to Albekizan, I will spare you from bondage."

"So be it," Zanzeroth snarled. "Our precious king may have his prize. But you must tell him I was the one with the plan that snared him. Speak for me, tell him that I deserve to be appointed as Bitterwood's executioner."

"I shall grant this," Kanst said, rising back to his hind-talons. Then, to Pertalon, "Let him go."

"My apologies," Pertalon said as he helped Zanzeroth to his feet.

"You had your orders," Zanzeroth said, brushing dirt from his skin. He looked down at his worn and torn body. This impromptu wrestling match had not only reopened some of his wounds, it had also cost him many more scales. Faded, rust-colored flakes littered the ground like leaves. He sighed, then raised his head to address Kanst once more. "One last thing, Kanst. We must retake the castle. The body of Vendevorex lies in the throne room. It is a prize for which the king will reward both of us highly."

"Agreed," Kanst said. His polished armor gleamed in the light of the morning sun. "Our retreat from the castle to gather the villagers came as our victory was imminent. We shall retake it within the hour."

JANDRA TURNED FROM the wall, running back toward the throne room. She had gone looking for Pet and arrived in time to witness the turmoil as a sky-dragon had tackled Zanzeroth. She couldn't make things out clearly from this distance, but it was apparent that Bitterwood had surrendered. The executions had stopped. So why didn't she feel any better?

As she ran through the corridors she had to constantly step around the bodies of the dead. She wanted to think the protectors of the castle had been defending more than the walls. They had died opposing Albekizan's cruelty and his vision of a world without humans. As shocking as it had been to watch the boy die at Kanst's blade, she knew that atrocity paled before what was to come.

When the other sun dragons learned of the assault against Chakthalla, would they be galvanized to rise against the king? Or would they instead cower before him, acquiescing to whatever mad scheme he might conceive? She feared the latter. Only Vendevorex could make a difference. He would listen to her now. He had to.

But as she entered the throne room she gasped in horror. Vendevorex had lapsed back into unconsciousness, causing his aura of invisibility to fade. Now an enormous sun-dragon crouched above Vendevorex's helpless figure. Hearing her distressed cry the dragon turned his face toward her. He wore a black hood, hiding his features, so that only his eyes could be seen. Jandra had never seen a dragon in such a mask before. She thought it looked sinister, evidence enough that this was a servant of Albekizan—another assassin, no doubt.

Jandra knew that she stood little chance against a sun-dragon, even if she wasn't exhausted already. Despite her sense of impending defeat she clenched her fists and braced herself for one last battle. She again summoned the illusion of flame around her hands.

"Get away from him," she growled, stepping forward with all the menace she could muster.

"Jandra," the dragon answered, stepping backward. "I mean no harm. I'm here to help."

Jandra paused. She didn't recognize the dragon's voice, slightly muffled by the hood. "How do you know my name?" she asked. "Who are you?"

"A phantom," the dragon said in a weary voice. "A faint echo of the being I once was. I heard whispers of a plot against Albekizan and came to investigate. It looks as if I came too late."

"We've lost this battle," Jandra admitted. "But no war is decided by a single battle."

"Perhaps. But news of the slaughter here today will squelch any thought of rebellion among other sun-dragons." The masked dragon sighed, his voice full of despair. "Albekizan need not rule with the respect of his subjects when all he needs is their fear."

"Fear you must possess in abundance," Jandra said. "You say you want to stand with us but you hide your face. You want to protect yourself if the war is lost. Obviously you fear for your name, or your power."

The dragon shook his head. "I no longer have a name, or power."

"Then you have nothing to lose," said Jandra. "At the moment, I'm short on allies. Can I count on your help?"

"I am at your service," the masked dragon answered with a courtly bow.

Suddenly, the blast of battle horns could be heard from the castle gates.

"Sounds like they're coming back in," Jandra said. "We'd better move Vendevorex."

"Why was he brought to the throne room to start with? With such serious wounds he should never have left his bed."

"He received his wounds here."

"When? How?"

"Zanzeroth almost killed him. This happened only hours ago."

"Hours?" The dragon sounded as if he thought Jandra was crazy. "These wounds are days old."

"Listen, Phantom, this isn't the best time to explain. No one's left to defend this place. Kanst's soldiers will sweep through here. We need to get moving."

Vendevorex moaned. He turned his head toward Jandra's voice. His eyes fluttered open as he whispered, "What's the point?"

Jandra ran to his side. She dropped to her knees and placed a hand on his fevered brow. "You're burning up, Ven. Phantom, go get him some more water!"

"Don't bother," Vendevorex said. His voice sounded utterly defeated. "I-I heard the battle horns. I'm too weak to move. It's time to accept... I'm going to die. Save yourself, Jandra."

"I'm not going to let you die," Jandra said. "I won't abandon you, Ven."

"You m-must," the wizard sighed. He closed his eyes. He arched his back in response to some internal agony. His belly was twisted and distorted with ugly tumors of scar tissue. His skin seemed to be crawling. "It's o-over. I'm too sick to move. You could make us invisible, but what's the p-point? Zanzeroth will bring in ox-dogs. We've lost."

"Don't be so willing to surrender, my friend," the phantom said, reaching for a large pack he had left on the floor. "Let Jandra make us invisible to their eyes and I will make us invisible to their noses. I can carry you both from here with ease." The phantom pulled a crystalline atomizer from his pack.

"You're going to save us with perfume?" Jandra asked

"Hold your breath until the mist settles to the floor," the hooded dragon said. "This is filled with the essence of hot peppers. The dogs won't even enter this room."

The phantom sprayed the fine pink mist around the room. Jandra fought aside her own exhaustion to concentrate on her role in the escape. She needed to create a circle of invisibility large enough for all three of them to hide in; this was no small task, given the sun-dragon's great size. The phantom looked back as he neared the door.

"Where?" he whispered, looking around.

"Here," Jandra answered, certain now that the invisibility was working. "Follow my voice."

The phantom hurried to her, stopping with a shock as he entered the circle and saw them again. "I've always wondered how this was done," he said. He looked at his skin. "Some sort of reflective dust. Interesting."

"Keep quiet," Jandra whispered. "Someone's coming!"

"In here, Pertalon," came a voice from the outer chamber. *Oh no*, thought Jandra. *Zanzeroth*.

Jandra held her breath as the hunter's head appeared in the doorway. The phantom froze where he stood. Zanzeroth moved into the room slowly. He was a mass of fresh white gauze bandages. He walked with the assistance of another dragon, a sky-dragon who stood beneath Zanzeroth's shoulder to support him.

"Damn," Zanzeroth said. "We're too late, Pertalon."

"What's wrong?" Pertalon asked.

Zanzeroth motioned toward Jandra. "This is where I left the body. It's gone now."

"I thought he was too wounded to move."

"Jandra must have taken his corpse," Zanzeroth said, sounding disappointed. "Damn Gadreel's incompetence. She should have been an easy kill."

Pertalon asked, "Who's Jandra?"

"The wizard's pet," Zanzeroth said. His eyes were following her bloody footprints from her earlier trip from the throne room to the armory. Ven's blood had been freshest then; it was the most obvious trail in the room. Zanzeroth twisted his neck around to follow the trail back into the hall. He continued his explanation of Jandra's role in Vendevorex's life as he studied the clues before him. "The wizard raised a human girl from infancy. The little bitch treated Vendevorex like a god. She never suspected the truth."

"What truth?" Pertalon asked, supporting Zanzeroth as they stepped back into the hall.

"The girl was an orphan by Vendevorex's hand," said Zanzeroth. "The wizard killed her parents with as little thought as you or I would give to killing a fly."

Jandra raised her hands to her mouth to silence her surprise. Zanzeroth had to be lying. But why? Why would he lie if he didn't know she could hear? Was this a trick? Perhaps he wanted her to cry out, revealing her location.

"Let's see where her trail leads," Zanzeroth said. "She can't have taken him out of the castle. We'll come back with the ox-dogs."

Jandra turned to Vendevorex as the voices of Zanzeroth and Pertalon faded down the hallway. The wizard lay with his head facing away from her. The phantom studied her face, his eyes sad, as if he knew some awful truth.

"Ven?" she said.

"What t-terrific luck Zanzeroth didn't come further into the room," the wizard whispered, looking at the wall. "We have a chance after all."

"Agreed," the phantom said. "I will carry you. If we can remain invisible we can slip through the gates unnoticed."

"Ven?" Jandra said, placing her hand on his shoulder. "Why won't you look at me?"

Vendevorex twisted his neck around to face her in a swift motion. Pain etched lines onto his face as he hissed, "Because it's t-true."

"What?"

Vendevorex sighed. He closed his eyes. His whole body slackened and sagged. "Years ago, when I arrived in the k-king's court, I was nobody," he said softly. "I had no allies to convince Albekizan to take me in. I had to p-prove my abilities, to convince him I was a worthy member of his court. Albekizan tested me by having me destroy a cottage near the castle."

Jandra shook her head, not believing what she was hearing.

Vendevorex continued. "Setting the structure ablaze was simple. Killing the man and woman who defended it was simpler still. To further prove my power I walked through the burning house, showing that the heat and smoke couldn't harm me. I heard your cries above the roar of the flames. I hadn't known they had a child."

"You killed my parents?" she said. "As... as a demonstration?"

"Yes," he said. "But I spared you. I... I saw you in your burning bed and you looked so... innocent. That night I knew I was committing murder solely for my own selfish needs. I never lied to myself. I made the cold, calculated decision to end your parents' lives to improve my own. But when I saw the innocence in your eyes... that was the first moment in my life I ever felt shame."

"I can't believe this," she said, choking back tears.

"I-I've tried to make amends," Vendevorex said, sounding as if he, too, were on the verge of tears. "I have used my powers more wisely, I hope. I try to protect life when I have the opportunity. I use my powers aggressively as little as possible. You've taught me that *all* life is precious, Jandra." He closed his eyes and shook his head remorsefully. "I made a horrible mistake that night. I only hope the intervening years have proven that I've since learned compassion."

Jandra kept her eyes fixed upon his face. It was true, his words, his feelings. Remorse for the deed filled him, but didn't change the fact. He had killed her parents. He had raised her all these years to appease his own guilt. Her relationship to him now seemed so clear. He kept her by his side to convince himself he was something better than a cold-blooded murderer.

She stood up. The cloak of invisibility around them dissolved. She turned her back on her former mentor.

"Goodbye," she said.

"Jandra," Vendevorex said, reaching out a feeble wing to touch her back. "I truly am sorry."

Jandra recoiled from his touch, stepping beyond his reach. "Sorry? You think that an apology now makes up for a lie you've told all my life? It's not enough, Ven. Nothing you can say will ever be enough."

"I understand you're hurt," he said. "And once this is over, I understand you may desire some time apart. But you can't leave now. Our circumstances require us to stick together, at least a while longer."

"I think leaving now is an excellent option," Jandra said.

"Where would you go?" he asked.

"Where I belong," she said, running for the door as tears burst from her.

ZEEKY COULDN'T STOP shaking. She'd been singled out with the other children earlier, into a group the dragons would eventually execute. Now the other girls and boys were free, threading back through the crowds to their parents who desperately called out their names.

No one called for her. She wasn't so far from her home village—twenty miles at most—but she knew no one here.

She had lost Merria in the confusion so she called for her now. To her relief, Merria called back. Then Merria's voice was cut short. Still, Zeeky headed in that direction.

"Merria!" Zeeky cried out as she spotted the girl held in Hodan's arms. The farmer had placed his hand over Merria's mouth. He scowled at Zeeky.

"Go away, child," he said.

"Hodan," Alanda whispered, "couldn't we...?"

"Be quiet, woman," Hodan said.

"What's wrong?" Zeeky asked. "You said you'd look after me."

"The evil that has fallen on our village arrived with you. The man who left you is mad, claiming to be Bitterwood. I don't understand what has happened, but these things taint you. Kamon warned against the evils outsiders can bring."

Zeeky couldn't believe what she was hearing.

"But—"

"Go," Hodan said, his eyes narrowed to hard slits.

Zeeky shut up. She saw that Hodan was serious. Alanda looked uncertain but Hodan would never let Zeeky stay with them. She wished Poocher were here now. He needed her so. She felt stronger when she cared for him. Now she had no one.

Unless Hey You was here. She thought she had heard his voice earlier but she couldn't see a thing from where she had stood. If she could find him, he would be nice to her.

She didn't have to look for long before she found him. His arms and legs were bound with rope and he lay on the dirt. The people of the village looked away from him, ignoring him, making a circle several steps around him for him to lie in, alone.

No one moved to stop Zeeky as she walked to him. But when she got there, his eyes were blank, staring straight ahead as if he didn't see her.

"Hey You," she said, crouching next to him. "It's me. Zeeky."

The old man didn't answer.

Zeeky said, "I don't know anyone. You were nice to me. Can I sit here with you?"

Still he didn't answer.

Zeeky's eyes blurred with tears. She said, "Please talk to me. I'm scared."

"Hello," a woman said from behind her as she placed her hand on Zeeky's shoulder. "Don't be afraid."

Zeeky turned. The woman was beautiful, with long brown hair held back by a silver tiara. She was dressed in white cotton though her clothes were covered with dark stains. Zeeky couldn't even say hello, however, as tears choked her voice.

"Hey," the woman said, crouching before her, wiping her cheeks. "What's wrong? Have you lost your mom and dad?"

"And my pig." Zeeky swallowed, then sobbed. "I'm all alone."

"Me too," the woman said. "So why don't we stay together. You can help me, okay?"

"O-okay."

"So what's your name?" the woman asked.

"Z-Zeeky. What's yours?"

"Jandra," the woman answered as she swept her up in her arms. Jandra looked at Hey You and said, "I'm surprised they don't have you under guard."

The old man shifted his eyes toward her. His lips barely moved. "I'm not the man I thought I was."

"What do you mean?" Jandra asked.

"I am no longer Bitterwood," Hey You said, continuing to lie as still as death. "Another now answers to that name."

"I don't understand."

At last, Hey You lifted his head from the ground. He frowned as he said, "Your boyfriend stole my name. I may let him keep it."

"My boyfriend?" Jandra asked, sounding confused. Then she raised her eyebrows. "Pet?"

The man Zeeky called Hey You lowered his cheek to the dirt once more and said nothing.

A commotion came from the edges of the crowd. The shouts of dragons could be heard, barking orders for the people to line up.

"Stick close to me, honey," Jandra said to Zeeky as she lowered her back to the ground. Then she moved to Hey You and said, "Let me help you up."

"Why bother?" the old man complained. "Let the dragons carry me or kill me."

"Don't be like this," Jandra said, placing her hands on the ropes that bound him. Her hands glowed in the morning light and the ropes fell free. "I'm going to save these people. You're going to help me."

"I tried to save them," the old man said. "I failed. I'm too tired to go on."

Jandra took him by the shirt and with a grunt lifted him to a sitting position. She stared into his eyes and said in a low voice, "No matter what the dragons or these people believe, I know who you are. You do too. You aren't going to simply give up."

"You don't know me," he said. "I've fought for so long. Now another has agreed to die for my sins. You could never understand what that means."

"Then you can try to explain it as we go," Jandra said, struggling to pull him to his feet.

The old man sighed, then stood, shoulders hunched.

"I need to borrow your cloak for a second," Jandra said, picking it up from where the dragons had thrown it to the ground. She looked around; no one even looked in their direction. "Zeeky, I need you to keep secret what you're about to see."

"Okay," Zeeky said.

Jandra took Bitterwood's cloak and placed it over her, hiding her face in the hood. By now the guards had reached them and forced them into the column of people that formed across the field. Zeeky noticed that other green dragons had herded the animals from the village at the back of the column, and she wondered if Poocher was with them.

"There," Jandra said, handing the cloak back to Bitterwood.

Zeeky gasped. Jandra's hair was no longer long and brown, but was now short and black. Zeeky wondered what had happened to Jandra's tiara. She thought it might be hidden behind the fringe of hair that hung across Jandra's forehead. Her dress was neither stained nor white but a uniform beige. Zeeky could hardly believe the change.

"How I have fallen," Bitterwood grumbled, "that I keep the company of a witch."

"Don't mind him, Zeeky," Jandra said. "I'm not a witch."

"Villagers!" Kanst again stood on the wagon, shouting through the wooden cone.

"Chakthalla, the tyrant who held you all in bondage, is dead. I have liberated you in the name of the great King Albekizan. The king has ordered me to take you to a new home, a better place, called the Free City. There you may live your days free from the worries of daily labor. In the Free City, food and shelter are provided at the king's expense. Chakthalla resisted the king's plan to shower you with wealth and comfort, preferring to keep you in servitude. Now she's paid the ultimate price for her cruelty. The journey in the days ahead will no doubt be hard. We will be walking during all the hours of daylight so that we may bring you to your new home as quickly as possible. But be strong, good people. You will have your reward."

Confused voices rose all around Zeeky.

"It makes no sense," a man said. "They threaten us with death, then say they've come to help?"

"My cousin in Richmond sent word of the Free City," another said. "He says he's been employed in its construction and that the wages were the highest any man could earn."

"It's God's will, my children," said an old man with a shrill voice.

"Kamon speaks!" A ripple of excitement ran through the villagers. "It's Kamon! He's broken his silence!"

The crowd turned and Zeeky caught a glimpse of an ancient withered figure clothed in rags. He was bald save for a fringe of thin white hair that hung around his shoulders like a wedding veil. He had a long braided mustache that hung six inches below his chin. His eyes looked twice the right size for his wrinkled, spotted face.

The villages were all jabbering now, whispering back and forth about the significance of Kamon speaking. They drew into a large circle around the old man. The ragged figure silenced the crowd with a raised hand.

"For years I have kept silent, waiting for the sign of our redemption," Kamon said, in a dry, scratchy voice. "In the blood of the child, all is revealed. We must obey the dragons. The murder of the boy, the taking of our homes, the fall of the castle: these are signs that the land is cursed. Though even they don't know the truth, the dragons lead us from this place to the Promised Land, where we will finally be free from sorrows. The day of redemption is now at hand!"

An earth-dragon pushed his way through the circle of villagers. "Break it up," he ordered. "We're leaving."

Male villagers, including Hodan, rushed to form a protective line in front of Kamon.

"Stop," Kamon said to his impromptu defenders. "Now is not the time to fight. These dragons are mere servants of fate. The day will come when they will pay for their sins against our people; today is not that day."

The dragons jostled the people into a long column, no deeper than three abreast. The people began to move forward, guided by the dragons across the broken fields. Zeeky looked back, trying to see the animals that some of the earth-dragons had gathered from the nearby farms. She watched the dragons herd the beasts together behind them. She hoped she might catch some glimpse of Poocher, but there was no sign of him.

Then they started marching, and the only animals she could see were the crows descending in great dark clouds, shattering the morning air with their harsh caws, forming a black wake as they fell on the battlefield, covering the dead with a living shroud.

BOOK THREE

RIVER

Take the millstones, and grind meal:
uncover thy locks, make bare the leg,
uncover the thigh, pass over the rivers.
Thy nakedness shall be uncovered,
yea, thy shame shall be seen:
I will take vengeance,
and I will not meet thee as a man

Isaiah 47:2-3

LIES

1078 D.A., The 47th Year of the Reign of Albekizan

"BANT BITTERWOOD! COME forth!" Hezekiah's loud voice echoed through the spare cabin. His daughters flinched at the noise. Adam, in his crib, began to wail. Bant went to the crib and leaned over to kiss his son on the forehead. The motion distracted Adam from the shout. He fell silent and stared up at Bant with wide, wet eyes. Bant turned away and faced his daughters. He scooped them into his arms as they rushed to him.

"Why do you have to go away?" asked Ruth, his eldest daughter.

"Hezekiah says we must spread the word of the Lord," Bant said, squeezing them with all his strength before lowering them once more to the dirt floor. "I'll think about you every day."

Recanna stood by the door, holding his pack.

"Be careful," she said as he took the pack from her hands.

"I will," Bant said, embracing her. "I'll miss you."

Ruth tugged at his pant leg.

"Promise you're coming back?" she said.

"I promise," Bant said, smiling. He wished he knew when that promise would be fulfilled. Hezekiah insisted they would be gone only as long as needed, but he also firmly refused to say how long that might be. Bant knew that his journey might last a season, or it might last years. He wished he could refuse the duty. However, after witnessing the miracle of Hezekiah being unharmed by the spear, he knew beyond question the man was a true messenger of God. Refusing Hezekiah would be like saying no to God Himself.

Bant's greatest fear was what might happen as a consequence of slaying the dragon. Yet over a month had passed with no sign of the king's armies. Perhaps Hezekiah's performance had been enough to scare them off forever.

With one last kiss Bant pulled away from Recanna's arms, then walked outside. Hezekiah waited, his wagon loaded and ready, his ox-dog pawing impatiently at the ground, its breath fogging in the morning air. Bant shivered as the breeze played with his cloak. The bright sun just over the trees hinted at a warm day to come.

"It looks like a good day to travel," Bant said, placing his pack on the wagon.

"Every day is a good day to do the Lord's work," Hezekiah replied.

Bant took his seat next to Hezekiah. "Have you decided our destination?" he asked.

"We shall head north, further into the heart of ignorance. The Lord will decide when we reach the site of His next church."

Hezekiah flicked the reigns. The ox-dog gave a low bark and began dragging the heavy wagon forward. Bant looked back at his home, at his wife and children standing in the doorway. Their forms shimmered as his eyes filled with tears.

They passed through the now-bare peach orchards. The air smelled of dry leaves. In the distance some of the village boys were rounding up a herd of goats for milking. Soon the women would turn their attention to the art of cheese making. Bant found himself reviewing all the things that still needed to be done in the village. The past month hadn't been enough time to finish everything. The necessities were taken care of, but he knew Recanna would have liked to have the house freshly painted, the widow Tabe's barn needed mucking, and the men could have certainly used his help with digging the second well.

Most of all, he hated leaving Recanna to care for the children alone. When next he saw Adam, no doubt the boy would be walking, perhaps even talking. He wanted to witness these things. He wanted to share his thoughts with Hezekiah but over the years he'd learned to anticipate the prophet's consistent message. The greater he suffered in this world, the greater his reward in the next.

"This is all part of God's plan," Bant said, meaning it as an affirmation, though it struck his ears like a question.

"Everything is part of God's plan," Hezekiah said.

* * *

THE OX-DOG WAS slow but steady. Moment by moment the distance between Bant and his home grew.

They were five miles from Christdale, with the sun high in the sky, when they saw the earth-dragons. This time only two of the dragons rode on the great lizards, but they led scores of soldiers, a long, single file which blurred together in the distance like an enormous emerald serpent slithering among the autumn foliage.

"Hezekiah—"

"I see them, Bant Bitterwood," the cleric answered.

"What do you think this means? What should we do?"

"Proceed with our journey," Hezekiah said, and he did so, keeping the cart on the road, drawing ever closer to the advancing regiment.

As they drew within a few hundred yards, the dragons halted and formed into a line across the road three dragons deep, spears thrust forward. Behind the line, one of the mounted dragons drew up in his saddle. Bant recognized Mekalov, the dragon who had visited Christdale the previous month.

"Isn't this a pleasant surprise," Mekalov said.

"Stand aside," Hezekiah said. "We go to spread the word of the Lord."

"Spreading your manure is of no importance to us," Mekalov answered, his eyes narrowed in anger. "We were charged with collecting the taxes of your village. Since you refused the king's generous offer to keep half of your labors, we come with new terms: we will take anything the king may find of value and destroy everything else."

"What?" Bant said, standing up on the wagon seat. "Are you mad?

"These are Albekizan's orders. To call us mad is to call the king mad. Hold your tongue lest I cut it from your treacherous lips."

"But—"

Mekalov raised his talon, silencing Bant. "Your protests are meaningless. Nothing you can say will spare your village."

"So be it," Hezekiah said. "Their souls are readied. Now, stand aside."

"What?" Bant said. "You're telling them it's okay?"

The prophet tilted his head up to face Bant. His eyes remained hidden beneath the broad black rim of his hat. "My work there is done. All have been saved. What true harm can come to those who have immortal life? Have faith, Bant Bitterwood. The Lord shall provide."

Bant was speechless.

"Your submission is the only wise course," Mekalov said. "Step down from the wagon. The ox-dog will be spared for he can be used to carry the tax back to the king. To ensure his strength we shall keep him fed on human flesh. A beast like this... I would say he requires at least two human males to feed him on his journey ahead."

"Dragon, I have no quarrel with you," Hezekiah said. "But if you attempt to interfere with our journey, you will surely die. Stand aside."

"Why?" Bant asked, finding he was angrier with Hezekiah than afraid of the dragons. "Are our lives worth more than Recanna's? It's okay for my children to die as long as we live?"

"We shall discuss the matter later, Bant Bitter-wood."

"No, you won't," the dragon hissed, raising a huge battle-axe above his head. "Kill them!"

The dragons rushed forward in one wave. The ox-dog snarled and jumped at them, breaking their line in half. The sudden movement toppled Bant backward from the flat wagon seat into the jumbled cargo. Hezekiah's strong hand reached beside Bant's face, and the prophet's fingers closed around the handle of his oversized axe.

The earth-dragons swarmed around the wagon. A spear bit into the wagon bed an inch from Bant's throat. The wagon shuddered as Hezekiah leapt into the tray, bringing his axe down with a force that severed the nearest dragon's arm. Two more dragons leapt on Hezekiah, grabbing his arms. Hezekiah swung the dragons who held him like rag dolls as he viciously hacked a red path through the green swarm.

The wagon continued to bounce around as the ox-dog fought until one of the giant mounted lizards pounced into its side. The wagon tilted and Bitterwood clutched at the shifting cargo as he struggled to stay aboard.

Suddenly, Mekalov cried out a command and the dragons that surrounded Hezekiah jumped clear as the leader's mount thundered ahead in a charge. Hezekiah struck first, burying his axe deep into the brow of the behemoth that crashed toward him. Momentum carried the monstrous lizard forward, with Mekalov leaning out from his saddle, slicing his broad, flat axe sideways with a savage shout, catching the black-robed cleric by the neck, severing his head from his shoulders.

Hezekiah's body staggered backward as his head spun through the air. Instead of blood gushing from the stump of his neck, a beam of red light brighter than the sun shot to the heavens.

"WHEREFORE THE KING SAID UNTO ME, WHY IS THY COUNTENANCE SAD, SEEING THOUGH ART NOT SICK? THIS IS NOTHING ELSE BUT SORROW OF HEART," Hezekiah shouted, his booming voice emanating from his headless torso.

Everyone turned to witness the spectacle, giving Bant temporary relief from the threat of spears. The great lizard and the ox-dog continued to struggle, jostling him among the cargo.

Mekalov jumped from his dying lizard, which now writhed in agony, with Hezekiah's axe still buried deep in its brow. Hezekiah's head fell at his feet. Mekalov jumped back as the head began opening and closing its jaw furiously, pushing itself around in a slow circle.

The prophet's body continued to stagger about, shouting mouthlessly: "THERE IS NO HEALING OF THY BRUISE; THY WOUND IS GRIEVOUS. Data set 1034. Syscheck failed."

The body swayed, looking ready to fall, then straightened itself and announced, "AND WHEN THEY HAD EATEN THEM UP, IT COULD NOT BE KNOWN THAT THEY HAD EATEN THEM; BUT THEY WERE STILL ILL FAVOURED, AS AT THE BEGINNING. SO I AWOKE."

The body began to walk in circles as all the dragons watched, slack-jawed.

At last, Hezekiah's head worked itself around to face the wandering body. The body stopped suddenly and said, "System initialization. Stabilized. Syscheck positive. Begin command."

His body then stepped purposefully toward his head, leaning down to grab it with his left hand while he pulled the buried axe free of the dead lizard with his right. He placed his severed head upon his shoulders. Sparks and smoke flew as they connected. Hezekiah turned to face Mekalov, straightening his coat.

"By the bones," Mekalov muttered. "What are you?"

Hezekiah stared at the earth-dragon as white smoke continued to rise from his neck. Then, with blinding speed, the prophet raised his axe high in the air and shouted: "TO ME BELONGETH VENGEANCE!"

Hezekiah struck the axe directly through the center of Mekalov's skull, continuing down in its vicious slice until its tip was buried in the ground. Mekalov's bisected body fell to earth in equal halves.

Just then the ox-dog let out a pained, wet, yelp as the lizard sunk its teeth into the dog's throat. The lizard pushed forward, forcing the ox-dog to fall to its back and sending the wagon completely over. Bant smashed his head against a rock as the heavy contents crashed down upon him. Bright spots danced before his eyes, and when they faded, all was dark and quiet.

BANT AWAKENED UNDERNEATH the stars next to a crackling fire. His head throbbed. He tried to raise a hand to touch it but his arms were tangled under blankets. Hezekiah sat next to him, running a whetstone along the edge of his axe. Behind the prophet lay a pile of reptilian corpses.

"I feared for your life, Bant Bitterwood," Hezekiah said.

Suddenly, Bant remembered. He kicked aside his covers and jumped to his feet.

"Do not flee," Hezekiah said. "You may be confused by what you witnessed today. Put it from your mind. You are still called by the Lord to do His work. Do not falter."

"You... you aren't human," Bant said.

"No," Hezekiah said.

"Are you angel, or devil?"

"Neither," the cleric answered, keeping his eyes fixed on the edge of his axe. "I am a machine. For over a thousand years I have performed the duties my maker charged me with, the duties His maker gave unto Him."

"I don't understand," Bant said.

"Understanding isn't required, Bant Bitterwood. All that matters is that you have faith. In my long centuries wandering this world, I have seen many men loyal to the Lord lose their faith after events like this. I hope you will prove stronger."

"You've lied to me all these years!"

"I never claimed to be human, Bant Bitterwood."

"What have I done?" Bant said, cradling his head in his hands. "I've given up everything to follow you."

"You've given up nothing," Hezekiah said sternly. Then, more softly, "The Lord will provide."

"Don't talk to me!" Bant shouted. "You were willing to let the dragons kill Recanna!"

Hezekiah shrugged. "I have sown the seeds of the word. Your fellow villagers have grown ripe in their love of the Lord. Perhaps the Lord has chosen to harvest the crop."

"I'm going back," Bant said, looking around the camp for his pack.

"That would be inadvisable," Hezekiah said. He sat aside the whetstone and began to polish the axe with a piece of soft leather.

"I don't want your advice."

"My mission requires me to purge uncooperative nonbelievers. Refuse to carry out your missionary duties and I will be forced to regard you as fallen. You stand with the Lord or you stand against Him. There is no middle ground."

"You're threatening me?"

"I'm informing you," Hezekiah said, holding the axe so that the firelight danced along its polished surface. He looked satisfied with his work. "With proper care, a good tool can last forever," he said.

"You can't stop me," Bant said, looking over his shoulder into the darkness. He was disoriented, but he thought he recognized enough of the landscape to know where he was. "I'm going home."

"I doubt that is possible," Hezekiah said. "Christdale may no longer exist. Thirty dragons fled and they moved in the direction of the village. I watched the smoke rise from that direction as night fell."

"You're lying," said Bant.

Hezekiah shook his head. "If your family is dead, Bant Bitterwood, it is now vital you remain faithful. You wish to reunite with them in heaven, do you not?"

"You son of a bitch," Bant growled. He turned and ran into the night, following the rough road back to the village. The night was moonless and the stars glittered like frost clinging to the sky. Dark shadows chased him, raced before him, thrust across the path to trip him. Each time he fell, he lifted himself once more and ran. His heart pounded in his ears. His lungs burned with each rasping breath. Hot daggers pierced his side. At last, after running for an eternity, he smelled the familiar scents of his home fields.

Then he smelled smoke.

He ran through the orchards, remembering the night so long ago when he had searched the darkness to find Recanna. He could see the red glow of light from ahead. He raced from under the thick trees into the starlit field. In the distance the embers of Christdale smoldered in the night breeze.

"No!" he shouted as he saw the charred remains that had once been his home. His legs gave out and he fell to his knees, weeping.

"Recanna!" he cried. "Recanna!" No one answered. He crawled into the black ash, burning his hands and knees as he dug through the hot rubble. He could barely recognize the shards of his life. Was this charred and broken clay the plate he'd eaten his breakfast on? Was this mound of smoldering cloth the bed he'd slept in the night before? Blisters formed on his fingers as he dug, looking for any sign of his family. He coughed and wheezed in the smoke rising from the rubble; he could barely see anything through his tears. His random path through the ruins at last led him away from the coals and onto a patch of dry earth that had once been his front yard. He collapsed, his raw and bleeding hands and knees no longer able to support his weight.

He lay there, breathless and numb, hearing only the crackle of embers. He had no strength to even open his eyes. After a long time he heard footsteps.

"You see now the truth in my words, Bant Bitterwood," Hezekiah said, his voice calm and even. "There is nothing left for you here. The Lord has cleared all obstacles to our mission."

Bant rose and turned to face the prophet he had followed all these years.

"Lies!" he shouted, rushing forward, pounding his blistered fists against Hezekiah's stone-hard chest. "Every word from your lips is a lie!"

"You are distressed," Hezekiah said, showing no pain from the blows.

"God damn you!" Bant cried, falling to his knees. It felt as if his fingers were broken. "God damn you."

"Watch your tongue," said the prophet. "Blasphemy risks your immortal soul."

"Go to hell!"

"Bant Bitterwood, I have walked this world for over ten centuries. I am capable of patience. This morning you were a true servant of God. You cannot renounce your faith so quickly. I will attribute your blasphemy to your distress, and spare you, for now. I will go and leave you to your grieving."

The black-robed prophet turned away, becoming a dark shadow against a dark sky. His voice seemed to come from nowhere and everywhere as he said, "I shall return in three days. Prepare yourself. If you have sought the forgiveness of the Lord at this time, I, too, shall forgive you. We shall never speak again of your shameful behavior. But be warned: if you continue down the sinner's path, or if you fail to meet me here on the appointed day, I will slay you when next I meet you."

"Kill me now," Bant said, his head hung low. His broken hands lay useless on the ground before him. "Everything I loved is gone. Everything I believed has been a lie."

"I have given you my judgment. I go now to rest. My maker built me well, but it will take time to repair the damage done. Three days, Bant Bitterwood."

The prophet's shadow dissolved into the night. Bant couldn't stop weeping. He crawled over the broken ground toward the ash that had once been his home.

Was it all a lie? Hezekiah's promise of a Lord watching over him, of a heavenly reward? Had he devoted his life to some absurd fiction? Could he believe in anything now?

In the dim light Bant could just make out the footprints of the dragons that had stood before the door. Seeing the truth of what the beasts had done didn't require even a mustard seed of faith.

His most fundamental beliefs were shattered.

All that he cherished, lost.

He no longer wanted to live in this barren world.

In the absence of love and faith, a single realization filled him as he stared at the dragon's footprint, pouring into his body in a hot wave like strong drink. He turned his face toward the starry sky and cursed till his voice trailed off in laughter. He still knew how to hate. And hate, he knew, could change the world.

CHAPTER FIFTEEN

BLASPHET

1100 D.A., The 69th Year of the Reign of Albekizan

METRON, THE HIGH Biologian, descended the dark stone spiral that led to the deepest tombs of the library. He carried a lantern but kept it shuttered. He didn't need his vision to walk this familiar path. He'd spent over a century within the library. He was the guardian of all the wide-ranging and ancient knowledge contained within the walls. No dragon alive had read more books than Metron; no dragon was more in love with their musty smell or their yellowed pages. This made his present descent into darkness all the more troubling. Today Metron's mission was to destroy the collection's most sacred books.

He'd been drinking wine all evening, with three bottles drained and a fourth, nearly empty, clutched in his gnarled talons. His courage, he knew, would never be greater. If he didn't destroy the books now he never would.

At last he arrived in the basement. He paused before the display case that held one of the dragons' most cherished artifacts. It was a slab of white stone, etched with the feathered fossil of a creature long since vanished from the earth. Half bird, half reptile, the winged beast looked for all the world like the smaller, more primitive ancestor of the winged dragon. A copper plate beneath the case bore the word "Archaeopteryx." Replicas of this stone hung in the halls of sun-dragons and in the towers of biologians throughout the kingdom, in testament to the dragon's long and rightful domi-nance of the earth

Metron knew it had not been a dragon who exhumed this fossil and engraved the letters into the copper.

"Guardian of the secrets," Metron said, his speech slurred. "Bah. Guardian of lies is more like it."

With no reverence at all for the artifact before him, Metron leaned his shoulder into the case and used the full weight of his body to push it aside. He paused, taking another drink from the flask, study-ing the iron door revealed behind the display, its hinges caked with rust.

Beyond the door was the forbidden collection, to be seen only by the High Biologian. Metron wished he had never read the terrible truths held in the books behind this barrier. He hung his lantern on the wooden peg near the door and placed the tar-nished key into the deep lock. With a strain that hurt his aged wrist, he twisted the key until the lock clanged open. Clenching his teeth, he grasped the ring that opened the door and dug his feet into the cracks in the floor stones. Needles pierced his heart as he strained and struggled against the weight, but at last, with a shudder, the door creaked open.

Light seeped from the growing crack. Metron frowned, unable to comprehend what could cause the brightness from within. He looked inside. The wine bottle slipped from his clutch, crashing to the stone floor.

Blasphet, the Murder God, waited for him, resting on all fours before an immense wooden table strewn with dozens of books and glowing candles. The chamber, which always seemed so open to Metron, seemed cramped when occupied by a sun-dragon, even one as thin and withered as Blasphet. The rear of the chamber was gone; the stone wall had been carted away, revealing a dungeon chamber beyond.

Metron swallowed, his throat suddenly very dry. He wished he had more wine. "How did you—"

"In my years in the dungeons, I grew quite sensitive to sounds," Blasphet said. "I knew there were other chambers set here upon the bedrock of the castle. I used to fantasize about what I might discover were I to have access to an army of earth-dragons armed with sledgehammers."

"I see," Metron said. "So much effort, only to discover a chamber full of lies."

"Lies?" Blasphet said, holding up a small, leather-bound volume entitled *The Origin of Species*. "Most of what I've read parallels your own teachings... though with one significant twist. Still, while this is an interesting discovery, it's not what I'm looking for.

I'm disappointed. I was certain this sealed chamber would hide something worth knowing."

"Nothing in here is worth knowing," Metron said. "It's why these books aren't kept with the others. You'll find only fables and heresies here."

"I'm rather fond of heresies," Blasphet said.

"No doubt," said Metron. "Still, I must ask you to leave. No one is allowed into this room save for myself. It's the law."

"Oh, dear me, another law broken," Blasphet said, his eyes brightening.

"The books here can be of no value to you," Metron said. "Half are written in lost tongues. You waste your time."

"I am a quick study," Blasphet said. "I am also the best judge of what interests me."

"The only thing that interests you is death," Metron said.

"Ah, but you're mistaken, Metron." Blasphet sat the book back on the table. "Life is what fascinates me. Life and the lies we are told about it. For instance, how many times have I been witness to a funeral pyre and listened to the legend of Asrafel? We are taught that life is flame."

"So it is written," Metron said.

Blasphet shook his head. "My experiments tell me otherwise. If life is flame, why is it that when I burn my subjects in a pit of fire, they die? Shouldn't they, in fact, prosper? In the legend of Asrafel, we are asked to believe that breathing smoke reconnects us to our ancestors. I have tested this. I have placed my subjects in airtight rooms and filled the rooms with smoke. They cough. They die. There seems to be no spiritual connection at all."

"Just because our mortal minds are unable to comprehend the paradox of flame is no reason to dispute the holy truth," Metron said.

"'Holy' is a word used to conceal a great deal of nonsense," Blasphet said. "If we disregard the evidence of our senses, won't that lead to madness?"

"Perhaps our senses are limited while confined to flesh," said Metron. "And you are already mad."

"No. Not mad. I merely trust the senses I possess. My eyes tell me that flame is not beneficial to life, despite your 'holy' teachings." Blasphet raised himself from all fours to place his weight on his hind claws in the more common posture of the sun-dragons. His shoulders scraped the stone ceiling of the chamber. "Unlike my fellow dragons, I have the intellectual honesty to reject an idea simply because it's labeled 'holy.' I've pondered the mystery of life for many decades. I thought perhaps it's not flame but heat that gives us the vital force. I've slit open many a dragon. The core of a dragon is undeniably hot—much hotter than the air around it. Perhaps heat is the key. However, when I place subjects in a steel box and heat it to a cherry-red glow, again they expire. Save for a brief burst of activity from the subject early on, heat has no invigorating effect at all."

Metron rubbed his chin. Perhaps the wine mellowed him. He knew Blasphet was confessing to disturbing crimes, but he still found the observations intriguing. He often thought of heat as invigorating. Standing beside the fireplace in the morning did wonders for his old bones. Blasphet must be overlooking something obvious in his experiments.

"Life also requires air," Metron said, latching onto the missing element. "Perhaps the heat drives out the air, extinguishing life."

"Air may be a key," Blasphet admitted. "My subjects do die in its absence. Yet fish are undeniably alive and they live without air. This showed that water might be the key—obviously, we expire if long deprived of it. But when I place subjects beneath the water, they do not live long."

"Then there must be a mix," said Metron. "Life isn't one thing. It's a mix of fire, of heat, of air, of water. All these things combine to animate our base matter."

"If this is true, I believe there must be some perfect mixture of the elements. Some ratio of flame and water that gives birth to unquenchable life." Blasphet sounded excited to be discussing this issue with someone who could follow his reasoning. Blasphet snaked his head closer to Metron, bringing his yellow teeth near the biologian's ear. He said, his voice soft, yet quivering with anticipation, "Tell me, Metron, do you believe in immortality?"

"In truth?" Metron asked, summoning the courage to look into the Murder God's blood-rimmed eyes. "No. It's idle fantasy."

"I believe," said Blasphet. "When I lost the contest to my brother, I was castrated; the normal path to continuing one's bloodline is simple procreation. With that route closed to me, I began to contemplate the alternative. It was in these very libraries that I gained the first knowledge of substances that could hasten death; by simple symmetry, isn't it likely there are also compounds or formulas that can extend life? I believe our bodies can be perfected. I believe it's possible to live forever."

Metron sighed. "I am old, Blasphet. When I was younger I occasionally entertained the thought of life without end. Alas, the years roll by. The body breaks and bends. The mind fogs day by day. Eternal life may not be a blessing."

"I refuse to accept that," Blasphet said. "The life force is a mystery, yes, but one I will solve. I will not go willingly into the final darkness. I will find the key to life and unlock eternity."

Metron nodded. Perhaps it was possible. Blasphet certainly seemed convinced. Then the biologian's stomach grumbled and knotted. This was Blasphet who spoke. This was a butcher before him, not a philosopher.

"This is fine talk," Metron said. "But I believe not a word of it. I think you kill because it gives you some deep gratification that I will never comprehend. I think all this talk of the mystery of life is meant to mask your vile actions. If you truly believe yourself engaged in some noble quest, you are only deluding yourself."

"You think me deluded? Hypocrite! You are the one who knows the truth yet lives a lie. The time I've spent here convinces me these books aren't forgeries. You know the truth about the origins of dragons."

Metron frowned. How much had Blasphet read? How many of the ancient languages did he know? "Don't believe everything you read here, Blasphet. You are making a common intellectual mistake that confounds many an otherwise brilliant student. You assume that just because information is old, it must be true."

"You are in a poor position to speak to me of intellectual mistakes," Blasphet said, his voice mocking. "You've counseled three generations of kings, telling them it is natural to kill the humans, as nature has decreed we are the superior race. How can you live with yourself?"

"You are hardly in a position to make me feel guilty," Metron growled. "I nourish the myths that allow dragon culture to flourish. You are the one with blood on his claws."

"Yes. Blood. And poison." Blasphet drew his fore-claw close to Metron's eyes. He flexed his bony talon, displaying the black, tarry substance caked beneath the nails. "Or perhaps you are speaking metaphorically? Implying I should feel remorse? Your own teachings contain the doctrine that organisms do what they must to survive. I devote my life to this central principle. If I must strip the planet of all life to learn how to ensure my own immortality, so be it. I'll never shed a tear."

"Have care, Blasphet. Push too far and Albekizan will recognize your true evil. You'll find yourself in chains once more," Metron said.

"Evil? What a quaint idea, unworthy of a scholar such as yourself. For the true intellectual, good and evil are mere hobgoblins. All that matters is the quest for truth. Perhaps your century of scholarship can end my quest. What is the animating force? What is the source of life?"

"What I know, I have told you," Metron said, looking at the floor, away from Blasphet's intense gaze. "Life is flame."

"Still you insist on that lie?" Blasphet grabbed Metron's face, turning his eyes once more to meet his own. "If you truly do not know, admit it. You may not be the most intelligent dragon who lives, but you are, perhaps, the most educated. Give me the answer or I'll sink a single claw into your neck, putting an end to your miserable life."

"Kill me if you must," Metron said, not daring to blink. "I do not know the answer you seek."

Blasphet released him. Metron staggered backward. Blasphet sounded more frustrated than angry as he said, "There is not a book in this library you have not studied. If you were to join me in my quest for truth, I know I could find the answer more rapidly."

Metron paused, considering the words of the Murder God. Metron truly had no special insight into the secret of immortality. Nevertheless, as long as Blasphet thought he might, perhaps he held some advantage over the wicked dragon.

"I don't have the answer you seek," said Metron. "But that doesn't mean I cannot discover it."

"Then you will research the answer? This is not the only library on the planet; the College of Spires has a collection that rivals your own. I know you biologians have a network of contacts. Will you not help me search?"

Metron rubbed his cheek where Blasphet's claws had rested. His scales crawled where he'd been touched. "Am I to believe that if you found the secret of life, you would give up your murderous ways?"

"You can believe whatever helps you sleep at night," Blasphet said.

"I believe that even if you were to change your ways, it would matter little in the grand scheme of things. Albekizan will continue to execute the humans with or without your help."

"Hmm." Blasphet studied Metron's face. "It bothers you, the genocide. Interesting. I hadn't guessed most dragons would object. However, if it's any comfort, when I gain the secret of immortality, I won't be sharing it with my brother. Albekizan won't live forever. I'll see to that when the time is right."

"Your words hint at treason."

"*Tsk. Tsk.* Those pesky laws."

Metron found himself in curious admiration of the monster before him. It occurred to him that a being unconstrained by laws or morality might prove useful. He said, "I do not lightly enter into treason. Give me time to consider your words."

"Of course," Blasphet said, his eyes glittering with the light of victory. "But I already know how you will answer."

DESPITE HER EXHAUSTION, Jandra couldn't sleep. Kanst had marched them nonstop through the day with no break for food or water. Any who stumbled or fell behind had been quickly motivated with whips to keep up the pace. When night fell Kanst had allowed them to drop, too weary to fight or protest, beside a small, muddy pond in the middle of a pasture. For dinner, the dragons passed around sacks of half rotten seed potatoes they'd scavenged from the village. The dragons slaughtered the cows they found in the pasture and the smell of charred meat hung in the air. The humans would get no taste of this.

The dragons set up tents for themselves, but no shelter, not even blankets, had been provided for the humans. The villagers all huddled together for warmth. Jandra wrapped her arm around Zeeky who was now sound asleep. The child hadn't complained once during their long march.

Jandra studied the stars, trying to make some sense of Kanst's reasons for the forced march. What did this talk of a "Free City" mean? Why hadn't Kanst simply slaughtered the villagers where he found them?

A sky-dragon circled high overhead, a dark blot against the night sky.

Vendevorex?

No. Most likely it was one of the aerial guard, flying on routine duty. If Vendevorex had followed, he would certainly be invisible. It was foolish to think he would follow. Never mind that he'd been too weak to even stand when she left him; he'd proven by word and deed that he was too cowardly to fight. Jandra pushed back thoughts of her former mentor. This was the problem with being raised by someone who knew how to become invisible: every time she looked over her shoulder to see nothing, it only fueled her suspicions that he was, in fact, there. Perhaps in time she would stop seeing him in any small flicker of shadow. She had to accept the reality that she would be better off never meeting Vendevorex again.

She couldn't believe how good the dragons' meals smelled. The aroma taunted her.

Carefully, Jandra slid from Zeeky's embrace. She spread her cloak over the child then, glancing around to make sure no one watched her, she tossed a handful of silver dust into the air.

Jandra moved invisibly among the sleeping humans, toward a small circle of five guards gathered around a fire for warmth. They were gnawing on charred bones.

"Can't be him. Seeing what they want to see," one of the guards said.

"He's supposed to be a ghost," another said. "How can chains hold a ghost?"

The third grunted. "Who cares if it's him or not? If Kanst and Albekizan are satisfied by killing him, our lives will be easier."

"It must be him," said another. "He had the arrows."

"Should've killed him where he stood," said the fifth dragon, tossing a gnawed thighbone over his shoulder. "I can't believe Kanst is actually sharing a tent with the mummy."

Jandra grabbed the bone from the dirt. There was still quite a bit of meat on it. Earth-dragons were sloppy eaters. She shoved the meat into a pocket in her cloak and moved on.

She went in search of Kanst's tent. That task proved simple enough—his was the largest and surrounded by the most guards. Unfortunately, some of the guards held ox-dogs on chain leashes. Invisibility wouldn't fool an ox-dog. Still, the guards and dogs looked as worn out and ready for sleep as the villagers were. Indeed, one of the dogs was already snoring. She held her breath and tiptoed between them.

She moved toward the tent flap. As she reached for it, the flap took on a life of its own, pushing outward. She jumped back as Kanst emerged from the tent. Jandra scrambled to move out of his way. Invisible or not, it wasn't difficult to be discovered if a creature with a forty-foot wingspan brushed up against you. Kanst's whiplike tail swung toward her and she skipped over it like a rope.

"Make sure no one gets in," Kanst said to the guards. "I go to consult Zanzeroth."

Kanst lumbered off into the night. Once the general was safely out of earshot, one of the guards muttered to another, "Going to consult that keg of goom in the hunter's tent is more like it."

Jandra slid between the gap in the tent flaps.

In the dim light she could barely see Pet lying prone on Kanst's huge battle chest. Manacles held his arms and legs to the four corners of the lid, and a steel collar was fastened around his neck.

He lay still as death. Her heart sank.

But why would they bother to chain a dead man?

She moved closer until she could hear his breathing. She had expected to find him bruised and bloodied but he looked unharmed. Kanst apparently wanted his prize delivered in good health.

Becoming visible, she carefully placed her hand over his mouth as he slept. He stirred to wakefulness.

"It's me," she said. "Don't be scared."

"Jandra," Pet whispered as she removed her hand. "What are you doing here? And what on earth have you done to your hair?"

"I'm not here to discuss hairstyles. I've come to rescue you."

"Don't," Pet said. "I've made my choice."

"Pretending you're Bitterwood isn't going to solve things. You saved the hostages for the moment, but Albekizan's death warrant on all humans is still in place. I need every ally I can muster to stop him. I need you free and fighting."

"I'm no warrior," Pet said. "We both know that. I'm only an actor, a pretender. I told you, if I could help people by acting, I would. Who knew I'd get my chance so soon? When they take me before Albekizan, I know he'll kill me. Perhaps my death will assuage his anger. He might call off his order of genocide."

"Or maybe you'll have died in vain."

"Your words of encouragement are a great comfort to me," Pet said.

"Sorry. But you don't have to die. I'm working on a plan to stop Albekizan."

"How?"

"The first step is to rescue you. Then..." Jandra hoped for inspiration. It didn't come. "To be honest, I'm still fleshing out the rest of the plan."

"If you're here, Vendevorex must have come to your way of thinking," Pet said. "What help can I be compared to him?"

"Ven isn't with me," Jandra said.

"Oh. He didn't pull through?"

"I'd rather not discuss it."

"But, if Vendevorex—"

"Stop," Jandra said, raising her hand. "I'm not here to discuss Vendevorex. I'm here to save you so you can help me in my fight to save mankind."

"As an army of two?" Pet said. "I think I currently have the better plan."

"When did you get so brave all of a sudden? I think I liked you better when you were—"

"Cowardly?" Pet interjected.

Jandra shrugged. "More protective of your self interests, shall we say."

"I didn't do this for you. I told you, the villagers weren't strangers to me. I've done what I could over the years to help them. And they... well, some of them... some of the young women... have, um, been grateful."

"What are you saying?"

"Chakthalla would never have allowed me to select a permanent mate from among the villagers but she couldn't know everything I was up to. If I had allowed Kanst to slaughter the village children he might have been killing my offspring."

Jandra's heart sank. Of course, she should have known that he'd use his privileges and talents to seduce the village girls. He'd tried to bed her after ten minutes of conversation. She was shocked to find an icy vein of jealousy running through her body. Why? She didn't have any romantic feelings for him, did she?

Pet seemed to sense her disappointment. "I'm sorry. I haven't been a saint. Maybe what I'm doing will make up a little for the self-centered way I've lived. Don't worry about me. This is just another performance, one last moment on the stage. You know I love being the center of attention."

Jandra nodded. Her eyes blurred with tears. "You do what you have to," she said, her voice wavering.

"Don't cry."

"I'm sorry," she said.

"It's okay," Pet said. "But you need to go. Kanst could return at any time."

"Good-bye," Jandra said, leaning down and placing a kiss on Pet's cheek.

"Good luck with your plan," Pet said.

PET WATCHED JANDRA step away. A swirl of tiny stars engulfed her in the darkness, and when they fell away, she had vanished. Turning his eyes toward the door, he saw at last the flap sway aside before falling back. Only then did he let tears fill his own eyes. He'd done well playing brave before her. He prayed he could repeat the performance when he finally faced Albekizan.

JANDRA KNELT BESIDE the sleeping form of the real Bitterwood. He'd been silent all day, marching sullenly, looking as if he'd lost all will to live. First Pet decided to become a hero, then Bitterwood lost his will to fight. Were all human males this prone to mood swings? Ven had his faults but at least he was predictable.

Bitterwood lay so still she wondered for a second if he was dead. She could see the slightest movement of his chest, rising and falling beneath his threadbare clothing. His shirt was a mass of patches, stitches, and stains; it looked as if it hadn't been laundered in months. Not even the humans that lived in the hovels around Albekizan's palace had worn such rags. Furthermore, Bitterwood stank; he smelled of sweat, road dust, and dried blood. Holding her breath she reached out her hand to wake the sleeping dragon-slayer. When her hand was still an inch from his shoulder he said, quietly, "I'm awake."

"Good," she whispered. "We need to talk."

He continued to lay perfectly still, his eyes closed. He sighed, with breath ripened by rotting teeth, then said, "Say what you must."

"I want to know what's wrong with you. Twenty-four hours ago you were this cold-blooded dragon-slayer. Now, all day you've been shuffling around, blank-eyed, looking half dead. Are you faking this? Are you just waiting for the right moment to strike? Because if you are, I want to help."

He waited a long moment before answering, "You should get some sleep."

"In preparation for battle?" she said, hopefully. "You *are* planning to fight."

"I am planning on walking however far the dragons command us to walk tomorrow," said Bitterwood.

"This isn't like you," she said.

He turned toward her voice and opened his eyes. He fixed his gaze upon her.

"You cannot judge me," he said. "Long ago, I was taught that the greatest thing a man could do was to lay his life down for another. I was taught that if struck, I should turn the other cheek. If anyone harmed me, or trespassed against me, I was commanded to love and forgive them. Love and forgiveness were the greatest virtues. I believed these lies for almost a decade."

"Why are love and forgiveness lies?" she asked, aware of the irony as she said it. She certainly had no intention of forgiving Vendevorex, or ever loving him again.

"I was taught that there was a god who loved us so much, he gave his own son in sacrifice. Imagine that foolishness... sacrificing your life to redeem others."

"It sounds noble to me," she said.

"As it did to me, once. Then I learned that the man who taught me these things wasn't what I thought he was. I met him when I was young; I almost thought of him as a father. You can't know how his betrayal wounded me."

Jandra nodded. "I might have some idea."

"After his betrayal, I vowed never to be weak again. There would be no love. There would be no forgiveness. I would never turn my cheek if struck. I would match every blow with double the force. I would never love. I would never show mercy."

"But you turned yourself in to save the villagers. You still have a good side."

"I still have a weak side," Bitterwood said. "I once... I once had children. Two daughters. An infant son. The night before the attack, I met Zeeky. She reminded me of my own long-lost daughters. On any other night, Kanst's gambit would never have caught me. But I couldn't get Zeeky's voice out of my head. In the end that lingering trace of compassion destroyed me. I surrendered myself to the dragons to save others."

"Just as you'd been taught to do," she said.

He nodded. "Yet my sacrifice was in vain. I was rejected. The dragons would have slain me and slaughtered the villagers."

"If Pet hadn't intervened."

Bitterwood didn't respond to this. He closed his eyes and turned back on his side.

"He gave himself selflessly," he whispered. "The villagers were spared. Now I wonder, were the lies of my youth true after all? Can a man love others so much he will surrender his life to save them? Was my sacrifice rejected because I am unclean, corrupted by my hate? I am guilty; Pet was innocent. Was his sacrifice accepted because his heart was pure?"

Jandra said, "Pure isn't a word I would use to describe Pet. I spoke to Pet a minute ago. He's intent on getting himself killed. It doesn't have to end like this. I can get your bow and arrows back. You were magnificent in the castle. Think how much damage you could do with me by your side, keeping you invisible. We'd be the ultimate dragon-slaying team. You can save Pet and everyone here. You're my only hope."

Bitterwood lay motionless once more. His breathing was even, as if he had actually fallen asleep. She reached out to nudge him, and once more, he spoke before her fingers reached him.

"Life is more bearable when you live without hope," he said.

VENDEVOREX WOKE INTO darkness. For hours he'd pitched and turned, burning with fever. Now his fever had broken. He touched his belly, probing softly. His wounds had vanished. Once he'd set the healing in motion, his unconscious mind had been able to guide the process.

Smoke hung in the air. The smoke had a touch of pine to it. The air was moist and... he could hear water boiling. He sniffed again. Sassafras? Vendevorex looked around. He wasn't in Chakthalla's castle anymore. He lay next to a small fire pit and, across from him, basking in the fire's glow, was a sun-dragon, his face hidden beneath a black velvet hood. Vendevorex had a brief flash of memory. He'd been carried from the throne room by this dragon.

"Where am I?" Vendevorex asked.

"In a cavern. I've hidden here before," answered the masked dragon as he stirred the coals beneath a blackened kettle. "You lost consciousness not long after we slipped past Kanst's army. I brought you here to recover."

"How long have I been asleep?"

The masked dragon motioned toward a stalactite. A tall, slender glass cylinder etched with lines sat beneath it, catching the water that dripped from its tip. "If my clock is accurate, you've been unconscious nearly thirty hours."

"Where's Jandra?"

"Don't you remember? She ran off, angry with you."

"She didn't come back?"

"I'm sorry. I couldn't wait. I know of no way she could find us now. We've eluded even the ox-dogs."

"I see," Vendevorex said. "Then I should go and search for her."

"Perhaps she doesn't want to be found," the masked dragon said.

"I must find her. I had hoped to convince her to avoid Albekizan's schemes. I see that is no longer an option. But I can't let her fight single-handedly against your father."

The masked dragon grew suddenly still. Then, after too long a pause, he asked, bemused, "My father?"

"Come now, Shandrazel. You can't fool me. I've known you for too long. You have nothing to fear. I'm definitely not going to carry out your father's death order."

"No," Shandrazel agreed, grabbing his mask and pulling it from his head. "I suppose you won't."

"Nor, I suspect, would Chakthalla. She would have welcomed you to her planned rebellion. Why hide your identity?"

"Because," Shandrazel answered, "I've no desire to be king." He lifted the kettle from the coals and poured pungent, oily liquid into clay cups. "This drink will help revitalize you. It's—"

"Sassafras," Vendevorex said. "I know my medicinal herbs. It's made from the roots of a tree that grows here in the eastern mountains. It's similar in odor and taste to the European licorice root."

"European?" Shandrazel asked, offering the clay cup.

Vendevorex shrugged as he accepted the drink. The rough, unglazed ceramic warmed his talons. "I'm not trying to be obscure, but it really would take a long time to explain. Let's just say that your father may not have been the best source for you to learn your geography from."

"I concur," Shandrazel said, then stopped to take a drink.

Vendevorex inhaled the steam from his own cup. The vapors were sour, with a fragrant kick that made the deep recesses of his sinuses tingle.

"So," he said. "What have you been up to besides digging roots and hiding in caves?"

"I also made a clock and sewed a mask," Shandrazel said. "These haven't been the most glorious months of my life, to be honest. I probably wouldn't have made it this long except, after I fled the College of Spires, a student followed me and pledged his loyalty. He visits me from time to time with news and supplies. Through him I learned that Chakthalla was harboring you, and heard the whispers of rebellion. I thought it might be time for me to once more seek the company of sundragons."

"You came to help overthrow your father?"

Shandrazel shook his head. "I came hoping to prevent violence. I believe, despite all that has happened, that it is not too late for cooler heads to prevail. My father ordered my exile during horrible times. Bodiel... Bodiel was his favorite. I know this. But now that father's had time to grieve, his reason may have returned."

Vendevorex sighed. "You didn't know your father at all, did you?"

"Of course I did," Shandrazel said, sounding offended. "As his son, who could know him better?"

"Precisely because you're his son, you cannot see him plainly. I've advised Albekizan for many years. Trust me when I tell you the king is bull-headed and stonehearted. He'll not be talked out of his plans. Your exile will only end with your death, or his."

Shandrazel opened his mouth as if to argue, then shook his head. The wispy white feathers around his nostrils wafted like steam as he sighed. He stared at the flickering coals within the stone circle.

"Killing him would be the same as killing myself," said Shandrazel.

"A noble sentiment," Vendevorex said. "If only your father displayed half your compassion."

"So what now?" asked Shandrazel. "I'd rather not live the rest of my life hiding in caves."

"Nor I. What's more, I have Jandra to think about. I must save her and, to satisfy her, I must save the entire human race."

"No small task," said Shandrazel.

"True," Vendevorex said, stroking his chin with a fore-talon. "Fortunately, I'm not without resources.

I see now that open revolution will only bring further destruction. What's needed is some candidate for the throne who will assume the duty with a minimum of bloodshed. If you aren't volunteering, I believe our best hope may be Kanst. I didn't like that possibility before but we are running out of options. We could play upon his vanity; if I play my cards right, I might even wind up as his most trusted advisor, and help the kingdom see better days."

"The armies would accept Kanst as king," Shandrazel agreed. "He certainly possesses ambition. But he's also known for his ruthlessness. In any case, I fear his loyalty to my father is too great."

"You may be correct," Vendevorex said. "Right now, my first duty is to find Jandra. Once we are united with her we can focus our energies on approaching Kanst and stopping Albekizan."

CHAPTER SIXTEEN

HEART

T HE SUN WAS low over the mountains to the west as the villagers marched through the green valley. Zeeky felt as if she couldn't take another step. She wished Jandra would carry her but her mysterious friend looked as tired as she was. She certainly couldn't ask Hey You. The man who had been so friendly to her in the barn now kept everyone at a distance with his stern countenance and silence.

Zeeky's stomach growled. The dragons fed them only one meal in the mornings and water at night. She'd eaten better during the days she'd been on her own as a runaway. Of course, she hadn't really been on her own then. She'd had Poocher to care for and his needfulness had kept her going. She was far more alone and scared now, surrounded by a crowd of strangers, than

she had been when wandering across the countryside.

How nice it must be to be Kamon. The aged
prophet wasn't suffering at all on this journey. The
village men carried him when he grew tired, and
everyone gave him food until he'd had his fill. The
villagers adored him but wouldn't even look at her.
She grew dizzy with anger thinking about it.

Or perhaps she was dizzy with thirst or exhaustion. Whatever the cause the world was definitely
spinning, the path tilting sideways around her,
until she fell face forward into the dust. She tried
to stand up but didn't have the strength. All she
could do was lie there as the villagers stepped
over and around her. She felt as if she should be
angry with them but all she felt was shame at her
weakness.

A bony, rough hand slid under her shoulders,
turning her over. Hey You knelt over her, placing
his strong, wiry arms under her knees and behind
her back. Without a word he lifted her, placing her
head on his shoulders.

From her new vantage point, Zeeky looked back
down the trail at the line of humans. Along the line,
dragons herded humans, making sure none strayed.
Following behind the humans were the farm animals the dragons had also gathered. It was difficult
to tell in the diminishing light, but she squinted, and
sure enough, she could see him. There among the
predominantly pink pigs, Poocher's black and white
hide stood out.

Zeeky knew then that she would live through
this. She had to. She didn't know when, and she
didn't know how, but she would escape and save

Poocher, and go someplace far away where she would never have to see another dragon again.

AFTER VENDEVOREX FLED, Albekizan gave Blasphet his chambers. The star-shaped room in the high tower suited Blasphet's needs. Blasphet was one of the few dragons in the kingdom who understood the contents of the beakers and vials that lined the shelves along the room. What lesser creatures might think of as magic, Blasphet recognized as natural substances. There was nothing mystical about an acid that ate away iron, nothing strange about liquids that burned. Blasphet had yet to learn the secret, but he was convinced the wizard's most amazing feat, his ability to turn invisible, was based in some as-yet-to-be understood physical principle rather than in the supernatural.

Over the weeks, Blasphet had made many modifications to the star chamber and the rooms beneath it. To start, the main chamber was too cluttered and crowded for a sun dragon to move comfortably in He had most of the treasures and oddities in the room packed and carted to the chambers below to await further study. He kept the large, central oak table. With the addition of manacles, the table was perfect. A series of lanterns and mirrors lit the oak surface to high-noon brightness, even in the chill, dark hours of the night.

"You will probably want to scream," Blasphet said to the naked young man shackled to the wooden slab. "I hope you won't. Think about how nice it would be to die with a little dignity. Instead of howling and begging for mercy you will not receive, resolve to let your death serve the quest for knowledge. Tell me if you have an increased sensation of warmth, or perhaps of cold. If anything, anything at all, makes you feel even the slightest bit stronger, tell me at once. Do you understand?"

The human didn't speak but his angry, defiant eyes were a comfort to Blasphet. Perhaps this one had the will to survive the vivisection long enough to be of some use.

Blasphet reached to the onyx tray at the edge of the table and retrieved his scalpel, its razor edge glowing in the focused light. Blasphet made three cuts across the man's chest with practiced precision, one down the center, then one each across the top and bottom of the first cut. The man arced his back from the agony and ground his teeth, but did not cry out as Blasphet took the two flaps of skin and peeled them back, exposing the man's rib cage. The salty scent of flesh and blood invigorated Blasphet, as did the realization that his victim was still holding on to some last faint glimmer of hope that he might survive.

He'd picked this subject well. It hadn't just been the firm musculature and overall good health the human had displayed; he'd also recognized courage within the man's eyes, a spirit of defiance. He congratulated himself on his perception. His foolish brother could never have recognized the value of this specimen. Albekizan thought all humans looked alike.

Setting the scalpel aside, Blasphet sank his sharp, strong claws into the tissue just beneath the man's sternum. With a grunt he tore open the man's rib cage, exposing the organs within. The man opened his mouth to scream but no sound came out. His eyes closed and his head fell suddenly limp. Blasphet knew the man hadn't fully lost consciousness. The stimulant draught he had forced the man to swallow earlier would prevent sleep until the very end.

At that moment there was a knock on the door of the chamber. Blasphet grimaced, hesitant to leave his work but certain he knew who was visiting. He'd been expecting him for some time. Licking the red blood from his ebony talons, Blasphet went to give his visitor admittance.

"Have patience, Metron," he called out. "I'm coming."

He pulled the door open, revealing the High Biologian.

"How did you know it was me?" Metron asked.

"No one else dares visit. Moreover, I knew you would accept my offer. You and I value knowledge—we need not let petty morality interfere with that quest. We are kindred souls, my friend."

Metron shook his head. "We are nothing alike. You are a wicked, hateful thing that thrives on death. You use the gloss of intellectual pursuit to mask your vileness."

"Yet still you've come to help me, yes?"

Metron hesitated, then looked to the floor as he whispered, "Yes." The aged dragon then raised his head. "But unlike you, I am driven by a hatred of death. I see dark times coming upon the kingdom, and an alliance with you may be my only hope of preventing greater bloodshed."

"Of course," Blasphet said. Then he gave a little bow, and said, "Where are my manners? Keeping you in the doorway... please come in, my honored guest. We have much to discuss."

The High Biologian followed him through the lab, his feathery scales trembling at the sight of the man shackled to the table, the exposed heart still beating.

"This disturbs you," Blasphet said. "It shouldn't. Think of this body as a book. There is much to be learned by studying its pages."

"What can you possibly hope to learn from this?" Metron said, sounding choked.

"I am presently studying hearts," Blasphet said, motioning toward the feeble pulses of the purple blob that lay between the gray lungs. "There is no question that a beating heart is essential to the life of a man. Yet their eyes have been known to follow me for several seconds, even after I've removed the heart entirely. Life endures, however briefly. Often when I remove a heart it will beat in my hands for some time. Curious, yes? I have even devoured hearts still beating; the muscle expands and contracts as it rolls on my tongue. These are pieces of the puzzle, I'm certain."

Metron looked as if he were about to faint.

"Perhaps you would benefit from some fresh air," Blasphet said.

Blasphet opened the door that led to the sitting room. A light breeze stirred the curtains that led to the balcony, letting pale moonlight spill across the polished wooden floor. Strolling to the curtains, Blasphet pulled them aside and stepped onto the balcony overlooking the huge city under construction.

The Free City had a gem-like symmetry, a diamond encased by high wooden walls, with wide avenues dividing the structures within into perfect squares. Even though the sun had set long ago, the sound of hammers and saws rose from the city, which glowed with the light of a thousand lanterns.

"Magnificent, is it not?" Blasphet asked as Metron joined him on the balcony. "Say what you will about my brother, he does have a talent for motivating his workers. Construction is well ahead of schedule."

Metron nodded. "It is impressive. I admit, it does look more like a dwelling than an abattoir. I don't understand why you've gone to such an elaborate ruse, promising humans a life of ease when the plan is to slaughter them."

"The humans would only flee were we to wage unfettered genocide against them. It's much easier to draw them all together in one place. When I am through, there will be no men left in the kingdom." Blasphet leaned against the stone rail and said, dreamily, "Who knows what will take their place?"

"What do you mean?" Metron asked.

"Once it's complete, the city before you could comfortably house perhaps a hundred thousand humans. I plan to fill the city with over a million. I will kill a steady number of them daily, of course, so that the king won't grow too suspicious of my true plan."

"Which is?"

Blasphet spread his wings in a gesture that encompassed the city. "To study life on a grand scale! Imagine what we can learn with a million subjects to observe. Food will be limited so fights will take place constantly as the strong take the food from the weak. Soon there will be no pretense of lawfulness anywhere within the Free City. The strongest men will take what is needed to live and breed with the women most capable of survival. Their children will add to the population pressure within the city."

Metron shivered in the cool breeze that blew up against the tower. "This is a nightmarish vision," he said.

"Compared to their waking life, the humans within these walls will pray for nightmares. Diseases will flourish in a city so bloated with corpses. The corpses of their kind will become the humans' only sustenance and rainfall their only water. Yet I am certain some will survive, even flourish. I do not think they will be human anymore, but something much hardier, something that can survive any suffering. What secrets will such a being hold, Metron?"

Metron turned away from the city. He stepped back inside, his wings wrapped tightly around him to fend off the chill. He said, softly, "What if, before then, I can give you your answer? I learn the secret source of life and reveal it? You will stop this plan?"

Blasphet cocked his head. "You've found the answer?"

"No."

"My experiments will continue, then."

"By my very profession, I am one who places faith in books," Metron said. "It is true that I haven't found the answer in my studies, but there are still great stores of ancient knowledge kept by other biologians throughout the kingdom. I shall consult them. I ask only that you hold off on your experiments until such time as I can complete my search."

"Bring me your answer when and if you find it, fellow conspirator. But I won't stop my research while I wait."

Metron started to speak, then stopped. Blasphet knew the old dragon had no choice but to agree to his terms.

"Very well," Metron said. "I will go. The quicker I begin my search, the quicker I can halt this madness."

"Of course," Blasphet said. "May the flames of the ancestors bring you luck in your quest."

"I didn't think you believed in the flames of the ancestors," Metron said.

"No. Neither, I suspect, do you. Now hurry on. My subject in the next room is most likely dead by now, but I wish to weigh his organs while they are still fresh."

Metron hurried from the room, passing through the lab without turning his face toward the pale body on the slab. Blasphet locked the door behind him but didn't return to his work, which suddenly bored him. He returned to the balcony to look at the Free City. Soon, the sound of construction would give way to the constant cries of men in torment as his city filled to overflowing. How pleasant it would be to sleep to such music.

PET STIRRED FROM sleep. He wasn't alone. He opened his eyes and found Zanzeroth looming over him. Pet glanced to the door of the tent. The guards were gone.

Zanzeroth bent his face close to Pet's. His wounds were terrible. Stained gauze was stuffed into the gaping hole in the center of the aged dragon's snout. Black blood caked between his teeth. His eye patch was gone, revealing a scarred, ragged hole where his right eye should have been. His left eye was fixed on Pet's face. Pet's eyes watered as Zanzeroth breathed. The old dragon's breath reeked of gore and goom.

In his claw, Zanzeroth held one of the arrows that had been pulled from his body. He raised it to his bloodied face. His tongue flickered out, licking the notched end of the arrow where the fingers would hold it against the string.

Then Zanzeroth moved his head to Pet's chained hands. Pet squirmed as the hunter's raspy tongue danced along his fingertips for a long moment.

The aged hunter then sat back, contemplating Pet in the darkness. He reached out a claw and, one by one, undid the buttons of Pet's silk shirt. He pushed the cloth open, exposing Pet's bare chest.

"Not a scar on you," Zanzeroth whispered. He pulled Pet's shirt closed. He leaned down and said, so softly that Pet wasn't sure of the words, "I wanted to make certain."

Zanzeroth turned and moved back toward the tent flap, half limping and swaying like a drunkard. He cast one last glance back as he pushed open the tent flap. Pet could see the body of a guard sprawled in the mud outside. Zanzeroth nodded.

"Sleep tight," he said before the tent flaps closed behind him, leaving Pet alone.

CHAPTER SEVENTEEN

SATISfACTION

A WEEK AFTER his visit with Blasphet, Metron restlessly flipped the pages of an illuminated tome, waiting for sunset. Earlier, he'd watched Kanst returning, leading a band of captured humans to the Free City. Little time was left to avert the impending atrocities. Fortunately, his fellow biologians had pledged their assistance in researching Blasphet's question. Today held the appointed hour for their responses.

As the last rays of daylight faded, Metron closed the tome before him. He straightened the green sashes that hung across his chest, then descended from his private chambers into the main body of the library. Here the long, high bookshelves were arranged in twisting rows, forming a maze in which even experienced biologians might find themselves lost. The narrow passageways between the shelves barely allowed room for sky-dragons to creep between them; sun-dragons never ventured into this area of the library. Metron often wondered if this was by accident or design.

Metron navigated the rows with a speed born of experience. He entered into a side chamber that was filled with crates of uncataloged books and looked around to make certain no one was watching. Then he pushed aside the crates along the far side of the room, revealing a smooth stone wall. The illusion of solid rock would have fooled Vendevorex himself. The builders of this place had access to many secret arts. Metron stepped forward, the wall rippling as it swallowed him.

Beyond the false wall, Metron's scales bristled. The air here was thick and electric, ice-water cold yet smelling of heated iron. From all directions came a *buzz* of angry bees. Most unnerving of all, the room had no floor, no walls, no ceiling. All around him was a uniform, blank whiteness. It had been seven decades since he first stepped foot in this strange space, and still the sensation of toppling into an unending void threatened to overwhelm him. Despite the information his eyes gave him, he knew his feet rested on a solid surface. He tapped his staff against the unseen floor to assure himself.

This was the Snow Room, the secret meeting chamber of the biologians. There were thirty such chambers throughout the kingdom, and all predated the libraries that surrounded them. From this point, it was possible to see all who stood in those distant chambers, though hundreds of miles separated them. As he stared into the nothingness, he soon began to see the image of another biologian, materializing beside him like a traveler emerging from a fog.

It was Daknagol, the only biologian older than himself. Daknagol had initiated him in the secret of the Snow Room all those long years ago.

"Cursed place," Daknagol grumbled. The fine scales around his eyes crinkled into a mask of disgust. "How this chamber filled me with wonder in my youth. Now, following every visit, I'm seized with prodigious vomiting. The humans who built this place must have been wicked indeed."

"Hold your tongue, honorable Daknagol," Metron said.

As he spoke, a second dragon emerged from the mist. It was Androkom, the youngest of the initiated biologians and, some said, the most brilliant. Despite his rank, Androkom still had the air of a student. This was due in part to his youth and the brightness of his feathers, but also because of the deep ink stains that covered his claws; scribe work was usually left to the novice biologians.

"Why would you have him hold his tongue?" Androkom asked. "Everyone present knows the truth. We live in a world of lost wonders. We scavenge among the miracles of a vanished human civilization. The pathetic, ignorant beasts we use to tend our fields once strode this world like gods."

"Yes," said Metron. "And they destroyed themselves with their own dangerous technology. Let me remind you, we aren't here to debate the ancient past. We are here to discuss a more urgent question: what is life?"

By now, ten or more dragons had appeared. The question set them all talking at once. Metron banged his staff on the floor, regaining order. All fell silent save for Androkom.

"Exalted brothers," Androkom said, raising his inky talons, "I have the answer that eludes the High Biologian. I know the secret source of life!"

Metron wasn't surprised by this response. Androkom was famed for his intelligence—and his arrogance.

"Speak," said Metron.

"Nothing contradicts the Book of Theranzathax. Life is flame." Androkom held his head high as if to dare any of his fellow biologians to challenge him.

A cacophony of voices arose instantly, shouting in protest.

"Brothers," Metron urged, banging his staff. "Restrain yourselves."

When the assembly regained order, Metron said, "Androkom, why insist on the validity of the Book of Theranzathax? All here know that the book is a fabrication, composed not in ancient times but mere centuries ago."

"I am aware that the biologian Zeldizar created the book," Androkom said. "He wrote in the belief that dragons would only be truly liberated when they lost the knowledge of their lowly origins and embraced his new mythology. However, my studies lead me to believe that Zeldizar didn't simply fabricate these myths. Rather, he disguised truth with metaphor and parable. His assertion that life is a flame is based on his knowledge of chemistry, for life and flame are analogous chemical processes."

"Blasphet won't be content with such a broad answer," Metron said. "Many processes are chemical."

"Acknowledged," said Androkom. "The full details of my answer are not easily grasped, but I can provide evidence of their truthfulness."

Metron nodded, then addressed the assembly as a whole. "Brothers, have any others among you found another answer?"

Daknagol was next to speak. "I, too, arrived at the answer that life is a chemical process. It is described in many ancient texts. But the writings are arcane and complex. Though we have insights into the true answer, understanding will no doubt forever elude us, despite young Androkom's boasts."

"I agree," Metron said. "My own studies tell a similar tale. The words and symbols lie before me on the page, but their context has been lost over the centuries."

"Not lost," Androkom interrupted. "Not any more. I understand the context. For too long we biologians placed our faith in books alone, searching them for secrets and wisdom, growing frustrated at the contradictions we've discovered. I have moved beyond books and followed the experiments described in the texts. Though I lack much of the equipment available to the ancients, I believe the experiments I have conducted to be valid. Let me travel to Albekizan's palace. I can demonstrate my knowledge to Blasphet. He will not be able to deny the truth."

Metron contemplated Androkom's offer. He envied the young dragon's confidence, and the fearless way he desired to enter Blasphet's presence.

"Very well," Metron said. "Leave your post and travel here at once, my brother. How quickly can you arrive?"

"I anticipated your approval. I have already gathered the texts and materials I will need. My flight will take two days, perhaps three, for my load is a heavy one."

"Bring only what you must," said Metron. "The Free City begins to fill. Time grows short if we are to prevent the coming tragedy."

Metron said farewell to his brother biologians and turned from the white chamber, stepping toward an unseen door. As he emerged into the library, he was greeted by a frightened cry and a flurry of papers thrown into the air. Wentakra, one of his newer assistants, stumbled away from him, looking prepared to run.

"Do not be alarmed," Metron said. "It is only I."

"B-but... the wall!" Wentakra said. "You passed through it like... like a-a—"

"Ghost? Yes. Try not to let it haunt you. Tell no one you witnessed this."

"Y-yes, sir," Wentakra said. Then his eyes brightened as if remembering something important. "Did Flanchelet find you? He searched for you in this chamber only moments ago."

"No. I haven't seen him. What did he want?"

"Albekizan wants to see you at once. Kanst has returned."

"I know of his return. I witnessed it earlier."

"They say he's captured Bodiel's killer."

Metron needed half a second to fully grasp the importance of the statement. "Bitterwood?" he asked, his voice betraying his excitement. "They've captured Bitterwood?"

"So Flanchelet said."

Metron turned at once from his subordinate, feeling a glimmer of hope as he hurried back through the maze of books. Perhaps Albekizan might change his mind about the genocide he had ordered once he had his revenge against Bitterwood. With any luck, Blasphet might be back in his cell before Androkom arrived.

BLASPHET DISMISSED THE messenger with a wave and turned back to the balcony overlooking the Free City. The balcony was decorated with pots of a dozen colorful species of plants, most of them poisonous. Normally, he felt something akin to peace standing in his little garden. Now, watching the new arrivals entering the city, peace was replaced with a cold anxiety. Bitterwood captured. Would Albekizan break his word and spare the remaining humans after slaking his thirst for revenge with Bitterwood's blood? Many influential dragons spoke against the king's plans. The labor of humans provided the wealth of the kingdom. They tended the fields, toiled in the mines, and harvested the sea. Perhaps in the afterglow of Bitterwood's death, his brother's reason would return. Blasphet couldn't allow this.

Blasphet leapt from the balcony, feeling his feathers catch the wind, and for an instant all his worries vanished in the joy of flight as he slipped between the stars above and the ragged darkness beneath. For long years this pleasure had been denied him as he moldered in the dank recesses of the castle dungeon.

As he thought of the dungeon, the sensual pleasure of the air racing across his wings faded, the memory of the cruelty of cages returning to his mind. The bars of a cell could restrict humans in one plane—the horizontal. For a dragon, the pain was squared, the inability to walk about on the earth being secondary to the denial of flying above it. He added this thought to the list of debts to be repaid to the fellow members of his race once their usefulness to him had been exhausted.

As he turned a wide circle in the moonlight, his eyes caught movement outside the walls of the Free City. A handful of earth-dragons marched away from the gates, herding before them a mixed collection of cattle, sheep, and pigs. Blasphet turned the edges of his wings upward, slowing himself to descend into their path.

"You there," he said to the apparent leader of the earth-dragons who flinched at his sudden appearance. "Who are you? What are you doing with this livestock?"

The earth-dragon looked confused. "I'm Wyvernoth, sir. This livestock was taken from a human village. The citizens were taken to the Free City earlier today. We're taking the spoils back to the barracks to stock the larders."

"I gave no orders that the humans were to be deprived of their livestock. Take this herd back inside. The humans raised them and shall feast upon them."

"Begging pardon, sir," Wyvernoth said. "That don't make no sense. Blasphet plans to kill all the humans. Why feed them?"

Blasphet realized that Wyvernoth had no idea who he was speaking with, which amused him. He said, "The reasoning is simple, my thick-headed friend. The food supply will remain constant in the Free City. Those now within the walls, and those arriving in the next few weeks, will want for little. As more humans arrive, their shares will grow smaller and smaller. Due to the simplicity of the human mind, the humans who were here first will blame their hunger upon the new humans who arrive, rather than the dragons who once fed them so generously."

"They'll be at each other's throats, then," Wyvernoth said. "They'll be impossible to control, fighting and squabbling among themselves."

"Precisely," Blasphet said, then realized from Wyvernoth's expression that the earth-dragon had raised this point as an argument against, rather than in support for, the plan.

"Whatever, sir," Wyvernoth said. "I don't recognize you, but if a sun-dragon wants something done, I do it. If you want the livestock inside, it goes inside."

Blasphet again took to the air, disgusted by the encounter. Wyvernoth had obeyed him simply because of his race and rank and not because of his reason. There were days when Blasphet felt like the only intelligent being in the world. No wonder he found the lives of others to have so little value. They were simply too stupid to live.

BREATHLESSLY, METRON CLIMBED the stairs leading to the king's hall. He remembered wistfully the days when coming to this hall had been effortless, when it was just a simple matter of stretching his then-young wings and letting the wind carry him to his destination. He felt a slight envy for the earth-dragons who would never have age steal the freedom of the sky away from them.

As he entered the flame-flickered hall, all eyes turned toward him.

Only the king's most trusted advisors were present. Kanst stood before the throne platform, bedecked in full uniform, the steel plates and chainmail draped across his body in such a way as to reveal the well-defined musculature of a warrior still in his prime. Beside him stood Zanzeroth. A horrible black scab dominated the center of his swollen snout. Metron noticed the bandages on the hunter's shoulders and legs, and the slight crook in his posture, as if standing caused him pain.

Like a chill in the air, Metron sensed the presence of one other. He turned to the far corner of the room where the torches cast deep shadows. Blasphet waited there, his dark scales blending into the gloom with only the red glow of his eyes in torchlight to reveal him. The Murder God's gaze briefly acknowledged Metron's glance, then looked beyond him to the arrival of the royal family.

Albekizan walked forward slowly, his untrimmed claws clicking on the marble floor. Tanthia followed Albekizan, her wings trailing long, lacy ribbons, the feather-scales around her eyes newly dyed in a rainbow of colors. Metron noted a faint blurring of the colors, however, as if recent tears had been shed and wiped away.

Albekizan took his place on the pedestal throne. Weeks had passed since Metron had been in the king's presence. He was startled by the change. When he'd last seen the king, his hatred of humans still flashed in his eyes as lightning illuminates a storm. He'd spoken with passion about the great deeds that lay before him. Now Albekizan's eyes looked dark and tired. Indeed, everything about the king seemed weary, from the rarely seen downward turn of his neck to the heavy way he slouched onto the throne pedestal and hissed, "Speak."

"Sire," Kanst said, his voice deep, strong, and vibrating with anticipation. "I apologize for calling this assembly at such short notice. I have returned from my mission earlier than planned to bring you a gift."

"A gift?" Tanthia said, with barely concealed anger. "You come to report the death of my sister-in-law, do you not? What possible motivation could you have had to perpetrate such an outrage?"

"My queen, I regret the loss of Chakthalla, but she was harboring the fugitive, Vendevorex. There was no time to send for further orders. We had to launch a daring assault, relying on surprise to best a superior—"

"Kanst," Albekizan interrupted, raising his bejeweled claws dismissively. "I know this. The news traveled more swiftly than your army. Save your battle tales for the amusement of others. I am only interested in the heart of the rumors. Did you capture Bitterwood?"

"Sire," Kanst said, "honor requires me to speak of the role the cunning hunter Zanz—"

"Pay attention," Albekizan said, again cutting the general short. "Your answer requires only one word. Is Bitterwood your prisoner?"

"Yes," Kanst answered. He turned toward one of the side halls leading from the throne room and shouted, "Bring forth the prisoner!"

Pertalon, a sky-dragon Metron recognized as a victor from the martial games, marched into the room, his sinister teeth flashing in the torchlight as he barked, "Faster, worm!"

The command was a cruel one, for its target was a human who had little choice in his speed. His long, powerful legs were manacled, with barely enough chain to let him hobble along. His well-muscled arms were shackled behind him with chains as thick as those used on ox-dogs. Pertalon controlled the prisoner by means of a long pole capped with a metal ring which was in turn connected to an identical ring on a steel collar locked around the captive's neck. Aside from the metal that bound him, the prisoner was unclothed. Human faces were often deeply lined with emotions—fear, anger, shame—that Metron could read as simply as he read the written word on a piece of parchment. This man was different, his lips and eyes locked into utter blankness. What else would he expect from the legendary Bitterwood?

"Bow to your superiors, dog!" Pertalon said, swinging his tail around to smack his captive behind the knees before pushing him forward with the neck pole until he was prostrate.

Metron looked again at the king, expecting to see the lightning return to his visage. However, Albekizan still appeared lethargic, and if he received any pleasure at all at seeing his enemy humiliated, his face failed to show it.

"This is he?" Albekizan asked, sounding bored.

"Yes, sire," Zanzeroth said. "I am the one who bested him."

"So I see," Albekizan said. "It's obvious by the numerous wounds you bear, and the absence of wounds upon him."

"I defeated him with wits, sire," Zanzeroth said.

"No wonder he's unbruised," Albekizan said.

Tanthia suddenly rose, tears now plainly visible in her eyes. "Lies!" she cried. "This is not the murderer of my son!"

"But, my queen," protested Zanzeroth, "I witnessed this man as he took my eye. I struggled with him in mortal combat in the throne room of Chakthalla's castle. No dragon alive can speak more authoritatively as to the identity of this prisoner. I tell you, this is the man."

Tanthia looked as if she might charge across the room and strike Zanzeroth in her anger. She half shouted, "You fool! This is Chakthalla's personal slave. She calls him 'Pet.' I've seen him before, many times. You recognize him, don't you?" she said, addressing Albekizan.

"I pay little attention to slaves. Perhaps he does look familiar."

"As I should!" the human said.

"Silence!" Pertalon shouted, twisting the pole to choke his prisoner.

Albekizan shifted on his pedestal. "Let him speak."

"It's true I disguised myself as Chakthalla's slave," Pet said, rising to his knees. "How better to infiltrate your castles? Chakthalla was present at the ceremonial competition between Bodiel and Shandrazel. I was to wait in her quarters during the ceremony. Instead I slipped out to perform the murder!"

"For one who's spent long years hiding in shadows, you seem eager to confess," Albekizan said.

"I have nothing to be ashamed of," Pet said, throwing back his muscular shoulders. "I am proud to have killed Bodiel. Set me loose and give me my bow, and I'll kill you all where you stand!"

Metron held his breath, expecting Albekizan's rage to at last ignite. Instead the king asked only, "Why?"

Metron noted a crack in Pet's demeanor, a look of confusion as if he hadn't expected to be asked the question. Then the cool mask again claimed his features as he answered, "Because I hate you. I hate how humans are made slaves. I seek to kill dragons until such time as men live free."

"How noble," Albekizan said. "Fighting for your fellow men."

"I do what I must," Pet answered. "I would fight you now, at this moment, if I were free."

"I believe you," Albekizan said.

"Sire," Zanzeroth said, "I have a boon to ask of you. I crave to be this man's executioner. With your word, I will end his life."

"I will consider the request," Albekizan said. "Now, all of you, go. Take Bitterwood to the dungeons and secure him while I consider his fate."

"Yes, sire," Zanzeroth said. As he turned, Metron felt sure he witnessed a look of sly satisfaction in the hunter's good eye.

Pertalon dragged Pet away.

Tanthia grumbled. "This is an outrage, Kanst. You've murdered my sister-in-law and abused her property. That man is too young to be Bitterwood. You've lost your senses."

"He was caught with incriminating evidence," Kanst said, holding forward a bundle wrapped in silk. Albekizan took the bundle and unwrapped it. It held a bow and three arrows, fletched with the crimson wing-scales of a sun-dragon. Bodiel's?

"This is damning evidence," Albekizan said, flatly. "Well done, Kanst. Now go. I have much to consider."

Kanst and Zanzeroth left, soon followed by Tanthia. Metron wondered at the king's somber mood. Could it be that the anger that had burned so brightly within the king had at last burned itself to ash? He had to know.

"Sire," he said.

"What is it, Metron?"

Metron glanced back toward the shadows. Blasphet remained there, silent and still as a statue. "May I speak with you in private, sire?"

"We shall speak at another time," Albekizan said.

"But—"

"Metron, your ancient office is owed a great amount of respect, even by a king. But don't presume to question my orders. I told you to leave. Your request for an audience is noted. I will summon you when I'm ready."

"Yes, sire," Metron said, turning away. *But you'd do well to speak to me soon,* he thought. *Before I'm forced to rely on my alliance with your brother.*

ALBEKIZAN WATCHED THE High Biologian shuffle slowly from the hall, wondering why he'd been so easy on the old fool. He often felt he allowed his advisors to be too familiar with him. The accursed Vendevorex was to blame, no doubt. He should have snapped the wizard's slender neck a decade ago. It would have spared him much grief.

The door closed behind Metron, leaving Albekizan with the torches that blazed throughout the hall, the life-flames of his ancestors, now joined by the flame of a descendent. Albekizan looked at the torch that had been his son burning beside the throne, and wondered if Bodiel had been witness to Bitterwood's presence in the room. He wondered if his son retained the full senses he had possessed in life, and suddenly he wished that Metron were still here, for it was his job to know the answer to such a question.

"I've seen this look upon your face before. Something troubles you, Brother."

Albekizan looked away from the torch into the shadows. His eyes adjusted to make out Blasphet's dark form.

"I told you to leave," Albekizan said.

"So you did. Yet, I remain. Your words may be law to others, brother, but I do as I wish."

"I was just thinking how useful it might be to throttle one of my advisors. It would keep the others in line. You tempt fate by taunting me."

"You'll not find my neck so easy to throttle, I fear," said Blasphet. "Today I have coated my claws with a most efficient poison. One scratch and you'd be dead within a heartbeat."

"You threaten me?"

"No. When I decide it is time for you to die, you will die, but today is not that day. Not if you give me the correct answer to a most urgent question."

"I know your question," Albekizan said. "Bitterwood's capture changes nothing. You may continue your work in the Free City."

"It feels hollow, doesn't it?" Blasphet asked, approaching.

"What do you mean?"

"It looks as if you haven't eaten or slept in days. I deduce you lost both your appetite and your restfulness when you learned he'd been captured."

"I care nothing for your speculations," Albekizan said.

"I will make them anyway. I believe you are feeling a disappointment I am long familiar with: the hollowness of death. How can you hurt Bitterwood now that you have him? Death will only take him from your grasp. You want him dead, and you want him to suffer, and the two are mutually incompatible." Blasphet shook his head as if saddened by the poor options. "What shall it be, brother? Torment or dissolution? The ache of knowing he still lives, or the frustration of knowing he no longer suffers?"

"You... may be right," Albekizan said. "You surprise me with your wisdom, brother. So, tell me, what is the answer? How do I hurt him even beyond death?"

"I don't know," Blasphet said. "Even if I did, why would I choose to end your agony? One reason you still live is that I enjoy your suffering."

Albekizan felt, not for the first time, an admiration for the cold, twisted mind of his sibling. Suffering or death: he framed the problem so eloquently. If only there were some way to have both...

Albekizan chuckled. Suddenly, the solution was obvious.

"Have I amused you?" Blasphet asked.

"You've inspired me, my brother," Albekizan said, feeling fire return to his limbs. "You've inspired me indeed."

CHAPTER EIGHTEEN

REFLECTIONS

J ANDRA HADN'T KNOWN what to expect from the Free City, but she certainly hadn't expected this. Thousands of freshly built houses in neat, orderly rows were furnished sparsely but adequately. The homes were modest by the standards of the dwellings she had lived in among the dragons, but they were far better than the hovels that used to surround the palace. The city also smelled better than any human dwelling she'd ever visited; Richmond always smelled of fish guts and dung. The Free City had the pleasant smell of fresh pine sawdust and new paint. There were even freshly planted flowers blooming in window boxes.

Jandra had anticipated cruel guards and chains for everyone inside. She expected at least more of the starvation and thirst of the long march here. Instead, there were banquet halls, where meals were served three times a day in heaps of roasted meats and fresh vegetables, and gallon upon gallon of fresh, clean water. At first she'd worried that the food was poisoned... but after seeing other people digging in, her hunger had overcome her caution.

Perhaps the most disturbing thing about the Free City was that Jandra felt very much at home. She'd lived her life in a castle built to accommodate sundragons. She was used to tables twice her height. At mealtimes, she was often confronted with dinner platters as long as she was. A dragon's cup was a bucket to her. In the libraries, she sometimes encountered books so large and heavy she couldn't lift them from the shelves. She had simply never fit into the dragons' world. The Free City was being built by humans (though supervised by dragons), for humans. There was something cozy about being able to climb a flight of stairs simply by stepping up, rather than actually climbing.

The nearly empty streets of the Free City, with no guards in sight, offered a surprising refuge for Jandra. She could wander among the alleyways for hours, trying to make sense of the events of the recent days, attempting to divine some truth from them that would give her guidance.

Foremost in her mind was Vendevorex and his lie. She wasn't surprised that he'd been able to keep the truth hidden all these years. Other dragons feared Vendevorex. Who among them would have cared enough about her to tell her the truth at the risk of the wizard's wrath? She could see him more clearly now that she was distant from him for the first time in memory. He was a cold, cruel manipulator, who always acted only to increase his power and wealth, never for any noble purpose.

Even his seeming kindness toward her had a selfish origin; Vendevorex wanted to assuage his own guilt. Caring for her had been his path to a clean conscience.

So why did she miss him so? Why, the more her mind argued all the reasons she should hate him, did she feel only longing? Had she made a mistake by leaving him?

No, she thought. He killed my parents. This is the central fact. He admitted it. I will hate him until I die.

Her longing for her mentor's company was amplified by her lack of human companionship. In the midst of the thousands of humans already at the Free City, she found no kindred spirits. Bitterwood was closed to her. He wasn't hostile, but he was distant, as if he were still struggling with his own internal demons. Zeeky was too young to truly be called a friend, though she spent more time with her than with anyone else. And the villagers... the villagers were incomprehensible. They seemed completely in the thrall of the prophet Kamon who had convinced them that their passage to the Free City was foretold by his visions.

Jandra knew the Free City was meant to kill them, but doubted she could convince anyone of this. She'd never persuade people the dragons were the enemy while all the residents of the Free City slept with full stomachs on clean linens. The humans were more a threat to themselves than the dragons were, as the only violence she had seen since arriving in the city was a brawl between the

followers of the prophet Kamon and the followers
of a rival prophet named Ragnar, whom she had yet
to meet.

At last, she had walked the streets until she was
weary enough to sleep, no matter how troubled her
thoughts. With a sigh she returned to the small
house she shared with Zeeky. Perhaps in the morning her mind would be clearer.

ANDROKOM WEARILY GLANCED over his shoulder
once more. No one followed, though the spiky
fringe of scales on his neck still tingled with the sensation that he was being watched. The sky was
crystal clear; if anyone was behind him, he would
certainly have seen him.

"You're paranoid," he said to himself.

Maybe, he thought. *But I still think I'm being followed.*

At length, thirst crept into his awareness, over-
powering his caution. He was only hours away
from Albekizan's palace but could go no further. He
needed water, a good meal, and a long nap.

In the distance a fat river gleamed like a band of
silver. He spied a small, tree-covered island in the
middle of the waters and knew this would be the
perfect spot to rest. No one could sneak up on him
there. Besides, who would want to? Only Metron
and his fellow biologists knew of his journey. Certainly none of them would have set pursuers after
him, would they?

If only Metron hadn't uttered that cursed name:
Blasphet, the Murder God. What could the High
Biologian be thinking in dealing with such a dis-
turbed mind? Moreover, was he a fool for helping?

Could this be some elaborate scheme by Blasphet to lead the biologians to their deaths?

"You're paranoid. Only an idiot could dream up such concerns," he said. He often talked to himself on long journeys. He wished, if he must talk to himself, that he wouldn't be so insulting.

Androkom swooped down, gliding along the moist air above the river, watching fish dart and scurry beneath the ripples. His blue hide was reflected in the surface of the water. He tilted his wings up to slow himself, then swung his legs forward to land on the island's sandy bank. The bank faced north, shaded from the sun, and the sand was cool and soothing beneath his talons. The damp sand carried an aroma that reminded Androkom of the ocean and the Isle of Horses, where he'd trained with the biologian Dacorn. Androkom unstrapped the pack he carried on his chest and set it gently on the sand, careful not to jar the equipment he carried. He walked to the water's edge and knelt, craning his long neck forward until his chin touched the water. With one last glance over his shoulder to confirm he was alone, he stuck out his tongue and lapped up the cool, fresh water.

That's what I needed, he thought.

The water was exceptionally still in the little cove he had landed in, so still his own face looked back at him as he drank, distorted only by the small wavelets his tongue created. Again, he felt the strange sensation that he wasn't alone and looked behind him. Shrugging it off, he lowered his head to the water once more. Suddenly, he began to choke as his reflection was joined by two others, a sky-dragon and a sun-dragon, standing on the bank next to him.

Androkom jumped forward into the knee-deep water and spun around. To his dismay, he recognized one of the intruders.

"Shandrazel!" he shouted. He'd heard about the reception the banished prince had received at the College of Spires and feared that Shandrazel might not feel warmly toward biologians.

"Don't panic, Androkom," Shandrazel said. "You have nothing to fear from us."

Androkom straightened himself, raising his wings for balance. "You remember me, Prince? I'm flattered." He'd met Shandrazel almost five years ago, while the prince was still under the tutelage of Dacorn.

"Of course," Shandrazel said. "I was impressed by your argument that books often contain falsehoods and contradictions. So many of the biologians seem fixed on the notion that if it's written, it must be true. It helped guide me to the view that the form of government we dragons have chosen might not be the wisest one."

"A surprisingly enlightened view for the only surviving prince of the realm," Androkom said. He cast a glance at the sky-dragon beside Shandrazel. A biologian? Why didn't he recognize him? Unless... could it be him? "Who, may I ask, is your companion?"

"I am Vendevorex," the sky-dragon answered.

"Of course," Androkom said with a knowing nod. The wizard. "I've tried to make your acquaintance before now. I wanted to discuss your so-called 'magic.' I have theories as to its origins. Did you not receive my letters?"

"I received them," Vendevorex said. "I ignored them. The source of my powers is my secret. If I won't reveal it to the king, you can't expect that I'd reveal it to you."

"I heard rumors you'd taken ill," Androkom said. "I took this to mean you'd fallen out of favor with Albekizan. I assume you've joined Shandrazel's quest to overthrow his father?"

"I've not come to overthrow my father," Shandrazel said.

Vendevorex added, "Albekizan knows nothing of our alliance. With luck, he thinks I'm dead."

"I see," said Androkom, walking back onto the shore, shaking his tail and wings to dry them.

"We're sorry if we frightened you," Shandrazel said. "We were traveling back toward my father's castle when we spotted you. We followed you until you came to rest. Knowing your reputation as one who is unafraid to challenge authority, I felt that I could trust you."

"Your instincts serve you well," Androkom said. "I'm at your service. But, may I ask, where were you? I felt I was being watched but saw no sign of pursuit."

"I used my magic to make us invisible," Vendevorex said.

"I believe you were invisible," Androkom said, "but I don't believe you use magic. I've read tomes describing ancient technologies. I believe you are in possession of a Magnetically Integrated Rapidly Rotating Optical Reversal System."

The wizard looked stunned. "I've never met another dragon I could discuss this with. I'm impressed. You're right. It's all done with M.I.R.R.O.R.S."

"But how did you come to be in possession of the technology? Having the information is a far leap from having the artifacts."

Vendevorex glanced at Shandrazel, then back at Androkom. "For many years I have guarded such secrets and recently, I paid a great price by having one such secret revealed. I must ask that you trust me when I say it could prove dangerous to tell you all I know."

"Your secrets may not be as secret as you think," Androkom said. "For years, we biologists have known the truth: the humans who live among us are the degenerate remnants of a once ascendant human civilization. They possessed knowledge beyond our imaginations. They had technology that we cannot distinguish from magic. They walked upon the moon. They traveled in great machines to the deepest depths of the oceans. They possessed other machines so small they could not be seen by the naked eye, devices that could transform matter from its most basic components into refined, priceless treasures. Most impressive of all, they knew the secret code of life itself."

"Astonishing," said Shandrazel. "Can it be true?"

"It is," said Vendevorex. "Their civilization peaked over a thousand years ago. Much of what they created has decayed over the years. My magic is accomplished using what they referred to as nanotechnology. The silver dust in my pouch is composed of these tiny machines, powered by the sun itself. They respond to thoughts, transmitted via my skullcap, or Jandra's tiara."

"This... this technology could change the world," Shandrazel said. "Why have you kept this secret?"

"Because," said Vendevorex, "I gave my word."

"To whom?" Shandrazel asked.

Vendevorex looked around, as if he, too, were worried someone might be listening. "Not all of human civilization collapsed to its present, degenerate state. Far beyond our shores exists a city where men live as gods. I have visited there and seen wonders beyond description. These men travel to other worlds. They fly through the air more gracefully than dragons. They have conquered death. They reshape matter with the most casual wish. The secrets I have stolen from them are so trivial as to be beneath their notice. My so-called magic wouldn't impress an infant in this wondrous city."

"How can this be?" Shandrazel asked. "If there are people with so much power, why don't they help their fellow humans? Why aren't they here right now?"

Vendevorex motioned Androkom and Shandrazel closer, drawing them into a conspiratorial huddle. "For all we know they might be here. They need not rely on the illusion I use for invisibility, they possess the power to recalculate the equations of space itself, and walk above, beside, and beneath what we know as reality. However, it is their practice not to interfere with the fates of their fellow men. Once, long ago, the ancients gave little thought to changing the world. They grew in such power that even their most casual actions shook the planet. They changed the map of the world by changing the levels of the oceans. Cities were drowned. Entire countries vanished beneath the waves. They nearly destroyed themselves with their own tools."

"To say nothing of their toys," Androkom added.

"What do you mean?" asked Vendevorex.

Androkom felt a chill run through him. He was certain the wizard had known. Did he dare tell them? Did he dare reveal the most terrible secret of the biologians?

Before Androkom could decide, Shandrazel said, "While this discussion of ancient history satisfies my intellectual side, I fear it doesn't help us solve our problems. Tell me, Androkom, why were you flying toward my father's fortress?"

"The short answer is that I go to give information to the most wicked dragon who ever lived. However, you may require more than a short answer. I'm unsure what you know of events that have transpired since your exile. Did you know that Blasphet has been freed?"

"I've heard. He's now my father's most trusted advisor, I'm told."

"What information do you have for Blasphet?" Vendevorex asked.

"Metron says that Blasphet kills only so that he may search for the secret of life. I go to provide that answer."

"You know the secret of life?" Vendevorex asked, his voice somewhere between amusement and astonishment.

"Indeed. Tell me, do these words mean anything to you? Double helix."

Vendevorex wrinkled his brow. "This is a mathematical form."

"So you don't know all the secrets of the ancients, eh?"

Shandrazel said, "I feel like you two are trying to one-up each other. I ask you to put this aside for the moment and use your great intellects to ponder the situation before us."

"Of course," said Androkom. "I think I have solved one problem. When I explain the source of life to Blasphet, and convince him of the answer via my experiments, he will no longer be a threat. The question that drives his evil will be sated."

"Or he'll use the knowledge to kill every last being on the planet. I can't allow it," said Shandrazel.

Androkom narrowed his eyes, annoyed by Shandrazel's attitude. He didn't recall asking for permission. Perhaps arrogance was transmitted genetically. Still, arrogant or not, he was pleased to be in the company of two dragons whose intellects approached his own.

"Good dragons," he said, "I think better on a full stomach. Come, I have food in my pack. Let us break bread while we decide how best to save the world."

As NIGHT FELL over the Free City, a youthful earth-dragon named Torgoz trudged toward the front gate for guard duty. As he approached, he saw the guard he was supposed to replace, an old-timer by the name of Wyvernoth. He raised a claw in greeting. Wyvernoth didn't respond. He drew closer and tried again. Again, the old-timer gave no hint he'd noticed him, though he was now less than a spear thrust away.

"Wyvernoth!" said Torgoz.

The old veteran jumped as his name was spoken.

"Asleep on your feet again?" Torgoz chided.

Wyvernoth shook his head. "I wasn't sleeping. I was thinking."

"Thinking's not your best skill, old-timer. When you try, it only causes more of your scales to fall out."

Wyvernoth scratched his scarred head as Torgoz spoke. A shower of moss-green scales fell with the motion.

"It's a waste of my know-how to be pulling watches," Wyvernoth grumbled. "All these years of duty and the best they can do is stand me next to a gate. Me, with command experience. Why, once I—"

"—Led your unit on to victory after the commander died," Torgaz said. "You've mentioned it once or a hundred times."

"I deserve better is all," Wyvernoth said.

"What you deserve is a thump on the skull. But since I'm here to relieve you, what you'll get is a good night's sleep in a bunk. That is, if you still remember how to sleep lying down."

"Oh. I remember," Wyvernoth said, in a tone that let Torgoz know the old-timer considered it a clever retort.

Taking his spear, Wyvernoth marched off stiffly, as if all his muscles weren't fully awake yet.

Torgoz took his place and sighed. Wyvernoth might not deserve better duty, but Torgoz certainly did. The Free City was a prison. Guards on the inside made sense. Guards on the outside were useless. They weren't even supposed to stop the humans who showed up wanting to get in; they only had to make sure that they didn't have weapons.

It still amazed him how many people showed up each day. He'd heard that the king planned to forcibly round up humans after the harvest. So far, that was proving unnecessary. The rumor of the Free City had spread, and now a steady stream of fools showed up voluntarily each day. The villages must be truly awful to produce people desperate enough to walk away from their old lives and come to a city not even fully built.

Torgoz noticed a wagon coming toward him on the road, which struck him as unusual. Most of the voluntary arrivals came on foot, too poor to afford a cart, let alone an ox-dog like the one approaching. As the wagon drew closer, he could plainly see that there was a human at the reins, apparently alone. He was dressed all in black and was possibly the biggest human Torgoz had ever seen.

"This is the Free City?" the man asked as he came within a few yards. The man's face was dusty from the road.

"Indeed. Welcome," Torgoz said.

"You will not block my entry?" the man asked.

"Of course not. We want you to enjoy all the pleasures of the Free City." Torgoz fought the urge to snicker. "Come, step down from your wagon. I'll call someone to take your ox-dog to the stables where he'll be fed and cared for. You look as if you've traveled a long time to get here."

"Centuries," the man said, stepping down from his seat.

Torgoz assumed this passed as humor among humans. He said, "Your journey is over. Welcome home."

The man nodded. "Your hospitality is unexpected. Dragons normally treat me with hostility."

"King Albekizan has commanded an end to old rivalries, friend."

"I care nothing for the commands of earthly kings," the stranger said, fixing his stern gaze upon

Torgoz. "I do care, however, for the safety of my animal. I will hold you responsible should harm befall him. What is your name?"

Torgoz bristled at the man's haughty attitude but decided he'd play along. It wasn't as if the man would get away with anything once he was inside. "I'm Torgoz. And you?"

"I am Hezekiah," the man said as he lifted a pack from beneath the wagon's flatboard seat. Torgoz noticed an axe strapped to the side of the pack.

Torgoz said, "The king wants peace inside the city. You'll have to leave the axe in your wagon, and I need to check your pack."

Hezekiah turned his shadowed gaze toward him. He said, in a stern tone, "I do not recognize the authority of your king. I serve a higher power. Within my pack is a Holy Book containing the words of the one true Lord. It is sacred. You shall not look upon it."

Torgoz gritted his teeth, nearly ready to lower his spear and run the insolent bastard through. With a second glance at Hezekiah's broad hands, he paused. Hezekiah looked like he could snap a spear like a toothpick. Worse, Hezekiah had an ox-dog by his side. If the beast defended its master, Torgoz would have a real fight on his hands. He decided to pretend he hadn't seen the axe.

"I guess I stand corrected," Torgoz said, opening the gate. "Go on in." The human strode through the opening. Torgoz closed the gate, hissing with soft laughter. The fate that awaited Hezekiah would more than repay the debts the fool had incurred with his tongue. As for the axe,

Torgoz didn't see a real threat. How much damage could one man do?

CHAPTER NINETEEN

RECKONING

THE MORNING SUN seeped through the open window, its rosy fingers touching Jandra's face. She sat up, stretching her arms, blinking the sleep from her eyes. Something about the small, nearly bare room seemed wrong.

"Zeeky?" she said, realizing how still the girl lay beneath her blanket.

Zeeky didn't stir. Jandra moved to her side and pulled back the covers, revealing a second blanket balled into the outline of a sleeping child.

Jandra rose, dressing quickly. She knew the fear that gripped her had little basis in reason. Zeeky was half her age but had spent more time fending for herself than Jandra had. Still, she couldn't help but wonder what had happened to the child.

Rushing down the stairs of the small building, she was surprised to find Bitterwood waiting outside on the steps. He looked more worn out than usual, and she wondered if he had been awake all night.

"Have you seen Zeeky?" she asked.

"When?" Bitterwood asked.

"This morning. She was missing when I got up."

"No," Bitterwood answered. "I've been sitting here since before dawn."

"Where can she be?" she asked, looking down the empty street.

"Don't worry," Bitterwood said. "She can't have gone far."

"She's been talking about the animals ever since we got here. I wonder if she's gone to the animal pens?"

"We can go look."

"Okay," Jandra said. Then she was struck by the strangeness of their conversation. Bitterwood was actually speaking without her having to drag words out of him, and now he had offered to help her.

"What's going on?" she asked. "Why were you waiting for me?"

"We can speak as we walk," Bitterwood said, stepping away without looking back to see if she would follow. "The pens are several blocks from here."

Jandra hurried after him. "You must be in a better mood. A different mood, at least."

Bitterwood nodded. "I've given your words a great deal of thought. Your request that I help you fight dragons. I came to give you my decision."

"Then you'll help me? It's still not too late. For whatever reason, it looks like they want to round up people here before killing them. Here's my plan: we sneak out invisibly and find weapons.

Albekizan's castle isn't far. I know its layout by heart. We can walk right into the throne room and you can shoot him."

Bitterwood didn't answer at first as they walked down the nearly empty streets. Then he shook his head. "That's not the decision I've made. Killing Albekizan is futile. All dragons hate us. Slaying the king will only prolong the inevitable."

"The inevitable? You accept it as inevitable that we're going to lose?"

"For twenty years I've slain dragons. What good have I done? There are as many dragons today as when I started. They breed as fast as I kill them."

"You were only one man," she said. "I'll stand beside you."

"It's too late." Bitterwood sighed. "My life has been utterly wasted."

Jandra wasn't shocked to hear his words. Bitterwood's despair had been obvious to her ever since his capture. However, she took heart that he had come to her to talk about his decision. She took it as a sign that he wanted her to change his mind.

"You're wrong," she said softly. "You think that you can't win the war unless you kill every last dragon on earth. I agree that can't be done. Don't you see that's not needed for true victory? Humans and dragons have lived side by side for centuries. Most dragons don't hate humans, and would gladly embrace a return to our peaceful coexistence if Albekizan were removed."

Bitterwood shook his head. "You think that peace was my goal? You don't know me. No one does."

"I know you're a strong, willful man who fights for what he believes is right."

"No," Bitterwood said.

"Come on. You're Bitterwood. You're a legend to these people, even if they are too blind to recognize you. You're a hero."

"They call me the Ghost that Kills. I'm a dead man. I died when dragons killed my family. When I saw what they had done, it was like my heart froze within me. I've not been warm since."

"I'm sorry," Jandra said. "I, too, lost my family to dragons. It happened so long ago I don't even remember them. I don't even know their names."

"Memory's a curse," said Bitterwood. "You are lucky to have escaped."

"Lucky," Jandra said, noting how sour the word tasted. "I don't think luck had anything to do with my survival."

"I don't mean it's lucky you lived," Bitterwood said. "I mean it's lucky you don't remember. Memories will burn you and sear away all that's soft inside, leaving only hard, hot hatred. Hate can feel like passion, like life, in the absence of anything else. It makes you feel strong and focused, eager for action against the source of the hate. But now…"

His voice faded away and he turned his face from Jandra.

"Now?" she asked.

"Hate was all I had. I see that my greatest strength was also my greatest weakness. My hate kept me going, gave me purpose. But it corrupted me. I've become an instrument of darkness, my every action bringing only ruin. If I had foreseen that murdering Bodiel would bring about the genocide of the human race, do you think I would have let the arrow fly? The time has come for me to surrender to the inevitable and do no more harm."

Jandra contemplated his words, surprised at how they seemed directed at her. She wanted to hate Vendevorex. She was certain that he deserved only her fury, and that there could be no room for forgiveness. Did she want to become like Bitterwood? Could she hate Vendevorex forever and not lose her soul?

Suddenly, Bitterwood stopped. Jandra raised her head, looking down the street toward the focus of his attention. An aged earth-dragon, its tail raised high, charged toward them, screaming, kicking the ground so hard in his haste that he trailed a cloud of dust.

"My god," Bitterwood said. "It's one of them!"

Jandra recognized the passion that had returned to his voice. For some reason she couldn't guess at, the sight of this dragon had ended his despair.

WYVERNOTH YAWNED AS he left the barracks and headed for his assignment. The sky was still dark though tinged with the faintest red of the rapidly approaching day. Wyvernoth was still tired despite having just arisen. He actually looked forward to his assignment today—guarding the animal pens. Not much action there. He'd have plenty of opportunity to catch a little extra sleep.

The sky had brightened by the time he reached his post near the pens. Borlon stood by the gate to the swine yard, his eyes wide and alert, his shoulders drawn back as if ready to fight the entire world.

"You don't fool me," Wyvernoth said.

Borlon jerked his head toward Wyvernoth's voice and barked, "Sir!" Then he relaxed. "Oh. It's you."

"I used to be that good," Wyvernoth said. "But now that I'm older, I find my eyes tend to shut."

"I wasn't asleep... Ah, who cares? Of course I was sleeping. By the bones, if I ever needed proof that any dragon with wings is insane, this job provides it. Pigs! We're guarding pigs!"

"We'd have eaten them ourselves if I'd had my way," Wyvernoth said. "The fact that I'm not a captain with my leadership experience is all the proof I need that our commanders are crazy."

"Leadership experience?"

"It was twenty years ago. My first time out. I was assigned to a tax enforcement unit in the southern province. We met up with some resistance. They slaughtered the commanders. But I led the survivors on to victory and completed the mission."

"Ah," said Borlon, nodding. "I have heard about that. Only, the way I heard it, you and the others ran blindly from battle and by luck found the village you were headed for. Nothing but women and children and wooden shacks. Easy to burn. Some leadership..."

"Hmmph," grunted Wyvernoth. "You weren't there. You didn't see the horrors I did."

"Nightmares most likely," said Borlon. "Why don't I get out of here so you can get some sleep?"

"You do that," Wyvernoth said, no longer sparing the younger dragon from the full force of his wit.

Borlon headed off, leaving Wyvernoth alone.

Wyvernoth muttered curses as he took his position before the pens. He braced his tail against the ground and locked his muscles, ready for a little nap. As he settled in, closing his eyes, he heard someone sneeze.

He looked around. No one was there. Had he imagined it?

He went into the large barn. The structure was long, opening out onto several pens that held pigs. Could pigs sneeze? He thought they could, but he wasn't certain. He was a soldier, not a farmer.

He walked down the center of the barn, peeking over the stall doors. Pigs. Pigs. Pigs. Girl. Pigs. *Hold on*.

He stepped back a stall and pushed open the door. A human child, a little blonde girl maybe eight years old, huddled in the corner of the stall, her arms wrapped around a small black and white pig.

"Um, hi," she said, then wiped her nose.

Wyvernoth didn't answer.

"I just wanted to see him. For a visit," she said.

"Why do you think I care?" Wyvernoth said, reaching down and grabbing the girl by her arm.

"Ow!" she yelled.

Instantly, the pens and stalls erupted in a cacophony of squeals. Seconds later, the rest of the animals in the neighboring barns joined in; a chaotic chorus of moos, baas, and clucks filled the air. The ox-dogs held in the nearby kennels began to yelp and howl, a sound that brought back bad memories for Wyvernoth.

"See what you've done," he said. "Set 'em all off. You're in a heap of trouble."

"You're hurting my arm," she cried as he lifted her from the ground and carried her outside. Given the noise, he guessed other guards would get here soon enough. He'd have one of them watch his post while he took her in to the captain. He could wind up looking good for this, especially if he trumped up the charges. He could blame her for the goat that'd gone missing yesterday. That way he'd get to enjoy not only his full belly, but also the fun of pinning the blame on someone else.

As he walked out of the barn, he noticed a figure approaching. He looked up, expecting to see a fellow guard. Instead he saw a tall, dark-robed man, his eyes hidden by the broad, black brim of his hat.

"You there," the man said. "What upset the ox-dogs?"

Wyvernoth noted that the man had a pack slung across his shoulder, and strapped to the pack was an axe, which worried him, for the man seemed familiar. Had he let this man in? What would his superiors say if they learned that he'd let someone bring in an axe?

An axe.

A broad-brimmed black hat.

An ox-dog.

Suddenly, Wyvernoth recalled quite clearly where he'd seen this man twenty years before.

"Y-you?" Wyvernoth said, his voice trailing off in a little squeal. He dropped the girl who fell roughly to the ground.

"You were one of the soldiers on the road to Christdale," the man said. "It's been many years."

Wyvernoth turned, lowered his head, raised his tail, dropped his spear, and shot off like an arrow.

* * *

"You!" Bitterwood shouted, unable to believe this turn of fate. Even after twenty years, the faces of the dragons who'd surrounded the wagon that night and thrust spears at him were burned into his memory.

Bitterwood braced himself as the dragon barreled toward him, wondering why his opponent was charging without a weapon drawn. He could plainly see a sword in the sheath on the dragon's hip.

The dragon swerved as he approached, his eyes not fixed on Bitterwood but on the path beyond him. Bitterwood realized the dragon wasn't attacking him, but planned instead to run past him.

"No you don't," Bitterwood said, sticking his leg out as the dragon raced by. The impact of leg against leg nearly toppled Bitterwood, so great was the dragon's speed.

Only a balance honed by years of combat kept him on his feet while the dragon hit the hard-packed earth beak-first. The dragon's legs flipped over his shoulders and he rolled three times before sliding to a stop on his back.

Bitterwood pounced, landing on the dragon's chest, locking a hand around the beast's scaly windpipe while his free hand drew the sword from the dragon's scabbard.

"Let me go! He's after me!" the dragon whimpered.

"He's caught you," Bitterwood said, looking down into the dark terrified eyes of the dragon. "After all these years, we meet again."

"What?" the dragon cried. "Are you mad?"

"Yes!" Bitterwood said, tightening his grip on the dragon's throat. "Don't pretend you don't remember. The village of Christdale!"

The dragon's eyes opened wider. "You! You were with him! The young man in the wagon!"

"Bitterwood," Jandra said, placing her hand on his shoulder.

"Go away!" Bitterwood snarled. "Don't try to stop me. He's one of the ones who killed my wife and children! He dies now!"

Bitterwood raised the sword.

"Please!" the dragon squeaked. "We killed no women or children that day! All but the men were taken into slavery! Please spare me!"

Bitterwood felt his heart skip one beat, two. "What?" he said, lowering the sword.

"Spare me!"

"Slavery?" Bitterwood said, studying the dragon's eyes. "You sold my family into slavery?"

"Yes. Oh, please let me go, let me go, let me go. He's after me!"

Bitterwood felt his heart resume beating as hope sparked within him. Recanna could still be alive. And Ruth, and Mary, and Adam.

The dragon beneath him suddenly stopped squirming. His eyes opened even wider until they looked as if they might pop from his skull. He opened his beak wide to scream but no sound came out.

A long, dark shadow draped over Bitterwood. Suddenly, he understood he wasn't the one causing this dragon to feel such terror.

"Bant Bitterwood," a voice said, deep and familiar as thunder. "Your day of reckoning has come."

BITTERWOOD GRIPPED THE sword in his hand so tightly it trembled. The dragon he held had information he couldn't afford to lose. He couldn't let the dragon go, he couldn't kill him, and he couldn't take time to think about the problem with Hezekiah stepping closer.

"Jandra," Bitterwood said. "Run."

"Why?" she asked, sounding confused. "Who is this?"

"The devil," Bitterwood said. "Go!"

"Bant Bitterwood," Hezekiah said, "the Lord is merciful. If you will confess the error of your blasphemy those long years ago, I will spare you."

"By the bones," the dragon whispered, tears welling in his eyes. "Let me go. He'll kill me."

"You'll stay until I'm done with you," Bitterwood said. With a grunt he brought the sword down. The dragon screamed, arching his back in pain, as the tip of the sword was driven through his right shoulder and deep into the hard earth, pinning him.

Bitterwood rolled off the dragon and onto his feet, facing the giant who stood only a yard away and was casually drawing an axe from his pack.

"Who are you?" asked Jandra, who hadn't run.

"I am Hezekiah, child," the prophet answered. "I have come to bring the word of the Lord to the people of this new city. The man beside you has turned his back on the Lord and, unless he repents, he must be removed, lest he poison the minds of others with his blasphemy. What say you, Bant Bitterwood? Will you accept the Lord's mercy?"

"Go to hell," Bitterwood said, the tight muscles of his legs uncoiling to drive him forward into the breast of the demon.

Hezekiah stood steady as a rock, just as Bitterwood had anticipated. His hands closed tightly around the axe the prophet carried and he leapt up, curled his feet under him, then drove them both into his foe's stomach. He knew the blow would cause Hezekiah no pain, but at least he could pry the axe from the demon's grasp.

Unfortunately, the axe didn't budge. Bitterwood dropped back to the ground, continuing to push and pull against the axe handle. It was like trying to remove a stone from a wall.

Then Hezekiah moved, pushing his arms forward with a snap. Bitterwood was thrown backward. He landed on his back, hard, but years of experience allowed him to roll with the force so that the momentum carried him to his feet. Jandra was running now, not fleeing, but moving to his side as she tossed a handful of silver dust into the air.

"Stay quiet!" she whispered as the morning sunlight dimmed.

"What witchcraft is this?" Hezekiah shouted. "Where have you vanished to, Bant Bitterwood?"

Bitterwood started to speak, uncertain of what was happening, but Jandra placed her fingers on his lips and whispered, "Shh."

"There," Hezekiah said. He hurled his axe in the direction of Jandra's whisper. The tool raced more swiftly than an arrow. Bitterwood tried to push Jandra from its path but succeeded only partly, for the steel tip grazed her ear, spinning her around. Her body went limp and she fell into Bitterwood's arms. Bitterwood lowered her to the ground and looked up, expecting to see death hovering overhead. Instead, Hezekiah had turned his attention toward the pinned dragon, wrapping his thick hand around the hilt of the sword.

"It's best you not speak of what you've witnessed," he said, and effortlessly drew the buried blade from the dragon's shoulder. He lowered the blade again, swinging sideways, silencing the dragon's sobs suddenly and permanently.

Bitterwood went numb as if the sword had pierced his own throat. The dragon was his only lead, his sole hope of learning Recanna's fate. He turned and raced to where the hurled axe had fallen. His muscles strained to their limits to move the heavy weapon. Perhaps its weight would tilt the scales toward the justice due him.

He looked over his shoulder and gasped as Hezekiah stood mere feet from him, raising the sword above his head. Bitterwood leapt sideways as the demon drove the blade down in a savage blow that left a long crack in the packed earth of the street. Before Hezekiah could recover his balance, Bitterwood struck, bringing the axe down with all his strength into the center of his opponent's back.

Sparks leapt into the air. The axe clanged and quivered as if it had struck metal, numbing Bitterwood's hands with the vibration. The blow was sufficient to knock the sword from Hezekiah's hands.

The black-robed prophet needed no weapon. Hezekiah struck sideways with his fist, catching Bitterwood in the chest, sending him spinning. The axe flew from his grasp. He landed on his stomach, skidding in the dirt. He blinked through the dust of his landing, looking sideways. He spotted the fallen axe and extended his arm toward it.

As his fingers touched the handle, a heavy black boot dropped onto Bitterwood's hand, grinding a cry of pain from him as Hezekiah's incredible weight crushed down. He tried to pull free but he was pinned and could only watch helplessly as the prophet bent over and lifted up the axe.

Bitterwood could hear the beating of the mighty wings of the Angel of Death. The dust around him rose in a cloud as Hezekiah raised his axe heavenward. With a surge of fear-driven strength, Bitterwood pulled his hand loose and rolled to his back, hoping to avoid the blow, but knowing the cause was lost. Hezekiah towered over him, the axe held high in both hands, his body tensed to deliver the killing blow.

The moment lingered, frozen in time, with Hezekiah waiting to strike, his body motionless, as if he considered the perfect placement of the axehead. The dust in the air began to settle. The axe did not lower. Hezekiah stood still as a statue. Bitterwood scrabbled back from his enemy. Hezekiah's eyes didn't follow.

Bitterwood could see a trio of glowing threads floating in the air behind Hezekiah, writhing like snakes striking at an unseen opponent. The air beyond their reach shimmered like heat over hard ground on a summer day, then broke into countless tiny shards that vanished as they fell. In their place stood a sky-dragon, his eyes fixed upon a small silver sphere no larger than an acorn that he held in his talons. The dragon wore a silver skullcap similar to the one worn by the dragon that Jandra had asked him to spare. His wings were studded with jewels in an identical pattern. Nonetheless, this dragon's blue belly didn't have a scar on it. This couldn't be the same creature.

"Intriguing," said the dragon, snaking his neck forward to closely study Hezekiah's frozen face. "I haven't encountered one of these since I escaped Atlantis."

"Atlantis?" Bitterwood said. The word triggered memories. The southern rebellion... The dragon's tongue beneath his fingertips... The kudzu-draped grove... His eyes widened as he studied the face of the sky-dragon before him. "You were in the cage," he said, "in the City of Skeletons."

"What a small world," said the dragon, glancing toward Bitterwood. "I wouldn't have recognized you. You've aged poorly. In retrospect, you did me a favor not opening the cage."

CHAPTER TWENTY

SKELETONS

G LANCING OVER HIS shoulder, it seemed as if the whole world was on fire. Bitterwood whipped his horse to have it run faster along the cracked, vine-covered stones of the ghost line. He looked back once more, still clinging to the hope that he might see one of his men following. All that lay behind him, though, was the black tower of smoke rising from the fort. No living thing traveled the cursed ground with him. Most likely, everyone he'd fought beside was dead.

For the last few years, Bitterwood had stirred up rebellion in the southern reaches of Albekizan's kingdom. It hadn't been difficult. The king's unreasonable taxation had planted the seeds of the resistance. Bitterwood's tale of the king's injustice and cruelty, which he'd told from town to town, had helped bring the rebellion to harvest. Albekizan's tax collectors for the last two years had faced an increasingly hostile population, until at last the town of Conyer had built a wooden fort and declared its independence from Albekizan completely.

Now, Conyer was burning. Albekizan's dragons had swarmed the place in unimaginable numbers, ruthlessly slaughtering men, women, and children. Bitterwood had fought as long as he could until a small band of his fellow rebels had announced a plan to fall back and retreat to the ghost lines. They would reband and continue the fight on more favorable grounds at the City of Skeletons. Two dozen of them had fled on horseback. One by one, in the dark of night, dragons had swooped from the sky and picked off Bitterwood's companions. Now, Bitterwood alone raced into the twisted, rusting towers of the City of Skeletons.

This was haunted ground. Legend said it had once been a great city of men. Now it was deserted, a maze of ruins countless miles across covered in avenues of cracked concrete and crumbling, oily-black stone. The shells of countless buildings still stood, walls of brick and glass, over towering frames of rust-red beams. Thick blankets of kudzu covered much of the remains, softening the edges, hiding pits and jagged glass and snakes. Bitterwood rode into the heart of the city, the one place he hoped the dragons wouldn't dare follow.

A shadow passed over him. He recognized the leading edge of the shadow as that of a great wing. He knew then that he'd been wrong about any safety the city might offer. There was no place in the world Albekizan's forces wouldn't follow.

Suddenly, a talon dug into his left shoulder. He was jerked up from his horse. His leg tangled in the stirrups. With a yank so forceful it lifted his horse, Bitterwood was snatched upward. His ankle snapped as the dangling horse twisted around. His knee felt as if it were torn from his body entirely. Bitterwood rose, a dozen feet in the air, two dozen, three… then the talon released his bloody shoulder and he plummeted feet-first toward the gray ground below. He looked up to see the bright red plumage of a sun-dragon pass over him. He glanced down in time to see his horse crumpling against the ground and his own feet inches from impact.

A moment of darkness followed. The heavy thump of giant wings woke him. He was propped against a mound of torn meat. His legs lay crumbled before him, as limp and boneless as the limbs of a rag doll.

Twenty feet away, a sun-dragon stood.

"You're going to wish the fall had killed you," said the dragon.

Bitterwood looked around for a weapon. By chance his bow and quiver lay within reach, still strapped to what remained of the horse. He snatched them up and with quivering, scarred fingers placed an arrow against the string. He pulled with what remained of his strength. His shoulder felt as if it had a knife through it. His vision blurred as stars danced before him. He could barely see the outline of the dragon as he let the arrow fly.

He closed his eyes and sagged back against the dead horse. If he'd still believed in a merciful god, he would have prayed that the arrow he'd just fired had found its target.

Hot, stinking breath blew against his cheek.

"You missed," the dragon whispered into his ear.

Bitterwood opened his eyes and found himself staring straight into the nostrils of the dragon. The white wispy feathers around the snout wafted with the dragon's breath. Bitterwood fumbled to draw a second arrow from the quiver.

The dragon lowered his snout to intercept Bitterwood's hand. A sound that was half a slurp, half a crack, echoed through the stony wastes. Bitterwood felt a numb pressure at the end of his arm.

The dragon once more brought his face level with Bitterwood's eyes. In his dagger-like teeth lay Bitterwood's severed hand. The dragon began to chew leisurely.

Some last remnant of resistance stirred in Bitterwood and he raised his good hand to the dragon's snout, punching it. He drew back to punch again. The dragon spit out Bitterwood's hand. The drool-covered palm slapped Bitterwood's cheek. The dragon caught Bitterwood's second punch in his mouth. Bitterwood's arm was in the beast's maw up to the elbow. The last sensation he felt was of his fingers against the dragon's raspy tongue. Then the beast clamped his jaws together and Bitterwood felt nothing at all.

He slumped against his bed of bone and flesh, life draining out of him, aware of each fading beat of his heart. The dragon's red scales shimmered like fire as the beast drew near to watch him die.

Then the dragon jumped backward. Bitterwood's eyes reflexively followed the motion. The beast's scales no longer shimmered like flame—they were actually on fire. The dragon yelped like a scalded puppy as bright white flame danced over his whole body. The dragon fell in seconds, its hide and muscle boiling away with a terrible heat. Foul, oily smoke rolled over Bitterwood, reeking of burnt feathers and charred meat. In under a minute the flame died away, leaving only a mound of jumbled, black bone, which cracked and crumbled to dust.

Bitterwood knew what had happened. The gates of hell had opened for him, and the heat of the infernal furnace had caught the dragon. It was time to pay for all his sins. Silently, he closed his eyes, and surrendered to the glowing green devil that walked toward him. The last sound he heard was the buzz of flies.

BITTERWOOD WOKE SLOWLY to soft music that was played on instruments he couldn't recognize. The sound was ephemeral; a woman's voice sang wordlessly in harmony. The air was cool and dry, and smelled of freshly washed cotton. He opened his eyes to the cleanest room he'd ever seen. Light seeped from every direction through pale, translucent blue walls. The room was dome shaped, as best he could determine. In the absence of shadows and corners, it was hard to judge its scale. Raising himself for a better look, Bitterwood discovered he was naked, resting beneath a cotton sheet on a firm, white mattress. He raised his right arm to his face. To his bewilderment, he found a hand there. A strange, new hand, plump and pink as baby skin, nailless, hairless, and itching like mad.

He raised his left arm to scratch... and discovered a second fresh limb, also sporting pale, white fingers. His hands felt as if they were being swarmed by ants, as did his legs. He kicked aside the sheets to find his legs restored. Not even a bruise remained as evidence of their earlier mutilation. He noticed something strange about his toes. He could see them quite clearly. Although he was looking at them from a distance of about five and a half feet, they may as well have been an inch from his face.

Behind the walls the shadow of a tall, slender man moved. The shadow grew closer. The wall shimmered as the figure passed through.

He gasped as the figure turned out to be not a man, but a woman, the glowing devil he'd seen before he'd died. Now that he wasn't seeing her through the haze of smoke, she didn't look as fearsome as she had earlier. Still, she didn't look fully human, either. While she had a lovely face, beautiful by any measure, her skin was a bright jade green. Her hair was a darker shade, like moss. She wore a golden gown that hung closely to the curves of her body. She smiled with pearly teeth. Her lips were a shade of green darker than her hair, nearly black.

"You'll grow nails in a few hours. Hair, too," she said. "Until then, it will itch like crazy."

"Where...?"

"We're still in Atlanta," the woman said. "My name is Cynthia. I used to live here, a long time ago. I know I look strange but I'm human, like you. What's your name? Where are you from?"

"Christdale," he answered. "My name is Bant Bitterwood."

"Hmm," she said, setting down on the edge of the bed. "Interesting. Christdale. I'm always amazed at how Christianity has endured over the centuries. Of course, when I lived here, this whole state was in an area known as the 'Bible Belt.' If the old time religion was going to survive, it makes sense that it endured in what used to be Georgia."

Bitterwood stared at the woman, at her flawless features. Despite her odd coloring, she was the most attractive woman he'd ever seen. Her face reminded him of the face of the Goddess statue that used to dwell in his home village, long ago. She smelled like honeysuckle and mint. He asked, "Are you the Goddess? Is this heaven? Was Hezekiah wrong about my damnation? Was that only another lie?"

"No," Cynthia said. "I mean, no, you're not damned, but, no you're not in heaven either. I have no idea who Hezekiah is or what he told you. But I'm just a person like you." She paused a moment and glanced down at her hands with their dark green nails. "Oh," she said. "You might be thrown by my skin tone; it's just a fashion choice where I come from. You're still on Earth."

"But, the dragon…" Bitterwood held his hands before him. His skin continued to itch.

"Is dead. I've broken all sorts of rules," Cynthia said, brushing her long hair back from her face. "I'm here as part of an ecological survey. My job is to capture a few dragons and take them back to Atlantis for further study. Still, I saw that dragon toying with you and something just snapped. I'm not supposed to intervene but I felt guilty. I knew I had to save you."

"Guilty?" asked Bitterwood.

"About a thousand years ago, I was one of the people who decided we should leave the dragons alone. They were ecological nightmares, yes, the epitome of everything wrong with genetic modification. However, I argued that it would be unethical to exterminate them all after they'd escaped into the broader environment. They were sentient beings, after all. I had no idea where that would leave the world a thousand years later."

Bitterwood shook his head. "I don't understand what you are saying."

"No. I'm pretty sure you don't," Cynthia said, smiling. "You don't have the proper social context to understand what we did a thousand years ago. The simple story is that mankind went through a century or so when we had unraveled the genetic code—the building blocks of life itself—and we used it to make all kinds of fun things. Some were benign: drought-resistant crops, cancer-eating bacteria, allergen-free cats. Some weren't so great, though. We made weapons out of micro-organisms, for instance. Nearly killed half the people on earth in the last war with those. And, of course, somebody had the bright idea of making dragons."

Bitterwood sat up further in the bed. He wasn't sure what she was trying to communicate, but thought he got the gist of her final statement. "People made dragons?"

"Yeah. By the early Twenty-First century, all the big game animals on the planet were extinct or protected. So my employers sidestepped the law by creating new game animals. We pulled creatures out of mythology: chimera, hydras, unicorns and, of course, dragons. Filled up a big game park in the middle of the Ozarks. Charged wealthy hunters a million dollars a day to hunt there. We turned a profit inside of five months."

Bitterwood tried to make sense of what Cynthia was saying. Individually, he understood about half of her words. Strung together, the words were meaningless to him.

"We wanted the dragons to be smart," Cynthia said in a tone that sounded like a confession. "We already had the genetic code to build the most effective mind generator the world had ever evolved—the human brain. Around the time I was born, our early genetic tampering let us put jellyfish genes in monkeys. By the time I entered the field, we were putting human cerebral cortexes in warm-blooded bird-lizards. There was something of a moral slippery slope in between the two. In fairness, we only wanted the dragons to be smart enough to be challenging prey. We didn't really plan on them escaping and organizing the way they did. We set out to make entertaining monsters; we wound up making man-eating politicians with feathers. Talk about the law of unintended consequences."

Bitterwood shook his head. "I don't know what you are trying to tell me."

Cynthia shrugged. "It's not important. I'm just babbling about old times. I get nostalgic whenever I come back to the mainland."

Bitterwood rubbed his eyes. "I must be dreaming," he said. "I have a clear memory of my legs breaking. My hands... they were devoured."

"Yeah, that was pretty gross," she said. "I'm not supposed to help people, but really, when the dragon spit out your own hand into your face, I kind of snapped. After I killed the dragon, I figured in for a penny, in for a pound, and decided I'd save you. I pumped you full of nano and nutrients to fix your legs and regrow your arms."

"Nano?"

"Tiny machines. Don't worry about it. Think of it as magic. And, hey, you're in for a treat. Your old arms and legs looked pretty banged up. I examined the hand the dragon had spit out. It looked like you'd broken almost every bone in it at one time or another. Your new arms and legs are going to be as finely tuned as your genetic code can support. You'll be crazy fast and crazy strong, at least for a few years until you wear them out again."

"Oh," he said. "Will they always look this strange?"

"Once they age a few hours, they'll look more like the ones you had. I also had them tune up your eyes. You were a teeny bit nearsighted; you probably didn't have a great picture of what your feet looked like most of the time. Now I've got you set to about twenty-ten. The next time you shoot at a dragon from a couple of yards away, maybe you'll hit him. I just wish I could do something about your brain."

"My brain?"

"Yeah. It's a mess. Alas, I have to tap into a different database before I can program any kind of brain alterations. I'll get grief if they find out I gave you new fingers. If I start rewiring your brain, wow, I won't be let back out of Atlantis for like, another thousand years."

"Atlantis?"

She motioned toward a wall. It faded away, revealing a great golden city beyond. Angels flitted through the air, darting among slender spires taller than the highest mountains. The music shifted from the light, ethereal tones to a more dramatic, brassy rhythm.

"This is a picture of where we live now," she said. "It's where we went, once we became immortal."

"Then this *is* heaven, after all," said Bitterwood.

"I can see why you might think that. Atlantis is the city we retreated to after we decided that tinkering with the world always led to more harm than good. We had reached such power with our technology that we changed the planet faster than we could react. We had the footprints of giants, and we were stumbling around as aimlessly as toddlers. After we beat death, we had the most dangerous technology of all in our hands. The fact that humans died off easily was always a nice brake on our ability to harm the world. If all the billions of people in the world were allowed to live forever and keep breeding, we'd wreck the planet. So we had to make choices. Not everyone could be allowed immortality. In the end, a select few retreated to a place where we wouldn't do any further damage, and let the rest of the world go feral."

Bant scratched the backs of his tingling hands against the raspy stubble of his cheeks. He asked, "If you are human, and you have this power, why do you allow the dragons to kill your fellow men? Why don't you save us?"

Cynthia nodded toward the wall which faded back to blue. "Actually, we're considering it. Some of us think it's time to tinker again. Bring the gift of knowledge back to the rest of humanity, slowly and carefully. Unfortunately, the downside of immortality is we'll probably debate this another century or two."

"A century?" Bitterwood asked.

"Or more," she said. "We like to carefully consider all ramifications."

"Humans are dying now," Bitterwood said. "Dragons killed my family. Their king starves humans with his unreasonable policies. He currently wages war... I may be the only survivor of his last atrocity. What is left for you to consider?"

She sighed. "Look, don't hassle me, okay? It's not like things were so different when humans were in charge. We killed a lot more people than dragons can even dream of. You're just going to have to have faith that we'll do the right thing."

"Faith is a foul word in my vocabulary," said Bitterwood. "I've suffered only betrayal when I acted on faith."

"You're certainly not a very grateful person are you?" Cynthia asked. "I save your life, fix your hands, tune up your eyes, and I don't even get a thank you?"

Bitterwood looked around. Without looking in her direction, he asked, "Where are my clothes?"

Cynthia handed him a neat stack of folded linen. "I had to nano patch and clean your stuff. I also fixed up your bow and arrows. Get dressed, then follow me."

Cynthia walked back out the wall. Her shadow paused on the other side, then moved away.

Bitterwood pondered the clothes she'd handed him. They looked like his, only as clean and crisp as if the cloth had just come off the loom. Was this witchcraft? Was he endangering himself by taking this gift? He thought the matter over and felt dumb; he was afraid of his own clothes. Shaking his head at his foolishness, he put his clothes back on. The clean linen against his new skin was disturbingly pleasant. It smelled as if it had been dried in warm sun in a spring breeze. His boots had been restored. The leather was cotton soft and fit like a second skin as he pulled them on.

He reached out to touch the wall Cynthia had exited. It felt like a curtain of falling water, though when he pulled his fingers back they were dry. He noticed pale half moons near the end of his fingers. His nails were growing back.

He held his breath and walked outside. Hot, humid air instantly soaked into his clothing. He raised his pink arm to the blazing summer sun He was in a grove of fragrant, dark green kudzu, humming with yellow bees, aflutter with iridescent black butterflies. A trio of crates stood before him holding three dragons: a sun-dragon, a sky-dragon, and an earth-dragon. Two of the dragons lay still as death within their cages. The sky-dragon alone was awake. He pressed against the slender silver bars of the cage when he saw Bitterwood.

"Help me," the dragon pleaded, extending a blue wing through the bars.

Bitterwood studied the creature's face. This dragon seemed younger than the sky-dragons he'd fought in recent weeks. His scales bore the faint white speckles of late adolescence. His accent was strange to Bant's ears. Perhaps it was only because he'd never heard a dragon ask for help before.

The dragon's golden eyes held a look of utter terror. "Before she comes back," the beast begged, "unlock the cage."

"I'm not in a mood to help dragons," Bitterwood said, walking away from the crates. He now saw Cynthia standing at the outer edge of the kudzu grove. She held his restored bow and arrows and offered them to him as he drew near.

"I can't believe this isn't a dream," he said as he took the weapons into his newly minted fingers.

"Maybe it is," Cynthia said, walking back toward the kudzu. "Maybe you should live as if it is, at least. You've got a new lease of life. What do you want to do with it?"

"Kill dragons," he said.

She giggled. "Well, it's important to have a goal in life. Maybe you can make all the studying and debating we're engaged in back in Atlantis moot. Get out there and wipe out all the dragons single-handed."

"I won't let you down," Bitterwood said, pushing aside a veil of kudzu and stepping beyond the grove. "I just have one more question."

Cynthia didn't answer.

Bitterwood stepped back through the emerald veil. The crates were gone. He called out her name. All he heard in reply was the breeze rustling through leaves.

Bitterwood took shelter from the sun in the shade of a vine-draped wall. He sat until nightfall, staring at his hands, watching his nails grow back, until all was restored. He thought about what Cynthia had told him, trying to fit the words into something that made sense.

It all boiled down to this. Humans had created dragons. Dragons had no rightful claim to the world. As the sun sank, Bitterwood closed his strong, young hands into fists, digging the nails into his palms, until the pain would most surely wake him.

He didn't wake up. Bitterwood opened his hands, then picked up his bow and arrow. He fixed his eyes on a single purple kudzu bloom across the grove thirty yards away. He fired an arrow, neatly severing the stem. The flower dropped, vanishing into the blanket of dark leaves.

For the first time in ages, Bitterwood grinned.

CHAPTER TWENTY-ONE

HOMUNCULUS

V ENDEVOREX STEPPED BACK from the now-paralyzed body of the prophet. The three smartwires continued to snake toward the silvery command homunculus he held. He reached out his free claw, fusing the tips of the three wires together so that they fell dead. The human whose life he'd just saved stood looking at him, slack-jawed.

"This is a very dangerous toy," Vendevorex said. "Did you bring this with you from Atlantis? Are you still working with Cynthia?"

"No," the man said. "I never saw her again. You're Vendevorex? You survived?"

"Yes and yes," Vendevorex answered. "And if you aren't working with Cynthia, who are you?"

"I'm Bitterwood," the man answered.

"I see," Vendevorex said, furrowing his brow. "I expect you'll be trying to kill me, then."

Bitterwood shook his head. "I agreed to spare you. I gave my word. To Jandra."

"Jandra," Vendevorex said, remembering his reason for being here. With a thought, he encased the homunculus in a thin coat of lead, then turned away from Bitterwood and moved toward his fallen student. He knelt next to her, reaching out his hand to feel the pulse in her throat, then gently touched the gash above her ear. Jandra moaned slightly and turned her head away.

At that moment three guards ran around the corner of the nearest building.

"Halt!" one cried.

"No," Vendevorex said, reaching into his pouch of powders. He flicked his dust-coated claws in the direction of the three green dragons. "My friends and I will be left alone." Vendevorex closed his claw in a deliberate, dramatic gesture. Suddenly, the spears carried by the dragons began to glow. Then Vendevorex flapped a wing, sending a breeze across the dusty ground. The spear shafts crumbled to ash and were carried off by the gust.

The leader of the three dragons looked confused. His eyes glanced down to his empty hands, then looked toward the decapitated body of the slain soldier, before turning to the frozen form of the black-garbed man, then fixing, finally, on Vendevorex. The leader's face flickered with sudden recognition.

"You're the wizard!" he yelped.

"You're right," Vendevorex answered.

"Yaa!" they shouted in unison. Their scales suddenly stood on end as they spun about to flee.

"Stop!" Vendevorex commanded. "If you try to run, I will disintegrate your legs as easily as your spears. I want us to come to an understanding."

The three guards didn't take another step. Vendevorex could see their muscles trembling as if resisting an invisible spring that threatened to snap them away.

"You should know that now that I have seen your faces, I can kill you at any time with just a thought," Vendevorex said. "I can make it as quick and simple as I did with your weapons, or I can prolong your agony, depending on my mood. I spare you on one condition. You must speak to no one of what you've witnessed today. Understood?"

"Y-y-yessir."

"Then go," Vendevorex said.

The three dragons tripped over one another as they raised their tails high and raced back down the side street.

"It was foolish to let them go," Bitterwood said. "To silence them, you should have killed them."

"I didn't see the need for bloodshed," Vendevorex said. "I fear there may be blood enough spilled in the coming days. Now be a good fellow and carry Jandra for me, will you?"

"I'm not a slave to be ordered around by your kind," Bitterwood said.

"No, of course not," said Vendevorex. "However, given your status as a legendary hero, I assume you are too gallant to simply let Jandra recover from her wounds in the middle of the street, yes?"

Bitterwood glowered. "I'll help her, but don't try to manipulate me."

"Understood," Vendevorex said. "I hate to even ask the favor of you. I'd carry Jandra myself but I doubt you have the strength to carry our friend here." Vendevorex moved to the frozen body of the axe-wielding man and tilted him backward, catching him with a grunt.

"What did you do to Hezekiah?" Bitterwood asked as he slid his arms beneath Jandra's shoulders and knees.

"It's a little hard to explain," Vendevorex said, his voice strained as he tried to get a grip on Hezekiah's heavy form. "I suppose you might say I've taken his soul from his body." Vendevorex looked up and down the row of buildings. "I'm surprised your fellow humans haven't been drawn to the commotion. Are most of these dwellings still empty?"

"My 'fellow humans' tend to cluster together. I stick to this area because I like my privacy," Bitterwood said, carefully lifting Jandra. He tilted his head toward an empty building. "Follow me."

BLASPHET PULLED THE weed from the soil and tossed it aside. Laboring on the balcony beside the trellis full of poison ivy, he had occasion to contemplate the sunlight on his skin, still a novel sensation after his years in the dungeon. The sensual pleasures the world offered thrilled him anew each day. How could others be so insensate to a world full of life? Blasphet doubted that Albekizan felt even one-tenth of the satisfaction when he looked out over his kingdom that stretched as far as the eye could see as Blasphet felt while simply tending this small potted garden. He reached for the watering can, tilting it, releasing a shower of fresh human blood to nourish the soil in a pot that contained a belladonna shrub. Ah, the simple pleasures of gardening.

Sometimes, while contemplating the life that burst from the soil, the answers seemed so close. The dark, wholesome earth was made rich by decay and excrement—surely a key to life's mystery. But what lock did this key fit?

A shadow passed over him. He looked up to see his brother descending from the sky. Blasphet drew back to allow his brother room to land.

"Blasphet," Albekizan said as he came to rest on the balcony, knocking over potted plants. "Thanks to your sage words, I've made a decision."

"I see," Blasphet said, wincing as his brother crushed flowers beneath his heavy talons. "Odd. I don't recall advising you to come here and wreck my garden."

"I speak of Bitterwood," said Albekizan. "I've decided his fate. But first, I need information about the Free City. Everyone tells me it's filling ahead of schedule. How many now dwell there?"

Blasphet shrugged. "Hard to say. The numbers increase daily, though the real influx will begin after next week's full moon. The harvest moon, the humans call it."

"You did not answer my question. I want a number. How many humans are within the Free City?"

"Why do you need this information so urgently?" Blasphet said, crouching to turn a potted nightshade upright once more. Its pink blossoms were horribly mangled. "You said you'd made a decision about Bitterwood. Is it possible you've decided upon a course of action before you've gathered the relevant information?"

"I grow impatient, Blasphet."

"Very well, if it will get you to leave my balcony quicker. The total at present is eight thousand, approximately."

"A fair number," said the king. "And how many guards are currently stationed in the city?"

"Right now, most of the guards are out in the countryside preparing to herd the humans here," Blasphet said.

"But in the city itself? How many?"

"Kanst could answer this for you," Blasphet sighed.

"You know everything about the city. Don't pretend otherwise," said Albekizan.

Blasphet felt contrary, wanting instinctively to hold back any information that Albekizan might consider useful. However, a second part of him was curious. What did Albekizan have in mind? "By my count, there are six hundred earth-dragons. Fifty sky-dragon officers. What are you planning to do with them?"

"There is a square at the center of the city? Large enough to hold a crowd of eight thousand?"

"Not comfortably," Blasphet said.

"Order the guards to gather the humans in the square tomorrow morning. During the night, Kanst's army will join with the city's guards, bringing the force of dragons to two thousand. This should be more than enough."

"Enough?" Blasphet asked. "For what? To keep order?"

"You'll find out tomorrow," said Albekizan.

"You are no good at being coy," Blasphet said. "There's only one reason you could want to herd the humans together. You plan Bitterwood's public execution."

"A public execution, yes," the king answered. "You're right; I shouldn't be coy. A public execution is precisely what I desire. Order the guards to cooperate with Kanst's troops."

"Of course," Blasphet said, disturbed by Albekizan's intrusion into his affairs, but feeling it unwise to press the issue now. Most likely, upon Bitterwood's death, his brother's interest in the Free City would wane. He said, in his most sincere tone, "I live but to serve you."

"You live to torment me," Albekizan said, turning away and spreading his wings. "But you live because I allow it. Remember that."

"Have no fear about my memory," Blasphet said as his brother leapt into the air. The king's long tail whipped around, knocking over another flowerpot. Blasphet looked down at the shattered terracotta and crushed blossoms that marked his brother's visit. He glanced back up at Albekizan's retreating form. He said, softly, "I remember everything."

THE BLACK CURTAINS that shrouded Jandra's mind parted. She opened her eyes with a start, expecting to find Hezekiah towering over her, preparing to kill her with a final strike in the middle of the dusty street. Instead, she found herself alone in a darkened room on a scratchy wool blanket. Her head throbbed as she sat up. She raised her hand to discover bandages around her brow. In the next room, she could hear a muffled but familiar voice.

"Ven," she whispered.

She rose on wobbly feet and tiptoed toward the door. She paused, listening to her former mentor speaking with someone else. A human's voice. Bitterwood?

Feeling unready to face Vendevorex, she steadied herself with her palms against the wall and peeked through a small crack in the door. She could see Hezekiah propped against the far wall, his body rigid, his eyes unblinking. Vendevorex walked into view holding a small metal sphere in his claws.

From beyond her view, Bitterwood said, "Hezekiah hasn't aged a day in all the years I've known him."

"Understandable," Vendevorex said, pulling free a yellow wire from the clump he had fused earlier. "He isn't really alive. He's a simulacrum."

"I don't understand."

"Long ago, people were able to make copies of themselves, or anyone, really." Vendevorex pried open the left eye of the paralyzed prophet and examined it closely. "The artificial bodies were practically indestructible, could mimic the human form perfectly, and were designed in such a manner that the maker of the simulacrum could feel and see and hear anything his double did. More, actually." He let the eye close. "This one sees into the infrared and ultraviolet, I think." He turned back to face Bitterwood. "Humans once used these doubles for sport. Normally, the simulacrum only did what its maker told it to do, but a few were fitted with the ability to think and act on their own. That's where this comes in," Vendevorex said, raising the sphere. "The homunculus. The soul of the machine."

"This is a soul?" Bitterwood asked. "I've cut open many dragons and never seen this organ. Are dragons truly soulless?"

"You won't find these in people, either. 'Soul' is merely an analogy." Vendevorex turned back to the black-garbed prophet and picked up one of the three wires draped over its shoulder, a yellow one. He said, "It's more accurate, perhaps, to say that this is Hezekiah's mind. It's the source of his intelligence and what passes for free will. For us," Vendevorex said, touching the yellow wire to the sphere, "it's the source of answers."

"Online. Testing," Hezekiah said, though his lips didn't move and his body remained motionless.

"Skip diagnostics," Vendevorex said.

"Diagnostics aborted. Activating personality core. Activated."

Vendevorex spoke toward the orb he held. "What is your mission?"

"To spread the word of the Lord," answered Hezekiah's seemingly disembodied voice.

"Who gave you this mission?"

"I was programmed by Jasmine Danielle Robertson."

"When?"

"In the year of our Lord 2077."

Vendevorex glanced toward Bitterwood. "He means A.D. The numbering system of years that preceded the Dragon Age." Then addressing the sphere once more: "Hezekiah, do you know why Robertson gave you this mission?"

"The world was falling into chaos and decadence. Few people remembered the word, and my maker believed it likely that the world would be cleansed once more, just as the Lord had cleansed it in the days of the flood. I was created to survive the coming cataclysm, and to spread the word among the survivors."

"I see," said Vendevorex. "Somehow this mission involves chopping off people's heads?"

"I am designed to remove any obstacles to the success of my mission."

"Excellent," said Vendevorex. "As long as you're programmed to be capable of violence, I think you should put that programming to good use. Only your mission will change when I let you go."

"Let him go?" Bitterwood said. "You can't mean to release him from this spell you have on him."

"I can," Vendevorex said. "Don't be afraid. He'll be no threat to you when I'm done with him."

"No threat?" Bitterwood said, moving forward into Jandra's line of sight at last. His fists were clenched. "Hezekiah's not human!"

Vendevorex looked impatient. "That's been established. However, being inhuman doesn't make one a threat to humans. I'm proof of that. Hezekiah is too useful a tool to discard. As a fighter, he's nearly unstoppable. He'll be the perfect weapon if things turn ugly with Albekizan."

Hearing this, Jandra decided the time had come for her to make her presence known. She pushed open the door and said, "So. Now you plan to fight."

"Jandra," Vendevorex said, looking startled. It gave her a slight tinge of satisfaction to realize that he wasn't ready to speak to her yet. "I apologize for not keeping our voices down," he said. "We shouldn't have disturbed your rest. You've suffered serious trauma. Even with the treatment I've given, I recommend allowing several hours to heal completely."

"It's funny how you pretend to care," Jandra said. "Why did you come here, Ven? Not to apologize, I hope."

"Yes," he said, sounding sad. "I am here to apologize, whether or not you'll accept. I've made horrible mistakes, Jandra. I'd be foolish to think that things can go back to the way they were."

"That *would* be foolish," she agreed.

"I'm hoping that the last fifteen years of my life count for something. I've tried to be the family you never had."

She crossed her arms. "You did a poor job."

"Yes. I can't deny it. But if I can't win your favor with my past deeds, I still hope I may influence your opinion with what I'm doing now. I've decided to fulfill your wishes and go to war against Albekizan."

"Don't do it because you want to earn my forgiveness. You won't receive it," she said. She was surprised to realize how deeply she meant it. She had practiced the words often enough in her mind in recent days. Now that she'd said them, the truth sank in. She would never forgive him.

"For what it's worth, it's not only your forgiveness that has led to my reassessment of my actions. I've gained new information since we parted which makes me believe a revolution can now be successful."

"Oh?"

"I saw little hope in revolution before. If Albekizan fell, the candidates for the throne were unattractive. Now, Shandrazel has returned. He's perfect for the job. I feel that placing him on the throne will return peace and stability to the kingdom. Assuming, of course, I can change his mind."

"Whose mind? Shandrazel's? About what?"

"Shandrazel is perhaps a bit too idealistic and kind for my purposes. The prince doesn't want to rule, nor does he want his father killed. I'm not sure that can be avoided, however."

"You would know about killing fathers," said Jandra.

Vendevorex turned his face away from her. Jandra knew her words had stung him.

Bitterwood, who had listened intently to the conversation, suddenly stiffened. He said to Vendevorex, "You killed her father?"

"Yes," the wizard answered.

He turned to Jandra, "Why did you beg me to spare him?"

"He's... I didn't know then, but even so, I want you to spare him. Let him live with his guilt."

Bitterwood approached her. "If you've lost your father to a dragon, then you must understand how I feel. I lost my whole family to dragons. For years I thought them dead—"

"I suppose, in that light, you're almost happy to learn they were sold into slavery," she said. She almost instantly regretted the words. They sounded so callous. Like something Ven might have said.

Bitterwood didn't look as if he took offense, however. "The possibility that my family is alive is something I can't ignore. If only Hezekiah hadn't killed my only lead. I don't know where or how to search for them."

"I might be of use," said Vendevorex. "If your family was sold as slaves during Albekizan's reign, there will be written records. By law, all transactions are documented for taxation."

"But it was twenty years ago," Bitterwood said.

"That won't matter," said Vendevorex. "Albekizan never destroys any records. The king built his empire with blood, cunning, and paperwork."

"Where would these records be?" Bitterwood asked.

"In the castle. In the library. You'll probably need a biologian to navigate the maze, unfortunately."

Jandra realized this was a chance to hurt Vendevorex once more. She said, "I can take you there. I've spent enough time studying in the libraries. I know where those records are kept."

"Very well. We can all go there," Vendevorex said, "after I've changed Hezekiah's mind."

"We'll go alone," Jandra said. "I don't want your help."

"No, but you'll need it," Vendevorex said. "The castle's too dangerous. Suppose you run into Zanzeroth?"

"Suppose we do? How will you being there help? Bitterwood and I both run while Zanzeroth guts you again?"

"I'm only saying your invisibility will be no defense. I've learned that."

"No dragon within the castle walls is a threat to me," Bitterwood said, picking up the slain guard's sword which rested on the table. He moved toward the door and looked back at Vendevorex as he said, "I've waited long enough. As for you, wizard, if you plan to make Hezekiah your ally, you can count me among your enemies. I want nothing more to do with this demon."

"I'm ready," said Jandra, walking to join him in the doorway.

Vendevorex sighed. "Please reconsider. I've come a long way to find you, Jandra. I don't want you placing yourself in further danger."

"I don't care what you want," she said. "I can take care of myself. Let's go, Bitterwood."

"Please," Vendevorex said, but Jandra paid no mind. She placed her hand on Bitterwood's arm, both to show her solidarity with the dragon-slayer and to steady herself, for the wound to her head hurt worse than she dared reveal. They stepped outside. Vendevorex came to the door and said, "You're being very unreasonable."

And reason's all you know, she thought, but held her tongue, knowing that silence hurt him more. The pain in Jandra's head paled next to the pain in her heart. Vendevorex would never understand her, and she would never understand him. Bitterwood was right. Men and dragons could never share the world.

Bitterwood led her away. She glanced back over her shoulder, hoping to see the look on Vendevorex's face. But her mentor didn't follow and now turned back inside. As Jandra watched his deep-blue tail vanish into the shadows of the building, a chill ran through her. This might be the last time she ever saw her former mentor.

"Are you okay?" Bitterwood asked, noticing her shudder.

"I'm fine," Jandra said. "But I just thought... what about Zeeky? We never found her."

"We'll have to hope she's okay," Bitterwood said. "She's a tough girl."

"True. And it's not like we could take her with us. So. Any ideas on how we get out of here?"

"Follow me," Bitterwood said. "I've found a rope and hidden it. I know of several places on the wall where we can climb up then use the rope to rappel down. We'll need to wait for night before we can move safely, though."

Jandra looked at the sun high in the sky, the bright light making her head throb even more. "It's several hours until sunset. Why don't we scale the walls now? We can cross invisibly then make our way to the castle. By the time we get inside it will be nightfall. That will give us several hours to search the records while the biologians sleep."

"Invisible?" said Bitterwood, sounding disdainful. "I dislike relying on your witchcraft."

"Would you stop that? I'm not a witch. I just happen to have fancier tools than most people. Trust me on this, okay?"

Bitterwood looked into her eyes for a long moment. "Very well. If I must. Follow me."

Bitterwood led her behind one of the empty buildings. He pushed aside a half-filled rain barrel, then pulled up a loose wallboard that the barrel had pinned down. He reached inside the wall and retrieved a long coil of hemp rope.

Jandra splashed some of the water from the rain barrel onto her face. The cool water helped greatly. Taking a deep breath, she felt strong and calm enough to make them invisible—but for how long? She tore a strip of cloth from her dress and wetted it to dab her brow as she needed it.

"You sure you're okay?" Bitterwood asked.

"I'm feeling better," Jandra said, trying to make herself believe it. "I just need to keep moving."

"If you're certain. We can go up the wall here," he said. The alley they were in ran along the outer wall of the city.

"Let me get ready," Jandra said, reaching into her pouch. "We'll still be able to see each other, but we need to stay close if you don't want others to see you."

Bitterwood nodded, then turned the rain barrel over and placed it against the wall. He hopped on and extended his hand to help Jandra up. Jandra activated the invisibility as she stood next to him. But now what? The wall stood twenty feet high, made of logs driven into the ground.

Bitterwood didn't share her hesitation. He placed his hands and feet between the gaps in the logs and scaled the wall as quickly as if he were walking across flat ground.

"Wait!" she said. "You're out of range!"

Bitterwood didn't stop. He placed his hand on the top of the wall and pulled himself up. He straddled the wall and turned around, looking down at her. He cocked his head.

"You really are invisible," he muttered.

"Yes," she said. "But you're not. Someone will see you."

"Then we should make haste," Bitterwood said, tossing one end of the rope toward the sound of her voice. "Don't even try to climb. I'll lift you."

Jandra wrapped the rope around her hand and arm and Bitterwood began to pull her up. She helped him by using her feet to climb the wider cracks when possible.

"I see you now," he said as she neared the top of the wall.

He reached down and took her hand and lifted her the rest of the way. Jandra looked around for guards and noticed a nearby guard tower, but the guards within weren't looking in their direction. Instead, the guards watched the sky. Jandra looked up and gasped. Sun-dragons!

"I see them," Bitterwood said. "I don't think they've seen us."

Jandra soon realized this was true. She'd gotten him into the invisibility field just in time. The dragons weren't headed directly toward them. They weren't even looking in their direction. They seemed to be heading toward the center of the Free City, to the square.

Albekizan himself led the way. It had been months since Jandra had seen him. The king was breathtaking in flight, with broad, crimson wings driven by a deep, well-muscled breast. He flew with powerful, precise movements, showing his mastery of the air. Tanthia followed. The queen was smaller than the king, sleeker, and her wings trailed yellow silk ribbons that flashed in the sunlight. If anything, she looked even more graceful in the air than Albekizan. In contrast to the elegant royal couple, Kanst followed behind in his slow, jerky motion. Weighed down by his heavy armor, the great bull dragon beat the air mightily, raising himself higher one flap at a time before holding his wings stiff and gliding down, losing the height he'd gained. He didn't so much fly as climb and fall through the sky. Zanzeroth lagged even further behind, the stiff movements of his wings betraying his half-healed wounds. Another dragon would have stayed in bed with such injuries, Jandra suspected, but the tough old hunter was too proud ever to admit to weakness. A single sky-dragon completed the procession, Pertalon. Despite his youth and strength, Pertalon trailed behind Zanzeroth, for he carried a burden, a cocoon of white cloth wrapped around what looked to be the body of a man.

Could it be Pet? Could it not be? She should have freed Pet when she had the chance. Now that Vendevorex was going to fight the king, there was no need for Pet to sacrifice himself. As much as she hated Vendevorex she respected his abilities, and knew that if he was intent on overthrowing the king, he would. The white bundle struggled as the dragons banked. She felt heartened that Pet was still alive. Jandra would help Bitterwood for now. When she found the information he needed, she would make him return the favor and rescue Pet.

CHAPTER TWENTY-TWO

MYTH

METRON WATCHED ALBEKIZAN'S party fly from the grand hall toward the Free City. He'd received an invitation to join the king but had politely declined, stating that he was feeling under the weather. Metron had suspected the king wouldn't take no for an answer, and had been anticipating the appearance of a few guards. Knowing the king proceeded without him was humbling. Apparently, he wasn't essential to the running of the kingdom.

Despite learning that he wasn't as vital to the king's court as he sometimes fancied, he was also relieved. Whatever the king had planned, the timing couldn't have been worse. The note passed to Metron moments before he'd been summoned made it vital he stay; Androkom, the biologian who boasted of knowing the secret of life, had arrived.

The scholar and his equipment were waiting below in Metron's personal study.

Metron hurried through the stone corridors and stairwells that led to the maze of books below. When he arrived at his study he found the door ajar. It locked with a secret key that only another initiated biologian would possess.

"Androkom?" he said, peering into the dark chamber.

"I'm here," his fellow biologian said. In the darkness, there was a creak as the shutter of an oil lamp was opened. The light revealed Androkom sitting at the table in the center of the room, his pale blue form half-hidden behind a stack of books. A well-worn leather satchel rested on the table before him. Androkom clutched the strap of the satchel tightly in his ink-stained fore-talons as he nodded in silent greeting. Metron stepped into the room, pushing the door shut behind him. He gasped as the closing door revealed that they were not alone. The rich scarlet scales of a sun-dragon's breast filled his vision. A familiar face loomed over him.

"Shandrazel!" he cried.

"Please," Shandrazel said in a loud whisper. "Lower your voice."

"Sneaking back into the castle with a dragon of Shandrazel's stature wasn't easy," Androkom said. "You'll understand that we'd rather not be discovered."

"What's the meaning of this?" Metron asked, pointing his walking staff toward Androkom. "Are you assisting the prince? This is treason! He's duty-bound to kill the king!"

"Nonsense," Shandrazel said. "I never felt any obligations to the old ways. I feel even less now that I know how artificial the so-called 'ancient traditions' truly are. Androkom has told me much about the ways of the biologians."

"Tell me this is a lie, Androkom," Metron said. "You cannot have told him the initiated secrets."

Androkom nodded. "I did; at least, what I had time to tell. I respect you, High Biologian. But I no longer respect our ways. The higher I have risen in the ranks, the more I have learned that has troubled me. Shandrazel and I share an abiding faith in the redemptive power of truth." Androkom toyed with the shutter of the lantern as he spoke, opening it fully to cast as much light as possible over the chamber. The younger biologian glanced around at the dusty tomes and shadowed niches of Metron's private study. "The Book of Theranzathax speaks of using light to carve the world from darkness," he said. "We think it's time for the obscuring haze of lies to be burned away by the lantern of honest inquiry."

"Androkom," Metron said, stepping to the table, placing his fore-talons on the heavy oak for balance as he leaned closer. "You must reconsider this reckless path you've chosen. I've known you for years. I've watched you rise through the ranks at a nearly unequaled pace. Why destroy the very title you've worked so hard to earn?"

Androkom met Metron's condemning gaze without blinking. He said, "I entered the ranks of the biologians seeking knowledge. It disturbs me that my role has become one of concealing truths, rather than revealing them. Too much of what's taken as common fact by most dragons is merely carefully constructed fiction."

"Yes!" Metron hissed. "Carefully constructed! Designed by the most brilliant minds who ever lived to give dragons a grand destiny! You cannot brashly destroy the work of centuries!"

"Metron," said Shandrazel, "I will grant that you have only the best interests of dragons at heart. No doubt the most central myths of the dragons were crafted solely for the benefit of our kind. But we are not alone on this world... we share it. Would my father now be waging war against the humans if he knew the truth? The petrified skeletons that adorn our halls... these are not the remains of our ancestors. Our species is barely a millennium old. We owe our existence to humanity."

"We owe nothing to humanity," said Metron. "I've studied the manuscripts they left behind. When they ruled this world, they poisoned it with their own filth. They were like yeast in a corked bottle, growing until they choked in toxins of their own making."

"So you support my father's genocide?" Shandrazel asked.

Metron felt the anger drain out of him at this question. His whole body sagged. "No," he said softly. "No matter their past sins, I want to avoid the coming slaughter. In my studies, I have learned much of human ways. In their time of dominance, humans callously drove uncountable species into extinction. I would like to think that we dragons are above this."

"As would I," said Shandrazel.

"And I," said Androkom. "So, it seems we have some common ground to build upon."

"Yes," said Metron. "Still, you should not have shared our secrets, Androkom."

"I find your hypocrisy on this most intriguing," said Androkom. "You would withhold the truth from Shandrazel, who's known for his integrity. Yet you share our secrets with Blasphet, the Murder God?"

Metron scowled. "Blasphet has learned many of our secrets against my will. Showing him tomes written by humans will tell him nothing he hasn't already deduced."

Shandrazel said, "What Blasphet knows or doesn't know isn't important, in the end. Our course is clear. We must tell my father the truth about the origins of dragons. In light of the new information, he'll halt the genocide and imprison my uncle once more."

Metron felt his jaw hanging open. "You... you really believe that?" he asked incredulously.

"My father may be stubborn and stern, but he's bound to listen to reason."

Metron shook his head. "My prince, you are too idealistic. The biologians at the College of Spires did their best to craft you into a being that respects truth and fairness, in hopes of shaping a future king. But I fear they've left you ignorant of the way the world actually works."

"No. Not ignorant. Educated. Once my father learns the truth, he will see the folly of his war on the humans and rescind the death orders. We dragons pride ourselves on being the highest product of the laws of nature, the rightful rulers of the earth, while the humans follow religions that tell them that they are separate from nature, and were created independently of it. All along, the opposite was true."

"He'll never believe you," Metron said. "Furthermore, you'll never have a chance to make your argument. He'll kill you on sight. He'll throttle the life from you while you're standing there like an idiot trying to appeal to his reason."

"That's why we need a plan," Androkom said. "And why we need your help."

Metron inhaled slowly, contemplating his next words. They wanted his help. Shandrazel, at least, was foolish enough to trust the king. Did he have the same faith in Metron's own honesty and fairness? If so, Metron might still have a chance. Androkom's books and equipment were sitting on the table. Blasphet would find these very useful.

"We were thinking you could request a private conference with the king," Androkom said. "Such is your right. Then—"

"No," Metron said, raising his claw, unable to believe his luck. "I know a better way."

"We're listening," Shandrazel said.

THE SUN HUNG red and low in the sky when Jandra woke. From her resting place on the hill she could see the king's castle casting a long, sinister shadow across the land.

Bitterwood sat against a nearby tree, though it took her a moment to spot him. He sat so still that, with his drab clothing and tanned skin, he blended in against the tree trunk.

She asked, "How long did I nap?"

"Not long," he said. "Perhaps an hour."

"I only meant to rest my eyes for a minute," she said.

"I don't begrudge you the sleep. I know how hard it is to keep going with a head injury."

Jandra noticed that her head no longer hurt. She pressed the bandage that covered her wound with her finger and felt no pain. She pulled the bandage free.

"It's healed isn't it?" she asked, reaching for her pouch of dust.

"Yes," Bitterwood said. "In less than a day. Yet you say you aren't a witch."

"Even if I were, I couldn't do this," she said. She used the dust from her fingers to create a small mirror. For half a second she wondered who she was looking at in the mirror. She'd almost forgotten that she'd changed her hair color to black. Once past the mild shock of seeing a stranger's hair, she pushed the hair back and studied her brow. She lifted her tiara slightly. There was no bruise. The skin that had been beneath the bandage was pale white compared to the tan she'd developed with all the time she'd spent outdoors. Aside from this there was no sign she'd ever been injured.

"Healing is a skill I have yet to master," she said. "I can do superficial stuff, things I can see and concentrate on, but internal injuries, especially head wounds, are more than I can handle. One misrouted artery can cause a stroke. This is Vendevorex's work."

"He seems to genuinely want your forgiveness," Bitterwood said.

"He won't get it." She let the mirror crack and crumble back into dust. "At first, the lie hurt most of all, the idea that he had raised me while keeping such a secret. But more and more I find myself dreaming of the life I might have known. All my life, I've been an outcast. I lived among dragons but could never be accepted by them. When I go among people, I find that I don't fit in either. Vendevorex robbed me of a normal life. I could have had a loving mother and father. Instead I was raised by a cold-hearted killer. He can never set things right between us."

"I understand," Bitterwood said. "It's good that you hate him."

Jandra wasn't sure she'd heard him correctly. Telling her that it was good to hate was so contrary to everything Vendevorex had ever tried to teach her.

Bitterwood continued: "People will tell you that hate eats you from the inside. They tell you to let go of old pains, not to carry a grudge. Don't listen to them. Hate's all a person needs to get out of bed in the mornings. Hold onto it. Hate is the hammer that lets you knock down the walls of this world. You see what happened to me when I let it go. I lost my way when I allowed my hate to wane."

"But now you've got something better than hate," Jandra said. "You've got hope."

"Like you, I'm haunted by the life I might have had. Even if my family is alive, I've lost twenty years. There can be no forgiveness. If my family is alive then I regret only that I haven't fought harder and killed more dragons to make a better world for them."

Jandra contemplated his words. All her life Vendevorex had given her cold and analytical advice. He normally advised her to set aside her emotions, especially the darker ones. How strange to be told to embrace them.

Bitterwood nodded toward the castle which stood like a dark stony mountain in the sunset, casting a long shadow over the surrounding fields. "I've noticed a steady stream of dragons leaving the castle. The palace guards are heading for the Free City."

"Do you think we should go back?" Jandra asked. "If something's about to happen we should try to save Zeeky and Pet."

"You're free to go. My family must come first," Bitterwood said.

Jandra looked toward the Free City then back toward the castle. Lanterns and torches were being lit in the windows and balconies. She suddenly felt perversely homesick. Oddly, she didn't feel as worried about the residents of the Free City as she thought she should. Deep in her heart she took comfort from a single fact: Vendevorex was inside the Free City and he was there to stop the genocide. Vendevorex wouldn't be there without a plan.

"Okay," she said. "Fewer guards in the palace makes it easier for us," Jandra said. "We might get the information you want before whatever is happening in the Free City unfolds. Are you ready?"

"Yes," Bitterwood said.

Jandra rose and once more cast the circle of invisibility around them. They headed toward the castle where she had lived a lie for so long.

* * *

JANDRA HAD NO problem leading Bitterwood past the handful of guards remaining in the castle and up the steps to the king's hall. From here they could descend through the High Biologian's door into the library.

"Look there," Bitterwood whispered as they passed near the throne pedestal.

Following his outstretched arm, she could see a quiver of arrows and a bow hanging on the wall high above the throne. A few red feathers caught the pale moonlight.

"That's the bow Pet took from the armory," Bitterwood said. "But those three arrows are mine. Where did he get them?"

"I don't know," Jandra said.

Bitterwood looked lost in thought. At last, he said, "When the sky-dragon tackled me in the window at Chakthalla's castle, I lost several shafts. He must have found them. Perhaps this convinced Zanzeroth that Pet was me."

"Pet's bought you a second chance," Jandra said. "When this is done, you'll help rescue him, won't you?"

Bitterwood looked at her, his brow furrowed. His voice gave no clue to his feelings as he said, "Let's move on."

Jandra nodded. They moved toward the library door. She wondered if it was locked. The point was rendered moot as the door swung open at her approach. Whispered voices met them.

"It's time," one said. "The dark will hide us."

"Lead on," said another.

Drawing the cloak of invisibility as tightly around them as possible, Jandra took Bitterwood by the arm and rushed forward past the three figures who entered the corridor. Even in the dark she could recognize Metron... and Shandrazel? Why was he here? She had never seen the third dragon. She and Bitterwood slipped into the library seconds before Metron closed the door. Quickly, they made their way to the rooms where the slave records were kept. Her heart sank as she stepped inside. So many rows of files. So many slaves.

"It could take all night to search," she said.

"A night or a year, you've done your part," Bitterwood said. "I'll search alone if need be."

"No," she said. She had made a promise and intended to keep it. "Let's get started."

"Are you sure this is wise?" Androkom asked, slowing to allow Metron to catch up.

"Positive," Metron said, his voice strained with the effort of climbing the stairs. "Blasphet may be mad but I understand the source of his madness. He holds no grudge against us."

"Still," Androkom said, "do you know how many dragons this monster has killed? It's not like he's ashamed of it. He calls himself the Murder God. This would argue against an alliance, I think."

"Monster or not, Blasphet is currently the king's closest advisor," Metron answered testily. "It's not too late to turn back if you're afraid."

"We're not frightened," Shandrazel said. "While I question the usefulness of this visit, my uncle is no match for me, physically, should he attempt to betray us."

At last they reached the main floor and the star chamber. Metron entered without bothering to knock.

Blasphet awaited them, standing before a dying fire in the room's lone fireplace. He stirred the orange coals with a long iron poker, then placed a heavy copper caldron onto the hook above the coals before turning to greet his guests.

"Welcome, fellow conspirators," Blasphet said, and bowed ceremoniously. "Especially you, dear nephew. My, you've grown in the years since last I saw you."

"Do not refer to me as a conspirator," Shandrazel said. "I take this path out of love for my father and the kingdom."

"Ah! Nobility. I'm glad to see Albekizan's blood-line has produced a scion that possesses a touch of my own idealism," said Blasphet in a sincere tone. "You fill me with hope for the world, Shandrazel."

"I take it you received the note I sent you?" Metron asked.

"Yes," Blasphet said as he walked to the balcony doors. He closed them, sealing the room. "Now we can be assured of privacy."

"Is it true?" Androkom asked. "You have a poison that can temporarily paralyze a foe, but otherwise does no harm?"

"Indeed," Blasphet said. "Such a poison would be a perfect way to assure you of a captive audience from my brother, wouldn't it?"

"It's not my preferred approach," said Shandrazel. "But Metron insists it's the only way to speak to my father without him immediately going for my throat."

Blasphet stared at Shandrazel, studying his eyes. Shandrazel didn't turn away from the stare and met his gaze. Shandrazel noticed a family resemblance in the sharp, well-bred lines of his uncle's face, despite Blasphet's discolored hide and bloodshot eyes. It was like looking at some dark reflection of his father.

Blasphet asked, "You still think you can use reason to persuade him?"

"I hope so," Shandrazel answered.

"Truly, your idealism exceeds my own," Blasphet said.

"How is this poison delivered?" Androkom asked. "Via drink?"

Blasphet shook his head.

"The blood, then?" Androkom asked. "An... an injunction. Injection, rather." The young biologian's speech was slightly slurred.

Metron swayed on his feet. He mumbled, "Blasphet, I... I..." The elder biologian raised his talon to rub his brow.

"Yes?"

"I feel... light-headed. The exertion... of the stairs—"

"No," Shandrazel said, noticing his own breathing growing shallow. "I feel it too."

Suddenly the High Biologian's eyes rolled beneath his lids and he toppled sideways. Shandrazel moved quickly, reaching out to catch the aged dragon in his arms before he hit the stone floor.

"The air..." Androkom said, leaning against a wall to steady himself.

"Is it too warm in here?" Blasphet asked. "I would open a window but that would let the poison out."

"Betrayer!" Shandrazel shouted, letting Metron slide to the floor. He leapt toward his uncle, his claws outstretched. But the air seemed too thick, slowing him, as if he were moving through water. The room swayed and where Blasphet should have stood he found only a wall. Shandrazel collided face-first with solid stone.

"Feeling a little disoriented, nephew?"

Shandrazel turned around, his legs trembling.

Androkom now sprawled across the floor, as unconscious as Metron. Blasphet had moved back to the fireplace, once more stirring the coals with the poker.

Shandrazel rushed forward, fighting the fog in his mind to focus on the target of his uncle's throat. He opened his jaws wide.

Blasphet suddenly possessed supernatural speed. He drew the poker above his head, then chopped it down between Shandrazel's eyes in a blur.

There was a flash of light, a crash of drums, then darkness. The darkness broke with pale red light as Shandrazel opened his eyes once more. He was on the floor, looking across toward Metron's slumped body. The High Biologian's silver-tinted scales seemed surrounded by tiny halos. Why was Metron on the floor? Shandrazel's head throbbed with distant pain. He braced himself with his claws and slowly rose. The floor was spinning as if on a giant turntable. He could vaguely hear someone saying, "You're as hard-headed as your father."

Another crash and the floor raced up to meet him. Everything grew silent and still.

"WAKE UP," THE voice said.

No. Shandrazel ached too much to open his eyes. He pulled the blanket of sleep more tightly around his mind.

"Wake up!" the voice repeated, and this time the demand was met by a strong poke in Shandrazel's gut. Shandrazel tried to twist away from the pain but couldn't move. The rattling of chains provoked his curiosity more than the voice did. Then he remembered. Blasphet! His eyes jerked open.

"Ah," Blasphet said from somewhere near. "You're back. Good. The dosage affected you more than I would have guessed. You barely stirred while I was strapping you in."

Shandrazel tried to turn his head toward his uncle's voice but couldn't. His head was held fast by cold, hard bars. He shifted his eyes and flexed his limbs. His whole body was trapped in a narrow cage in which he lay flat, his wings pinned behind him with crossbars trapping his limbs, allowing not even a wiggle. The cage was suspended so that he faced downward. Below him sat a huge pool of black liquid. He noted that the cage bars weren't metal but were fashioned from thick rods of glass. He would have little trouble breaking them, if only he could get some leverage.

To the side of the pool he could see a wheel around which was wrapped a sturdy chain. Blasphet stepped into his field of vision, standing beside the wheel, grinning. On the other side of the pool Androkom was chained to the wall, his body slumped over, a stream of drool dripping from his mouth.

"I designed this for your father," Blasphet said. "But you'll do fine for practice. This way I can work out any kinks before I try it on my dear brother."

Shandrazel growled. He tensed and released every muscle of his body, struggling for even an inch of movement. The cage began to sway, but only barely.

"I'd love to stick around," his uncle said. "Alas, I'm pressed for time. With this device your death will take hours."

Blasphet turned the wheel. It clicked once and the cage dropped a fraction of an inch.

"The pool beneath you is acid. This device allows me to lower you into the pool using precise measurements, then raise you to examine the results. I'll do a detailed drawing at each step. It should make for fascinating reference material, as the interior of the body is revealed, layer-by-layer. Practicing on you will allow me to get the subtleties worked out for your father. I have this marvelous dream of dissolving his eyelids without touching the eyes," Blasphet said. "It probably won't work, but what is life without a dream?"

Shandrazel kept silent, contemplating his possible actions. His silence prodded Blasphet into talking further.

"This acid cauterizes wounds so you could live for several hours once we begin. Who knows? I might spend days on this project. Will you still be alive when we reach your heart? Oh, the suspense!"

Shandrazel relaxed his entire body. He tried to allow slack to build in the cage. Unfortunately, some mechanism took up the slack. He managed only to immobilize himself further.

Blasphet looked disappointed. "This is the point where you're supposed to scream, 'You're mad!'"

"Will you prattle on like this the whole time?" Shandrazel asked. "If so, could you dissolve my ears first?"

"I may be able to accommodate you," Blasphet said. "For now, I must bid you farewell. Your father has some business cooked up at dawn, which fast approaches. I believe he plans to kill Bitterwood. I must attend. It's important I remind him how shallow and meaningless his vengeance will be."

Blasphet raised his claw in a gesture of farewell, then turned and vanished from sight. A few seconds later, Shandrazel heard the rattling of a key in a door, then footsteps fading into the distance.

When he was certain his uncle was gone, he said, "Androkom?"

Androkom's eyes opened and he sat up. "I'm awake," he said. "I didn't want him to know."

"Have you already thought of a way to escape?" Shandrazel asked him.

"No. You?"

"Not yet," Shandrazel said, trying to turn his head. "My field of vision is limited. Tell me everything you see."

"You, mostly, the pool and the wheel. The chains holding me, of course. There are two pairs of manacles, one for my wings, one for my legs. They run through iron rings in the wall. They look well made. There are a few lanterns on the other side of the room. My tail's free but I can't reach anything of use."

To demonstrate, he pulled himself as far from the wall as the chains would allow and thrust his hips forward, his tail snaking between his legs and stretching out about a yard across the pool.

"Can you touch my cage with your tail?" Shandrazel asked. "If we can get it swaying enough to bang the ceiling, perhaps we could break the bars."

Androkom stretched, but his tail failed to reach the cage by several feet.

"Just as well," Androkom said. "If we did break the bars, you'd only plummet into the acid. There's not enough distance for your wings to catch the air."

Shandrazel stared into the acrid ebony fluid beneath him. The stench made his nostrils water. He rubbed his snout as much as he could against the cool, smooth glass. The motion pulled one of the delicate feathers that adorned his snout free. It drifted slowly downward. Against the perfect blackness of the pool, it seemed to fall forever, into a void, until it touched the surface. Then, with a *hiss*, it vanished into nothingness.

"HERE!" JANDRA SAID, raising papers over her head. "I can't believe it! After all these hours!"

Bitterwood rushed to her side and snatched the papers from her hand. The cover page read: "An Inventory of Human Slaves Captured in the Village of Christdale."

The first page contained a list of male children. He recognized the names, but one name was missing. What had happened to Adam? He turned the page and saw a list of names of women, and beside each was marked their fate. The widow Tate: dead in transit. His neighbor's wife, Dorla: sold to a noble dragon from the Isle of Horses. Then Recanna! Ruth! Mary! All had a "K" marked next to their names.

"What does this mean?" he asked, pointing at the mark. "Please tell me it doesn't mean 'killed.'"

"It means 'Kitchen,'" Jandra said, looking over his shoulder. "They weren't sold at auction, but were kept by Albekizan to be put to work in the kitchens."

She took a closer look at the names next to Bitterwood's fingers. All this time they'd searched for the name of his village; he hadn't told her the names of his family. Her mouth went dry.

"You can't mean…" Bitterwood's face broke into a look of joy. "They're here! My family is within these walls!"

Jandra didn't answer. She turned away from him. Perhaps the names were only a coincidence. Perhaps this was a different family. Perhaps…

Bitterwood turned around, the smile falling from his lips. "What?"

"It's… I knew them," Jandra said, still with her back to him.

"Knew? What happened to them? Why won't you look at me?"

Jandra spun around. "Because they're dead! Every human who worked in the palace is dead. Albekizan ordered them killed in retaliation the day after you killed Bodiel."

The papers dropped from Bitterwood's hands, fluttering to the floor around him like dying leaves.

ZEEKY WOKE TO the sound of voices from below. She had run to the closest building she could find after the dragon dropped her, and spent the day hiding in the attic, waiting for things to calm down so that she could sneak back to the barn.

But during the day, more residents had arrived in the Free City, and it was her bad luck that out of hundreds of empty buildings, some of the new arrivals had picked the building she hid inside to make their home.

It was dark outside. What time was it? Something about the smell of the air hinted that it wouldn't be long now before the dawn.

The words of the men speaking in the room beneath her were difficult to make out until she heard a now familiar name: Kamon.

"You can't mean it," the first voice said.

"I saw him with my own eyes," said the second. "I would have killed him then but he was surrounded by a dozen Kamonites."

"I'll stand with you," the first voice said. "As will my brothers. Kamon will pay for his poisonous lies."

The conversation was dropped suddenly as a loud *bang* shook the house. Someone had kicked in the door.

"Humans!" a dragon snarled. "Wake up! You must go to the square! Albekizan will address you!"

The men raised their voices in protest until a whip cracked, silencing them.

Suddenly, the trapdoor to the attic flew open and the beaked head of an earth-dragon popped through, looking straight at Zeeky.

"Get down here," he commanded.

There was no exit save for the hole the dragon was stood in. Luckily, she was small and dragons were slow. She leapt forward over the dragon's shoulder, sliding down his spine as he uselessly grabbed behind his back, trying to catch her. She grabbed his tail, swinging her feet down to land in a running position. But her feet stopped just inches from the floor. The full weight of her body hung by her collar. She twisted around to see a second earth-dragon holding her at arm's length, looking at her as if she were some awful bug.

BLASPHET WHEELED OVER the scene below. It was early morning; the sun was just peeking over the eastern horizon. All of the residents of the Free City had been gathered in the square, packed in tightly by the guards that stood in thick columns in the adjoining streets. They looked groggy, disoriented. Blasphet's research had taught him that humans were most sluggish and compliant in the predawn hours. Apparently, his brother knew this as well.

Toward the front of the crowd, a large platform had been hastily erected overnight. The platform was surrounded by dark green, heavily armored earth-dragons—nearly the entire unit of the Black Silences—separating the crowd from the platform by rows three dragons deep. On the unpainted boards of the impromptu stage stood Albekizan, looking too smug and satisfied for Blasphet's comfort.

Behind Albekizan stood Tanthia, her eyes dark and sunken with depression, a look that Blasphet found quite attractive in a female. A heavy wooden post protruded up from the center of the stage next to the king; beside this stood Pertalon, who was laboring to chain the captive Bitterwood with his back to the post and his arms stretched high above his head. Bitterwood's wrists were fastened to an iron ring, leaving his toes barely touching the platform. Completing the group on the dais were the hunter, Zanzeroth, and Kanst, dressed in his full ceremonial armor. With a turn of his wings and a rustle of scales, Blasphet dropped to the platform to complete the assembly.

Albekizan didn't acknowledge Blasphet's arrival. Instead he checked Bitterwood's chains as a leather strap was placed around the prisoner's head. He then tied the strap around the post in such a manner as to ensure that the human couldn't look away from the crowd.

The crowd murmured in speculation. Blasphet noted one voice in particular in which he could recognize madness, always an interesting quality.

"The prophecy!" the madman shouted. "It is as I said! Bitterwood must suffer this hour so that we can be free!"

Small chance of that, Blasphet thought.

"Well, brother," Blasphet said. "Today's your big day. Tell me, do you intend to kill him quickly? Or perhaps make it last hours, as if that will bring release from these endless days of mourning he has inflicted upon you?"

"His fate will be prolonged," the king said. He moved behind the post and reached his claws around, placing them on Bitterwood's face.

"Do your worst," Bitterwood said, though Blasphet's trained ear could hear the deep current of fear flowing beneath his brave words. "I don't fear death!"

"Nor should you," King Albekizan said. With his sharp claws he grabbed the skin above and below the captive's eyes and forced them open. "For it is not your death we are here to witness. This is a *public* execution."

Blasphet felt the scales along his back rise.

The king continued. "You'll watch their slaughter, an unspeakable tableau of gore and agony. When this crowd is exhausted, we will gather another, and another, and another, and all will die, day after day after day, all because of you. Only when the last human in my kingdom has been killed will I grant you the surrender of death."

"No!" shouted Bitterwood.

"No!" shouted Blasphet, rushing forward. He wouldn't allow his brother to ruin his plans for the Free City by killing everyone before the experiment had even begun. Before he could reach the king, Pertalon jumped into his path and held him from his goal.

As the two struggled, Bitterwood cried, "Kill me! My life for theirs! I'm the one who wronged you!"

"Kanst," Albekizan said, his eyes gleaming in the dawn light. "Give the command."

HEZEKIAH TWISTED HIS neck from side to side as Vendevorex sat back, exhausted. The artificial man flexed his hands, almost like a human would flex a limb that had been asleep. "My mobility is restored," Hezekiah said in a tinny, hollow voice. "I assume you're done with me?"

"You assume wrong," Vendevorex said, handing the prophet his broad-brimmed hat. As Hezekiah donned the hat, Vendevorex lifted the heavy axe with a grunt. He held it to the artificial man and said, "You and I are just getting started."

CHAPTER TWENTY-THREE

go!

K ANST LIFTED HIS gleaming ceremonial sword
high over his head, then sliced it down in a
swift arc.

"Kill them!" he commanded.

WHEN AT LAST Bitterwood spoke, Jandra could
barely hear him.

"What?" she asked.

"Go," Bitterwood whispered.

"Not yet," she said.

"Go," he repeated, more forcefully.

"But—"

"Go!" he screamed. "Go!"

The look on his face—a twisted mask of distorted pain and anger—told her he would never listen
to her words. Still she had to speak them.

"Fine," she said. "Blame yourself. Act as if nothing matters but your own guilt. Let Pet die in your place, let Zeeky rot away inside the Free City, let the whole world come crashing down. But I'm going to try to stop it!"

Jandra turned and ran, not bothering to render herself invisible. She had been a fool to trust him.

THE CROWD SCREAMED as the guards surged forward.

Zeeky hadn't seen or heard what had happened on the stage, for she was near the back of the crowd. She cried out, frightened, as the crowd pushed her about like a mouse batted by a dozen cats. "What's happening?" she begged.

Suddenly, the adults closest to her screamed louder, and the crushing pressure of bodies abated as the crowd parted. The people were fleeing from a snarling ox-dog, a whip-wielding earth-dragon mounted in the large saddle on its back. As the adults ran the gigantic beast locked its dark eyes on Zeeky's small figure and bounded toward her, barking, its teeth bared, its tan neck hairs standing up like brush bristles.

"Aw," said Zeeky, in an instant forgetting the confusion of the crowd. Here was something she understood. "Aren't you a big 'un?"

The ox-dog skidded to a halt before her, thrusting its face into hers, growling, its steaming breath foul with the smell of fresh blood.

"You're just a big puppy, ain't ya?" she said.

The ox-dog stopped growling. "Hrunmph," it snorted.

Zeeky reached out and scratched the dog above his big, wet, black nose. The hair on the dog's neck relaxed. It showed gratitude for her scratches with a big, wet lick of its pink tongue.

The dragon in the saddle lashed the beast's flanks with his whip. "Forward, Killer! Attack, brute! Attack!"

The ox-dog's right legs buckled and he rolled over, tossing the dragon from the saddle. As the dog rolled, he crushed the dragon with the whole of his massive weight before coming once more to his feet. The humans in the crowd scrambled to stay out of the beast's way.

"Damn you, Killer," the dragon wheezed as he struggled to stand. He raised his whip. "I'll thrash some obedience into you yet!"

Killer opened his huge jaws and leaned forward, placed his maw over the dragon's head, then closed his mouth.

"Ret goo!" the dragon shouted, his voice muffled.

The ox-dog shook his head from side to side, jerking the screaming dragon from his feet. Zeeky ducked as the dragon's feet passed just over her head. It was too awful to watch, even if it was happening to a dragon.

"Put him down!" she said, placing her hands on her hips and looking stern. "Right now!"

The ox-dog paused, looking at her. Then he flipped his head to the side once more, hard, and let go. The dragon sailed for a few brief seconds of flight, his wingless limbs beating the air in a vain attempt to control his motion. Then he fell among the turbulent crowd of humans and was gone.

The ox-dog again turned its attention to Zeeky, letting its foot-wide tongue hang from its mouth.

"Good boy," Zeeky said. Then her fear and confusion returned as the crowd continued to scream and mill about. Still, Zeeky was safe in a bubble that formed about ten feet around the ox-dog. Even panicked people steered clear of such a beast. All Zeeky wanted was to get away from here. She had to go to the stables to find Poocher then leave this terrible place forever.

She grabbed the stirrup of the saddle and managed to pull herself up. From her new vantage point she could see dragons killing people all around her. Tears filled her eyes.

"Get me out of here!" she sobbed.

Killer woofed in agreement. The ox-dog wheeled around, racing forward toward a gap that opened as dragons fell over one another to get out of Killer's way. Zeeky closed her eyes tightly and swore that if she ever got home, she'd never run away again.

A QUICK, INVISIBLE flight gave Vendevorex a view of the catastrophe. He'd heard the soldiers moving through the streets before dawn, commanding the humans to the gathering, but he never anticipated the scene below. Albekizan was on the platform, standing behind Pet, holding the human's eyes open. Behind the king a large black-scaled sun-dragon struggled with a sky-dragon. Blasphet?

Kanst continued to bark out orders. Hundreds of dragons tore into the crowd. Vendevorex needed to think the situation over but there was no time. The only thing that offered a brief glimmer of hope was that a few of the humans had managed to overwhelm the earth-dragons with their numbers and now fought back with stolen arms.

Vendevorex swooped back to the street and called out, "Hezekiah! Come!"

The black-robed figure emerged from the nearby building as Vendevorex landed on the dusty ground.

"Go to the square," Vendevorex said. Until this moment, he'd hoped that the situation might be diffused without bloodshed. Now there was no time for subtlety. He gave the command he'd hoped to avoid: "Kill every dragon you see."

"Even you?" the artificial man asked.

"No, except me."

"And other sky-dragons? Don't kill them?"

"Kill sky-dragons, except for me," Vendevorex said, wishing he'd had time to do a little more sophisticated job on the logic loops. "Kill sun-dragons, too, earth dragons, great lizards, and crawlbugs. Don't hurt people."

"I will obey," Hezekiah said. He turned, swung his axe up to rest on his shoulder, and marched off in the direction of the commotion.

"Hurry!" Vendevorex said.

Hezekiah began to run, streaking down the street with inhuman velocity. Vendevorex knew what Hezekiah was capable of. The automaton could kill every dragon in the Free City given time. Yet with each second that passed, dozens of humans died. Vendevorex needed to do something big to tilt the odds but felt a chill at the thought of making himself known. The presence of Albekizan and Kanst didn't bother him. Unfortunately, Zanzeroth stood on the platform as well.

* * *

BLASPHET WAS UNUSED to physical confrontations and quickly found himself in the humiliating position of being pushed to his belly by the much more skillful Pertalon. The sky-dragon twisted Blasphet's wings behind his back, causing him to cry out in pain. Blasphet whipped his tail up around Pertalon's neck but couldn't pull hard enough to dislodge his tormentor.

"Zanzeroth," Pertalon said. "Bring me chains."

Zanzeroth didn't answer. The pressure on Blasphet's wings shifted ever so slightly as Pertalon twisted around to see where the hunter had gone. With Pertalon distracted, Blasphet flicked the fake nail from his right fore-talon with his thumb, revealing the sharpened claw beneath, wet with poison. With his wrist twisted painfully, he could barely scratch his opponent, but the barest scratch was enough.

"Wha—" Pertalon began, but never finished the syllable.

The pressure on Blasphet's wings ceased as the weight fell from his back. He rose and turned to the already dead Pertalon who lay twisted in pain. Blasphet kicked the corpse, angry that he'd been forced to waste one of his poisons on such an insignificant fool. Still, Kanst's back was to him, for the general was busy shouting commands to the Black Silences that surrounded the platform. Zanzeroth had vanished, not that Blasphet had been overly worried about the hunter who was half-crippled from his wounds. As he'd expected, Albekizan was too busy laughing at the sea of carnage before him to pay any attention to Blasphet. Blasphet shuddered at the sound of elation in the king's voice. He'd hoped to never see his brother this happy again.

Then let him die happy, thought Blasphet. With a flick of his left fore-talon, his final poisoned claw was revealed.

HIGH ABOVE, ZANZEROTH circled, looking through the seemingly endless field of faces below him. The real Bitterwood had to be among them. Ever since his nose had healed enough to restore his sense of smell, he'd known beyond all doubt that the prisoner Albekizan tormented wasn't Bitterwood. He'd chosen the wrong man, no doubt due to his exhaustion and injuries. In retrospect, he couldn't have planned events better. The intervening days had allowed Zanzeroth time to rest and recover a bit from his wounds. He wasn't fully healed, but he felt strong enough to face any man, especially now that it would be he who held the element of surprise. Albekizan had his own victim to torment. This left the true Bitterwood as his prey alone. He need not share his revenge with anyone, not even a king. Alas, the carnage unleashed now threatened to steal Bitterwood once more from his grasp. He had to find the man, and quickly.

Then he spotted a human attacking from behind the line of the dragons, tearing through the rear troops like a demon. Bitterwood? Zanzeroth swooped for a closer look. The man below was dressed in black and fought with an axe, and continued to fight even with three spears embedded in him. The man stood ankle-deep in foul mud created by the blood and offal of slain dragons. The human wasn't Bitterwood, but Zanzeroth was impressed nonetheless. Who was this?

* * *

"No! I'll kill you!"

Blasphet didn't have time to turn and face the female voice that cried out behind him. A wave of patchouli washed over him. Blasphet crashed once more to the rough boards of the platform as Tanthia threw herself against him, her painted claws digging into the skin of his neck.

"You took my brother," she screamed. "You won't take my husband!"

Blasphet twisted in her grasp, bringing himself face to face. Her cheeks glistened liked jewels from her tears. Tanthia was strong and his equal in size, but no more used to combat than he. He pulled her claws from his neck with ease, taking care not to prick her with the exposed poison.

"Your devotion is commendable," he said through clenched teeth as he twisted her wrists backward, using the pain to force her from him. "Now be a dear and go gather wood for the pyre, hmm?"

"Murderer!" she shouted, and thrust her jaws forward, clamping her teeth deep into his shoulder.

"Aiigh!" Blasphet shrieked. Enough was enough. Albekizan would have to wait. He ran the sharpened, poisoned claw along Tanthia's slender neck. Her jaws slackened and she fell with a sigh.

Blasphet looked back. Kanst still hadn't noticed him. His attention was focused on a battle at the front of the platform, and he certainly couldn't have heard the struggle over the deafening cries of anguish that rolled through the air like unending thunder. The roar now washed out even Albekizan's mad laughter.

Spotting Pertalon's sword, Blasphet considered running his brother through from behind. But if his brother survived the blow, he'd fight much harder than Pertalon or Tanthia. The time had come to return to the tower for more poison. With luck, he would be back before Albekizan even noticed he was gone.

HE HAD GONE mad. He must be mad. Why couldn't he go mad? Pet screamed and could barely hear his own voice over the crowd's panicked shouts. The tears that blurred his vision rolled down his cheeks, across the sharp-nailed claws clamped upon them. Albekizan laughed wildly.

He would go mad. He had to go mad. But he couldn't. Pet could only watch through the teary mist as men, women, and children died before him by the uncounted hundreds, some at the hands of dragons, many more beneath the trampling feet of their fellow stampeding men.

"Stop it!" he shouted. "Oh please, stop it!"

"Your cries are music, Bitterwood," Albekizan shouted. "You wanted to save them! You killed in their name! Look what you've done! Look what you've done!"

Pet looked for he had no choice. However, he stilled his voice in his throat. He would not beg. Albekizan wouldn't have that satisfaction, at least. Albekizan released his eyelids as he had every minute, perhaps to make sure he wouldn't go blind. Pet clamped his eyes shut but to no avail. The king's claws upon his cheeks and brow quickly pried them open again. His vision fresh once more, Pet looked upon the violence before him. He noticed some intense fighting immediately

before the platform, where a group of men had wrest-
ed weapons from the Black Silences and now
defended themselves fiercely.

Tears robbed his sight of clarity before he could
be sure of what he had seen. Could the men truly
have been winning?

JANDRA BURST FROM the stables astride a dappled
mare, knocking aside the earth-dragon stable hand.
She dug her heels into the horse's flank and raced
toward the open gate. Even from this great distance
she could hear the cries from the Free City. What was
happening? Was she already too late to save Pet?

Then she saw the glow towering above the walls
of the Free City.

"SIRE," KANST SAID, placing his claws on the king's
shoulder. "We must go!"

Albekizan turned his head, fixing a gaze like daggers upon Kanst.

"What?" asked the king.

"Sire, the guards around this platform can't hold
out. The sheer weight of the humans is crushing
them. For every ten we slay, a hundred take their
place. I warned you that—"

"Kanst," Albekizan said, "it is not your duty to
warn me. It's your duty to see that your soldiers
fight on. Join the fray if you must, but do not inter-
rupt me again!"

"Sire, Queen Tanthia is dead," Kanst said, revealing what he had discovered only seconds ago.

"What?" Albekizan released Pet, spinning
around. His jaw dropped open at the sight of his
beloved queen, lying still, as if asleep. "How?"

"I don't know," Kanst said. "Both she and Pertalon are dead without a wound on them. Zanzeroth is missing, as is Blasphet. I fear betrayal."

Albekizan looked dazed. Then he looked up, his eyes wide. Kanst followed his gaze into the glowing sky.

ZANZEROTH COULDN'T RESIST. He might never find Bitterwood among the crowd, but there was no way he could lose the man with the axe. All his life Zanzeroth had craved hunting the most dangerous prey he could locate. Never had he seen a challenge such as this. Single-handedly, the human had broken an entire regiment, leaving a street cluttered with the bodies of a hundred dragons over which the humans now fled, spilling from the square like water surging through a hole in a dam. A few dragons fled before them, one mounted on an ox-dog—no, that wasn't a dragon in the saddle but a child. No matter. The axe-man chased down one of the remaining earth-dragons who tried to flee by climbing to the roof of a building. The man now stood on the rooftop as the soldier cowered before him, pleading for mercy. As the man raised his axe to kill his panicked victim, Zanzeroth made his decision. Here was the true test of his prowess.

He braced his spear in his hind claws and folded back his wings, angling into a dive. He noted the light brightening behind him, like the sun coming from behind a cloud. His shadow touched the black-robed man who turned his head in time to see Zanzeroth, his spear tip now inches away.

* * *

THE GLOW AROUND Vendevorex shifted, swirled, and coalesced as he mentally positioned the floating particles in the edges of the field. All below looked up, both men and dragons. Vendevorex activated the white plastic disk he'd removed from Hezekiah's torso. Stamped on the outer edge of the plastic were the words, "Voice of God."

"I AM VENDEVOREX!" he announced. His words boomed like a clap of thunder and the din of voices beneath him lessened. He swooped within the sphere of light that surrounded him, careful to maintain the motionless illusion that he had created. Vendevorex had grown to a hundred feet in height, his eyes bright with flame, lightning playing about his outstretched wings. He decided on a last-second improvement to the illusion, and suddenly his claws became the blue-gray of hardened steel as they grew as long as swords. "HEED ME, O DRAGONS! DROP YOUR WEAPONS, OR FACE MY WRATH! THIS BATTLE IS OVER!"

"THE HELL IT is," Pet heard a nearby man shout, and a dozen men joined him in a battle cry. The sound of blade against blade rung all around the platform.

"Sire," Kanst said behind him.

"I've considered your advice, Kanst," Albekizan said, his voice trembling. "I'll return to the castle now. Make sure your soldiers continue to fight. And kill that damned wizard! Do it personally!"

"Of course, sire," Kanst said.

The entire platform shuddered as Albekizan and Kanst leapt into the sky like sparrows before a cat.

Alone on the platform, Pet struggled to free himself, to no avail.

ALIVE, THOUGHT ZANZEROTH as he heard the wizard's voice. It was too late to turn back now. His spear struck the black-robed man squarely in the chest. Zanzeroth tilted his wings so that his great speed would cause him to swoop skyward, carrying the impaled human with him. Alas the human proved too heavy for the maneuver; he was more like a mound of stone than flesh. The spear shaft snapped. The human was thrown to his back by the force of the blow but Zanzeroth's momentum shifted as well. Instead of returning to the sky, he hit the rooftop hard. He slid across the wooden roof, splinters tearing away his bandages, until he collided with the brick chimney. His breath exploded from him in a pained cry.

"DRAGONS!" Vendevorex shouted. "RETURN TO YOUR BARRACKS AT ONCE! FEAR MY VENGEANCE!"

Alas, the dragons didn't seem to fear his vengeance as much as he'd hoped. Below him, the fighting resumed once more, though the dragons now fought more defensively as the humans surged against their ranks. To stop fighting was to risk death. But perhaps there was another way to stop the fighting. Albekizan had taken flight, as had Kanst who flew straight toward the illusion. If he could slay them here, in full sight of the troops, the war would be won.

Kanst reached the edge of the illusion and struck with his spear, then spun off balance when the blow connected only with air. Vendevorex knew he'd never have a better chance. He shifted his concentration to his hind-talons, allowing the illusion around him to crumble as he formed a boiling ball of the Vengeance of the Ancestors. He hurled the flaming orb toward his target.

Kanst recovered from the missed blow much faster than Vendevorex would have guessed. The general turned, steadying himself on outstretched wings, just in time to face the flame that raced toward him. He then did the worst thing possible from Vendevorex's view. He thrust his chest forward, straight into the path of the flame, allowing the deadly plasma to splash against his iron breastplate.

Iron. The one thing the Vengeance wouldn't burn.

ZANZEROTH SHOOK HIS head to chase away the stars. There was the faintest vibration on the boards beneath him.

Move.

He rolled aside as the axe sunk deep into the wood where he had rested. He kept rolling, tumbling from the roof's edge, letting the rush of air catch his wings. He pushed himself higher into the air, noticing Vendevorex attacking Kanst. There was no time to give thought as to why the wizard was still alive. He wheeled in the air, bringing himself around once more toward the roof. The man stood, his axe tightly gripped in both hands, his legs braced, his eyes fixed upon Zanzeroth. Zanzeroth passed over the rooftop well beyond the man's reach as he freed his whip from his belt with his tail, placing it in his rear talons.

"Let's see how formidable you are without that axe," he said.

The hunter climbed higher in the air then wheeled once more, diving straight at his opponent. The human raised the axe, preparing to strike. At the last second Zanzeroth pulled up as the human swung his axe forward. With a flick of his hind claws the whip snared the axe-shaft, ripping it from the man's hands.

KANST COULD SEE the look of consternation in the wizard's eyes. He hurled the heavy spear he carried in his rear claws. Vendevorex folded up his wings and dropped from the spear's path, then, spreading his wings once more, vanished.

"Damn!" Kanst shouted, flying to the spot where the wizard had just been.

"Lose something?"

A sudden weight on his back sent Kanst listing sideways. The wizard had latched onto him, securing himself with his tail around the general's waist and his claws on each of his wings, the only large expanse of Kanst's body not protected by armor. In horror, Kanst watched flames burst from his exposed skin. The air rushing over his wings pushed the flames rapidly along their entire length.

The weight on his back lifted as Vendevorex released him. Waves of excruciating pain swept over Kanst's mind but failed to wash away the realization that he was going to die.

But not alone...

He swung his tail about, hitting the wizard's leg. He constricted his tail with all his strength. Vendevorex struggled, but to no avail, as Kanst jerked him closer and clamped his rear claws into the wizard's shin. Then Kanst simply closed his blistered wings to his side and fell. The wizard's wings couldn't support their weight. The ground was a long way down.

Zanzeroth landed, brandishing the axe. The weapon was heavy, even for a dragon, and slick with red-brown gore. Zanzeroth felt his hunting spirit stir at the familiar scent of blood and excrement. The black-robed man charged across the roof toward him, as expected. Zanzeroth was ready. He pushed his tail around in a rapid arc, catching the man's legs while he was still two yards away. As his foe stumbled forward the hunter struck, bringing the axe down hard in the center of the man's back, severing the spinal cord. His foe fell to the roof, face-first. Zanzeroth relaxed. That had been easier than expected.

Then the human's arms thrust forward, grabbing Zanzeroth's ankle. Zanzeroth was startled more by the movement than by the pain of the man's incredible grip. How could he fight with his spine severed?

With a grunt Zanzeroth swung the axe against the man's elbow, severing the arm. But the hand that held him didn't release him. In fact, it squeezed harder still. With a sickening snap his ankle gave way and Zanzeroth toppled.

The human rose to his knees. Zanzeroth felt panic rising in him and struck out in fear, swinging the axe with one talon and landing a solid blow against the back of the man's head. His opponent ignored the blow and rose to his feet.

Zanzeroth sat up, getting into a position to better defend himself. The hand that held his ankle released him, and scratched its way toward the blood-soaked man, who casually lifted it and placed it back in its proper place.

"What are you?" Zanzeroth muttered.

"His name that sat on him was Death," the man said in a squeaky, hollow voice. He straightened the brim of his hat before advancing on Zanzeroth, then said, "And hell followed with him."

VENDEVOREX COULDN'T BELIEVE Kanst's will. Even with his wings engulfed in flames he wouldn't release his grip. Vendevorex beat the air but to little avail. The general's armored weight was too great. He was being dragged down into the crowd of humans below. From the corner of his eye he could see Hezekiah on a nearby roof, and Zanzeroth sprawled before him, looking seriously wounded. If only he could stay in the air long enough to guide the path of his descent, he could reach the artificial man who was more than capable of prying Kanst free.

With a mighty effort he turned toward the rooftop. As he stretched his wings to their fullest to slow his descent, something in his shoulder snapped from the strain. They plummeted earthward.

ZANZEROTH SAW THE ball of flame that had been Kanst blazing toward the roof. The unkillable man stepped closer. Zanzeroth kicked out and up with his good leg, catching him in the crotch. No look of pain passed upon the man's face, but the blow still had the intended effect, pushing his foe backward, straight into the path of the hurtling fireball.

AT THE LAST possible second, mere yards from the roof, Kanst's grip slackened. He'd finally lost consciousness. Vendevorex thrust his wings out once more, fighting the pain, pulling himself free of the sun-dragon's body. He watched as Kanst plummeted to the rooftop, smashing directly into Hezekiah's back.

Hezekiah staggered forward, the Vengeance quickly racing across his skin, engulfing him. Vendevorex swooped closer, mentally willing the flames to cease. Hezekiah was built out of much more advanced materials than simple iron. Vendevorex had no clue how the Vengeance would react with these materials.

The fire only brightened as chemical reactions beyond Vendevorex's control raced through the body of the artificial man. Vendevorex decided he didn't want to be around when the flames penetrated Hezekiah's power supply. He raced upward, only to have the shockwave lift him faster than his wings could. A thunderous explosion deafened him. An unbearable flood of heat engulfed him, singeing his scales, burning all air from his lungs.

A second wave of concussion slammed into him, then vanished. The atmosphere became too thin to support his wings, and he fell earthward once more, the world going black.

* * *

"FIGHT ON!" a dragon on the platform shouted, but it was too late. The humans charged the remaining Black Silences, cutting them down with the weapons taken from their fellows.

"Release the savior!" someone shouted.

Pet felt the leather strap that held his head slacken. His heart leapt as the post that held him shuddered with a loud crack of a sword striking chains. Pet toppled forward but he never reached the ground. Hands thrust in all around him, lowering him carefully to his feet.

Pet recognized a few of the dozen faces before him from Chakthalla's village. He was startled to see Kamon, the ancient mad prophet among them. How many men must have died to keep the old fool alive through all of this?

Kamon raised his hands toward the sky as he cried, "It is as I prophesied! We have freed the savior from his bonds so that he may free us from ours!"

"No!" someone shouted.

The men turned to face another small crowd of men who had climbed onto the platform. They, too, were armed with weapons taken from the bodies of dragons. Their leader was a tall, naked man with intense, angry eyes. His coal-black beard hung all the way down to his pubic hair. The only article of cloth on his body was a blood-red ribbon tied around his forehead, holding back a mane of dark hair that reached halfway down his back. He was thin yet well muscled, and tanned so darkly it seemed that his nakedness was a way of life. The naked man shouted, "I am the Prophet Ragnar! Bitterwood is the savior *I* prophesied! Release him, filthy Kamonites, and we'll grant you swift, merciful deaths!"

"We'll fight your blasphemy to our dying breath!" Kamon shouted.

"Then die, infidels!" Ragnar cried, brandishing his sword.

"Stop!" Pet shouted. To his surprise, they did.

"I don't believe this," Pet said. "The dragons are killing us by the hundreds and you fight among yourselves?"

"These heathen dogs are undeserving to breathe the same air as you," Kamon growled. "Let us remove their hideous faces from your sight."

Ragnar stamped his feet in anger. Purple veins bulged in his neck as he shouted, "They are the dogs! This abomination has tainted generations of men with the false doctrine of compliance with dragons. He has brought this horrible day upon us!"

Kamon shook his withered, age-speckled fist. "Fools! We were to obey the dragons until the savior arose! That day has come to pass, as I foretold! Now we must cleanse the awful stench of dragons from this world!"

"Shut up," Pet said, running his fingers through his hair in exasperation. "You think I'm some kind of mythic figure from prophecy? You're wrong. I'm not your savior. All I am is mad as hell. Albekizan must pay for what's happened today. If it's dragon blood you want, then follow me. I'll fight until there's no life left in my body! What we do this day may decide the fate of all mankind. Who's with me?"

"We are!" Ragnar shouted.

"We are!" Kamon said.

"For humanity!" Pet cried, grabbing the sword of a fallen dragon and lifting it high.

All around him they answered, "For Bitterwood!"

CHAPTER TWENTY-FOUR

DEATH

WRONG. IT'S ALL gone wrong...

Blasphet could see his dreams crumbling from the tower balcony. Albekizan had fled, Kanst and Zanzeroth had fallen, and now the mad mob of humans threatened to burst through the lines of the remaining, dispirited earthdragons. Damn Albekizan!

And damn himself. All of this, he knew, was his fault for letting his brother live despite a thousand opportunities to slay him. His fatal flaw, he realized, was his love of playing with his victims. It only brought him to ruin. But no more.

Blasphet stormed down the stairs of the tower toward the dungeon. Before he went to find Albekizan, he would kill Shandrazel. Nothing subtle. Nothing fancy. He'd simply slit his throat. The thought made him giddy. He felt liberated.

He turned the key in the lock and pushed the heavy door open, revealing the acid chamber. His jaw dropped at the sight. The glass cage lay in the pool with all but its uppermost bars submerged, revealing shattered glass at the joints where the iron chains had fastened. A slight mist hung over the pool, bearing the scent of burnt scales and boiled flesh.

Androkom still lay slouched against the wall.

Blasphet stepped into the chamber toward the acid pool. Only one thing could have happened. He'd misjudged Shandrazel's strength. The prince's struggles must have shattered the glass bars, dropping him into the acid. Blasphet noted the wheel that lowered the cage hadn't changed position. Wait. Something was missing. The long, iron handle that attached to the wheel had vanished.

The coolness rose along his back. He turned and saw the steel handle, wrapped in the sinewy fingers of a large red fist. Both traveled toward his snout at an incredible speed.

WRONG. IT'S ALL *gone wrong*

Albekizan dropped from the sky toward the open doors of the throne room. He thought of the last time he'd seen his son here, his beautiful Bodiel, his feathers gleaming as if they truly were fragments of the sun. Such joy he'd known. Joy turned to grief so quickly. Shouldn't grief turn to satisfaction, at least eventually? Didn't he deserve this one small comfort?

Perhaps it wouldn't be too late, once Kanst disposed of that meddling wizard. He would wait for the news of Vendevorex's death on his throne, surrounded by his remaining guards.

"Guards!" he called out as he swooped through the wide doors and brought his feet down on the polished marble. The hall was gloomy, dark and shadowy, even in the early morning light. Then it struck him. The torches were all extinguished. The spirits of his ancestors were gone.

"No!" he cried, and rushed forward, grabbing the charred stick of wood that sat in the golden holder beside the throne.

"No," he whispered, and touched the oily black tip, still warm. This faint heat was all that remained of Bodiel. His child of fire was gone forever.

"No," he said, dropping the dead torch, craning his head toward the ceiling. His body felt weak. His knees buckled, and he slid against the golden pedestal of his throne, knocking the silk cushions onto the floor.

"No," he said, though only the barest sound now escaped his throat. But he knew, despite his protests, that it was true. Even the soul of his son was now dead.

Albekizan trembled. He clenched his eyes shut and prayed that he, right then and there, would burst into flames. He willed himself to spark, to burn, to explode in a holocaust that would ignite the torches once more, would set the whole castle ablaze, and the forests beyond, and even the oceans would become fire!

But it didn't happen. It couldn't happen. His powerlessness to make it happen burned at him more hotly than the heat of a thousand suns.

He opened his eyes to the distant ceiling. He lowered his gaze along the shadowed wall above the throne, down once more to the blackened stick that lay at his feet.

"Oh, Bodiel," Albekizan whispered, his voice wet and weak. "Your father loved you."

Suddenly, the burning in his heart became a chill and he looked up once more to the wall above the throne, to confirm with his mind what his eyes had already seen.

The wall was empty save for the decorative tapestries.

The bow and quiver were gone.

"Guards!" he shouted, his voice echoing through the halls of the castle.

"They won't answer," someone said with a voice as cold as the winter wind. The last remnants of smoke from the dead torches swirled across the marble floor.

"Who?" Albekizan said, rising, spinning around, looking all about the shadowed hall. "Who speaks?"

"I, Bitterwood," the voice answered, echoing in such a way that it could have come from any of the doorways leading into the room.

"It can't be! You're in the Free City! You're chained to the post!"

"You captured only a man," the cold voice answered. "I am lightning striking forever against the earth. I am the Death of All Dragons, the Ghost Who Kills. I come this day for you, Albekizan. I do not meet thee as a man."

A faint whistle cut through the air.

Albekizan pitched forward at the impact to his shoulder. He regained his balance and looked at the arrow shaft jutting through the muscle. Red feather scales crowned the shaft. The pain was distant, unreal. The flame once more flickered within Albekizan's soul.

"It is you!" His voice trailed off into a laugh. "Is this your best? You'll never kill me!"

"I have two more arrows," the voice answered, mockingly.

Albekizan turned. The arrow and the voice had to come from the hall leading to what had been Vendevorex's tower.

"Stand before me," he demanded. "Kill me now, if you can."

He listened hard. The voice didn't answer but Albekizan was certain he heard footsteps. He ran into the hallway in pursuit of the fleeing ghost. He found the body of a guard and blood pooled on the stone… and beyond this, a mark in the shape of the human's boot. Any force of nature solid enough to wield a bow and leave footprints was solid enough to rip apart with tooth and claw.

"FORWARD," PET SHOUTED as his band of men rushed in pursuit of a squad of fleeing dragons. His forces had grown from two dozen to two hundred, as men gathered about him to serve the legendary Bitterwood.

Pet knew it was rage against the day's atrocities that gave the men the strength to fight, not his shouted commands. The men fought mercilessly, seeking vengeance against an oppressor who had held them beneath his heel their whole lives, only to have finally stumbled.

The fleeing dragons—a force of perhaps twenty— reached a dead-end and turned to face their pursuers. Pet was left behind as the majority of his men rushed into combat with them. A small force of Kamon's men stayed by his side, and they set to work on the dozens of dragon bodies that lay trampled in the street, liberating them of weapons and shields.

"Hey," one of the men said as he lifted the wing of a sprawled sky-dragon. "This one's still breathing!"

"Then make him stop," Kamon said. Pet looked at the dragon and thought he looked familiar. The man above the dragon raised his sword.

"Stop!" Pet shouted, recognizing the dragon.

"What?" the man asked, looking confused.

"Don't you recognize him?" Pet moved forward and placed his arm on the man's forearm, lowering the sword. "It's Vendevorex, the wizard. He's on our side."

Kamon sneered, his braided mustache twitching, and said, "We ally ourselves with no dragons. All must die."

"Look," Pet said. "I'm Bitterwood. You're Kamon. Which one of us is the unstoppable dragon-slayer, the last hope of humanity; you or me?"

Kamon grimaced. "You are," he said at last in a barely audible voice.

"Then hold your tongue and fetch some water. Let's see if we can revive him."

Kamon grew red, then turned around, heading for a nearby rain barrel.

Pet knelt next to the wizard, checking the pulse in his throat. It was weak and unsteady, but present. Except for a few scorch marks and some nasty gashes in his legs, Vendevorex was nowhere near as bloodied and torn as he'd been the last time Pet had seen him. If he'd survived what happened in

Chakthalla's hall, he'd survive this. Or would he? His body had footprints all over where men and dragons had trampled him. Who knew what injuries bled deep inside him?

"Help me," Pet said to one of the nearby men.

Together they turned the wizard onto his back, then carried him onto the closest porch. Vendevorex's breath came in wet gasps. Blood drooled from his limp jaw. His silver skullcap was missing. Pet noticed how quiet the Free City was becoming, with distant cries and the occasional clash of steel on steel growing ever more rare. They had won this battle, but at what cost? For every dead body of a dragon he had counted, he had counted two humans, mostly women and children. After this day, things could never be as they had been. Albekizan had to be removed from the throne, and he was the only one left to do it, unless the wizard could be revived. He wondered what Jandra would say if she could see him now.

Jandra. Had she, too, died among the crush of bodies? What use was it to turn invisible when death touched you from all sides? He couldn't help but hope she still lived. She was the most resourceful woman he'd ever met.

Kamon brought him a dirty rag, sopping with water.

"Thank you," Pet said, dabbing at the fallen wizard's brow. "Now, I have a new task for you and your men. I have reason to believe that somewhere in this city is a woman with long brown… I mean short black hair. Her name is Jandra. Go through the city and call out her name, and bring her to me when you find her."

"Yes," Kamon said. "At once. But where will you be?"

"Right here," said Pet, taking Vendevorex's foretalon into his hand and squeezing it. "If he's going to die, I'm not going to let him die alone."

THE HALL FLOOR was slick with blood. The horrified look on the severed head of the guard that lay before him told Albekizan that his foe had passed this way. How terrible Bitterwood must be to look upon.

The door to Vendevorex's tower lay battered from its hinges. Bloodied footprints led over it and into the absolute darkness beyond. Without warning, the second arrow streaked toward him.

"PET!"

Pet looked toward the woman's voice. At a nearby corner he saw a horse, its reigns held by one of Kamon's men who led it toward him. On the back of the horse sat Jandra.

"You're alive!" he shouted, releasing Vendevorex's talon and running to meet her.

"I've come to rescue you," she said, her voice full of jest. Then a horrified look passed over her face. "I'm sorry. How awful to make jokes at a time like this. I'm happy to see you again, but... all these people dead. I never imagined anything like this was possible."

Pet reached for her arms and helped her down from the horse.

"I understand," he said. "And you may rescue me yet. These men want a revolution. We've won this battle, but not the war. Albekizan must pay for this. He'll die much quicker if we can save Vendevorex."

"Save him? What happened? I was riding toward the Free City when I saw the light in the sky. I saw something that looked like him—"

"He was magnificent," Pet said. "He appeared in the sky, a hundred feet tall. He looked like a god. His appearance alone put Albekizan to flight, and then he slew Kanst single-handedly. The sight broke the morale of the dragons. But Vendevorex vanished after that, until now. We found him but he's not well."

"Take me to him," Jandra said.

BLASPHET FELT THE cold touch of manacles around his wrists and ankles, a familiar sensation from so many years waking from troubled sleep in the dark bowels of Albekizan's dungeon. The cold was great, greater even than he remembered.

He opened his eyes. Shandrazel stood before him assisting Androkom, wrapping fresh bandages around the blunt stub of the biologian's tail.

Blasphet rattled the chains, testing them. They held him securely but the locks wouldn't hold him for even a second. He reached to his legs, for the lock-picks hidden amidst his scales. He suddenly found out why he was so cold.

"Looking for those?" Shandrazel said, pointing toward the mound of translucent feather-scales. "I remembered your nasty reputation for hiding poisoned needles. I didn't want to take any chances."

Blasphet felt his face burn at the indignity. Still, his curiosity was greater than his embarrassment. "How did you escape?"

"It cost noble Androkom his tail, yet another crime for which you will be brought to justice. He reached the acid pool with his tail tip, soaked it, and then brought it back to eat away the iron chains which held him."

"It took many soakings," Androkom said. "Fortunately, after the first few, the nerves burned away. You may be interested to know that the acid cauterized the wounds, just as you promised. Still, you are lucky to have been apprehended in Shandrazel's presence. I would have tossed you into the pool without a second thought."

"We do have laws in this kingdom," Shandrazel said, "even if my father seems to forget them."

"You fool!" Blasphet laughed. "Albekizan is the only law. I'm too valuable to him. As long as he's king, I will be free!"

"You may be right," Shandrazel said. "Which is why he cannot remain king."

JANDRA CRADLED VENDEVOREX'S head in her arms and closed her eyes, concentrating. The tiny machines that swam in Vendevorex were controlled by his mental commands. If he had lost consciousness before willing the molecular engines to heal him, they wouldn't do so. Jandra wished she knew the skills needed to mend damaged tissue, to knit together once more the ruptured blood vessels. She couldn't bear to lose him. All that had happened today, all the death, all the sorrow, had made her understand the lesson of Bitterwood. Holding onto hate, even for the most-deserved cause, would kill your soul. Hate would grow until there was no room for anything else. She couldn't let that happen. Vendevorex had to live, not to kill Albekizan, not to fight to save mankind, but simply so she could tell him she forgave him.

Unfortunately, Vendevorex was unlikely ever to wake. His breathing grew even more labored, his pulse weaker with each beat. She began to cry as a wave of convulsions wracked his body. If only she could tell the machines what to do, she could…

Of course. Her head wound. Vendevorex had commanded the machines in her blood to heal her head wound. Not even a full day had passed—they might be active still.

"Give me a knife," she said to Pet.

Pet handed her a blade, shining and sharp. "What are you doing?" he asked.

"Quiet. I need to concentrate."

She cut a gash across her palm, releasing a ribbon of red. She took her mentor's talon and did the same, then placed palm against talon and squeezed.

"Go," she whispered. "Heal him."

A long time passed as the sun grew ever higher in the sky. Pet gave orders to Ragnar and Kamon, telling them to gather together the men remaining in the Free City and prepare them for the coming battle. Jandra couldn't allow the clamor to distract her. With sweaty concentration, she guided the active machines into Vendevorex's blood. There weren't enough of them. She told the machines to multiply themselves and, to her relief, they did.

As they spread, she blocked the outside world, listening only to the reports of the microscopic explorers in Vendevorex's body, plotting, in her mind's eye, a map of her mentor's wounds. After a time, she could see the extent of his internal injuries, as if her eyes could see through skin. She willed the machines to knit his ruptured blood vessels back together, and they obeyed. She found a clot of blood choking Vendevorex's right lung. As she willed it, the tiny machines began to eat away the blockage. There was too much fluid pooling around his heart. She stimulated his kidneys and opened his bladder to remove the excess fluid. She'd never concentrated on anything more intently. She trembled from the effort, sweat soaking her clothes. His wounds were closing but was she doing it right? Was she doing him more harm in ways she couldn't guess?

As if in answer, Vendevorex arched his back in pain and coughed blood. A blood vessel leading to his heart had ruptured.

Then, despite all her sweat and work and will, his heart fell silent. His body went limp. Jandra looked up at Pet who stared at her, his eyes reflecting her anguish.

The porch shook as someone ran onto it. It was one of Ragnar's men. He carried a metal bowl, dented, covered in mud. Its silver edge glinted in the light. Jandra gasped. It was Vendevorex's skullcap.

"I found this where he fell," the man said. "I thought it might be important."

ALBEKIZAN WAS FINISHED. The bandage he made from the tapestry torn from the wall had finally stanched the loss of blood from the wound of the second arrow that hit his right thigh. Albekizan pulled himself back to his feet, steadying himself against the wall to compensate for the loss of strength in the leg. The arrow had sunk deep, hitting bone. As he stepped forward the pain was sharp and focused, in contrast to the dull numbness of the wound in his shoulder.

"You look weary, Albekizan," the ghostly voice said from somewhere in the gloom.

Albekizan looked up the spiral stairwell heading to the tower's roof, high above. The voice had come from there but he saw no hint of movement in the shadows.

"Two arrows and already you're dying," the voice mocked. "It took so many to lay Bodiel low."

"I've strength enough to kill you twice!" Albekizan yelled. As his voice echoed throughout the tower, he listened to the words as though a stranger spoke them. Such bluster. Such boast. Was this all he'd become? Then he swallowed, and said, "Just as you killed my son twice, taking both body and flame."

"Then we have something in common," Bitterwood answered.

His voice seemed closer now. Albekizan limped forward. He clenched his teeth to beat back the pain, then climbed the stairs in pursuit of his tormentor.

"My family died twice for me as well," Bitterwood said from somewhere just ahead. "We killed them together, you and I, just as together we killed Bodiel."

Albekizan climbed faster now, driven by the nearness of the voice. He expected to catch sight of his foe any second.

"Hurry!" Bitterwood taunted. "Faster!"

"Cease your prattling!" Albekizan commanded.

"Soon enough," the voice said, trailing into the distance.

* * *

JANDRA PLACED THE misshapen helmet on Vendevorex's scalp. She placed her hands upon it, closing her eyes. The helmet was the interface between Ven's mind and the nano-machines. It was sensitive to his every thought. Could it allow her to reach into the last traces of his mind?

"Wake up, Ven," she said. "I need you."

"Jandra," he answered, his voice as strong as ever. "You've come back."

Jandra opened her eyes, expecting to see her revived mentor. But Vendevorex still lay lifeless and limp in her lap. Had it only been her imagination?

"No," Vendevorex answered, the voice coming not from his lips but from inside her mind. "Not your imagination. The skullcap is responding to my last flicker of life and relaying my thoughts to you. My soul stirred when I heard your voice. I'm so happy you've returned."

"I had to tell you, Ven," she said, blinking back tears. "I... I forgive you. You were right. Fifteen years of kindness and devotion do pay the debt of a single horrible decision. I love you, Ven. I had to let you know."

"Thank you," he said, his mental voice fading. "There's something I should say to you."

"Save your strength," she said. "Heal yourself."

"It's too late. You did good work, but my body was too torn. I may have only seconds remaining. I must say this. You've grown to be a good, strong, willful woman, Jandra. I have always thought of you as my daughter. You've made me very proud."

"Oh, Ven," she said, squeezing his talon, searching his face for any flicker of life.

"I will always love you, Jandra," he said, his voice faint, distant, vanishing, at last, into static.

ALBEKIZAN PRESSED ON, lifting himself up the stairs one step at a time, knowing that soon the stairs would end and his opponent would have no place to go.

"Do you hear it?" Bitterwood said, so near, so near. "The Angel of Death hovers above. He grows weary of waiting. The children are all dead, and the sins pass to the fathers."

Albekizan found a gray cloth stretched over the open trap door leading to the flat, circular roof of the tower. He pulled it aside and squinted as bright sunlight chased away the shadows.

He pressed the cloak to his nostrils. It bore the same scent as the cloak Gadreel had fished from the watery tunnel.

Albekizan rose through the door, and on the tower wall facing him stood a man, his hair gray, his eyes dark. His cheeks were moist with tears. So great was the grief etched in his features that Albekizan actually found his vision fixed upon the face, rather than on the bow held before it, and the red-feathered arrow aimed at him.

"You'll only live long enough to kill me," Bitterwood said, slackening the hand that held the bowstring.

The arrow flew home, catching in Albekizan's throat.

He tried to scream but managed only a gurgling *hiss*. In silent rage he leapt at his foe who made no move to avoid him. Albekizan closed his outstretched jaws around the human's belly.

Momentum carried them over the wall, and Albekizan stretched his mighty wings to the onrushing wind.

He couldn't breathe. The man in his jaws grew limp and Albekizan flew on, driven by the emotions piercing him more deeply than arrows. He was dying, and in that was fear. Bitterwood was dying but without a struggle, and in that was frustration. But the frustration gave way to joy as he looked at the earth below. The fall forest had turned bright red, the treetops swaying in the wind like flames dancing, and he was falling, falling, falling toward his eternal pyre, with all the world ablaze.

BITTERWOOD FELT THE king's jaws slacken as they spun toward the distant ground. What Albekizan's teeth hadn't ripped from his body, the ground would. Bitterwood could see the broad, deep river beneath them now, and found a song Hezekiah had taught him passing through his mind.

Shall we gather at the river?

With a splash the water took them, and Bitterwood fell through darkness.

Still alive.

Could nothing kill him? Could nothing end this?

"*You can end this,*" she said.

Bitterwood looked toward the voice and saw a distant light, and in the light she stood, her body aglow, her hair floating around her in a breeze Bitterwood couldn't feel.

"Recanna," he whispered.

"*You can end this,*" she said once more and turned toward the light.

Bitterwood tried to chase her but his feet had nothing to push against.

"Recanna!" he cried.

She glanced over her shoulder. Her face bore a cryptic smile. "*You cannot follow me, not yet. But we may still be together*," she said, as the light around her faded. "*You can end this.*"

"Recanna!"

She was gone. All was dark. Bitterwood opened his eyes. Sunlight flickered on the water's surface far above him, bubbles rising from where he had shouted her name. His shirt was snagged in Albekizan's jaws as the dragon sank to the bottom.

With a single movement of his hand, he could rip the shirt free and fight back to the air above where each breath promised further pain. Or he could sink lower and stop his struggles, and be free of pain forever.

The light grew ever dimmer.

CHAPTER TWENTY-FIVE

JUSTICE

"**F**ATHER!" SHANDRAZEL'S VOICE echoed throughout the throne room. Shandrazel felt his heart sink when he saw the dead torches throughout the hall. He didn't truly believe these torches carried the spirits of his ancestors, but it still filled him with sorrow to see them extinguished. Who would have done such a thing?

"Father!" Shandrazel shouted once more. He approached the throne. His nostrils twitched at the scent of blood: dragon blood. He knelt before the throne, spotting a dark, sticky splatter. The blood was now hours old. Perhaps it came from one of the guards? By this time they had discovered a dozen corpses.

"No one's here," Androkom said, looking around the chamber, sounding a little spooked.

Then, to contradict the biologian's observation, a familiar voice said, "I'm here. Your father won't be answering, Shandrazel."

"Show yourself," Shandrazel said, looking around the hall.

"I didn't mean to hide from you," the source of the voice said, stepping from behind a pillar. It was Metron, looking especially frail and weary as he hobbled toward them. "I wanted to be cautious. I escaped from Blasphet and returned here to report our plight to your father. I arrived to find everyone dead. I heard your father's voice and followed it to the roof where I saw him flying off with a human held in his jaws. The king crashed into the river and never came back to the surface."

"You lie," Shandrazel said.

"No," Metron said. "My words are truth. You're king now. You must respect the words of the High Biologian... sire."

"So I shall," Shandrazel said, with a nod of agreement. "However, I'll not be listening to you."

"What do you mean?"

"On this day, I accept that I am king. Though I do not intend to remain so for long, I will take advantage of one of the privileges by appointing a new High Biologian. Androkom is my choice."

"But," Metron protested, "you may not appoint a new High Biologian until my death."

"Or until you are convicted of treason. And who is the final judge in such matters?"

"The king..." Metron said.

Shandrazel held forward a slip of paper. "The note you sent Blasphet informing him of our visit and asking him to dispose of us. The penalty, as decreed by all previous kings, is death."

"But—"

"But," Shandrazel said, "I'm not like previous kings. Your sentence shall be exile."

"You must reconsider," Metron said. "I've faithfully served this kingdom for generations. I have nothing but the best interests of all dragons in mind. You cannot do this."

"I can. Now, speak the truth. Where is my father?"

"I did speak truth in this matter, sire."

Shandrazel stood silently for a moment, realizing that Metron was being honest, in this at least.

"So…" he said, sighing deeply. He moved toward the open door of the chamber to gaze upon the clouds beyond. "On this day, I have lost both father and mother, for Blasphet boasts of slaying her as well."

"I'm sorry," Androkom said.

"Thank you for your sympathy." Shandrazel sighed. "I fear I have no time for my own sorrow. Later, I will mourn. But now, I must prepare myself."

"For what?" Metron asked.

Shandrazel looked out toward the Free City, and the ragged mob that marched from it, headed toward his door.

"For the future," he said. "If there is to be one."

THE SUN HUNG low behind the castle yet seemed reluctant to set, on this, the longest day any man had ever seen. Pet felt the weight of the eyes upon him, the eyes of a thousand men, every man of fighting age who had survived the Free City. He looked to Jandra who smiled at him. She'd shown remarkable strength since Vendevorex had passed, moving among the injured, healing those she could. With her help Pet had assembled the men into something not quite an army, yet something more than a mob.

Pet climbed onto the wagon resting at the base of the palace walls. He raised an open hand and the men before him fell silent.

"Today," Pet said, "we've lost almost everything."

He watched their faces, saw the anger showing in the eyes of many, the emptiness in the eyes of most.

"Thousands dead. Wives. Children. Fathers. Mothers. Not a man stands among us who hasn't lost someone he loves."

The men in the crowd nodded in silent acknowledgement of this fact.

"We are far from home," Pet said. "We don't know if those homes even still exist. We have little food. We are weary from battle. We stand under a burden of grief more heavy than a mountain."

Pet paused, letting his words sink in. "Everything lost but hope."

The men looked at him, hanging on his words.

"We'll never bring back the dead," Pet said, clenching his fists. "Revenge will never bring us relief. But justice, aye, justice shall surely bring us hope. We attack this castle tonight not in the name of vengeance, but in the name of justice! King Albekizan will be brought low, and his kingdom will pass forever from this earth. In its place shall stand a new civilization, a land of truth and kindness, where atrocities like this day's will never happen again!"

Pet thrust his fists into the air. The crowd let out a loud cheer.

"Justice!" Pet cried.

"Justice," shouted the crowd.

Back and forth the word was called out until suddenly, a voice shouted down from the walls above, "Agreed! There will be justice!"

The army began to talk among themselves and point to the top of the wall. Pet looked up and saw a huge sun-dragon standing over him.

"It's Shandrazel," Jandra said. "He can be trusted, Pet."

Pet called out, "Bring us King Albekizan!"

A man in the crowd cried out, "Bring us his head!"

"Albekizan is dead," Shandrazel said. "We will drag the river for his body, but I won't allow its desecration. The war is over."

"Never!" someone in the crowd cried. "Not until we have our justice!"

"Yes," Pet said. "It's not over simply because he's dead."

"No," Shandrazel agreed. "It's over because I will not fight you. But I do not come to surrender. I come instead to help you create your kingdom of justice."

"We'll never live under a dragon's thumb again," Pet shouted. The crowd of men cheered.

"So you now intend to be the thumb?" Shandrazel asked, snaking his head down the wall so that his voice could be better heard. He looked into Pet's eyes and said, calmly, "If you seize the throne by force, the dragons will not consent to your rule. There will be further war."

"We will be ready," said Pet.

"There is another solution," Shandrazel said. "A compromise is possible. Will you listen to my proposal?"

Pet looked at the mob of men he led. He doubted they were in the mood for compromise. But Pet felt the responsibility of the role he played. He knew that his words could launch a war far bloodier than what he'd witnessed today. But was it possible that he could lead these men to peace? Would they accept him as a leader if he weren't marching them to war?

"We are not in the mood for compromise," Pet said. "Still, I will allow you to state your case."

"I propose," Shandrazel said, "that both a human and a dragon shall rule jointly, though neither as a supreme power. The age of kings is passing. If we wish to move forward, we will need new forms of government; a government where laws are based on reason rather than on the whims of a single king. A government where courts make decisions based on truth and fairness rather than tradition and prejudice. I have many ideas, though this isn't the proper place to discuss them. I invite you to join me in the castle, that we may peaceably discuss this proposition. What say you?"

"Never!" someone shouted. Pet recognized the voice.

"Kamon," he said, "come forth."

The old man left the crowd, marching as boldly as his frail limbs would carry him. Pet helped him rise to the platform.

"Everyone knows me," Pet said, "but you may not know Kamon. He was one of the men who freed me from the platform. I owe my life to this man. But we are of different minds on many things, I find."

"You dare to talk with this dragon?" Kamon said, his small body producing a surprisingly vital voice. "Human blood has been spilt this day, and the earth itself cries for vengeance!"

The crowd shouted in agreement, raising their weapons. Even Ragnar and his followers, long foes of Kamon, seemed ready to follow the aged prophet into battle.

They were ready to fight. Pet could see it in their eyes. If he gave the word, every last man before him was willing to put his life on the line to storm the castle.

As he stood in silence, considering his options, the crowd lowered their weapons and grew quiet, waiting for him to speak. At long last he took a deep breath. There was only one thing to say.

"Friends, earlier today, I said much the same thing as Kamon. I wanted to see dragon blood on my sword as badly as any of you. But the day has been long. It may be that I am weak. Or it may be that I am tired of death. I want justice, but I also want peace, and I'm willing to talk to anyone, man or dragon, to get it." Pet took the sword that hung from his belt and handed it to Kamon. He said to the aged man, "If you want blood, I won't oppose you." Then, to the crowd, "No one has made me your leader but yourself, and no one can stop you if you want to follow Kamon into this castle and kill every living thing you find. If I am to remain your leader, put down your weapons and wait while I speak with Shandrazel. By dawn, we may have our victory without further blood being spilled."

"You can't mean this," said Kamon.

"I can," Pet said. Then, addressing the crowd, "Now, choose. Kamon or Bitterwood. Vengeance or justice. Which path will you follow?"

Pet looked at Kamon who glowered at him, looking ready to run him through with the sword he'd just been handed. Yet, something stayed his hand.

"Bitterwood," someone in the crowd mumbled.

"Bitterwood," another said.

"Bitterwood!" the crowd shouted as one, as the last embers of the sun faded away.

HOME

KILLER GROWLED, CAUSING Zeeky to stir from her sleep. Poocher squealed as the ox-dog began to bark furiously. She rubbed her eyes. Zeeky scanned the darkness around them but saw no one. The air carried the smell of the last embers of the fire she'd built earlier in the night.

Killer continued to bark into the dark voids among the surrounding trees.

"Is that thing going to eat me?" a man said.

Zeeky recognized the voice.

"It's okay," she said, and Killer stopped barking.

"Come on, Hey You," she shouted.

The old man emerged from the darkness as the moon slid from behind the clouds. He walked stiffly and sort of tilted to one side. His left arm hung limply, swaying as he moved. Bandages had been wrapped around his chest.

Yet, as awful as he looked, Zeeky was happy to see him. She jumped up and ran to him, giving him a hug, though not a hard one, as he looked like he might not be able to take it.

He placed his right hand on her back and said, "You don't need to call me Hey You anymore."

"So what should I call you?"

"Bant will do."

"Okay."

Bant grimaced as he lowered himself to the ground. She helped him sit then sat beside him.

"I'm glad you're alive," she said. "After the—"

"Shh," he said. "Let's not talk about what happened back there. Let's talk about tomorrow. Where you heading to?"

"Home," said Zeeky.

"You aren't an orphan?"

"I hope not."

"Didn't think so," Bant said. "Bet your dad was going to kill that pig 'cause it was a runt, so you ran away with it."

"How'd you know?"

"I was young once. A long time ago." Bant shrugged. "Who knows? Maybe I'll be young again one day."

"Where are you going?" she asked.

"Don't know," he said. "If you want me to, I'll stick with you for awhile. I'm guessing you don't know your way back home."

"No," Zeeky admitted. "I'm so lost."

"So am I," Bant said. "But home's out there somewhere. Maybe, together, we'll find it."

DRAGONS
ON THEIR SPECIES AND LINEAGE

SUN-DRAGONS

Sun-dragons are the lords of the realm. They are huge beasts with forty-foot wingspans and jaws that can bite a man in half. Sun-dragons are adorned with crimson scales with touches of orange and yellow that give them a fiery appearance. They are gifted with natural weaponry of tooth and claw, but are intelligent tool users who often use spears and swords to enhance their already formidable combat skills. Politically, sun-dragons are organized under a powerful king who, by right, owns all the property in the kingdom. A close network of other sun-dragons, usually related to the king, manage individual areas within the kingdom. Sun-dragons of note are:

ALBEKIZAN
The king of the dragons.

TANTHIA
His queen.

BODIEL
Albekizan's youngest son, known for his courage and cunning.

SHANDRAZEL
Albekizan's oldest surviving son, known for his intellect and integrity.

CHAKTHALLA
The king's sister-in-law, the widow of Tanthia's brother.

ZANZEROTH
The king's closest companion, a grizzled old dragon known as the greatest hunter in all the kingdom.

KANST
The king's cousin and general of the king's armies.

BLASPHET
Known as the Murder God, Blasphet is legendary as the most wicked dragon ever to have flown over the earth.

SKY-DRAGONS

Half the size of sun-dragons, sky-dragons are a race devoted to scholarship. The culture and history of the dragons are protected by a group of sky-dragons known as biologians, who are part priest, part librarian, and part scientist. Sky-dragons have blue scales and golden eyes. Sky-dragons of note are:

VENDEVOREX
The king's wizard, also known as Master of the Invisible.

METRON
The High Biologian, over a century old and famed for his wisdom and scholarship.

GADREEL
A rarity among sky-dragons, Gadreel is a slave, belonging to the sun-dragon Zanzeroth.

ANDROKOM
A young biologian with a reputation for arrogance.

EARTH-DRAGONS

Wingless creatures, earth-dragons are humanoids with turtle-beaked faces and broad, heavy bodies. Seldom more than five and a half feet tall, earth-dragons are twice as strong as men, though also twice as slow. The king's armies are composed mostly of earth-dragons. Few can truly be said to be of note.

HUMANS

THE LESSER SPECIES

The bottom rung of the dragon society, humans exist as slaves, serfs, pets, and prey. While some humans have proven to be as smart as dragons, humans have never successfully shrugged off the chains of dragon rule. For the most part, they live in villages with little daily interaction with dragons, and are left alone as long as they pay their taxes. Human society is highly fragmented and tribal, organized around competing prophets who are constantly waging small wars against one another. A lucky few humans have escaped the squalor of the human villages and have been adopted as pets by dragons. Humans of note are:

BITTERWOOD
A legendary dragon-slayer.

JANDRA
A girl raised by the wizard-dragon Vendevorex who has been trained in many of his arcane arts.

PET
A dashing and handsome purebred human, Pet is the loyal companion of the sun-dragon Chakthalla.

ZEEKY
A run-away girl with a mysterious power over animals.

CRON and TULK
Two slaves who escape from a ritual hunt.

KAMON
An aged prophet who teaches men should be subservient to dragons until the savior arrives.

RAGNAR
A young firebrand prophet who teaches that men should struggle against dragons at every chance.

HEZEKIAH
A giant, axe-wielding prophet of the old-time religion.

ACKNOWLEDGEMENTS

BITTERWOOD WOULDN'T BE in your hands today without the help and encouragement of many, many people. I wrote an early draft of *Bitterwood* nearly ten years ago then set it aside. I felt like I had a good story idea, but didn't yet have the writing experience to give the story the treatment it deserved. A lot of people in the intervening decade have helped me get that experience. I wish my memory was strong enough that I could recall the names of everyone who looked at *Bitterwood* over the years. I'll have to resort to thanking people in groups. The early chapters of *Bitterwood* were written during my time as a member of the Writer's Group of the Triad novel critique group. I owe a huge debt to my fellow travelers from that time, including Karen McCullough, Rick Fisher, Julie Anne Parks, Mary Elizabeth Parker, Phillip Levin, Elizabeth Lustig, and Doug Hewitt. Anjela Indica was also an important reader of that early draft, and I got words of encouragement that I can still remember from Jeremy Cavin and Chris Woodcook.

IN ADDITION TO the Writer's Group of the Triad, another group that proved helpful in those early days in learning the writer's craft was the Odyssey Fantasy Writer's Workshop. There I worked with fellow students Sean Finn, Sharon Keir, Matt Rotundo, Rob Jones, Erica Tolley, Steven Prete, Walt Cuirle, Marty Hiller, Julia Duncan, Carrie Vaughn, Morgan Hua, Stephen Chambers, Stacy Dooks, Richard Bradford, Bryan King, Lea Braff, Samantha Payeff, and Rita Oakes. Jeanne Cavelos led the workshop, and I got advice from literary notables like James Morrow, Warren Lapine, and, of course, Harlan Ellison.

A FEW YEARS after Odyssey, I had the honor of attending Orson Scott Card's Writer's Boot Camp. Among the many people I met there was Luc Reid, who later went on to found *www.codexwriters.com*. My involvement with this group of writers has proven to be an invaluable source of writing and career advice. There are over a hundred members, but some Codexians who have proven especially supportive have been Alethea Kontis, Steven Savile, Bob Defendi, Douglas Cohen, Ed Schubert, Judson Roberts, Eric James Stone, Elaine Isaak, Jason D. Wittman, Ian Creasey, Tom Pendergrass, Nancy Fulda, John Brown, and Cat Rambo. Many of the people just mentioned read all or part of the manuscript, but a special note for the heroic efforts of Codexians Laurel Amberdine and Cathy Bollinger is in order. They provided detailed critiques of the final manuscript, and I truly appreciate their hard work and dedication. Bits and pieces of that final manuscript were also read by a local writers' group consisting of Paul Paolicelli, Nancy Hunt, Jessica Hollander, Brad Powers, Ken Alexander, Mark Cornell, Tania Osborn, and Richard Mocarski.

MOVING INTO THE homestretch, the following people will know why I'm mentioning them: Greg Hungerford. Cheryl Morgan. Various and sundry Kinkonoids (Anne Abrams, Chris Young, and Ian McDowell to name a few). Nadia Cornier. The Phobos crew of Keith Olexa, Christian O'Toole, John Ordover, and Sandra Schulberg who gave me my first shot at getting into print.

THE BOOK IN your hands literally would not exist without the terrific crew at Solaris Books. A big thanks is owed to Christian Dunn, Mark Newton, Nozomi Goto, Darius Hinks, and cover artist Michael Komarck. Cheers!

AND THEN THERE'S Laura Herrmann. I met her around the time my first novel, *Nobody Gets the Girl*, was catching the attention of Phobos Books. The story of my life between *Nobody* and *Bitterwood* is inextricably tied with her story. She was informed she had a metastasized cancer on the day I got my contract for *Nobody Gets the Girl*. The next three years taught me a lot about courage, dignity and love. She made me a better person; perhaps the most important step in becoming a better writer. During our brief time together she was an amazing source of inspiration and suppor. I miss her more than I can hope to express.

FINALLY, THERE'S YOU, the reader who's taken the time to pick up my book. Thanks! Hope you liked it. Feel free to drop me a line if you'd like; you can contact me via the boards at *www.solarisbooks.com*.

ABOUT THE AUTHOR

JAMES MAXEY LIVES in Hillsborough, NC, USA. After graduating from the Odyssey Fantasy Writers' Workshop and Orson Scott Card's Writer's Boot Camp, James broke into the publishing world in 2002 when he won a Phobos Award for his short story, "Empire of Dreams and Miracles." Phobos Books later published James's debut novel, the cult classic superhero tale *Nobody Gets the Girl*. His short stories have since appeared in *Asimov's* and numerous anthologies. For a listing of his currently available stories, and frequent rants about circus freaks, comic books, and angels, visit James on the web at *jamesmaxey.blogspot.com*.

The debut of a stunning new talent in the fantasy firmament

"Attractive characters and an imaginative setting combine in an excellent, fast-moving quest novel."
— David Drake, author of the Lord of the Isles series

GAIL Z. MARTIN

THE SUMMONER

Book One of the
CHRONICLES OF THE NECROMANCER

ISBN: 978-1-84416-468-4

The world of Prince Martris Drayke is thrown into sudden chaos and disorder when his brother murders their father and seizes the throne. Cast out, Martris and a small band of trusted friends are forced to flee to a neighbouring kingdom where he believes they can regroup and plot their retaliation. But if the living are arrayed against him, Martris must call on a different set of allies: the ranks of the dead...

www.solarisbooks.com

SOLARIS FANTASY

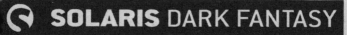

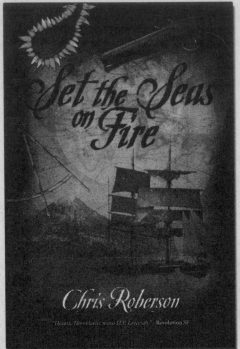